"Would you consider a short-term, exclusive relationship, with a predefined end date?" There, Charlotte thought. That sounded mature, sensible. No need to let emotions colour what promised to be a satisfying adult affair.

Justice straightened from the wall, looming to his full height. "Would this so-called relationship be strictly physical? Or could it involve social aspects as well?"

Once again, she sensed an underlying current of laughter, but she ignored it. "I can't see why not."

"And it would come to an end the same time as your contract?"

"Or earlier, of course, should either of us find it no longer meets our needs."

"I thought English professors were supposed to be romantic."

Romance. Love. That's what hurt you. Sex, on the other hand, was just sex. "Not all of us," Charlotte said.

Mom + Dad

When Time Falls Still

Brenda Margriet

Thanks for everything – and more

Brenda Margriet

This is a work of fiction. Names, characters, places and incidents are either the product of the author's imagination or are used fictitiously, and any resemblance to actual persons living or dead, business establishments, events, or locales is entirely coincidental.

WHEN TIME FALLS STILL

This edition published March 2016.
Copyright © 2016 Brenda Margriet Clotildes
Cover Art by **Steven Cote**
Editing services provided by Story Perfect Editing

ISBN 978-0-9950008-4-1 (print)

To my children.

And to everyone who gives me the courage to keep on writing.

CHAPTER ONE

"Damn it!" Charlotte Girardet pounded her gloved fist against the steering wheel, the soft thud-thudding a dull echo of her frustrated fury.

Jerking the gear lever into drive, she pressed the gas pedal firmly one more time. The engine whined, but her boxy little SUV went nowhere.

The university parking lot stretched ahead of her, black asphalt hidden beneath more than a foot of snow. The few vehicles scattered about were blanketed in white. Flakes drifted thickly down, treacherously beautiful in the ghostly glow of the tall overhead lights cutting through the gloom of the November afternoon.

She'd managed to pull out of her parking slot, but was now stranded between the rows. Every turn of her tires only made the situation worse, polishing the snow into ice. Charlotte bared her teeth. "Should have taken the all-wheel drive option," she muttered to the empty seat beside her. Of course, when she'd bought the vehicle she'd been living in Vancouver, where half this amount of snow meant everyone stayed home. Here in Northern British Columbia, most people took a storm like this in stride.

She wished she was like those people. Going inside to ask for help would be humiliating. It was sure to bring knowing grins, accompanied by condescending advice. "Silly southerner," they would think, "can't deal with a little bit of snow." It burned her that they might be right. Were probably right. God, she hated feeling ignorant.

Maybe she could back her way out. She dropped the vehicle into reverse. For an instant she thought it was working, could feel the tires catching, but then the back end slipped sideways and she lost whatever inches she had gained.

Her chilled fingers tingled inside her thin leather gloves, and cold liquid trickled down the backs of her heels where snow had made its way inside her stylish ankle boots. She'd had to clear the buried windshield using only her hands, as she hadn't thought she'd need a brush or ice scraper so early in the fall, and the damp had seeped into her bones. The heater, despite going full blast, hadn't managed to cut through the cold interior. Tucking her hands under her thighs in a futile attempt to warm them, she scowled out the window.

In any other circumstance, she would have been thrilled with the scene before her. The snow was blue-white, the flakes large and fluffy, the texture perfect for making snowmen. Unfortunately, it wasn't perfect for getting home without a fight.

Rat-a-tat-tat.

"Oh!" She jerked round, pulse scrambling. A beam of light sliced through the window, glaring in her eyes. All she could see was a large, black hulk.

"Need help?" asked a deep voice, muffled by the closed glass.

The dazzling brightness swung away, leaving spots before her eyes. She peered up, taking careful stock. The man outside was so tall he had to bend almost double to see through the window. He held a flashlight in one gloved hand, now directed upward under his chin, casting eerie shadows on his features. His head was covered in a snug black toque, incongruously spangled with glittering snowflakes. A scar cut through one thick blond eyebrow, and there was no way he had been born with a nose that crooked. A burnished gold beard did nothing to disguise a square jaw.

Surreptitiously, she reached for the door lock button, reassured by the solid sounding clunk.

"Need help?" he repeated. The flashlight tilted down and shone on the insignia stitched to the breast pocket of his parka. "Campus security. Should be able to push you out."

****

Justice Cooper waited patiently for Professor Girardet to answer. He stood quiet and still, holding the light on his uniform badge, and watched as the fright faded from her face. He hadn't meant to scare her, but knew his bulk and battle-scarred face was often unintentionally intimidating. Not that he wouldn't use his size and looks as weapons when he needed to. This, however, wasn't one of those times.

"I appreciate the offer." Professor Girardet's voice came through the glass tight and wired, not calm and confident as it did when she was lecturing. Justice attended her class on medieval poetry, but he always sat at the far back of the room, so he wasn't surprised she hadn't recognized him. The University of Northern British Columbia might be small, but it was still possible to lose yourself in the crowd if you wanted to. "I'm sure I'll manage just fine."

He doubted it. He'd watched her futile struggles as he'd trudged through the drifts toward her. Tired of talking through the glass, he motioned her to roll down the window. She did so reluctantly, shivering as the cold air whooshed in. She wore a useless little knit hat, a flat, white one that looked like a pancake, on her curly brown hair. Her dark eyes, now they'd lost their panicky look, were once again sharp with intelligence and more than a hint of temper. He suspected the colour in her cheeks wasn't just from the cold. Smart people didn't like admitting they didn't know everything.

"Keep your wheels straight. I'll push from the back. Give it a little gas, then ease off, give it a little more. We have to rock it out."

Her lips tightened, and then she gave a brisk nod. She pushed the button to roll the window up.

"Keep it open," he said. "So you can hear me. Once we get her going, don't stop until you hit the road." The plow had made one pass of the ring road that circled the campus, clearing a narrow lane. If he could get her there she should be able to manage the rest.

He set his shoulder against the back of the SUV, on the driver's side, bracing his feet in the slick snow. "Go," he called out.

She fed the gas and he strained his legs, feeling the tension run up his thighs, into his back, through his arms. She released the gas, as he'd instructed, and the vehicle settled back into the rut, but the next time she accelerated he could feel the tires catch. "Again," he shouted.

A few more back-and-forths and suddenly the SUV shot forward, skidding slightly. He watched with approval as she corrected the slide and kept her momentum until she reached the cleared roadway. Brake lights glowed as she pulled to a stop.

He followed her tracks, stomping in his heavy winter boots, clapping his thick gloves to rid them of damp snow.

As he approached, the driver's door opened and Professor Girardet stepped out.

She was a tall woman, slim despite the bulk of her black wool coat. Her dark-coloured trousers were tucked into low boots with high, narrow heels. She stood framed between the door and the body of the SUV and offered her hand. "Thanks so much. I hate to admit it, but I probably wasn't getting out of that on my own."

He clasped her hand briefly, conscious of the slenderness of her fingers even through the fabric separating them. "You need winter tires."

Her chin lifted. "I have all-seasons."

He shook his head. "Not good enough."

"Winters will cost me, what, a thousand dollars? I'm only here for one year. I just don't see the point."

It wasn't worth arguing about. He shrugged. She was a grown woman. She'd either figure it out or she wouldn't. "Drive safe."

He headed back toward the campus building, keeping an eye out for other stranded drivers. He'd spent the last hour pushing numerous vehicles out of the drifts, and it was a relief to see the lots were mainly empty. Maybe he'd actually make it back to the office this time. A cup of coffee, even the crud the guys in the office made, would go down just fine right about now.

Inside the vestibule leading to the university's main hall he knocked off the worst of the snow, brushing his jacket, peeling off his toque and slapping it against his thigh, stamping his feet. As he passed through the second set of doors, long, black mats squished damply beneath his steps, and then gave way to a polished concrete floor that arced in a wide, semi-circular path. Tall windows to his right revealed the wide-open outdoor space called the

Agora. Only six weeks ago, students had been scattered over the brick courtyard, lazing on the green lawns. Now it was hidden beneath a smooth carpet of white, pools of light from outside lamps chasing purple shadows into dark corners.

The security office smelled of bad coffee, damp clothing, and overheated photocopier. Shawn McMorris glowered at the machine and gave it a frustrated slap. "Damn thing's jammed again." He raised his glare to Justice, who ignored him and poured a cup of coffee.

McMorris, squat and stocky, with prematurely thinning grey hair shaved closed to his skull, opened the paper tray and rooted around inside. "Any more shit going on out there?" he tossed over his shoulder as he pulled crumpled sheets from the innards.

"A few more stuck, including Professor Girardet. Got everyone out okay." He switched the mug to his other hand, wrapping his chilled fingers around the warm ceramic.

"Freakin' in-tell-ect-u-als." McMorris slammed the drawer shut and grunted in satisfaction as chunking sounds indicated the machine was back in business. "Go to school all their lives, don't know nothing but books."

Justice lowered into his chair, settling his weight carefully as it creaked and groaned beneath him, and then swivelled to the computer monitor to begin writing up his end of shift report. The office was manned by at least two guards twenty-four hours a day, three hundred and sixty-five days a year, and he was just finishing up his fourth ten-hour shift. Three days off stretched ahead. He was looking forward to picking up Max on his way home and spending the weekend with his son.

McMorris sorted the pages he'd finally managed to

print and began filing them away in the cabinets across from Justice. "Professor Girardet's one of our new ones, isn't she? The tall, built one? Teaches in the English program?"

Justice made a noise of agreement without taking his concentration from his keyboard. He found typing with both hands awkward, his big, blunt fingers tangling on the keys, so he had perfected his own one-handed system that rivalled most others for speed.

"Aren't you taking an English course this semester? Something fancy about poetry?" McMorris didn't wait for an answer. "I don't know, I just don't get the deal why anyone would spend his time reading poems written by dead guys."

Now was not the time to try to explain the way his gut felt when he read words first written centuries ago. In fact, *never* would be a good time to discuss his fascination with poetry with McMorris.

He hit Ctrl-P and headed to the printer. The door at the back of the room opened. Curtis Nielson, director of security, stepped through and stood four-square in the entrance, as if preparing to repel attackers.

"You're off in fifteen, aren't you, Cooper? Where's your report?" A few inches shorter than Justice, Nielson was bulky and solid, his shoulders filling the door frame.

Justice pulled the still warm sheets from the tray and held them out. Nielson's lips thinned. He took them with a disgruntled huff and read them over.

Ex-RCMP, Nielson was new to the security team, having taken the management job in September. When the position had come open several months earlier, Justice knew his colleagues had expected him to apply. So had his father, his ex-wife, and maybe even his son. No one had thought to ask him whether he wanted it or not.

The answer had been not. He was happy doing what he was doing, had no ambition to change his role. He still didn't want the job. But that didn't mean he had to like the man who now held it.

Nielson peered at Justice over the frames of his heavy black glasses, the overhead light glaring off the closely shaved skin of his bald head. "Spent a lot of time pushing cars out today. You'd think people living up north would figure out how to handle a bit of snow."

As far as Justice knew, Nielson hadn't been out of his office all day. And as it didn't have a window, he wondered if his boss would still be calling it "a bit of snow" when he had to dig out his own vehicle.

Nielson rolled the report into a tube and gripped it at the end, like a club. "You're back on Tuesday at 7am."

Justice jerked his chin in a short nod. He hadn't missed a shift in eight years and didn't need reminding by a nit-picking, micro-managing control freak.

Nielson returned to his office, shutting the door firmly behind him. The atmosphere in the outer room slowly relaxed.

"Do you think he'll ever take the stick out of his ass, or is this as good as it gets?" McMorris grumbled.

****

Charlotte leaned against the door with a sigh of relief. She had made it home without any further excitement, and didn't have anywhere to go until Monday. The whole weekend stretched ahead of her—solitary, silent and hopefully productive.

She dumped her satchel and briefcase at the foot of the stairs leading to the second floor, tugged off her boots and placed them upside down on the heating vent to dry. The thin socks she wore went next. She bundled them into a damp ball and tossed them into the laundry room. The cuffs of her pants hung clammy against her ankles. She headed to the kitchen in her bare feet, desperate for a cup of tea.

The cell phone in the pocket of her blazer buzzed. She dug it out, saw her sister's face grinning up at her from the screen. Connecting the call, she switched to speaker. "How's it going, Sonny?" Sliding the phone onto the counter, she grabbed the electric kettle and filled it from the water cooler in the corner of the room.

"Oh, you know. The usual madness." Sondra's voice was tired but cheerful. "I had to stop Anthony from sliding Andrea down the basement stairs in the laundry basket."

Charlotte dumped a couple spoonfuls of loose leaves into her tea press, smiling as she pictured her impish niece and nephew. "I'm sure she was more than willing to give it a try."

"I distracted them by suggesting they fill the basket with their stuffed animals and give them a ride." A delighted shriek cut through the last word. "It's working for now, so I thought I'd give you call, see how you're surviving up in the great white north. I saw the weather report on the news."

"White is definitely right, at least today. I could barely see well enough to drive home." The kettle clicked off and she filled the pot. Leaving the tea to steep, she found a box of crackers in the cupboard and rustled out a couple. "I'm going to settle in for the next two days, do research, mark a few essays."

"Isn't that what you did last weekend? Maybe you should get out and have fun, meet new people."

The security guard's rough, rugged face flashed

across Charlotte's mind. She didn't think he was quite the person Sondra had in mind. Despite her current immersion into motherhood, her older sister was a brilliant corporate lawyer, and her husband, Thomas Huntsville, an equally brilliant attorney dealing with entertainment law. Before children, they had been a sophisticated urban couple mixing with Vancouver's high society. Charlotte had once thought she'd make the same sort of match—refined, intelligent, with a partner who matched her intellectually and sexually. "I'm not here to have fun. It's just a one-year contract. I come in, I teach, I work on my book, I get out."

"Doesn't mean you can't have a social life."

Charlotte depressed the plunger on the press and poured the steaming liquid into a brightly painted mug. "I see people all the time. I teach two classes every day, have office hours with students, mingle with the other staff. It's not like I'm stuck in a dark dungeon, studying by the dim light of a coal-oil lantern."

Sondra laughed. "That's not quite what I was envisioning, but I get your point." A high-pitched squabble pealed through the speaker. "That's my cue. Take care of yourself."

"You, too. Say hi to everyone for me."

When the connection ended, silence settled into the kitchen. Not the welcoming silence that had greeted her when she'd first stepped in the door. This quiet seemed edgy, empty. Charlotte rolled her shoulders, shrugging off the fancy. Carrying her mug, she collected her bags and headed upstairs to the small second bedroom she used as an office.

She had a lot she wanted to accomplish this weekend. It was time to get to work.

CHAPTER TWO

"While you might expect religious poetry of this age to be written in Latin, it may come as a surprise that much of the secular poetry was also written in Latin, not English." Charlotte surveyed the room before her. The faces looking back at her wore the typical mix of expressions—engaged, apathetic, entirely distracted—the same expressions that had confronted teachers since Socrates. "In medieval times, Latin was the language of the educated. Anyone with something to say would use it, in the knowledge it could be universally understood. Students would have used it to write the Facebook posts and Twitter tweets of the time—bawdy songs, drinking ballads, and poetic satire."

A ripple of interest rolled through the room, and Charlotte felt the atmosphere brighten. Monday classes often suffered from ennui, and three-hour long lectures on Monday evenings could be even more deadly, for both students and professors. She nurtured the faint shift, pleased when a lively discussion blossomed.

Comments and observations ranged freely, and she allowed them to continue without interference. Released from leading the conversation, her attention was caught by a large, still shape in a far corner of the room. The man sat alone, taking up more than his fair share of a table meant for two. His blond hair was cropped close to his head, his full beard neatly trimmed. He wore a plaid collared shirt, open at the neck to reveal a white cotton t-shirt underneath.

Even without his uniform, he was easy to recognize as the security guard who had helped her last Friday.

What was he doing in her classroom? She would have noticed if he'd arrived part way through the lesson, so he must have been there for more than two hours already. What purpose could he have for attending?

A student's direct question re-focused her attention, but her awareness of the guard's presence niggled away at the back of her brain for the remainder of the session.

"If anyone's interested, we can continue this in the online chatroom," she offered as students gathered their belongings. "Otherwise, I'll see you all next Monday."

The room emptied. As she closed her laptop and slid it into its case, she cast a surreptitious glance toward the desk where the security guard was sitting. He had unfolded from his chair and was shrugging into a sheepskin leather jacket.

The loose sleeve of her blouse caught the corner of a folder of notes on the edge of the desk and scattered pages across the floor. "For crying out loud," she muttered. She crouched down and began gathering them up.

A large shadow blotted out her own where it lay over the strewn-about papers. Charlotte jerked her head up. The security guard hunkered next to her, his battered face disturbingly close. "Here," he said, his low voice rough.

"Thanks." She took the pages he offered and straightened to her full height.

He stood as well. "Got home okay?" he asked.

"Yes, thank you." She had to look up to meet his eyes. At five-ten, she wasn't used to feeling physically overwhelmed by too many people. But this man was at least six inches taller than her, with wide, solid shoulders and a tapered but muscular torso. She took a small step away.

"Buy winter tires?"

She narrowed her eyes. "No."

"You want to be safe, you need winter tires."

"I appreciate your concern, Mr.—"

"It's Justice. Justice Cooper."

"—Mr. Cooper, but it is not necessary." His eyes were blue, a deep, greyish blue. They regarded her steadily. She tucked the pile of papers into her satchel. "Surely you didn't spend three hours in my class simply to check up on whether I followed your instructions."

He smiled, the movement of his lips so slight she almost didn't see it. But it was obvious in his eyes, which crinkled at the corners. "I'm one of your students. I've been in the class since September."

"No, you haven't." Her response was automatic. "I would have noticed you before."

The grin in his eyes deepened. Flustered, she clarified her comment. "I mean, I would have recognized your name. I haven't seen it on any assignments."

"I don't do the assignments. I'm auditing." His voice rumbled in the deserted room. Footsteps echoed in from the hallway, and then faded away.

Charlotte became aware of their isolation. The last classes of the day were over, and the lonely pall of a large institution settling for the night drifted down. The subtle scent of spicy aftershave and warm male teased her nostrils. Her belly tightened. Hurriedly she hooked the strap of her satchel across her body, gripped the handle of her laptop case and headed for the door.

"I've never understood the point of auditing." Her heels clicked loudly. "If you're going to attend the class, why not do the work and get the credit?"

"I don't care about the credit. I just want to learn." He pushed open the door at the end of the hall and held it wide. Her shoulder brushed his arm as she passed through.

Refusing to be unnerved by his nearness, she continued the conversation. "You'd learn more if you did the assignments. You don't take part in the discussions, either."

"I learn enough. And I like to listen." He spoke with a quiet firmness, neither defensive nor placating.

The halls leading to the Administration Building were empty, except for a security guard doing his rounds. Charlotte swept past without a second glance. She heard Justice offer a quiet greeting, but she was too irritated with him to observe social niceties.

They reached the elevator. "Well, goodnight. I'll see you next week."

"Are you working much longer?"

She looked over her shoulder. He loomed large behind her. Not frightening, just very—*there*. "I have to grab a couple of things from my office and then I'll be heading home."

"I'll stay with you."

"I'm on the third floor. There's no need for you to come up."

"You shouldn't walk to the parking lot alone at this time of night." He pushed the elevator button and motioned her inside when the doors slid open.

Short of refusing to get in, there wasn't much she could do. She waited impatiently while the car slid upward and strode out the doors without giving Justice another look. When they reached the open space just outside her office where Natasha Szpendyk, the administrative assistant she shared with a couple of other professors, had her desk, she tried again. "I might be longer than I thought. Please, don't stay on my account."

"Take your time. I'll wait here." He leaned against the wall and crossed his arms, the leather of his jacket creaking.

"I'm sure you have things of your own to do." She frowned in exasperation. "Don't let me take up any more of your evening."

"It's no problem."

She stared at him, baffled by his amiable persistence. He avoided her eyes, studying the bulletin board across the way, papered in tattered notices for "Roommate Wanted" and "Undergrads Unite!"

With a mild curse, she strode into her office.

*****

Justice had barely finished reading the poster promoting "5 Days of Homelessness" before Charlotte flounced out of her office and down the hall. He followed, hiding his amusement. She would probably insist she had never flounced in her life, but it was the first word that came to mind at the sight of her tip-tilted nose and squared-off shoulders.

"There's really no need for this. I walk to my car alone every night." Her thigh-length black coat swirled about her hips as she entered the elevator. The red scarf around her neck matched the colour in her cheeks, and her pancake hat once again sat frivolously on her curly dark hair.

"You shouldn't." The thought of Charlotte walking without an escort through a dark, deserted parking lot irked him. Not that the university was a particularly dangerous place. But why take unnecessary risks?

"I am perfectly capable of taking care of myself." The doors opened and she stepped out.

Sometimes words weren't enough. He clasped her wrist and spun her around so her back was to the wall.

"What the hell are you doing?" Temper flared her nostrils. "Let me go."

"Make me."

Her eyes widened. He held her loosely, his fingers circling strong yet delicate bones. Her skin was soft and cool. Under his fingertips, her pulse thudded rapidly.

"For God's sake." She tugged with force, but he easily kept his hold. "Exactly what are you trying to prove?"

"You may be capable. I'm stronger." He was all for women's equality, but reality was reality. He was six inches taller and thirty pounds heavier. Did she really think she could win?

"I'll be sure to avoid meeting you late at night, then." She renewed her efforts to get free, her eyes sparking with frustration. Trapped between him and the wall, and hampered by the laptop case she still carried, she could do little but wriggle.

The layers of winter clothing between them did nothing to disguise soft breasts rubbing against him, taut legs struggling to get leverage. He was so close her light scent teased his nose. His body reacted instinctively, his arousal distracting and disturbing.

Her expression changed a fraction of an instant before her knee jerked upward. It gave him just enough warning so he could turn his hip to protect his groin. His quick move reversed their positions, throwing her off balance and bringing her fully against him, his back to the wall. He wrapped one arm about her waist to support her.

"Nice try. Next time, don't telegraph your move," he said.

Her cheeks flushed and she squirmed. He knew the

instant she became aware of his erection. She froze, staring at him with wide eyes.

He released her immediately and stepped back. His hands felt huge and clumsy, club-like. He shoved them into his jacket pockets. "Sorry. I was just making a point." The distress in her face had him dropping his gaze, unable to meet her eyes.

Slender muscles in her throat flexed as she swallowed. "Fine. You've made it. You're bigger and meaner." She walked backward a few steps. "I'm going to my car now. Alone." She turned and strode away, back stiff and straight.

She passed through the doors at the end of the corridor. He cursed silently and followed. He didn't want to frighten her further, but damned if he was going to let her out of his sight until she was safe in her vehicle.

He watched from the foyer as she crossed to the parking lot. The snow from Friday, cleared from sidewalks and roadways, remained in high, heaping piles. She disappeared between the rows of parked cars and he jogged across the road until he caught sight of her again. Slots nearest the building were fairly full, but most of the huge lot was an empty expanse. He heard a quick double beep and saw the lights flash on her SUV as she hit unlock on her fob.

When the reverse lights brightened as she put it in gear, he headed for his own truck, parked one row over. He gave her a few minutes start, and then made his way off campus. He would be back at work tomorrow, but there was little chance he'd see her until next week's class. Maybe by then she'd have forgiven him.

****

Charlotte lifted her mug to her mouth and sipped air.

Empty? She stared at it in confusion. Hadn't she refreshed her tea a minute ago?

She returned the cup to the small circle that was the only clear area on her desk. Spread-eagled books fought to keep their foothold on the crowded expanse, battling for space among fat files, stacks of papers and her laptop. Along the wall to her right, more books were piled within comfortable reach, coloured post-it note tags fluttering in the breeze from the furnace vent. Document boxes rested on the single bed tucked into a corner. Originally a guest room, she had commandeered it as her office when she'd moved in at the end of August.

Knuckling her hands in her lower back, she stretched, groaning at the ache in her shoulders and neck. A glance at the clock in the lower corner of the computer screen revealed she'd worked straight through lunch. Her stomach growled, as if it had been waiting for her brain to catch up before notifying her. Straightening out of her chair, she did a few easy stretches to work out the kinks, and headed for the kitchen.

Brilliant sunshine glared off the glossy granite counters, caressed the dark oak of the small dinette suite, and created pools of warmth on the cozy sofa in the sitting area to her right. Wide windows overlooking the backyard revealed pristine snow and a copse of slate- and silver-coloured birches, delicately leafless against a flat blue sky.

She sat at the small round table and munched on canned tuna and the remains of a tossed salad she'd made the night before. The scene outside was picture-perfect, teasing her thoughts away from the work still to do upstairs. If she was serious about getting a teaching position at a larger university, one that could lead to tenure, she needed to complete her research, finish reworking her doctoral dissertation and get her monograph published. She didn't have time, even on a Saturday afternoon, to go for what would surely be a chilly walk.

Ten minutes later she was crunching across the yard, taking a childish delight in marring the smooth white expanse. Cold nibbled at her toes through her thin leather boots, but at least they were tall enough to keep the snow out. The air was startling in its freshness, and she buried her nose in the thick scarf she'd wound her neck.

At the trees, she turned to look back. During her year at UNBC, she was renting half of a recently built duplex. Two stories, with a garage and three bedrooms and a huge open living area, it was much bigger than she needed, but she was tired of living in tiny apartments. The retired couple who lived in the other side owned both units, and used her side as an income property. They had left a week ago for Mexico, where they would spend the next few months. While they were gone, she was getting a break on the rent in exchange for watering the houseplants, collecting the mail and keeping the driveway clear. It had seemed like the ideal plan, until she'd spent hours shovelling last weekend.

The thought of last week's snowfall brought Justice Cooper to mind. Restlessly, she headed deeper into the trees, finding a well-trodden but narrow path. She continued along its winding route, fists deep in the pockets of her coat. He would have been a lot easier to put out of her mind, if all he'd done was help push her out of the snow. But she'd been unable to forget their encounter on Monday night, reliving it at inconvenient moments all week long.

She barely felt the cold breeze nipping her ears as she recalled how he'd held her, snug against his large, solid bulk. He'd infuriated her with the negligent way he'd proved his point, but it hadn't been anger that had anchored her in place, fixed her startled gaze on his hard, roughhewn face.

It had been unadulterated, unexpected, unwanted lust.

The memory of it had heat flushing the back of her neck, set her pulse thudding. Disgusted with herself, she came to an abrupt halt and spun to retrace her steps. She'd enjoyed enough fresh air. Her head was clear now. It was time to get back to work.

Frenzied barking sounded up ahead. A huge black and tan form barreled around the corner, tongue streaming from its gaping mouth, feathery tail wagging. It darted toward her, dropped its front quarters low to the ground, and then bounced up, yowling and yipping.

She stopped in her tracks. "Good doggie." She wasn't afraid of dogs. Not exactly. Maybe a little—especially big, strange dogs. "Nice doggie. Where's your owner?"

Bright brown eyes gleamed up at her. He—she—it quivered with joy. At least, she hoped it was joy. "Good boy. Or girl." It plopped down and lifted a paw. Despite her caution, she smiled. "Well, it's nice to meet you, too."

With a sudden lunge, the dog leaped up, planting both paws firmly against her chest and knocking her to the ground. Hot breath fanned her face, white teeth gleamed. She shrieked and curled her arms over her head.

CHAPTER THREE

A high-pitched squeal echoed through the trees. "Damn it. Chaucer! Come!" Justice raced around the bend in the path in time to see his rock-brained dog bounding away from a dark figure supine on the ground. "I said *come*, damn you!"

Grinning as only a dog can, Chaucer galumphed to Justice, who quickly snapped on his leash and anchored him to a sapling.

His victim had struggled to a sitting position, dark curls tumbled about her face. Justice took a knee next to her. "Are you all right?"

The woman tossed her hair out of her eyes and stared at him. He stared back in dismay. "Professor Girardet?"

"It's you. Of course it's you." She closed her eyes briefly. "Is that your dog?" Her tone was not complimentary.

"He didn't mean to frighten you."

"He didn't frighten me. He knocked me down." She sounded breathless.

Justice glared at Chaucer, who ignored him and lifted a leg to pee against a tree. "Did he hurt you, Professor?"

"Only my pride. And since your dog just bowled me over, I think you're allowed to call me Charlotte." She motioned him out of the way.

"Let me help you." Justice rose and held out a hand. She stared suspiciously before accepting it and allowing him to haul her to her feet.

She pulled free as soon as she was upright, and stepped away.

"Sorry again about Chaucer."

"Your dog's name is Chaucer?" She arched an eyebrow. "As in the poet?"

He dipped his head in acknowledgement. Her dark brown eyes slid from him to Chaucer—now industriously licking his butt—and back. The tip of her nose twitched.

"It was—interesting—meeting you and your dog." She edged around him. "I'd better get home."

"You live around here?" He shouldn't have been surprised. Residents used the greenbelt trail often, but few strangers found their way onto it.

"Yes." She circled past Chaucer, who woofed as she neared. She jerked.

Damn it, his fool dog had scared her, no matter what she said. The least he could do was offer her comfort. "How about a drink?" he said.

She wasn't wearing her hat today, but a grey, bulky knit scarf puffed out under her chin. Sunlight gleamed on the dark strands of her hair. "A drink?"

"In apology. For Chaucer knocking you over." He didn't like the thought of her being scared. Maybe spending time with the dumb pup would help.

"I've got to get back to work."

He frowned. "It's Saturday."

"I'm doing research. Being a professor isn't only a Monday to Friday job."

"It won't take long to have a drink. Hot chocolate?"

A hint of humour creased the corners of her eyes. "With marshmallows? Mini ones?" She licked her lips.

His gaze zeroed in on her mouth, pink and unpainted. With an effort, he dragged his thoughts away from how she would taste, how her lips would feel against his. "Or Baileys, if you want to be grown up."

The rapid-fire rattle of a woodpecker cut through the forest. She looked over her shoulder, indecision on her face. Her coat was thigh-length, but he could see damp patches on her jeans.

"You're wet." His voice was hoarse and he cleared his throat. "From falling in the snow. You can warm up at my house."

"I really should go home." She took a step back.

"My place is right there." He jerked a thumb toward a wooden fence visible through the trees, the gate in the middle propped open as he had left it. Charlotte peered past him, indecision evident on her face

"Oh." White teeth worried her bottom lip.

The attraction he'd been denying flared. With a tug of one hand, he released Chaucer's leash from the tree. The pup reared onto his hind legs in delight. Justice jerked the leash firmly. "Off." When the dog was under control, he pointed to the snowy path leading to his gate. "I'll keep Chaucer away from you. Watch your step." He guided Charlotte toward the house, his free hand on the small of her back. She resisted at first, but then with a faint sigh, gave in.

"One drink. A quick one. And then I have to go."

****

Charlotte wasn't quite sure how it happened. One minute she was determined to return home and get back to work. The next, she was in Justice's living room, wrapped in a warm woollen throw and ensconced in a high-backed chair while warming her hands on a mug of hot chocolate—with mini-marshmallows *and* Bailey's.

"Sure you don't want to borrow a pair of sweats?"

Justice sat opposite her at one end of a squashy-looking leather sofa. Chaucer—*Chaucer* of all things—was curled on a large dog bed, gnawing happily on a red rubber toy.

"Honestly, I'm not that wet." The thought of wearing Justice's clothing sent a flush of warmth over her skin. She sipped her hot chocolate, wincing as it burned her tongue. The quicker she drank it, the quicker she could go.

"I usually keep him on the leash. But we were close to home, so I let him off for a run." Justice held a matching mug, his big hand dwarfing the porcelain. "He's just a pup and still learning to obey."

She studied the dog in disbelief. "How old is he? He looks full grown to me."

"Nine months."

"How big will he get?"

"Pretty big. He's a cross between a Saint Bernard and Bernese Mountain Dog."

She gaped. "Good Lord."

The dog lost interest in the chew toy and wandered out of the room. Moments later, Charlotte heard enthusiastic lapping coming from the kitchen. She'd seen the food and water dishes when Justice had brought her through the kitchen after leaving their outerwear in a small entry way near the back door. The front room where they sat was panelled in dark wood and had a wide picture window looking onto the street. A huge flat screen TV hung above a gas fireplace, and bookshelves filled another wall from floor to ceiling. More books were stacked on the square coffee table between the sofa and chair, including one of the texts she'd assigned for her medieval poetry class.

She used a spoon to fish out the last marshmallow and placed the empty mug on the coffee table. "Thanks very much. But I definitely have to be going." She rose, shook out the blanket and folded it neatly.

Justice stood as well. "What are you researching?"

"I'm expanding my doctoral dissertation into a book."

"Medieval poetry?"

She was struck anew at the oddity of this hard, physically dominating man's interest in ancient literature. "Yes. It's the next step, if I want to get a tenure-track appointment."

"At UNBC?" He took the blanket from her and draped it over the back of the couch.

"No. I'm only here on a temporary contract. I'd prefer a larger university. Toronto, maybe, or somewhere in the States."

"Big dreams."

He might think so, but Charlotte didn't. Tenure wasn't a dream, it was a necessity. Her career was very strictly mapped out, and the stability tenure would give her was only part of her future plans.

She moved toward the door leading to the kitchen. It was set in a wall covered with photos, prints and paintings. A black and white Ansel Adams hung next to the bold colours of an abstract oil-painting, an old-fashioned tin Coca-Cola sign beside an expertly matted and a framed shot of a hockey player, suspended in mid-air, expression delirious with joy.

Her attention focussed on an eight by ten print of a young boy. It was the traditional school pose—waist up on a nondescript background—but the glee in the child's face was impossible to resist. He sat, slightly hunched, mop of blond hair falling over bright blue eyes hugely enlarged by the thick lenses of his heavy, black-framed glasses. "Isn't he a cutie. Who is he?"

"My son, Max."

She shot a look of surprise over her shoulder. "You have a son?"

"Is that a shock?" Justice stood just behind, a soft look on his craggy face as he regarded the photo.

"Yes, a little. I don't know why." She was no expert when it came to children, but the boy looked older than her nephew, maybe eight or nine. "How old are you?"

A gleam appeared in Justice's eyes—also blue, but a harder, flatter colour than his son's. "Twenty-nine. How old are you?"

She suppressed a twinge of feminine dismay. What was age but a chronological marker anyway? It didn't define you. "Thirty-three." She turned back to the photo. "You must have been very young when he was born."

"Just turned twenty." He reached out and straightened the frame by a hair. "How about you? Kids, husband? The university grapevine has been remarkably silent on your personal life."

"No, no one." She spoke lightly, made sure to smile, so he wouldn't find her pathetic. "Your son—does he live with you? Where is he?"

"He lives with his mother, here in town."

She desperately wanted to ask more—had he and his son's mother been married? Why were they no longer together?—but felt she'd reached her quota of impertinent questions. "I should get back."

"You keep saying that. And yet—" He held out his left hand, palm up, in a questioning gesture. His fingers were long with heavy knuckles, the veins in his wrist prominent, leading up his brawny arm to a well-defined bicep revealed by the short sleeve of his black t-shirt.

Hunger to have that hand on her shuddered through her. Yes. Definitely time to get going. She strode through the kitchen and lifted her coat from the hook. "Thanks for the hot chocolate." Chaucer scrambled over and snuffled at her boots, around her knees. She hesitated, and then reached down and gingerly patted his head.

"No problem." Justice slapped his thigh, calling the dog away, and leaned down to give him a vigorous body rub.

Light shone on Justice's face as he tussled with the dog, glinted off his thick eyebrows, a softer gold than his beard. She studied the scar that bisected the brow over his left eye. How had he got it, she wondered, irrationally compelled to touch the old wound, soothe it.

He looked up suddenly and heat flushed her face, embarrassed to be caught staring. "See you Monday," he said.

"Yes." She grasped the door knob, turned it. "See you Monday."

Why did Monday suddenly seem so far away?

****

"Need help with that?" Justice crouched in front of Max.

"I got it." His son's face scrunched with determination, tongue poking from the corner of his mouth, as his small fingers hooked into the thick laces and tightened them up the ankle of his hockey skate.

"You sure?"

"Daaaad." The drawn-out syllable was long-suffering. Max pushed his glasses up his nose and frowned. "I can do it myself."

The bulky shoulder pads under his red jersey made his neck look slender and fragile. "Just asking." Justice ruffled Max's hair and moved on to the next player. The dressing room was crowded with small bodies, some struggling with their own cumbersome gear, others getting help from parents. It could have been any dressing room, on any early Sunday morning, in any small town across Canada. Justice knew—he'd seen most of them.

The scents of old sweat and musty gear had soaked into the breeze block walls, the wooden benches, the black matting on the floor. It was the odour of his childhood, one that spoke of hard work and friendly rivalry, crushing defeat and glorious victory. It never failed to comfort him.

"I'll meet you on the ice," he called out to the team. "You've got five minutes or everyone is skating lines." A groan of dismay followed him from the room. He grinned.

The heavy steel bar holding the gate closed clanged when he slapped it open. Shoving his hands into his well-worn gloves, so supple with age he barely felt them, he stepped onto the ice. His first stop was the bench, to drop off the bucket of pucks, the sack of triangular cones and his clipboard. Then it was time for a skate.

The sound of steel biting into ice was as familiar as his own heartbeat. He picked up speed between the blue lines, didn't let up as he cut hard behind the net and cruised up the other side. Though he was only coaching, he still wore a helmet, but no visor, and the crisp cool air stirred by his passage was sweet against his face.

His players started to make their way onto the ice. It was a Novice team, made up of eight- and nine-year old boys and girls. When he'd been nine years old, he'd already been scouted for Rep, but this was a House league team.

Justice didn't give a shit what level of skill these kids had. He was loving every minute of coaching them all. Especially his son.

The last player stumbled onto the rink just in time to

avoid the dreaded punishment of lines. Justice took the kids through skating drills, moved on to game strategy, and then divided them up for a quick scrimmage to end the hour-long practise.

He coasted along, acting as referee and linesman when needed. The play bogged down in one end and he waited near the players' bench, watching.

Dan Moffat, one of his assistant coaches and dad to Max's best friend, Devin, was working the gate nearest him. "Not quite what you were used to, I suppose," Dan said.

"What do you mean?" Justice nodded in approval as Max banked the puck off the boards and finally cleared the zone.

"Coaching eight-year olds isn't exactly the same as playing in the Western Hockey League." Dan rattled the steel bar of the gate, calling for a line change. "All those great players, one step away from the bigs."

Two boys who barely reached Justice's waist skated past him, hurrying off the ice to make way for their teammates. "Everyone has to start somewhere." He shook off the memory of those years, when hockey had stopped being fun. "First to the puck, boys, first to the puck!" he shouted to the players on the ice before turning back to Dan. "It's not all about making the National Hockey League." He wanted his kids to learn about being part of a team, how to work together for a common goal.

He skated away from Dan to direct one of his defense into the correct position. A few minutes later, he blew the play down. "Time's up. Do a couple of laps to cool off. And don't forget your water bottles when you leave the ice."

He came out of the change room ten minutes later to

find his ex-wife waiting in the hall. She hadn't sat in the stands during the practise, as most parents did, but he understood why. Tiffani Mason hated and feared hockey. It hadn't always been that way. But that was the way it was now. She'd only given in and let Max play after a long struggle.

"He's almost ready," Justice said, tossing his equipment bag onto the floor.

"That's fine." She slung a brilliant pink purse with rhinestone-studded straps over her shoulder. Her blonde hair was piled on top of her head in a messy knot, her faux fur jacket buttoned tight to her throat against the arena's chill. "He's been asking when you're coming for dinner."

"I told him maybe Wednesday."

"I work Wednesday."

The minefield that was a post-divorce relationship made Justice's head ache. The only way he could deal with it was to keep the goal in mind—giving Max a healthy, happy life, despite not having a father living with him. "We'll figure it out."

Other parents milled about, talking and laughing. The dressing room door opened and closed as kid after kid streamed out.

"See you next week, Coach," said Monica, one of his best defensemen. She grinned up at him as she dragged her hockey bag past.

"You bet." Frigid air swirled in as she pushed open the exterior door.

Tiffani waited as other players said their goodbyes. In a lull she asked, "Could you come by today? The tap in the bathroom is leaking. I was hoping you would take a look."

More than two years ago she had blindsided him with her demand for a divorce. With the luxury of hindsight, he could now see the signs he had missed in the months, if not years, leading up to her ultimatum. But he'd thought he could fix things, make it all right, if only he tried hard enough. God knows he'd tried. And failed miserably.

Separating from her, leaving Max, was one of the toughest things he'd ever had to do. He'd spent long, dark nights wondering where he'd gone wrong, plotting how to bring his family back together. But Tiffani had made it plain, in strident, no-holds-barred terms, that reconciliation was not in her plans.

Until recently, that is. Lately she'd been asking for help, encouraging him to stop by, reminding him of the good times they'd shared. He wasn't entirely sure what her motivation was, but he was determined not to get sucked into repeating a doomed relationship.

Yet he couldn't refuse her his help. "I have to bring Dad his groceries. I can stop by after that."

She rested her head against his shoulder. "Thanks."

"No problem." Strands of hair freed from her topknot tickled his neck. The high-heeled boots she wore gave her height, but in reality she wasn't quite five foot four. If Charlotte wore those same boots she'd reach his nose. He'd never dated a woman as tall as her.

Dated? What the hell?

Thinking about another woman while his ex-wife snuggled up against him did nothing to loosen the knots in the back of his neck. He tried to ease away, but Tiffani moved with him, tucking her fingers into the crook of his elbow.

She looked up at him, elfin face serious. "Honest. I don't know what I'd do without you."

"You'd be fine." He gave her hand an encouraging pat, then gently plucked it off his arm and stepped back.

No matter how much he wanted a family—wanted to be able to give Max a home with a mother and father, maybe even siblings some day—there was one thing he knew he could never do.

Get back together with Tiffani.

The toxicity of their relationship hadn't been cured by their separation—only neutralized.

CHAPTER FOUR

Somewhere in the depths of her purse, her cell rang. Charlotte dragged her attention away from the email she was writing and dug around until she found it.

Setting it to speaker, she tossed it on her desk. "I'm working, Sonny," she said absently, already back to the keyboard, compiling notes she needed to send to a student.

"When are you not?" her sister replied. "Are you at home?"

"No, the office." Her small, square space in the Administration Building had a large window overlooking a traffic roundabout and the student residences. The sun was setting behind the three-storey buildings, bronzing the snow and gilding the leafless trees. It was quarter after four.

"I can't keep your schedule straight. I thought you went home earlier than this on Tuesdays."

"Sometimes I do, sometimes I don't. I had a meeting with a student at three-thirty. We just finished." The essay they'd been reviewing was still scattered across her desk. She tried to keep her office here neater than the one at home, but it was a never-ending battle. What did it matter that it looked disorganized? She could always find what she needed.

"Maybe I should call you back," Sonny said. "I can hear you typing."

"Just finished." She tapped the last key with a flourish and sat back in her chair. "You've got me now. What's up?"

"It's just that—I was hoping you'd be home when I called."

Something in Sonny's voice finally cut through the myriad of thoughts buzzing in Charlotte's brain. The hairs on the back of her neck stood up. "You've got me worried. Is it Mom? Dad?"

"No, no, they're fine." Now she was paying attention, the strain in Sonny's tone was obvious. "I didn't want you to hear this through the grapevine. Or, God forbid, see it on Facebook."

Charlotte gripped the edge of her desk. "Sonny. Just tell me."

"Okay." A deep breath huffed through the connection. "Richard and Elyse are expecting."

A sharp stab of surprise pierced her. She sucked in a long, calming breath. It shouldn't matter. Not anymore. Yet it did. "They've only been married three months." She eased back in her chair, conscious of a new brittleness in her bones.

"They made the announcement at work this afternoon. Thomas called me right away, so I could—" She broke off.

"Warn me? Thanks, but it wasn't necessary." Her heart was still beating, her lungs still functioning. She could do this. "Make sure Thomas offers my best wishes when he sees them tomorrow."

"I know this has to be hard—"

This time it was Charlotte who cut Sonny off. "No, it's fine. I'm fine. Richard must be ecstatic."

"It's not your fault things didn't work out, Charlotte. You know that."

"Of course, I do." Richard had wanted something she couldn't give. It was no one's fault. It was just what was.

Charlotte gazed at the open, empty doorway and said, "My next appointment is here. I've got to go."

"Charlotte—"

"Thanks for telling me. I appreciate it." She cut the connection.

****

Justice's shift ended at five o'clock. Instead of heading directly to the parking lot, however, he detoured through the Administration Building.

Last night, during class, he'd sat at the back in his usual place and listened to Charlotte bring ancient, archaic poetry to life. She read selections from the old English version of *The Canterbury Tales*—one of his favourites— and he had absorbed the lilt and rhythm of her voice while watching her roam about the room, every inch of her tall, curvy body living the passion of the words.

He hadn't been able to get her out of his head, not since that errant, random thought on Sunday morning while standing in a frigid, drafty hallway with his ex-wife clinging to his arm. And certainly not after hearing her recite the raunchy, bawdy, joyful words of the Wife of Bath.

Date Charlotte—Professor Girardet? Between the two of them, he was certain he was the only one considering such an action.

He climbed the stairs two at a time until he reached the third floor corridor. Still thinking about dating Charlotte, he rounded the corner, almost bowling over her administrative assistant, coming from the other direction.

Natasha Szpendyk shrieked and clapped a hand to her chest. "Justice. Oh, my goodness."

"I'm so sorry," he said, steadying her. "Are you okay?"

She waved off his concern. She was whip-thin, just over five feet tall, had a database for a brain, and ran her professors with a firm hand. "I'm fine. Late to get my daughter to dance class, for which she'll never forgive me, but otherwise unharmed." She smiled and tossed him a half-frantic look as she rushed off.

His soft-soled shoes made little sound on the carpet tiles. When he reached Charlotte's office door, he stopped and looked in.

She sat in a high-backed chair behind a desk piled with papers and books. The overhead fluorescents were off, and a lamp cast a pool of amber light on the cluttered surface. He saw her in one-quarter profile as she looked out the window, the glow limning her nose and chin in gold.

She looked unutterably sad. And lonely.

He knocked softly on the jamb. "Charlotte?"

She bolted upright and twisted toward him. "You really have to stop doing that."

"Doing what?" He took a step into the room.

"Sneaking up on me. You and your dog." Her voice was tight, angry.

Surely she wasn't that pissed only because he'd startled her again. "Sorry," he said, positive he had nothing to apologize for but certain it was the right thing to say.

Jumping to her feet, she shoved papers and books haphazardly into her bag. Her coat was draped over the back of her chair and she pulled it off with such force the seat spun around. She jammed her arms in the sleeves, threw the strap of her satchel over her head and snatched up a small duffel bag.

Familiar with a female in a rage after his years with Tiffani, he watched Charlotte through narrowed eyes. She stalked three paces toward him and stared at him, nose raised in disdain. "I'm leaving now. Will you get out of my way?"

He didn't move. "What's wrong?" He'd grown wary of asking the same question of his ex-wife. But the set of Charlotte's shoulders, the thinness of her mouth spoke of hurt, of pain.

"It's nothing to do with you." Hectic patches of red glowed on her cheeks, and he could see her trembling. Her brows drew together in a fierce vee. "What are you doing here, anyway?"

As he wasn't sure himself, he hesitated. It went unnoticed. She charged on. "You didn't come to see me as a student. You don't do the assignments, don't care about grades." Bafflement filled her voice. "Surely you aren't here to walk me to my car. I made myself perfectly clear about that the last time you tried to be an overbearing, overprotective...*man*." She almost spit the final word, at last giving him a clue as to where her ire was really directed.

She stood rigid, back poker straight. Her eyes glistened in the dim light and panic rose in his chest. Was she crying? Over a guy? The thought burned. He wasn't even certain if there was a guy, but he wanted to break his nose for hurting her.

He shoved aside that confusing reaction. "Is that a gym bag?"

Her mouth dropped open. "A gym bag?" She hoisted the duffel and stared at it blankly. "Yes, but why do you care?"

If those had been tears in her eyes, they hadn't overflowed onto her cheeks. Thank Christ. "Are you going to work out?"

"Oh, my God." She scrubbed the heels of her hands against her temples. "I go to the gym in the mornings, before work. What's it to you?"

"You look like you need to burn up some energy." He didn't like the thought of her going home in this state. From her mulish expression, though, any suggestion she needed to be looked after might result in blood being shed. His blood. "Maybe you should do another workout."

She'd braided her hair into a thick, dense tail, and curly tendrils twisted about her ears, at the nape of her neck. "You think I should go to the gym again?" she asked, confusion clouding her forehead. It seemed to have defused some of her tension, and he took that as an encouraging sign.

"I've got a change of clothes in my truck," he said. "I'll meet you at the Northern Sport Centre." The university's gym was just across the road from the main campus.

A pulse tripped madly in her throat. For a moment he had the insane desire to place his mouth on it, feel that life force under his lips. She contemplated him with dark, furious eyes and barked out a despairing laugh. "Why not? I was going to go home, work on my book. But right now I don't think I'd accomplish anything useful." She gestured to the door. "Lay on, MacDuff."

****

"Anyone in the studio?" Justice asked the staff member at the reception desk.

"No, sir," the young man answered. From the size of his shoulders, Charlotte thought, he must have been trying to make up for his lack of height by increasing his bulk. "It's all yours."

Justice nodded at Charlotte as he swiped his magnetic

44

membership tag against the reader. "Meet me here after you change."

She beeped her own tag and followed him down the stairs to the locker rooms. As she swapped her dignified professor clothing for a pair of yoga pants and an athletic top, she argued with herself. What was she doing here? She should be at home, burying herself in her office, working to finish her book. A tenure-track appointment was even more precious now. It would validate everything she'd sacrificed.

But she couldn't bear to be alone. Not right now. Her muscles shook from suppressed tension.

Justice was waiting for her in the lobby. He wore a grey t-shirt that might once have had a graphic on the front, but was so faded she couldn't be sure. The sleeves had been ripped off, revealing impressive biceps. Basketball shorts hung loose about his hips, falling almost to his knees. Golden hair dusted his shins, his forearms.

Her anger burned brighter at her body's instinctive response. She didn't want to be attracted to this...this brute, this aggressively physical male. Her spine stiffened. Damned if she let biological chemistry control her.

He led her into a mid-sized studio. The floor was scuffed blond hardwood, springy beneath her feet. One wall was completely covered in mirrors. Hanging from the ceiling were various bags—some long and cylindrical, others fat teardrops.

She stopped in her tracks. "Boxing?"

"I thought you might want to hit something."

A vision of Richard's face as he'd broken off their relationship rose to mind. He'd been apologetic, sincere in his desire not to hurt her. He'd done so anyway. She could still feel the searing pain of his rejection, more than a year later.

Her fingers curled into fists.

Justice moved to a cabinet and took out a pair of blunt, blue boxing gloves and a roll of tape. He motioned her over. "Hold out your hand."

He swiftly wrapped her wrist once, twice, three times, and then looped the tape across her palm and between her fingers. His touch was deft and sure. "MacDuff?" he asked, his voice breaking into her wandering thoughts.

She had no idea what he was talking about, and then remembered her last words in the office. "Oh. A Shakespeare character. From *MacBeth*."

"I know." He leaned over her wrist and used his teeth to rip the tape. His beard brushed her fingers and she stifled a twitch. "It's what made me think of boxing. MacBeth, exhorting him to fight." He began wrapping her other hand.

Her eyes widened in surprise. "You know the quote?"

He finished the tape job and released her. "Yours isn't the first course I've audited." He returned the roll of tape to the cupboard and held out a glove.

Bemused, she shoved her hand in. "I'm pretty sure you're the first security guard I've ever had in my class, though."

He tightened the laces, held out the second glove. "How would you know?"

She sighed. "Fair enough." Holding her protected hands in front of her face, she twisted them back and forth, studying them as if they belonged to someone else. "Now what?"

"Now, you punch." He pointed at a heavy bag, suspended and still.

She approached it gingerly. "This really isn't me." She

tossed a glance over her shoulder. "I'm more of a treadmill kind of girl. Besides, I'm not angry anymore." The words were out of her mouth before she consciously thought them, and surprisingly they were the truth. Somewhere along the line, as she'd talked with Justice about boxing, about Shakespeare, her fury had drained out of her.

"Who upset you?"

"Nobody worth the trouble." And she meant it. Richard wasn't worth it. If he'd truly been the man she thought him to be, they'd still be together. But he wasn't, and they weren't, so what was the use in moping about it? But the news of his bride's pregnancy rankled, more than she cared to admit.

****

Justice watched Charlotte standing next to the heavy bag, tall and strong and goddamn gorgeous. He kept his gaze glued to her face, no matter how much they wanted to wander down her body. Her skin-tight pants and figure-hugging top left little to his imagination.

Not that it stopped him from imagining what she'd look like out of them.

"You're a parent, right?" Her blurted question had him raising an eyebrow. A slight blush tinted the back of her neck. "I mean, you have a son. Was it a planned thing? Or did it just happen?"

"It? Thing?" He couldn't help but tweak her about her word choices. For an English professor, her vocabulary seemed rather limited.

Her blush deepened and she continued to stare at the bag, refusing to meet his eye. "Did you and your wife sit down one day and say 'Let's have a child?' Did both of you want one?"

"No, Tiffani didn't plan to have Max. And I was

scared spitless about being a father." He still lost his breath sometimes, thinking about those early days. He'd been terrified of doing something wrong, of hurting Max with his big, clumsy hands.

"I don't get it." She nudged the bag with one glove. Her face showed vague surprise when it barely moved. "What is it about wanting to have a kid that changes people?"

"I guess you have to have one to understand." He moved around to stand behind the bag, facing Charlotte.

She tapped the bag harder, her face shuttered, closed. "Yeah, well, that doesn't help me."

He had no words to describe his feelings for Max. Maybe that's why he loved the rhythm of poetry. It, too, described things indescribable. "Do you want children someday?"

This time the punch she threw had enough weight to set the bag swinging weakly. She frowned at her fist.

"You need to step into it."

She turned her frown on him. "What?"

He spread his feet, left foot forward, right foot back, about shoulder-width apart. "Put your weight on your back foot, step forward and extend your arm. Get your body behind it."

She mimicked his stance with fierce concentration. Whatever was bothering her seemed to have come back in full force. While she no longer appeared angry, waves of upset and tension flowed from her. He figured she'd dodged his question about children for a reason. A reason that was none of his business.

"Hold your fists at your chin, elbows together." He demonstrated. "Now try."

Her next punch was a definite improvement. She

nodded grimly.

"Hit through the bag." He wasn't wearing gloves, so he mimed hitting the bag. "Reach past it, not just to the closest part."

She settled in again, knees loose, arms up. The thwack of leather hitting leather reverberated in the quiet room.

"Nice. Repeat that, ten times."

He paced her through a few more rounds. Sweat gleamed at her temples, the hollow of her neck, dampened the material between her shoulder blades. He could smell her, rich and earthy.

Finally, Charlotte sank to the floor, leaning against a wall. Her chest heaved with exertion. "I had no idea how empowering that would feel." She guzzled water from a bottle, the slender tendons of her throat flexing. "That was amazing."

Justice sat next to her, careful to keep his distance. "Feeling better, then."

"I am." She twisted her neck to check the time on the wall clock behind her. "If I'd gone home, I would have done nothing but mope. Now I feel like I could work all night."

A muffled beeping sounded to Justice's right. He snaked out an arm, dragged his sports bag closer and scooped out his phone. The campus security office number appeared on screen.

"Hey, Coop." It was Elizabeth Paxton, the only female security guard on staff. "Sorry to bug you."

"No worries. What do you need?" Justice's attention wandered as he watched a bead of sweat trickle over Charlotte's collarbone.

"I have a young lady here. She's got an odd story, and I'm not sure whether I should call Nielson in or not."

Elizabeth had been with the team for more than three years, and was a practical, no-nonsense woman. Since Nielson's arrival, however, Justice had noticed she'd started second-guessing herself. He hoped it was only difficulty adjusting to a new regime and that she'd soon be back to form, for her sake as well as the rest of the crew.

"Is she okay?" He rolled to his feet. Charlotte tilted her head and peered up at him.

"Yes, she's fine. But you know how Nielson wants to be alerted of anything out of the ordinary. This isn't over the top, but something just isn't sitting right. I wouldn't mind some advice."

"Who are you on shift with?"

"Brent. He's out doing a walk around now."

Justice grunted. Brent Parvat was the newest member of the team. He could see why Elizabeth wanted another opinion. "I'm at the Northern Sport Centre. I can be there in five."

"I appreciate it."

He tossed the phone into his bag and snagged a pair of track pants.

"What's going on? Nothing serious, I hope." Charlotte rose, a faint wrinkle between her brows.

"Not sure. I've got to go back to the office." He stepped into the sweats. "You all right?"

She waved a negligent hand. "Of course. Go on. I'll see you around."

"Don't walk to your car alone." He shrugged into his coat. Despite the urgency, he waited until she'd tilted her head in agreement. "Good. Sorry about this."

"There's nothing to be sorry for." She leaned against the wall and smiled up at him.

She definitely looked settled, steadier, certainly as

compared to when he'd found her in her office. He could put aside his worry over her—for the moment at least. With a nod of goodbye he hustled out of the studio.

CHAPTER FIVE

"Look, it's not that big a deal." Imogene Martinson's bewildered gaze met Justice's. "But my floor monitor thought I should tell Security, so I did. I really have to get back to my dorm. I've got an essay due tomorrow."

"I'll be as quick as I can," Justice said as he pulled a chair next to the girl.

There was no space for visitors in the small office, so Elizabeth had parked Imogene at a desk tucked against the far wall. Elizabeth herself sat in a glass cubicle that jutted out from the office into the hall, giving an unimpeded view in all directions. She had short, jaggedly-cut dark hair and a square build that the guard uniform did nothing to enhance. From her perch on a tall stool she flashed Imogene an encouraging smile. "Just one more time, then we'll let you go."

The girl rolled her eyes as only an eighteen-year old can and sighed heavily. "Fine. I'd been working in the library, and when it closed, I headed to my dorm." She spaced out her words as if talking to small children. Justice felt amusement flicker, but kept his expression noncommittal. "When I reached the road, I saw a car coming. The headlights were off, which was weird, but I just thought the driver had forgotten to turn them on."

"Did you step into the road?"

Imogene raised her eyebrows. "Of course not. I waited in case he hadn't seen me." She flicked her straight blonde hair behind her shoulders with an impatient gesture. "I guess he did, though, because he pulled up a little way away. I thought he was waiting for me to cross, but then the passenger door opened." She smiled. "He was listening to The Pretty Reckless. I love that band."

Justice smiled back. "Me, too."

"Really?" She regarded him with suspicion. "What's your favourite song?"

"I'm partial to "Heaven Knows" but haven't had a chance to really listen to the rest of the album yet." He ignored her open-mouthed surprise and continued. "Are you sure it was a man?"

Imogene answered with a bit less attitude than before. "That's the impression I got. I couldn't see into the car." The corners of her mouth turned down. "Doesn't a light usually come on when you open a door? I don't think it did, or I would have seen him better."

Brent Parvat entered the office. His questioning gaze flicked from Elizabeth to Justice to Imogene. Justice sent him a silent signal and he joined Elizabeth at the window without comment.

He continued his conversation with Imogene. "What happened then?"

She shook her head. "Nothing. I crossed the road and into the dorm."

"He didn't talk to you? Ask you to get in?"

"No." She drew out the syllable. "I told her that when I called in." She jerked a chin at Elizabeth.

"Can you describe the car?"

"I don't know. Dark, maybe four doors. I didn't pay attention." She shifted in her seat. "Look, I don't know what the fuss is all about. I didn't even want to call in the first place, and then you made me come here to tell you exactly what I said over the phone." She stood and zipped up her jacket. "I've really got to go and finish my essay."

"Thanks for talking to us, Imogene." Justice walked the few steps to the door with her. "It probably is nothing, but you did the right thing by calling. Mr. Parvat will walk you back to your dorm."

She flapped a hand and scuttled away, Brent following. Justice turned to Elizabeth. "Make sure you bring Brent up to speed when he gets back."

She nodded. "So, what do you think? Do I call Nielson?"

"I don't think you need to." He scratched his chin through his beard, absently noting it was nearly time for a trim. "Like I told Imogene, it's probably nothing. I haven't heard of any similar incidents, have you?"

"No."

"Write it up, including that you called me. Wouldn't hurt to send out a general reminder to all students to be aware of their surroundings, especially now it gets dark so early. Nielson can decide to do that himself. But I don't think we have anything to worry about."

****

She really needed to invest in a good pair of winter boots. She was tired of having her feet freeze while she shovelled.

It had snowed again, another layer of deceptively heavy white. People at work moaned about the early arrival of winter, assuring Charlotte that November wasn't usually like this. At least it hadn't been as big a dump as the previous storm. She'd manoeuvred out of the campus lot with relative ease, and made it safely into her garage without incident. Then, in a fit of ambition, she decided to tackle the driveway right away.

The wide, deep scoop of the shovel cut through the

drifts, the snow tumbling in front of it like a curling wave. The exertion raised her heart rate pleasantly, and she plodded back and forth, lifting and throwing each load with economic movements. Her research had led to a crossroads, and she needed to decide what direction to follow. The repetitive action was a soothing backdrop on which to consider the problem.

Half the drive was done before enthusiastic and familiar barking roused her from her reverie. She spun sharply, half crouching against the expected onslaught, and then relaxed. Chaucer bounced on the end of a leash, firmly controlled by Justice, tall and solid in the gloom. A measure of tension returned when she noticed a small figure at Justice's side.

The boy wore a puffy, padded coat in a silvery blue. A blue and white knit cap was pulled low over his ears, and matching mittens protected his hands. His cheeks were rosy from the cold, the lenses of his glasses misty. His laughter rang out sharp and clear as the rambunctious pup twisted in a tight circle and lost his balance, sprawling to the ground, four legs spread awkwardly.

"Evening, Charlotte." Justice's face was shadowed under the brim of a red ball cap with the words "Snow Cats" crossing the crown.

"Hello." She approached, keeping an eye on Chaucer, but he seemed content to lay in the snow, panting. "This must be Max."

Justice laid a hand on the boy's shoulder. "Max, I'd like you to meet Professor Girardet. She teaches at the university."

"Cool." The boy's eyes were wide, magnified by the strong prescription of his lenses. "I'm going to go to university someday."

Charlotte felt faintly nervous under his serious gaze. She cleared her throat. "I see. What would you like to study?"

"Engineering. I want to build things, like bridges and buildings." He looked up at Justice. "Dad and I are going to make a Popsicle-stick bridge for science fair this year."

"That sounds like fun."

"Yeah. We looked it up on online and everything. We want to build the longest one ever, right, Dad?"

Justice smiled down at his son. "We'll do our best." Chaucer scrambled to his feet and tugged at the leash. "I want to talk to the professor for a bit. Why don't you walk Chaucer to the end of the street?" He handed over the leash. "Remember, make him behave. He has to learn to walk properly."

"Okay." Max gripped the strap determinedly. "Let's go, Chaucer." They set off at a brisk pace toward the cul-de-sac at the end of the road.

Justice moved to stand by Charlotte's shoulder. He kept an eye on his son and dog as he spoke. "This where you live?"

"Yes."

"I figured you must be in the area, after we met on the path." He shuffled his feet, enormous in heavy black boots, scuffing at the snow. "We often walk the dog this way."

"It's a nice neighbourhood." A breeze blew up, nipping the end of her nose and sweeping strands of hair across her cheeks. She tucked them out of the way with a damp mitten.

He shifted toward her, taking his gaze off the boy and dog for a moment. "I meant to stop by your office today, but didn't have the chance. So, since coincidence led me here, I'd like to say I'm sorry for rushing off last night."

She slanted him a glance. Beams from the streetlight caught in his beard, sparking bronze and gold. "There's no need." She gripped the shovel, aware of the urge to brush the short strands, discover if they were soft or bristly. "I'm sure it was something important."

"It wasn't, but I didn't know that at the time." He reached for the handle. "Max and Chaucer will be a while yet. Why don't I finish this off for you? As an apology."

She backed away, held the shovel behind her. "I told you, no apology is necessary."

"As a neighbourly gesture, then." In a swift move, he plucked it away, leaving her empty handed and gaping. "You can return the favour."

"I can?"

"Shovelling is thirsty work. And Max loves hot chocolate. With marshmallows." He scraped the blade through the snow, tossed the load onto what would be lawn in June. "No Bailey's for him, though."

Charlotte crossed her arms. "I have work to do. On my book. And I don't have marshmallows. Or Bailey's for that matter."

"Do you have hot chocolate?"

"Yes."

"Good enough." He effortlessly tossed another scoop of snow.

"Didn't you hear me? I don't have time to entertain." She stood in his path. He sidestepped around her.

"I'm saving you the time it would take to clear this driveway. Surely you can spare a minute or two to give a couple of guys a hot drink."

Once again, his imperturbable will baffled her. She stomped to the front door. "Fine. I'll make the hot chocolate. But you're going to earn it." She pointed across the yard to the duplex's other drive. "I'm looking after that side as well. Don't come in until you've done both."

****

Max returned from walking Chaucer. He left the dog outside with Justice, who was still shovelling, and now sat at Charlotte's small dinette table. His feet, sporting mismatched socks, dangled, swinging as he talked.

She discovered he had a lot to say. Other than her niece and nephew, Charlotte had little opportunity to spend time with children. She found herself unwillingly fascinated by the developing personality present in her kitchen.

"My dad and I are going sledding this weekend." He folded his arms on the table top and rested his chin. She was no expert, but he seemed rather small for his age. Considering Justice's height, she guessed that wouldn't be the case for long. "There's an awesome hill at my school. We go a hundred miles an hour."

"Really? That's pretty fast." She popped open the hot chocolate container and spooned powder into three mugs.

"Well, not actually a hundred miles an hour." Concern filled his small face. "I was just ex-agg-er-ating." He pronounced the word carefully.

"I understand," she assured him. "What else do you do with your dad?"

"He coaches my hockey team. It's pretty cool, because he knows a lot of stuff about hockey. He almost played in the NHL."

Charlotte paused as she poured boiling water. "He did?"

Max's chest puffed out with pride. "He had a contract and everything. But then he had to come home and take care of Papa."

"Is that your grandfather?"

"Yeah. Dad's dad."

Curiosity won over politeness. "What happened to him?"

"He had an accident at work. He's in a wheelchair now." He spoke with the insouciance of youth, tragedy taken in stride. Why wouldn't he? Max had never known anything different for his grandfather.

"And your dad never went back to playing hockey?" She should have felt uncomfortable, pumping a child for information, but couldn't stop herself.

"Nah. He and Mom got married instead." He scrambled onto his knees on the chair and leaned his arms on the table. "Dad doesn't live with us now, but they're going to get back together soon. I know it."

Charlotte's heart cracked a little. Max sounded matter-of-fact, yet she could hear the longing in his voice. Without knowing more about the situation, she couldn't bring herself to agree with him. It would be too cruel, buoying his hopes, should it only be a young child's wish to have two parents at home.

"Is the hot chocolate ready?"

"Almost." She gave the last mug one last stir, tapped the spoon on the rim. "Do you want milk in it? It's hot."

"Yes, please."

A dark shape loomed through the glass as the back door opened a crack. Justice peered through, using his knee to stop Chaucer's determined rush. "Okay if I let him loose in the yard? I've closed the gate so he doesn't get out. Otherwise I can tie him up in the front."

"No, of course, it's fine."

Justice commanded the dog to sit and stay, and despite uncontrollable wiggles Chaucer did so, at least long enough to let Justice step through the door. He toed off his boots and left them on the mat, padding to the table in sock feet much larger than his son's. He joined the boy at the table.

Charlotte carried over both mugs. "Sorry, no extra goodies."

He lifted a shoulder in a "no problem" gesture and blew across the surface of the hot liquid.

Charlotte studied his face. She supposed he'd broken his nose and scarred his brow in a game. For some reason, she couldn't see him as a fighter, despite his size. His actions with his son, his dog, spoke of a gentle soul. Never mind the interest in medieval poetry.

Max nattered away, Justice listening with his head tilted forward, one elbow slung casually over the back of the chair. His eyes cut sideways and met Charlotte's, catching her staring.

A blush heated her throat and she lowered her eyelids, belatedly covering her thoughts. She sipped her own drink with concentration.

She certainly wasn't a hockey fanatic, but as a Canadian she couldn't help but be aware of the importance the sport had in the country's psyche. Playing in the NHL was every young hockey player's dream. What had Justice felt, having that dream snatched away from him?

A disturbing thread of connection wound through her at the thought. After all, she knew a lot about unattainable dreams.

****

A little while later, they headed home. Max trotted at Justice's side. "Professor Girardet must be really smart."

"Because she teaches at university?" Justice gave a sharp tug on the leash, bringing Chaucer to heel as they paused at an intersection.

"Yeah. She told me she went to school for ten years *after* Grade Twelve so she could be a professor." The wonder in Max's voice was a clear indication of how impressed he was.

A minivan rolled to a stop, and they crossed the road. "If you really want to be an engineer," Justice said, "you'll have to go to school for a long time, too."

"That would be okay. I like school."

Max walked along quietly. Justice glanced down. His son's mouth was pursed in a thoughtful frown. He waited.

Finally, the boy broke the silence. "Do you like Professor Girardet?"

Justice knew a loaded question when he heard one. He answered simply. "Yes."

"Like *like* her, as a friend or—you know." The snow crunched under their boots, Chaucer's happy panting accompanying the rhythm. Max kept his head lowered, the vulnerable back of his neck exposed to the cold night air.

Obviously he wasn't getting away with the easy answer. "I don't know," Justice said, determined to be honest. "Right now, I like her as a friend. But I might like her as something more, when I get to know her better." Wasn't his son too young to know about the different relationships between adults? Tiffani would never expose the boy to situations beyond his years, but God knew what he heard on the schoolyard. And now he thought of it, Max was only a couple years younger than Justice had been when sexually charged stories had started swirling through hockey dressing rooms, told by bragging boys on the verge of manhood.

Max stuck out a hand and trailed it against a leafless hedge bordering the sidewalk. Snow tumbled off the dried brown branches. "I only wondered, 'cause Mom said you might be coming home."

Justice hissed in a breath, the cold air sharp against his teeth. He stopped Max with a hand on his shoulder, shortened his grip on the leash and knelt down, face to face with his son.

His heart splintered at the wistfulness he saw in Max's expression. "Your mom shouldn't have told you that."

"Isn't it true?" He pressed his lips together.

"I'm sorry, Max." He pulled off his gloves and zipped Max's coat a little higher under his chin. "You know I love you, right?" Max nodded. "It doesn't matter whether you live with me or your mom, or if I live with you or on my own. I'll always love you."

"I know." His tone was resigned. Chaucer whined and rubbed against Max, causing him to stagger. With a small grin, he wrapped his arm around the dog's neck. "I just wish, sometimes."

"I just wish, sometimes, too." Justice missed the little, everyday things—tripping over small shoes in the entry way, listening to soft, even breathing coming from a darkened room, the smell of crayons and paint and children's shampoo.

He scrubbed Max's head, knocking his toque over his eyes. "Come on. If we hurry, we still have time for a battle to the death on PlayStation before your mom picks you up."

CHAPTER SIX

A couple of days later, Justice pulled into the drive of his father's house, Max and Chaucer keeping each other company in the backseat of his pickup. He opened the small rear door. Max hopped out, and Justice handed him a plastic grocery bag. "Here, take this into Papa's," he said before grabbing another bag and a case of Canadian from the front seat. Chaucer took the opportunity to slurp him lovingly from chin to temple. Justice pushed him away. "Back off, you goof. We won't be long. You wait here."

The dog barked in reply. Right in his ear.

"Damn it, you're going to make me deaf." He shoved the door shut with his elbow and followed Max up the ramp leading to the front of his father's bungalow.

"Papa, we're here!" Max called as he pushed open the door and stepped into the hall.

"Who's here?" shouted a gruff, gravelly voice.

Max giggled at the familiar game. "Us, Papa!" He traipsed ahead of Justice into a room opening to the left, the grocery bag dragging on the floor. "We've got your beer and beans."

"You better have, or you can just turn around and head on home." Whitman Cooper's wheelchair was parked in front of a large, flat-screen TV monopolizing most of one wall in the crowded space. A table at his side was covered in the scattered remnants of a newspaper, used coffee mugs, an open bag of pretzels and an empty but gritty ashtray. The air reeked of stale tobacco, flat beer, and old man.

Max dropped his bag and hefted himself onto Whitman's lap. "How are the Habs doing?" he asked over the patter of hockey play-by-play droning from the screen.

"Losing to the bloody Leafs."

"Don't worry, it's early days yet."

Justice grinned at Max's worldly-wise tone. "How you doing, Dad?"

"Fine," his father answered. Whitman's thick bushy brows of faded gold bristled over watery blue eyes set in a face seamed from pain, drink and more than twenty years working out of doors. His long frame, heavy around the middle, huddled awkwardly in the chrome and vinyl wheelchair.

Justice crouched down and used his little finger to hook the bag Max had discarded. "I'll put these away."

The case of beer fit comfortably in the fridge, along with a small bag of apples Justice was sure his father would ignore. As usual. But he figured while he was buying the groceries, the least he could do was give him the chance to eat healthy. The cans of beans, bread, and other staples found homes in cupboards under the counter, within easy reach.

The sink held dirty dishes. Justice left them alone, knowing his father would get to them when he wanted. He did clear the trash under the sink and take the box of empties to the big bin in the carport for recycling later.

By the time he returned to the living room, Max and Whitman were deep in a fierce Scrabble battle. Max's face pursed in a serious frown as he fiddled with the tiles on his holder.

"Ever gonna play there?" Whitman growled.

Max's concentration didn't flicker. "I think I can play

all my letters." He pulled at his bottom lip, and Justice's stomach twisted, recognizing the gesture as one of his own. At unexpected times, love for his son simply grabbed him by the throat.

Whitman pushed against the arms of his chair and lifted his torso into a new position.

Justice watched him clinically. "Pressure sores?"

"Nah, just stiff."

With little sensation below the waist, it was easy for Whitman's skin to chafe until medical attention was needed. "When did someone check last?" Justice asked. A homecare worker visited Whitman twice a week, pushed him through physio, helped him bathe, and monitored his overall health, but it was easy to miss the beginning of a bedsore.

"Yesterday, just like always. I tell you, I'm fine." Whitman's hand patted the breast pocket of his pale green shirt. Justice heard the crinkling of a cigarette pack. He knew his father wanted a smoke, but also knew he wouldn't light up in front of Max.

"How's that new boss of yours?" Whitman swung his chair away from the table, where Max was still muttering as he shuffled tiles.

Justice rolled his shoulders. "Same."

"Don't know why you didn't take it yourself."

"I didn't want it, Dad."

"And now look what you've got—an ex-cop who's frustrated at dealing with piddly issues like loud music and kids smoking where they shouldn't."

Justice's thoughts turned to Imogene Martinson's odd report. Nothing else of a similar nature had happened in the intervening days, but something about it still rankled.

Max had finally given up on his seven-letter word and

played. Whitman laughed, the sound phlegmy and loose. "Not bad, not bad, young man," he said. "But look at this." He set down EXCITE, making four two letter words and scoring more than forty points, giving Max no quarter simply because of his age. Justice often thought Max handled Whitman's high expectations much better than he had as a child.

With Max once again scowling at his letters, Whitman turned back to Justice. "Tiffani came by the other day. Wanted me to talk to you about getting back together."

Justice felt his expression freeze. He shot a quick look at Max, who gave no sign he'd heard Whitman. "Papa and I are going to the kitchen for a minute," he told Max. "You keep thinking."

The boy grunted and waved a hand without lifting his gaze from the board. Justice strode out of the room. Behind him, the rubber wheels on Whitman's chair squeaked on the vinyl flooring that spread through every room of the house.

In the kitchen, he swung around and glared down at his father. "Don't say things like that when Max can hear."

Whitman stared back. "You don't think she hasn't told him herself?"

"I know she has, and I've already told Max it's not going to happen. I don't need you raising his hopes again."

"Wasn't trying to." Whitman rolled to the fridge, snagged a beer and popped the top. His Adam's apple bobbed in his thin neck as he swallowed. His shoulders, once so broad and thick, were now bony and withered, as were his legs and arms. All his weight was centred in his torso.

"Then why mention it?"

"Wasn't sure you knew."

Justice snorted. "The way she's been making up to me, asking me to do little favours, inviting me to dinner? I couldn't miss it."

"Might be best for the boy." Whitman tossed the empty can into the box in the corner.

Justice leaned a hip against the counter and crossed his arms. "You think I haven't thought of that? But I can't do that again. I learned my lesson."

"Every man needs a woman. And every boy a mother."

Justice stared at Whitman. "Mom died when I was only a little older than Max is now. You never remarried, gave me a new mother." Not that he'd wanted a one, not right away. But after the grief had eased...

"We're not talking about then. Besides, we did okay on our own."

Was that really how his father thought of those long, lonely years? After his mother's death, his father had pushed him harder and harder at hockey. Sure, he'd loved the game. But sometimes he felt his only worth had been his ability on the ice.

Justice pushed off from the counter. "You know what, Dad? Sometimes okay isn't good enough." Without waiting for a response, he headed back to Max.

****

Madeline Donald switched off the gooseneck lamp that illuminated the podium in the small lecture hall. "So, now that you've been a here a few months, what are your impressions of our university?"

Charlotte placed her satchel on a table and rustled around inside it, making room for her crumbled pile of notes. She and Madeline, Chair of the English Department, had just finished hearing a graduate student defend his thesis. "I'm finding it very pleasant."

"Come now, you can do better than that." Madeline scorched her with a glance. "I'm interested in hearing your honest opinion, or I wouldn't have asked in the first place."

"It's not much different than other universities I've experienced, except for being smaller. It's easier to get to know the students and faculty."

"From what I hear, you're not exactly taking advantage of that fact," Madeline said as she ushered her to the door. Charlotte stepped through, towering over the diminutive professor, yet forced to step lively to keep up with her brisk pace as they headed down the hall.

Feeling rather like a stork being harried by a sandpiper, Charlotte replied, "I'm very busy, expanding my doctoral dissertation. And as I'm only here for one year..." She dodged a group of young men, faces streaked green and gold in support of the school's basketball team. "It doesn't feel necessary to immerse myself in the social aspects."

Madeline strode directly through the throngs of students, parting the crowd like a hawk swooping through a flock of sparrows. "Should the opportunity arise—not that I'm saying it will, but if—would you be interested in extending your contract with us?"

Charlotte shook her head automatically. "My goal has always been to move on to a larger centre." Aware she may have sounded ungrateful, she hurried to add, "Not that I don't appreciate the chance to be here."

"Do you want to be closer to family?"

"It's not really that. My sister is in Vancouver, and that's only an hour flight away from here. And my parents travel a lot. Right now, they're spending a year in England. My father is a freelance writer, and my mother a photographer. They work together, doing articles for travel magazines, newspapers, that sort of thing."

"Interesting."

Hearing a familiar deep voice rumbling from above her head, she paused, moved to the side of the hall, and raised her eyebrows. "It is, yes," she said to Justice, who once again had appeared without her noticing.

He wore his security guard uniform with an air of ease, like someone used to being part of a team. The black material emphasized the brightness of his bristly hair and short beard.

"Justice, how are you?" Madeline asked as she peered up at him. "Are you taking Modern Canadian with me next semester?"

"I haven't decided yet." The skin at the corner of his eyes crinkled as he regarded Madeline, hovering at his elbow.

"The joys of auditing," Madeline said. "No anxiety, no desperation. If you don't get one class, you simply choose another."

"Shouldn't you be encouraging him to actually register, get the full benefit of the course?" Charlotte frowned at the little round woman, caught Justice's sardonic gaze, and smoothed her expression. "Auditing has always seemed like a waste of time to me."

Madeline reached up and patted Justice's bicep. "Do you think I haven't tried? If you can ever get him talking, he's one of the brightest minds I've known. But he's buried it, buried it deep."

Charlotte watched, fascinated, as a rosy red blush stained Justice's cheekbones sharp crests above his beard. His only other reply was a grunt.

A chime sounded and Madeline checked her phone.

"I'm late for office hours. Must run. See you at the Christmas party?" Without waiting for an answer, she bustled off.

"What Christmas party?" Justice fell into step beside Charlotte as she followed Madeline at a more sedate pace.

She offered a faint shrug. "The English faculty. It's this weekend."

"Are you going?" They reached the end of the hall and entered a round, towering space. Metal sculptures of giant mosquitoes hung from the ceiling three stories above.

She shook her head. "My time is better spent working on my book."

He gripped her arm, his hand gentle but firm, and drew her to a halt at the base of a long, low ramp. The heat of his palm burned through the thin silk of her blouse. "You should go."

"Why?" she said absently, distracted by his touch. Pulsing sensation twined from their single point of contact, curled into her belly, her thighs. Her lips felt dry.

"I don't know," he replied. "Maybe just for fun?"

She dragged her eyes from the sight of his big, hard hand circling her forearm. His mouth was relaxed, with no hint of a curve, yet she had the feeling he was laughing at her. Her nose lifted and she stared at him down its length. "I have fun," she said. "And I don't need to go to a university function to do so."

"Dare you."

She gaped. "*Dare* me? How old are you?"

"I dare you to go with me."

Now her teeth clacked together. "With you?"

"I'll pick you up."

"No, you won't."

"Yes, I will." He stepped closer. His scent reached out,

wrapped around her. "Come with me to the party, Charlotte. All work and no play..." His husky voice drifted away.

He released her arm and rested his hand on her hip. A shudder of awareness rolled through her. She told herself to step back. Instead, her hand lifted, slowly, languorously. The crisp hairs of his beard abraded her palm, shooting sparks of tension down her arm. The air grew thick and heavy. Her lungs laboured.

His mouth touched hers and the ground undulated beneath her like an unmoored dock. His lips were warm, firm—confident, yet not demanding.

He was the first to move away. For a moment, the silence between them hummed so loudly she thought her eardrums had burst.

Or maybe it was the blood in her veins, thrumming.

"Be ready half an hour before the party starts." He stepped past her and was gone.

****

Justice's breath puffed out in white clouds and his collarbone, broken in an awkward fall his second year in the WHL, ached from the cold as he trudged around the campus. He was working evening shifts this week—one p.m. to eleven p.m.—and had met Charlotte and Professor Donald shortly after clocking in. Now he was making his second outdoor circuit in what promised to be a bitterly chill night.

He switched his flashlight to his left hand so he could tuck his right into his pocket for a bit of warmth, the thick gloves he wore no match for the December wind.

The curve of Charlotte's hip was still imprinted in his palm. He still savoured the soft warmth of her lips, the sexy sound she made as she leaned against him. A sound he was sure she hadn't known she'd made.

Maybe it was a good thing the night was so cold. It should cool off the desire raging through him.

Despite the dark, it was only about four p.m., and the parking lots were full. He circled the outer edge and paused for a moment. The University of Northern British Columbia sprawled on a hill above Prince George, and the lights of this city of eighty thousand spread below him, blue and orange and red and white, twinkling and glowing.

Daring Charlotte to attend her own Christmas party had been the impulse of a moment. His usual game plan—live and let live—seemed to be in abeyance every time he was near her. Something about her made him want to take care of her, protect her, encourage her to enjoy life. He knew how fleeting it could be—had personal experience of the fragility of the spark that was the human soul—and couldn't allow her to cut herself off. Her book may be important to her, but it shouldn't be everything.

He resumed his patrol. The snow under his feet squeaked like Styrofoam and the beam of his flashlight bobbed from side to side, glaring off the vehicles lining the aisle.

A black figure launched itself from between the cars ahead. "Help! He's getting away!" The woman screamed as she raced toward Justice, tossing quick glances over her shoulder. "There he goes!"

A dark-coloured sedan, headlights off, sped across the end of the road. It fishtailed on the corner and disappeared into the night.

Three long, quick strides had Justice by the woman's side. "Campus security. What's happened?"

"Damn it." The woman bent forward, put her hands on her knees, let her head hang. In the dim illumination he could see the sleeve of her coat, ripped at the shoulder seam, feathery white stuffing bursting loose. "He tried to pull me to his car. He was so strong." She straightened, wrapped her arms about her torso. Her voice was staunch and fierce, but a wildness in her eyes revealed the depth of her distress. "He said he was going to rape me."

CHAPTER SEVEN

Though the woman declared herself fit to walk, shivers racked her body and her face was icy pale, so Justice made sure to stick close as they headed inside. Elizabeth Paxton, enthroned in the glass-enclosed citadel of the office, watched them approach. She hopped off her tall stool and opened the door.

"What happened?"

"Another attack." Justice ushered the woman through the outer area into Nielson's office and settled her onto a couch against the wall. "Call the paramedics. And Nielson."

"I don't need a doctor." The woman squeezed her hands between her knees and huddled in on herself.

"Just a precaution." Justice crouched next to her. "What's your name?"

"Anna-Marie Prentice. I want to go home." She clenched her jaw, muscles flexing in her cheek.

"Hang tough a little while, okay, Anna-Marie? How about something to drink?"

By the time the Security Director and the paramedics arrived, neck and neck, Anna-Marie was wrapped in a grey blanket and sipping hot tea, liberally laced with sugar.

While the paramedics did their checks, Nielson drew Justice to the side and demanded a report. Shawn McMorris, who had just arrived for his own shift, and Elizabeth stood by, listening intently.

"She was heading for her vehicle in Parking Lot C. As

she walked down the row, a man got out of a car and headed toward her. She thought nothing of it, until she drew level with the vehicle and realized he'd left his rear door open. He'd already gone past her, so she turned, intending to call out and tell him. He was right behind her. He grabbed her by the upper arms and forced her to the open door."

"Can she describe him? What kind of car? Only one assailant or was there someone else?" Nielson's pale hazel eyes snapped with a ferocious glee behind the black frames of his glasses.

"I didn't ask," Justice said. "I needed to get her medical attention, treat her for shock."

McMorris scratched his chin, the rasp of whiskers grating. "What about you? Didn't you hear anything?"

"No, nothing." Justice clasped his hands behind his back and rocked on his feet. "Anna-Marie's on the basketball team, a point guard, not tall but plenty strong. She struggled, pulling so hard the sleeve of her jacket was ripped half off, and ran away, dodging between cars. I don't think he was prepared for her to fight back that hard."

Nielson reasserted control of the conversation before McMorris had time to open his mouth. "And you didn't see the vehicle, either."

"Not good enough to identify without a doubt." He explained how the car had shot out of the lot and vanished into the gloom.

Nielson was about to say something more, but one of the paramedics came out from the back office. "She seems to be fine, but we'd like to take her in, keep an eye on her for a little while. She says she's up to answering questions before we do, though."

The four security personnel entered the office.

Knowing Nielson would take the lead role, Justice stayed near the door, along with McMorris and Elizabeth.

Anna-Marie looked up wearily when Nielson sat next to her on the couch, careful to keep his distance. "Can you tell us what happened?" he asked.

Her head bobbled loosely on her neck, reminding Justice uncomfortably of one of Max's toy sports figures. "It was dark," she said. "We were far away from any of the lights. I didn't pay attention when he was coming toward me, and he grabbed me from behind, before I could turn. He wore a hat." Surprise lightened the fear lingering in her face. "I've just remembered. A dark ball cap, pulled low over his eyes."

"Can you describe the car?"

"I'm sorry, I'm awful at makes and models." Her voice lilted up at the end, as if asking a question. "It was a dark colour. And it had four doors, because that's where he tried..." She trailed off.

"Take your time." Justice had never heard Nielson's voice so calm and soothing. "I know it's hard. Was there anything special you might have noticed, about the man, or the car?"

"He wasn't particularly tall, not like—" She flapped a hand at Justice, the corner of her mouth lifting in a faint smile.

Nielson shot him a narrow eyed look and returned to his questioning. Anna-Marie did her best, but no new details were revealed. The paramedics took her away shortly after.

"We'll be taking this incident very seriously, especially after the event last week," Nielson said. He dropped into his black leather executive chair, while McMorris and Justice stood in parade rest position in front.

Elizabeth went back to her post. "I'll send out a memo, alerting everyone to this incident. Keep your eyes open for a vehicle fitting the description, as vague as it is. And if a similar incident happens, I want to be alerted immediately on my cell."

****

"Why am I doing this again?" Charlotte held up a black dress with rhinestones flashing at the waist and studied her reflection in the cheval mirror.

Sonny's disembodied voice rose from the phone lying on the cluttered dresser. "Because woman does not live on research alone."

Charlotte tossed the dress onto the bed. Standing arms akimbo, in only her bra and underwear, she glared into her closet. "I don't know why not."

"Have you decided yet?"

"I hate all my clothes."

"The complaint of women everywhere. Do you still have that blue satin skirt with the slit?"

"Yes." Charlotte shoved aside hangars and found it in the far back corner. "It doesn't seem right for a Christmas party."

"Everyone will be in black or red. Be different. Wear that big, chunky necklace with the blue and gold beads I gave you for your birthday and a white blouse. Toss on that pashmina you bought that day at Granville Island and you're good to go."

Charlotte eyed the slipper chair in the corner, almost hidden in pashminas of various colours and hues. She could see the one Sonny was talking about peeking out from the bottom of the pile. "Do you have my entire wardrobe memorized?"

"I'm living vicariously through you. These days I'm

thrilled if I remember to put on lip gloss."

"You wouldn't have it any other way."

"You're right, but that doesn't mean I don't miss dressing up for an evening of adult conversation."

Charlotte was ready five minutes ahead of Justice's peremptory deadline. Before heading downstairs, she gazed longingly into her office. The small blue light flashing on the side of her laptop called to her, promising an evening of quiet, productive solitude. She tightened her lips and straightened her spine. She didn't appreciate being manoeuvred into wasting an evening, and was prepared to tell Justice so in no uncertain terms. She would put in an appearance at this annoying social event, and then make a quick exit.

It had crossed her mind more than once during the last few days to call him and cancel their appointment—she refused to think of it as a date—but the memory of his concealed amusement stopped her every time. Damned if she was going to give him another reason to laugh at her.

Promptly at 7:30 p.m., her doorbell rang.

She took her time, sauntering to the entrance, her high-heeled pumps clicking on the honey-coloured wood flooring. A shadow crossed the narrow, opaque-glass window beside the door. Placing her hand on the knob, she took a deep breath, and opened it.

"Evening, Charlotte." Justice stepped through, cold air clinging to him, swirling about her.

Mechanically, she closed the door, shutting out the frigid December night. Leaning against it, she clenched her hands behind her back, and stared.

He wore a well-cut, dark wool coat which emphasized the strong breadth of his shoulders. Despite the freezing temperature, it was unbuttoned, revealing a crisply ironed light blue dress shirt stretching across his wide chest, bisected by a fashionable silk tie in complementing shades. Sleek trousers hung from his lean hips, and his large feet were shod in shiny leather loafers, damp with snow.

Her gaze swept back up to his face, and was met by a lift of his scarred brow. She realized she had yet to reply to his polite greeting.

She cleared her throat. "Good evening, Justice."

That indefinable air of amusement emanated from him, although his lips remained uncurved. "I left the truck running, so it will stay warm for you."

She nodded silently.

His amusement deepened, reflecting in his eyes. She took a step away from the support of the door and lifted her chin, ignoring the weakness in her knees. It was only physical attraction, her intellect told her, only chemicals and hormones and... Her thoughts trailed off when he lifted a lock of her hair, which she'd allowed to flow free tonight, and tucked it behind her ear. Goosebumps pebbled her skin and she suppressed a sensual shiver.

"You look beautiful."

She took courage from his voice, low and hoarse. "You're not so bad yourself," she said.

His eyes dropped to her lips. His fingers lay gently on her neck. She wondered if he could feel her pulse pounding. The force of it made her dizzy, and when he stepped forward, her hands automatically clutched his waist for balance.

His breath, warm and fresh, fluttered her bangs, whispered against her temple. His fingers trailed along her collarbone, tracing the deep vee of her blouse. Her skin flushed, her breasts swelled. She watched his face, fascinated by the way his lids drooped lazily as his eyes followed his questing hand. When he finally met her gaze, she sank into their flaming blueness.

He reached past her and lifted her coat, draped in readiness over the newel post. Silently he held it out for her. She slipped her arms in and buttoned it up with trembling fingers. Still in the same charged silence, he opened the door and gestured her into the velvet night.

****

Justice ushered Charlotte into the University's Atrium. The subtle murmur of erudite conversation drifted to the engineered wood beams gleaming three stories above. Tall, round tables draped in white linen were scattered about, the golden glow of red candles shielded by hurricane glass casting a flattering light on the assembled academics and their guests.

Neither he nor Charlotte had spoken on the short drive over. His body still thrummed with a wicked pulse of desire. He gave in to temptation and touched her whenever he could—guiding her with a firm touch on her elbow, helping her off with her coat, taking her hand to lead her toward a small grouping that included Madeline Donald.

"Charlotte!" The Department Chair was clothed in a black dress that spangled and sparkled in the low light. "And Justice." Her glance swung between them, friendly but sharp. "I am so glad you both could make it." She waved a hand at the bar. "Justice, go get Charlotte a glass of wine."

He released her hand, reluctant to let the slight connection go. "Red or white?"

Her gaze fluttered about his chin. "A Cabernet, if they have it. Thank you." She smiled vaguely, and then turned her attention to the others in the group while Madeline began introductions.

As he waited at the bar, he scanned the room. Most of the faces were familiar, although he wasn't certain of all the names. A tall, angular man joined the queue. If Professor Odili stood spine straight, he would have been close to Justice's height, but his shoulders stooped and his head tilted forward at a vulture-like angle. Curly black hair streaked with grey capped his skull.

"Cooper, isn't it?" Odili asked. He wore a neat grey suit and white shirt with a gaudily striped yellow, red, and green tie. "Had you in my Anthropological Perspectives on Inequality, didn't I?"

"Yes, sir." Justice shuffled forward and ordered two glasses of wine.

"Saw you come in just now with Professor Girardet." Odili smiled widely, white teeth brilliant in his dark face. "I must congratulate you."

"On what?"

"For rescuing the maiden from her tower." He leaned in and lowered his voice. "This is the first faculty event she's attended. Rumours were beginning to circulate she was either too haughty to join us Northern academics, or too dedicated to her research to waste time socializing."

"The second reason." Justice grasped the bowls of the wine glasses offered by the bartender and made way for Odili. "I guarantee it."

Odili placed an order for a vodka and tonic, and then turned back to Justice. "I've heard her dissertation was brilliant. If she does as fine a job on her monograph, she's guaranteed tenure-track wherever she likes."

Something oddly like fear clenched at Justice's belly. It couldn't be at the idea of Charlotte leaving, he thought. He knew there was no long-term future in their relationship. She'd been more than honest about her goals in life.

So why were Odili's words so disturbing?

****

Charlotte hadn't felt this awkward in years. Madeline had blithely and rapidly introduced her to the couples standing near and bustled off, leaving her vulnerable to a well-meaning but intrusive inquisition.

"And you did your graduate work where?" The question was posed by a petite blond woman wearing a cherry-red sheath. Charlotte thought she was the wife of one of the chemistry professors, but wasn't sure.

"York," Charlotte replied. "I studied under Arthur Ross-Moore." Justice appeared at her side. She took the wine he offered and buried her nose in the glass in relief.

"I do admire women who go on with their education." The blonde's giggle set Charlotte's teeth on edge. "I met my husband while doing my BA. We had our first child less than a year after I graduated, and I just haven't had the chance to go back. The munchkins do keep me busy."

"I imagine they do." Charlotte smiled woodenly, her lips stiff. She was viciously aware of Justice next to her. What was his opinion of women, education and children? And why did she care?

"You simply can't imagine it, if you don't have any of your own." When Charlotte didn't volunteer any details, the blonde lifted an eyebrow and continued with an air of martyrdom, "I haven't had a moment's peace since the first day. I no longer call my life my own."

Charlotte narrowed her eyes, but was prevented from replying by Justice's smooth intervention.

"Will you excuse us?" He inclined his head. "I'd like to introduce Charlotte to a friend of mine."

His hand, warm, dry, clasped hers. She moved away

willingly, her stride easily matching his. He drew her behind a huge palm fern and into a small alcove leading to a darkened office.

She looked around, irritation roughening her tone. "You said you wanted to introduce me to someone."

A corner of his mouth quivered. "I lied. You looked like you were going to snap. Thought it best to get you away."

She stared, startled that he had seen her so clearly. "Oh. Thank you."

"Why?"

"Why was I going to snap?" She took another swallow of wine, wondering how much to tell him. "I don't like it when women use children as an excuse for not furthering their education, or their careers."

"Kids take up time." Justice leaned a shoulder against the wall and swirled the ruby liquid in his glass.

"Of course they do. My sister has two and I'm amazed at how busy she is with them. But she doesn't blame them for changing her life. She chose to have kids, and now she accepts the fact her life is different." She lifted her wine glass to her mouth again and was startled to find it empty.

"Wait." Justice plucked it from her hand and disappeared, returning moments later with it refilled.

The wine was full and rich, and the bouquet tickled her nose. "It annoys me when someone uses kids—or a spouse or a parent, anyone, really—as the reason for not doing something."

"A successful career is more important than family?"

The edge in his voice cut through her wine-fuddled emotions. She belatedly recalled Max telling her of his grandfather's accident, how Justice cut short his hockey career to care for him. "That's not what I meant. Some circumstances are impossible to change, no matter how much we wish we could." She drained the last of her second glass. "I just think some women enjoy presenting themselves as self-sacrificing, even when it's not true, or necessary."

"Wouldn't you put someone you love ahead of your goals? Your book, say? Or tenure?" His blue gaze held hers, daring her to look away, to prevaricate.

She swallowed, her throat raspy. From the wine, nothing else. "Your question is moot. Those I love will not suffer if I concentrate on my career."

"Use your imagination. What if someone would suffer? What would you do?"

A tension she didn't understand energized the air between them. She licked her lips and his eyes dropped to her mouth. Her mind went blank, drowning in a swirl of confusion. She took a hesitant step forward.

CHAPTER EIGHT

"I thought I saw you come in, Cooper."

Justice dragged his gaze away from Charlotte's pale, wide-eyed face and focused on Curtis Nielson. His head was freshly shaved, gleaming in the subdued light, and he wore a dark pinstripe suit.

"Nielson." Justice said curtly, breaking free from the fog of sensuality in which he'd been about to lose his way.

"I didn't know you attended these sorts of events."

"I came with Professor Girardet." Justice pressed his hand to Charlotte's lower back. Her muscles quivered and she moved stiffly, but allowed him to draw her to his side. "Charlotte, my boss, Curtis Nielson."

"Pleased to meet you." Her voice was husky, and Justice had a sudden, detailed, flash fantasy—Charlotte, naked below him, panting in just that tone. Blood surged to his groin. He beat back a feeling of possessiveness. She shouldn't talk to anyone but him that way.

Nielson exchanged pleasantries, displaying an unexpected charm. Charlotte relaxed, the rigidity easing from her body. When she smiled at Nielson, deep brown eyes sparkling, Justice quelled the savage urge to push his nose in.

Charlotte asked Nielson how he'd come to work at UNBC.

"I put my thirty in on the force. Decided it was time for a change. This position came up." He raised a heavy, squat tumbler of golden liquid in Justice's direction.

"Rumour has it the guys in the office would have preferred Cooper. But he didn't apply, and I was in."

She tilted her head at Justice, cutting him a sidelong glance. "You didn't even try for the promotion?"

He lifted a shoulder, shrugging off her question.

"And you don't do courses for credit." Charlotte shook her head, a teasing light in her eye. "One would think you have no ambition whatsoever."

"Not everyone is cut out to lead," Nielson said, the light in his eye not nearly as friendly. Justice knew Nielson resented the respect the other guards offered him, but generally he hid it better. "Being a hockey player doesn't exactly prepare you for the real world."

Charlotte hadn't missed the insult. Her chin lifted. "Research has shown that people who participate in team sports communicate better, are more disciplined and are better decision makers."

"Which means nothing if the person doesn't actually use those skills."

If Charlotte had been a cat, Justice was sure her fur would have ruffled. She raised her brows at Nielson, expression full of disdain. "From what I've seen, Justice uses those skills on a daily basis." She turned to Justice, her gaze sweeping over him, and he felt his biceps and thighs tighten, as if preparing to snatch her up and run away with her. "Perhaps, for now, he prefers to lead by example, as one of a group, and not the one heading the charge."

Startled by her perception, Justice narrowed his eyes. Ignoring his scrutiny, she bade Nielson a polite but chilly farewell, and moved past him into the main space. Justice followed, amusement at her imperious exit quirking the corner of his mouth.

"How can you work with him?" She hissed the question, hiding behind her empty wineglass as she surveyed the room.

"I just do my job and go home."

"A boss like that must make your life miserable."

Instead of answering, Justice plucked a full glass from a server circulating the room and offered it to her.

She said absently, "I really don't need another," but took it anyway, sipped, and then returned to her argument. "You had the chance to improve your life, move forward in your career, and you didn't. Why not?"

"I like what I'm doing. I saw no reason to change."

"Do you really see yourself as a security guard for the rest of your life?"

"I don't know." He stared into his own glass—still his first of the evening—and watched the ruby liquid reflecting the lights high overhead. Nielson was right—not everyone was a leader. Justice had been honoured to be named an assistant captain for many of his hockey teams, but he'd never been captain. Supporting roles suited him just fine. "It's a job I'm good at, and one I enjoy. For now, it's enough."

****

The zing of frigid air dissipated some of the delicious wine buzz tingling in Charlotte's cheeks and fingers, but not all of it. She dodged a small drift of snow and teetered on her heels, giggling. "I should have worn boots."

Justice wrapped his arm around her waist. "Certainly more practical."

"But not nearly as pretty." She lurched to a stop and stood on one leg, waggling the other foot. "Aren't they pretty shoes?"

"Very pretty."

Charlotte knew she was tipsy, but she wasn't drunk enough to miss his dry tone. She peered at him, her nose now level with his chin, thanks to the added inches her high heels provided. "Are you laughing at me?"

"Of course not." He kept his arm around her as they negotiated the slippery sidewalk. "But now I know why you don't go out very often."

She clutched her coat around her throat in a vain attempt to shut out the icy wind. "You do?"

"You can't be trusted around alcohol."

"That's not a nice thing to say." She waggled her finger in his face. He grabbed it, his hand wonderfully warm despite the cold. "And if I am a little befuddled, it's your fault. You're the one who kept bringing me drinks."

They reached Justice's truck. Charlotte regarded it dubiously. She'd had enough trouble climbing into the cab when she was sober. While she considered the ascent, she was lifted by two large hands on her waist and dumped onto the seat.

She straightened her skirt and grumbled as Justice slid behind the wheel. "A gentleman shouldn't toss a lady around like that."

"A lady should learn to hold her liquor better."

"I am not drunk." She shot him a triumphant glance when she clicked her seatbelt the first try.

The truck's heater barely made a dent in the raw cold of the cab by the time Justice pulled up outside her house. "Wait. I'll help you."

Ignoring his command, she pushed open the door and swung her legs out. Before she had a chance to wriggle to the ground, though, he hefted her off the seat, one arm under her knees, the other behind her back.

"Put me down." She struggled impotently against his

hold. He made her feel small, delicate. Feminine.

"The path is slippery." His arms tightened around her as he made his way to the front door.

She peeked at him through her lashes. In the soft glow cast by the porch light, his irises were slate-coloured, the crooked bluntness of his nose cruelly defined, the ridges of his cheekbones flushed.

Later she would blame it on the alcohol. Whatever the reason, she gave in to impulse and cupped his jaw with her hand, as she had the day he'd coerced her into going to the party.

The hairs of his beard were wiry yet soft. Despite the freezing temperature, heat radiated from his skin, burning the chill from her fingers.

He turned his head toward her, bristles tickling her palm. The blaze in his eyes made her want to stretch and purr. Confident in his strength, she burrowed closer, caressing his chin, his neck, feeling the pulse thundering in the big vein lying so close to the surface.

He shifted her, allowing her legs to stretch downward, yet holding her snugly against him, her toes still inches from the floor. The long, thick layer of her calf-length coat, his heavy wool jacket, combined to create a frustrating barrier between their bodies.

Except for the embers behind his eyes, his face was still and blank. In the tautness of his hard body, the immobility of his large frame, she sensed a ruthless determination held strictly in check.

"I'm going to kiss you," he said.

A delicious shiver shuddered down her spine. Not "I want to kiss you" or "May I kiss you?" She should have been insulted. Instead her body molded itself even more closely to his.

Slowly, ever so slowly, he lowered her until she was standing firmly on the floor. Well, perhaps not firmly. Her knees felt loose, her thigh muscles lax. Her lips parted and she waited breathless, edgy.

The first touch of his mouth was startling. She'd been so certain his lips would be hot, fiery, matching the fever of his skin. Instead they were chilled, frosty.

But only for a second.

She lost herself in the splendour of being held, the glory of mating tongues. The unfamiliar sensation of whiskers was oddly exciting, adding a layer of surprise and delight. An unconscious moan of pleasure vibrated from her throat.

****

Now this, Justice thought hazily, this was a woman. Through the heavy concealing layers of winter clothing he could sense her softness, her femininity. Yet she was sturdy in his arms, strong and resilient. He didn't have to hold back. She matched him, size for size.

He leaned into her and she moaned again, the soft sound of approval hardening him further. The crisp scent of the wintry air mingled with the lush, sensual scent of woman, intoxicating him in a way alcohol never could. He wanted to rifle under her coat, her skirt, rip clothing out of the way, lose himself in her body. He wanted to cradle her gently, caress her face with his fingertips, explore the delicacy of her shoulders, wrists, breasts.

He wanted her every way, any way.

An arctic wind blew up his back, followed by the burning brand of Charlotte's fingers, as she wormed her way under his coat, yanked his shirt from the waistband of his trousers. The glacial breeze cut through his lust-crazed brain, and recalled him to the fact they were standing on her front porch, under a light, in full view of the neighbourhood.

He dragged his mouth from the feast of her lips. "Where's your key?"

"Hmmmm?" She ducked her head under his chin, nibbled the side of his neck.

Blood roared in his ears. "Your key." He gripped her shoulders and stepped away. She stared at him from under heavy-lidded eyes, her mouth swollen, the skin around her lips slightly reddened from his beard.

"Oh." She held up empty hands and looked about her in confusion.

Spying her flat, book-sized purse by her feet, he swooped it up and handed it to her. She pulled out the key and unlocked the door. She'd left a lamp burning on the flimsy semi-circle table set against one wall.

She held out a hand. "Come in. Stay." Her voice was low, breathy.

Every atom in his body bellowed to do as she asked. His hand lifted, ready to accept her invitation. He conquered the impulse. "Not a good idea."

"Why?" She pursed her plump, luscious lips as she unbuttoned her coat.

He held back a groan. "You may not be drunk, but you're certainly not sober." He took a step back, his feet obeying his will reluctantly. "When we sleep together for the first time, you should have a clear head."

She rolled her shoulders, her coat sliding off her arms. Her nipples jutted under the thin fabric of her white blouse. "I want you now."

Justice retreated down the steps. He breathed deeply and evenly and considered shoving his head into a nearby snowbank to clear his brain. Behind him, the low growl of his truck idling reminded him of his original chaste intent to bring Charlotte home. And leave her there. Alone.

"Shut the door, Charlotte." He couldn't escape without making sure she was safely locked in for the night.

Her eyes had lost their sleepy, sexy look. "You're not coming in, are you?"

He shook his head.

Her lips thinned and her chin lifted. "Fine. Thank you for a wasted evening." The door slammed, echoing down the darkened street.

He waited for the click of the lock, and then climbed slowly into his truck and made the short drive home. Aching, irritated and horny.

****

Tremors of lust and rage, desire and humiliation, shuddered through Charlotte as she stared at the closed door. Her body hummed with tension, her mind whirled with dismay.

She'd been rejected. Again. Perhaps not quite as brutally as Richard had dismissed her—at least Justice had tried to sugar-coat it by using her tipsiness as an excuse—but the end result was the same. The back of her throat burned. She swallowed the tears, refusing to give her mortification physical form.

She retrieved her discarded coat and hung it up, her movements slow and deliberate. Removing her shoes with the same careful consideration, she padded up the stairs, nylons slippery on the slick laminate. After placing the pumps side by side on the floor next to the dresser, her fingers moved to the buttons of her blouse. She slotted it and her skirt into the closet, paying strict attention to the straightness of the seams and the natural creases of the cloth. Draping her bra neatly over the back of the slipper chair in the corner, she moved to the bed, and wearing nothing but a pair of flimsy panties, slid between the cool cotton sheets.

Any traces of her wine buzz had burned out of her blood. She was coldly sober, eyes dry, lungs so tight the air razored in and out of her chest. Nothing blurred the memory of Justice back pedalling off the porch so fast he almost fell. Even Richard hadn't shown his eagerness to get away so clearly.

Her bedroom overlooked the street. Light from a passing car tracked across the ceiling, the crunch of tires on snow fading as it passed by.

She'd known from the first time she'd seen Justice that they were ill-suited to each other. He was a man who lived by brawn and force, physically dominating others without even trying. He was the exact opposite of the intellectual, scholarly man she'd always imagined spending her life with. But she'd been irresistibly intrigued by his mental acuity, fascinated by his sheer size, drawn into his controlled energy.

The furnace whirred to life, humming and churning as it poured heated air through the quiet house. Charlotte huddled deeper in the bed, rolling to her side and pulling the covers to her chin.

She blamed it on the wine. If she'd been in her right mind, she never would have given in to temptation. Justice had been right about that, she admitted bitterly. He was probably congratulating himself for being chivalrous, for using the truth as a means of escaping a distasteful situation.

Her stomach seethed as she recalled how blatantly she'd offered herself. Her courage may have been fortified with alcohol, but it had still taken a great deal of resolution to invite him in. Into her home, into her life. Into her body.

And he'd said no.

Thank God only her pride had been bruised, this time. She *hated* feeling stupid, but she could survive that. She didn't know if she could survive a second broken heart.

CHAPTER NINE

Justice paced the hall, stretching out his already considerable stride as he hurried through his rounds. When he reached the closed door of the lecture room where Charlotte's medieval English class was writing their exams, he paused, leaned a shoulder against the wall, and waited.

Two hours ago, he'd watched Charlotte enter the room, her steps brisk and confident, classically elegant in a sleek pair of navy blue slacks and a cream-coloured blouse buttoned at the wrists. Though he'd seen her a couple of times since the disastrous faculty party last weekend, it had always been at a distance, and never when the opportunity for discussion presented itself. She had ignored his phone calls, and simply knocking on her door—office or home—and demanding she speak to him struck him as heavy-handed and crude.

Which had reduced him to skulking in the hallways, hoping to "accidentally" meet her. He figured she wouldn't make a public scene, and maybe the shock of the ambush would give him enough time to say what he wanted to before she froze him out.

The door opened and a young girl slipped through. She carried the students' ubiquitous backpack over one shoulder and a parka in eye-straining green over her arm.

"Many left inside?" he asked.

She looked up, noted his uniform, and shook her head. "Only two. Who you waiting for?"

"Professor Girardet."

"She gave the fifteen minute warning a little while ago, so she shouldn't be long." She pulled a cell phone from her pocket. "Merry Christmas," she said absently, flicking at it with her thumb.

"Merry Christmas to you, too."

The girl sauntered away, head down, checking the screen as she went.

A few minutes later the door opened again, and two students left together, chattering indecipherably in a language Justice guessed was Japanese. He continued to wait, still and watchful.

Finally, Charlotte appeared. She saw him, hesitated, and then straightened her shoulders, adjusted the satchel strapped across her body, and stepped forward, eyes focused down the hall. As she passed, he swung into place beside her, matching his stride to hers.

"You're mad at me." Why beat around the bush? He could think of no other reason for her avoidance of him, especially after the scorching kiss they'd shared. Lying in bed at night, he could still feel her body, sinuous with silky strength, pressed against his, taste the flavour of her lips on his tongue.

"Why would I be mad at you?"

Justice had been married long enough not to be fooled by her flat, bland tone. "Because you invited me in, and I refused."

She stopped abruptly and glared at him. He took a step back at the fury blazing in her eyes.

"Yes, I did. And, yes, you did. Obviously, we have nothing to talk about. So why are you here?" She whirled away without waiting for an answer.

Justice followed. "You'd been drinking. I couldn't

stay." He kept his voice low, conscious of the interested gaze of a student cloistered in a reading nook, books and binders and bags strewn about.

"I'd had a couple glasses of wine. I was feeling buzzed, not bombed. I knew what I was doing." She stabbed the up button on the elevator repeatedly, staring at the floor indicator with fierce intent.

"I didn't mean to hurt your feelings."

Small patches of red bloomed on her cheeks. "I don't want to discuss this." The bell dinged and the doors slid open. She stepped inside, turning to face him. "Goodbye, Justice."

The doors began to close. "Damn it." He jammed his shoulder into the gap and forced his way in.

She gaped. "What do I have to say to get you to stay away from me?"

The car jolted as it began its ascent. He pushed the emergency stop button.

Her eyes widened further, white showing in a full circle around her mahogany irises. "What the hell?"

"I need your undivided attention. We have thirty seconds before the alarm goes off." Her mouth opened and closed. Was it wrong of him to enjoy shocking her this way?

He closed the gap between them, forcing her to tilt her chin to keep his face in view. "You seem to think I said no that night because I didn't want you. That I walked away without a second thought." Her scent wrapped around him, heady, womanly, with a hint of midnight. The tip of her tongue traced her upper lip. His body went on alert, straining with awareness. "The truth is the complete opposite."

Her hair hung over her shoulder in a thick, luxurious

braid, glossy in the subdued light of the elevator car. He gripped it lightly, sliding his hand down the satiny length. "Do you remember what else I said to you?"

She jerked her head from side to side, the rest of her immobile, a breathing statue.

"I said when we sleep together for the first time, you should have a clear head." He touched a fingertip to the pulse pounding in the side of her throat. "When, Charlotte. Not if."

He pressed the emergency button again, and the car lurched upward, the silence between them stretched, taut, volatile. He'd said what he wanted to say. The rest was up to her.

****

Charlotte braced herself against the motion of the elevator, but not before her breasts, protected only by thin fabric and thinner lace, brushed Justice's chest. He was standing so close she felt overwhelmed. Not intimidated—he didn't scare her—just...swamped by his nearness.

Or maybe it was the heat in his eyes.

Ocean depths had nothing on the blueness searing into her, she thought wildly. Vertigo weakened her knees, but she couldn't look away.

"I—" She broke off, swallowed, and tried again. "I don't know what to say." He toyed with the end of her braid, and she swore she could feel the touch of his fingers fizzle up the strands, down her spine and into the soles of her feet.

"Did you honestly think I wasn't attracted to you?" His voice rumbled, low and sexy.

The doors slid open. Thank God the hallway was empty. Her legs felt disconnected from her body, but she managed not to stumble. She unlocked her office, seeking refuge inside. Justice followed.

"Charlotte?"

He wasn't going to let it go. Perseverance was his greatest strength—and his most irritating habit, she thought peevishly. "I threw myself at you and you walked away."

"I just about took you up against your front door." Frustration coloured his tone. He scrubbed his hands over his close-cropped head.

"Fine. Maybe you were right." She lifted her satchel off her shoulder and tossed it into a nearby chair. "Maybe I wasn't thinking clearly enough."

"Maybe." He crossed his ankles and leaned against the wall, the casual stance belying the tension evident in the fists jammed in his pockets, the set of his shoulders. "Now what?"

"I don't know." The collar of his uniform jacket had kinked up on one side. Without thinking, she stepped forward to smooth it down. He caught her hand and held it. Her fingers curled into his.

The connection felt good. It felt right. Maybe she should stop thinking altogether, and just go with her gut.

She never did that. She planned and researched and debated and planned some more. Trying to regain her equilibrium, she tugged away and escaped behind her desk.

"Let's look at this rationally," she said. His scarred eyebrow arched and amusement flickered in his face, but she battled on. "We are both healthy, single adults. For some reason, we seem to have strong physical chemistry."

"Some reason?" The amusement was uppermost, now. His lips remained firm and straight, but she could see it in his eyes, as usual.

"Don't take this the wrong way, but you are not the kind of man I ever thought I'd be attracted to."

He lowered his lids and regarded her through narrow slits. "Right back at you."

She bristled, but took her own advice and let it go. "Regardless, we could take advantage of this mutual appeal."

"There's the professor I know and...admire," he murmured.

She ignored the sarcasm. "I'm only here for a few more months." The exam today was the last she needed to invigilate. As soon as they were marked and the results submitted, she was flying out to spend Christmas with Sonny and family, returning a few days before the start of the winter session. "Are you in any of my classes next semester?"

He shook his head, watching her closely.

"Would you consider a short-term, exclusive relationship, with a predefined end date?" There, she thought. That sounded mature, sensible. No need to let emotions colour what promised to be a satisfying adult affair.

He straightened from the wall, looming to his full height. "Would this so-called relationship be strictly physical? Or could it involve social aspects as well?"

Once again, she sensed an underlying current of laughter, but she ignored it. "I can't see why not."

"And it would come to an end the same time as your contract?"

"Or earlier, of course, should either of us find it no longer meets our needs."

"I thought English professors were supposed to be romantic."

Romance. Love. That's what hurt you. Sex, on the other hand, was just sex. "Not all of us."

"And when would this contract, should I agree, begin?"

"I'll be out of town for a few days. I could call you, when I return."

He looked down at her, head tilted slightly to one side. She tapped her fingers against her thigh, and then stilled them.

"Professor Girardet, you have a deal."

****

Charlotte did her best to push all thoughts of Justice and the arrangement she'd brokered out of her mind. The task became a little easier a few days later when she arrived at Sonny's, and found the family in the grips of a nasty flu bug. Her nephew, Anthony, had been struck down first, and was making a slow recovery, but not before he had generously passed on his illness to his younger sister. With relief, Charlotte stepped in to lighten the load on her beleaguered sister.

Her niece's body rested limply in Charlotte's arms as they rocked back and forth, the chair creaking in a comforting rhythm. Andrea's room was a tribute to her love of Disney princesses, including a pink comforter decorated with the smiling image of her favourite, Cinderella. Frothy dresses in yellow and blue peeked out of her closet.

Charlotte tucked the blanket around the small, heavy form, felt the heat of the fever radiating through.

"Comfortable, pumpkin?"

"I'm hot, Auntie."

"I know, sweetie. You're sick. But Mommy gave you medicine that will make you feel better soon."

"Will it still be Christmas, even if I'm sick?" Andrea asked, her plaintive, tiny voice hoarse with fever.

"Of course it will," Charlotte said, although the poor thing probably wouldn't be able to enjoy it much. "Santa comes tonight, and tomorrow we'll have a wonderful turkey dinner." Charlotte could hear the sounds of preparations floating up the stairs from the kitchen on the main floor. Not particularly at home among steaming pots and roasting pans, Charlotte had offered to take sick child duty to free up her sister.

The rasping rattle of Andrea's breathing grew slow and steady as she slipped into sleep. Charlotte kept rocking.

She swallowed at the knot in her throat, and only succeeded in lodging it lower down, in her heart. As much as she loved her niece and nephew, the older she grew, the more she ached to hold her own child. She thought she'd been reconciled to the fact that could never happen, and during her late teens and early twenties she'd barely given a thought to the life-saving operation that had rendered her infertile. But her body didn't seem to know its own limitations, and her biological clock ticked louder and louder.

She carried the sleeping child to the bed and tucked her under the protection of her heroine. Then she made her way down the stairs to see how the battle waged.

Sonny wore a smear of flour on her nose and a harried expression. Her abundant hair, as curly as Charlotte's but amber gold, was knotted on top of her head. She looked up from rolling out pie crust when Charlotte entered the kitchen. "How's my baby doing?"

"Sleeping. I'll check her in a bit. What do you need me to do?"

"Eggs need to be devilled. Can you start shelling?"

They worked in amicable silence for a few minutes, broken only by Sonny's occasional curse as she wrestled with the apple pie.

"Why don't you just buy one?" Charlotte asked.

"Get behind me, Satan." Sonny slipped the pie into the oven and shut the door with a grateful sigh. "Any other holiday of the year, I'm first in line at the bakery. But this is Christmas. And nothing smells more like Christmas than a pie overflowing in the oven."

Charlotte laughed. "Mom will be proud to know you're following in her footsteps."

"I miss them both." Their parents had decided to stay in England for the holidays. "But I suppose we should be happy they are still so active."

"You talk as if they are in their dotage. They're barely in their sixties."

"I know. But the time seems to fly so much faster, now I have kids."

Usually Charlotte only felt joy that Sonny had two such beautiful children. Today, a stab of sorrow kept her silent.

A shadow fell onto the neat row of eggs she had peeled.

Sonny's hand rested on Charlotte's shoulder in mute apology. "I'm sorry. Sometimes I forget."

"It's getting harder for me to forget, especially at holidays." Charlotte did her best to smile. "I love Anthony and Andrea, and I'm so happy that you and Thomas have such an amazing family. So don't worry about me." She reached up and squeezed Sonny's hand. "I have a good life. And it will only get better."

Sonny squeezed back, then released her hand and

snagged a potato from a Kilimanjaro of spuds. She began peeling it with deft, clean movements. "How's your book going?"

"Not bad. I wish I was further along, but I should be able to catch up, as long as I schedule my time wisely." She wiped up the crumbled shells and shook them into Sonny's ecologically friendly compost container.

"What do you mean? Do you have something other than teaching that is going to interfere?"

Charlotte selected a knife and picked up a potato. The skin was smooth and clear, and she could smell the starch as she cut into it. The urge to tell Sonny about Justice was strong.

"I might be seeing someone." She said the words slowly, testing them out. They felt right—vague enough to cover almost any eventuality.

Sonny dropped her potato into the water-filled pot with a surprised splash. "Really? Who?"

Charlotte found herself explaining her odd relationship with Justice. "I don't know what it is about him," she said as they cleaned up the remains and tidied the kitchen. "He won't take no for an answer, but he's so polite about it I find myself doing exactly what he wants. He's a security guard, for God's sake. I shouldn't even be attracted to him."

"It's not what a man does, it's who he is." Sonny's eyes danced. "You need to step out of your comfort zone. Dating someone other than a stuffy academic is perfect. Is he hot?"

Charlotte bent over the trash bag and tied the knot, her hair loose, swinging down to hide her heated cheeks. "I suppose."

"Have you kissed him yet?"

"Maybe." She headed for the garage door.

"Maybe?" Sonny blocked her retreat. "How can you not know?"

"Okay, fine. Yes, we've kissed. Yes, he's hot. He's tall and built and an ex-hockey player. He has a broken nose and a scarred eyebrow and a beard." Sonny's eye widened as Charlotte's voice rose. "He's big and burly and I want to jump his bones. Happy now?"

"You bet." Sonny smiled in satisfaction. "After Richard the jerk, I worried about you. You hid inside your shell, and I wondered if you'd ever come out." All laughter gone from her eyes, she tucked a strand of hair behind Charlotte's ear and added, "Are you going to tell Justice you can't have children?"

"It's not that sort of relationship. He knows I'm leaving in a few months, and when I do, it will be over. There's no need to tell him."

"Keeping it from Richard didn't go so well. Of course, if he'd been the man he should have been, it wouldn't have mattered when you told him. Still..."

"Whether I can or cannot have children can't matter to Justice," Charlotte said, remembering the mischievous eyes of his son. "It's not like we're making long-term plans."

CHAPTER TEN

Whitman rolled into the living room, a giggling Max perched on his knee. Chaucer bounded alongside, nipping at the wheels. "Get away, you stupid mutt." Whitman batted at the pup, his actions gentle despite his gruff tone. "Max and I think we've waited long enough. Are we ready to open presents?"

"Presents, Papa, presents!" Max wriggled down and headed for the tree.

Justice made a grab at Chaucer's collar as he dashed to the tree with Max. "Sit." The dog's butt hit the floor with a thump. Justice rewarded him with a piece of cheese.

Max lifted a shoe-box sized gift and rattled it. "I want to open this one first."

"Wait for your mother," Justice cautioned. "She's on the phone with your Gramma."

Tiffani's parents lived in a small town a few hours north of Prince George. Since the divorce, she'd made the trek to their home every Christmas, taking Max with her, but Justice hadn't been surprised when she'd suggested they spend the holiday together as a family this year. It was an obvious move in her campaign to reconcile. While he hadn't changed his mind about that impossible possibility, he was willing to accept the offer in order to spend the time with Max.

Tiffani hung up the phone and joined Max on the floor near the awkwardly decorated tree in the corner. Due to the limited reach of both Max and Whitman, most of the baubles dangled in the bottom half of the branches—those that had survived Chaucer's wildly waving tail. "Your Gramma sent you this," Tiffani said. She tackled Max and dug her fingers into his ribs. He shrieked with glee. "And this." She covered his face with kisses.

"Eww. Mooooooommmm!" Max wiped his cheeks vigorously.

Justice grinned. Despite his worries, moments like these helped Justice believe he and Tiffani were doing a good job with their son, no matter their personal differences.

"I've got a gift for you, too." She crouched next to Chaucer and held out a large rawhide bone. The dog almost levitated in his excitement. "Come lay down over here and you can have it." With the now enthusiastically crunching and slurping dog out of the way, she perched on the arm of the couch next to Justice and watched Max tear into his first present.

"*Star Wars* Lego—cool!" Max exclaimed. He poured the pieces out. "Papa, you read the instructions. I'll put it together." He shoved his glasses up with one sturdy finger.

As the old man and the young boy concentrated on building the V-wing Star Fighter, Tiffani handed Justice a gift bag frothing with tissue paper. "I know we don't give each other anything, but I thought you'd like this."

It was a five-by-seven print of Justice and Max at centre ice during a hockey practise. Justice was on one knee, pointing out of the frame, as Max listened intently. His face was visible through the cage of his helmet, eyes bright with intelligence and joy.

"It's great," Justice said sincerely. "Did Dan take it?" His assistant coach was a talented amateur photographer, and often had a camera with him at the rink.

"Yes. He showed it to me a couple weeks ago. I thought you'd like it."

"I do."

Her shoulders moved in an odd little squirm. "There's another one." Although she spoke to Justice, she kept her eyes on Max.

Justice's breath caught at the sight of the second framed photo. Also taken on a hockey rink, this one captured a moment in time Justice would never forget.

If he closed his eyes he could still remember the glory of that day. His WHL team had clinched a place in the Conference Championships, on the strength of an overtime goal by Jake Newton, assisted by Justice. In the photo, the two of them stood on the ice, arms about each other's shoulders, hair sweaty and tangled, smiles a mile wide.

Jake Newton. Max's biological father.

Justice gripped the frame tightly to hide his trembling hands. "Where did you get this?"

"His mom gave it to me. I used to have it on my nightstand. But after the accident—" Her breath caught and she clutched his shoulder. After a moment, her grip eased and she continued. "I put it away. I found it a few weeks ago, when I was cleaning out a closet."

He and Tiffani had argued more than once about whether to tell Max his real father had died only months before he was born. The boy had known no other dad but Justice, and Justice loved him as if he was his own—damn it, he *was* his own son, regardless of blood—but Tiffani worried the truth would only confuse Max.

Whitman's voice cracked through Justice's abstraction. "What are the two of you whispering about?" Max was still absorbed in construction, but Whitman peered at them from under wildly sprouting eyebrows, suspicion wrinkling his forehead.

Justice slipped Jake's photo under a crumpled sheet of tissue paper while handing Max's photo to his father. "Look what Tiffani gave me."

The old man harrumphed grumpily, one horny finger tracing the surface of the photo. "It's not a bad shot. The young one here doesn't look too dumb."

"Let me see." Max scrambled up and leaned in. "Hey, Dad, it's you and me."

"Yes." *Dad.* That's who he was to Max. Yet didn't Jake deserve recognition, too?

He would have to talk to Tiffani again. But not today. Today was Christmas. It had waited almost ten years. It could wait a little while longer.

****

Contented snores rumbled up from Chaucer, sprawled across his dog bed in gluttonous abandon. The gas fireplace flickered with characterless blue and orange flames. Justice rarely used it, but tonight, late on Christmas night, he wanted the company.

Tiffani had taken Max home after the festivities at Whitman's. Justice returned to his house, alone but for Chaucer, and wandered restlessly through the rooms, unable to settle.

The two photos were propped up on the coffee table in front of him. Justice and Max—the present, the future. Justice and Jake—the past.

God, they looked so young. Justice picked up the photo and cradled it in his hands. Small white scars on his knuckles caught the light as he held the frame in the glow of the table lamp. Yet another reminder of those days, when hockey was everything.

At the age of sixteen, he and Jake had joined the same

WHL team. Jake had been the shooting star, the forward who skated like lightning with the hands of a surgeon, deft and sure. Justice had been chosen much lower in the draft—a solid, stay-at-home defenseman. On road trips they'd been paired together, and by the end of their first season had earned the nickname J Squared for their off-ice friendship and on-ice compatibility.

Three years later, it all went to hell. Justice swallowed away the taste of fear, remembering the sickening skid, the explosion of glass, the smell of leaking diesel.

The screaming silence from the empty seat next to him.

Without analyzing his action, he searched for Charlotte's contact info in his phone and sent a quick text.

Merry Christmas.

He slid down on the squashy leather sofa, stretched his legs toward the fire, laid his head back and waited. If she didn't respond in a minute or two he'd go to bed. It would probably be a sleepless night, but he had to spend it somewhere.

The phone lying on his thigh vibrated.

Same to you.

What to reply? Impulse had sent the first message. Now confusion stymied his next move. While he dithered, Charlotte sent another message. *Is Max still up?*

That was an easy one. *He's with his mom.*

What are you doing?

He hesitated again, deciding finally on a half-truth. *Thinking of you.* He couldn't get her out of his head for long. Even thoughts of Jake hadn't pushed her away completely.

The pause this time was so long he almost gave up. Then—

I was thinking of you, too.

His whole body tightened with longing. The urge to share his turmoil with her was almost overwhelming. He controlled the weakness and a typed four letters. *Good.* He hit send, waited a few moments, and typed *Night.*

Chaucer whuffled in his dreams, his legs jerking.

****

Charlotte's sense of homecoming was surprisingly strong and unexpectedly welcome. She shut the duplex's door against the arctic chill and leaned against the panel with a relieved sigh. The air was bitter enough to crisp the hair inside her nostrils, but the sky was an unearthly blue, the sun a pallid gold. Both were a refreshing sight after the damp, grey mist cloaking Vancouver.

She allowed herself only moments to enjoy the light, however. Her comment to Sonny a few days earlier echoed. She needed to schedule her time wisely if she wanted to stay on track with her book. An opportunity like this—solitary time, without distractions—could not be wasted.

A few hours later, she looked up from her computer screen to discover deep dusk had fallen. She checked the clock, disoriented. This close to the winter solstice, the sun disappeared below the horizon before four o'clock. She was relieved to see it wasn't as late as she had feared. She still had plenty of time to work.

The doorbell rang.

She was out of her seat and down the stairs with an alacrity that belied her stern vow to put work first. Jehovah's Witnesses wouldn't be canvassing in such weather. It wasn't the right time of year for Girl Guide cookies. It could only be—

Justice stood on the doorstep, appearing even more

massive in a dark blue parka with a tunnel-like hood rimmed in fur. Chaucer sat properly at his knee, tongue lolling, breath puffing.

"Come in." She resisted the urge to grab his sleeve and drag him over the threshold. Justice lowered his gaze to the dog. "Chaucer, too."

He wound the leash tighter about his mittened fist and stepped in. "I saw fresh tracks on the driveway." He shoved back his hood with his free hand. The cold air clung to his coat, a fresh, brittle scent.

"Do I have you to thank for clearing them?" It was the first thing she'd noticed. Despite the evidence of another layer of snow blanketing the front yard, both sides of the duplex boasted neatly shovelled surfaces leading to the garages.

He shrugged, frost-bitten nylon crackling. His eyes met hers, calm, confident, with the hint of a question burning in their depths.

Charlotte bit her lip and heat rose to her cheeks. Other than that brief, cryptic text conversation while she was away, they hadn't spoken since she'd offered him sex. Had he come because she'd said their affair would start when she returned? She hadn't thought he'd be quite so— prompt.

The silence stretched. Unable to hold his gaze, she stared at the vee of his parka zipper, lowered just enough to reveal the pattern of the heavy wool sweater he wore beneath. Her heart pounded heavily in her chest. Chaucer whined.

"Want to go for a walk?" Justice asked, the question rumbling like thunder through the chasm between them.

She drew in a gasping breath and dared to shoot him a glance from under lowered lashes. "I should really keep working." She jerked a thumb over her shoulder.

"When did you get home?"

"Around eleven."

"When did you start working?"

"Around eleven thirty."

"I think you've earned a break. Let's walk."

Chaucer galumphed, knocking into her knees. Justice steadied her with a hand on her arm and helped her into her coat. She closed her eyes and breathed deeply, his warmth overriding the residual iciness adhering to his parka, his spicy, woodsy scent disturbingly familiar. He handed over her scarf and waited with unruffled patience as she wound it about her neck and dug gloves out of her pockets. He pulled up the hood and with one large finger tucked her hair out of the way. She slid her feet into her warmest, tallest boots. Then he held open the door.

With a sense of inevitability, Charlotte stepped out into the dark.

****

Justice took Charlotte's hand as they headed down the front steps. Her gloves were thin leather, completely unsuited for the frigid temperature, and he hoped the added warmth of his heavy suede mitten would help. At least her boots and coat looked decently warm. Regardless, he wouldn't keep her out too long, just enough for the air to bite some colour into her cheeks. She'd looked far too pale when she first opened the door.

With the heavy, enclosing hoods they both wore to protect them from the glacial breeze, he couldn't see her face. Yet he was entirely aware of her tall, well-made form, swinging briskly next to him. No one sauntered in these temperatures.

The late afternoon was sapped of colour, darkness

leeching green and blues and reds away until only shades of white and grey and black remained. "This way." He motioned her ahead of him to the pedestrian walkway between two homes, the path a narrow valley trudged into the snow by many feet. He and Chaucer followed, the dog snuffling at the wooden posts marking the start of the trail.

The lack of light stole his depth perception. Charlotte must have suffered the same lack of sensory input. She teetered, one foot sinking deep into the unpacked snow along the edge of the path. He threw out a hand and caught her sleeve, her body swinging around to collide with his. She clutched his parka.

Chaucer thought it was a great game. He gambolled around, not caring where he bounced, barking madly. Absently, Justice brought him to heel. The dog subsided, grumbling.

Charlotte's eyes were ebony in the moonlight, the hollows beneath her cheekbones sooty, etching the bones into sharp relief. Her mouth opened in a surprised O, her breath escaping in clouds of moisture.

He dipped his head, cocooning their faces between their hoods, twilight deepening to midnight as the little light surrounding them was blocked out.

What the hell. He hadn't really wanted to go for a walk anyway.

He kissed her.

A small part of his sanity ensured he kept Chaucer tightly controlled. The rest of his mind was lost in the luxury of her lips, her tongue. She moaned faintly, a sound he felt rather than heard, and her arms clung to his waist. He pressed his free hand into the small of her back, a futile attempt to feel more of her through too many layers of clothing.

His hood rustled against his ears. Or maybe it was the blood rushing from his brain, settling in his groin. The scent of her, soap and woman, made him light-headed. Her tongue darted into his mouth, tempting him to taste deeper. He felt invincible and weak-kneed, unstoppable and vulnerable.

The tug on his arm almost re-broke the collarbone he'd smashed during a game. Justice hissed and jerked away from Charlotte's warm mouth. Chaucer, growing tired of waiting, had darted off in search of other amusement, ignoring the confining leash.

"Heel!" Justice shouted, his voice harsh with discomfort as he rubbed his aching shoulder. Chaucer cowered, dark puppy eyes pleading for forgiveness. "Oh, stop it, you ass. I'm not going to beat you."

Charlotte cleared her throat. "I suppose we should keep walking. He looks like he needs a run." She took a hesitant step back, cold air rushing to fill the gap between them.

"To hell with that," Justice replied. She started at his tone, eyes wide. "I walked him for an hour in this godforsaken weather before we stopped at your place. It was you I thought needed air." He grabbed her hand and dragged both her and the dog toward the street, all three of them stumbling among the snow drifts. "He'll be fine locked in your back yard."

"He will? Why? What for?"

Icy air scraped his teeth when he smiled. "It's the best place for him while I do to you all the things I have in mind."

CHAPTER ELEVEN

She was not turned on by this aggressive side of Justice, Charlotte told herself sternly. She was *not.*

Oh, but she was. Heat fluttered down her spine and curled between her legs. Her breasts ached, her mouth dried. Her head was spinning, and not only because of the speed at which he hustled her down the street and into her house.

She stood at the bottom of the stairs in aroused bemusement as Justice impelled a reluctant Chaucer through the kitchen and out the back. She heard a pitiful whimper as the door clicked shut.

"Maybe we should let him—"

"No." Justice unzipped his parka and shrugged out of it, tossing it carelessly over the newel post. "I will not have him whining at the bedroom door." He toed off his boots. "Your porch is sheltered." He pulled the heavy wool sweater over his head, revealing a white t-shirt that clung to his chest and arms. "I sacrificed one of your patio chair cushions to be his bed." His fingers moved to the buttons on her coat. "He'll be fine."

"Oh." She lowered her chin to watch him undo the fastenings. Her coat joined his on the rail. She felt faint at the rapidness of his motions, drugged by the sensations pounding through her. He knelt before her. Grey spots blurred her vision. She reached out a hand and laid it on his head to balance herself, his short hair silky between her fingers.

He cupped her calf with his left hand and her heel with the right. She raised her foot and allowed him to draw off one boot, then the other. He remained crouched before her, his hands caressing the back of her knees through the fleece leggings she wore under a pale blue jersey tunic.

It was odd, looking down at his upturned face. It made him less dominating, more approachable. As she'd longed to do since almost the first day she noticed it, she traced the slashing scar bisecting his brow, trailed her finger down the crooked bridge of his nose.

"Hockey?" she asked quietly.

"Yes. Not exactly."

Before she had time to consider the oddness of his reply, he nuzzled his face into her belly, the crown of his head brushing the undersides of her breasts. She gasped as his hands slid up the backs of her thighs and cupped her buttocks. "You smell good."

She gave a shaky laugh. "Thanks." His hands kneaded her lightly, the heat of his large palms burning through the thin fabric separating their skin. He lifted his head and brushed his mouth over her hidden nipples. She gripped his shoulders, the muscles in her legs shuddering as she struggled to keep upright.

He rose slowly, his mouth whispering along the low, round neck of her tunic, his tongue licking her collarbone with teasing flicks, his teeth nibbling at the straining tendon in her neck.

She turned her head, seeking his lips, and the world caught fire.

His mouth was a storm of needs, of desire unleashed. She trembled at the power, the power he'd been holding in check until this moment. He consumed her, burned her to embers, leaving nothing but electric nerve endings ready to absorb every touch.

****

If they didn't get to a bedroom soon, Justice was going to take her here in the entrance. On the floor, against a wall, he didn't give a damn. He needed to be inside her, inside her hot, slick body. And her frantic motions as she pressed against him told him she felt the same.

He broke away from the temptation of her mouth. "Upstairs." He paused only long enough to snatch a box of condoms out of his parka pocket. He'd bought them at the local corner store while walking Chaucer tonight. And thank God he had.

She blinked at him, dark eyes heavy lidded, mouth lush and moist.

"Your bedroom, Charlotte." He could at least pretend to be civilized. What he really wanted to do was beat his chest and drag her off by her hair. Her glorious, curly, silky hair.

Without a word, she preceded him up the stairs, which put her ass immediately in view. He swallowed a groan. She was rounded and firm and her muscles clenched and released as she climbed. He assumed a man could actually survive with no oxygen in his body, no blood in his brain— if not, he'd be dead on the floor right now.

Her bed boasted an over-sized mattress, tall as well as wide, so the surface was unusually high off the floor. A vision of Charlotte lying face down on it, naked, bent at the waist, feet on the floor, melted what little sense he had remaining into a useless puddle.

And then that puddle evaporated into nothingness as Charlotte wriggled out of her tights and pulled the long shirt...short dress...whatever the hell it was...over her head and tossed it to the floor.

A lacy bra cupped her breasts, as his palms itched to do. The material was cut low, revealing the upper circle of her nipples. His gaze drifted lower, and then stopped, arrested by a long, thick scar marring the smooth, pearly skin of her stomach.

He reached out, one finger tracing the obscenely neat ridge. "Charlotte."

"It's nothing. An operation, a long time ago."

He carried his own scars, tidy ones on the outside, vicious ones on the inside. "Tell me."

"No. It's nothing." She reached up to release her hair from the tie holding it back, her breasts lifting erotically.

He needed to know what had happened, but could wait. Right now he wanted nothing more than to feel all that luscious, heated skin against his naked body. His shirt joined her dress and he shucked his underwear and jeans in one motion.

Her panties were cut high, showing off the long, slim line of her thighs, barely hiding the dark, secret place at their junction. Her hands went to the narrow lace ribbon that was all that held them on her hips.

"No." He swallowed, throat dry and rough like a man lost in the desert. "Not yet." Her hands stilled.

She stood before him, proud and tall, arms loose at her sides. Her scent enthralled him. He lowered his face to the curve of her neck, breathing deeply.

Her hands stroked his chest, cool and tantalizing on his heated skin. Slim fingers circled his nipples, traced the muscles of his stomach, wandered lower.

Justice didn't consider himself a talker. He said what needed to be said and no more. But he couldn't seem to stay quiet with Charlotte's hands on him.

"Oh, God," he choked out. She fisted his cock loosely,

gently rolled his balls with her other hand. "That feels so damn good." He grabbed her ass, pulled her tight against him, trapping her hands and his cock between them. She wriggled her pelvis and he growled. "If you want this to last more than the next thirty seconds, you better stop that."

She giggled, gave him a playful squeeze.

He unwrapped her fingers, clamped her hands to her hips and flung her on the bed. She squealed, eyes sparkling. He followed, the mattress dipping beneath his hands and knees.

He scraped his beard lightly across her abdomen, deliberately caressing the evidence of battle, of survival. Goosebumps rippled across the tender skin. Her laughter cut off abruptly and she arched toward him. Sliding his hands under, he undid the clasp of her bra. Using his teeth, he bared her breasts.

She slipped her arms out of the straps and the scrap of fabric disappeared. Her fingers danced on the back of his neck, urging him, seducing him. He teased a bit longer, using the rough bristles on his chin to bring her nipples to hard, engorged points. Her breath came in gasping moans, and she thrust her chest forward, begging without words.

When he finally took one rosy tip into his mouth, her whole body stiffened, then collapsed. He reached down, cupping her mound, and found her incredibly wet, unbelievably ready. She writhed restlessly.

"Shhh," he soothed, moving to the other breast, kissing and licking her softly. "I'll take care of you." Her hand pressed his, commanding his fingers to explore her deeper. "Have patience."

She whimpered. "Justice..."

"Shhh," he whispered again.

****

Charlotte was on fire. Any water poured on her right now would simply steam off her skin. Justice's mouth on her breasts, his hand between her thighs, ignited feelings she'd never experienced.

Feelings she didn't know how to contain.

His voice rumbled, murmuring endearments, encouragements, but her brain was too muddled to understand the words. The first flickers of her orgasm coalesced at the base of her spine, the tops of her thighs. His fingers moved against her, against the lace of her panties, now a useless, sodden barrier between their flesh. Keening sounds escaped her helplessly, her hips lifted, her head arched...

...and she exploded in a sparkling firework, the atoms of her body separating in a brilliant burst. For an instant, the world went dark, and then a million stars formed on the back of her eyelids, dancing like fireflies.

A satisfied chuckle breathed into her ear. Her limbs sprawled, slack and sated. As sanity and breath returned, she grew conscious of a heated, heavy weight laying against her hip, a warm palm flat on her abdomen. She dragged her eyes open.

Justice looked down at her, a smug expression on his face. "Enjoyed that, did you?" he said as he flexed his groin, his hot shaft nudging her.

She stretched luxuriously, lifting her arms above her head and opening her thighs in invitation. Air hissed between his teeth, but instead of accepting her offer he rolled off the bed, searching the floor with a scowl. With a grunt of satisfaction, he seized a small black box, ripped it open with a few sharp movements and removed a condom packet.

A twinge of irritation chipped at her sensual haze.

Wasn't he just the little Boy Scout, ever prepared? If she'd had the chance, if he hadn't shattered all her carefully thought-out plans with his actions tonight, she would have told him not to worry about getting her pregnant. Although, she supposed—

Her temper vanished as he settled between her legs, and the rounded, ready head of his erection found its place at the opening of her body. She hooked her heels behind his calves and lifted her hips.

Inch by inch, he thrust into her, a welcome invader, her body softening as she accepted him. She widened her thighs, urging him deeper, her hands on his buttocks, making sure he joined her completely.

He wrapped his hands under her shoulders and rocked into her. She could feel him in her abdomen, moving inside her with force and rhythm and urgent desire. His eyes blazed into hers, trapping her in their steely blue. She ran her fingers hard up his spine, bumping them along his vertebrae. He arched into her, the muscles in his biceps trembling, the tendons in his neck sharply defined, lips pulled back from his teeth in a soundless snarl.

She closed her eyes and held on, riding the thunder with him. His movements lost their powerful grace, grew sharp and jerky, until with a throat-tearing groan he buried himself deep.

He held himself above her, chest heaving, head hanging. Despite the continuing intimacy of their position, she felt bereft. She wished he would lower his body to hers, abandon himself to the sensual aftermath. She wanted to be covered by him, be surrounded by him, revel in his weight bearing down on her. Instead he slowly disengaged and dropped to the bed at her side.

She stared at the ceiling, embarrassment rustling over

her skin like spider's feet. Now what? Her only other sexual encounters had been within the familiar framework of a long-term relationship. What did you do after having sex with someone you had no commitment to? She shifted away from the heat of his body.

"I can hear you thinking." Justice's voice was low and lazy. She stole a glance. He lay, one arm cocked over his eyes, his hand open and relaxed. Knowing he wasn't staring at her gave her enough courage to scoot off the bed and grab the robe hooked on the headboard.

"Yes. Well." She tied the sash at her waist and felt a modicum of confidence return.

He rolled his forearm just high enough so he could peer at her from under it. "Are you going to make this awkward?"

"What do you mean?" She picked an imaginary thread from the lapel of her robe. It gave her somewhere to concentrate other than his naked body, sprawled out for her perusal.

With a quiet groan, he lifted into a sitting position. He scrubbed his knuckles over his skull and studied her with narrowed eyes. "This was your idea."

"I know." She bit her lip, caught herself doing so, and stopped. "And it was great." His eyes narrowed further. She hurried on. "Amazing, stupendous."

He raised his hands to check her. "I wasn't fishing for compliments."

A flush heated her cheeks. She lifted her chin. "I'm just a bit...unsure. I don't how to handle this. After. You know."

He rose to his feet, nonchalantly naked, and cupped her nape. His thumb traced the side of her neck. "All I know is, this may have been our first time together"—he leaned in, brushed his lips lightly across hers—"but it won't be our last." She shivered as his teeth nipped along her jawline. "Unless you have any objections to repeating the experience?"

Wordless, she shook her head.

"Good." He patted her on the ass, a saucy grin cutting through the crisp bristles of his beard, and disappeared into the ensuite. Water ran, the toilet flushed and he returned, reaching for his jeans.

She glared at him. "I wouldn't be so flustered if you hadn't rushed me. I know I said we'd get together when I came back after Christmas. But I thought we would sit down first, have a rational discussion, lay the ground rules."

"Sometimes you have to go with instinct." He buttoned the waist of his jeans.

She dragged her eyes away from his flat stomach. Unfortunately, with all the good bits from his hips down now clothed, she couldn't avoid his chest, covered in a light mat of dark blond hair. Her nipples tightened, remembering how it had felt brushing against her.

Dazedly she focused her attention back on Justice's voice in time to catch the end of his sentence. "...blame it on Chaucer," he said as he worked his arms into his t-shirt and pulled it over his head.

Her mouth went dry. What the hell was wrong with her? Her brain felt full of cotton wool. "Chaucer?"

He shot her a sardonic look. She flushed. The last thing she wanted was for him to recognize the power he seemed to hold over her. "I was saying, if only I didn't have Chaucer with me, we'd have time to have that rational discussion, lay down those ground rules. But I really should get him home before he tears up your porch."

She'd completely forgotten about the dog. "Of course."

"I'll call." He strode to the door, spun on his heel and returned. Clasping her face, he kissed her, bruising, possessive. "I'll call," he repeated and stalked out.

She lowered herself to the bed. The scent of their lovemaking rose from the sheets, and a traitorous rush flooded her belly.

A dog's grateful barking sounded under her window. She pictured Justice's big hands ruffling Chaucer's ears, watched in her mind's eye as he unlatched the back gate and headed out, the dog trotting at his heels.

Her head dropped into her hands. He'd been gone scant seconds and she wished him back. That wasn't good.

Not good at all.

CHAPTER TWELVE

Even during the Christmas break, the security office at UNBC was manned twenty-four hours a day. With the vast majority of students and staff on holiday, it could be excruciatingly boring. Justice never minded. He enjoyed the sense of expectation, as if the buildings were holding their breath, treading water, waiting patiently for the return of youth and vitality.

Today, as he sat in the glass box with a view down three hallways, the quiet only gave him time to think of Charlotte. Too much time to wonder why she was once again avoiding him. He hadn't seen her since the night they'd had sex, four evenings ago. Four frustrating, solitary evenings.

He wanted to make love to her again. But he also wanted to talk to her. The cruel scar marring her body was a burr in his brain, raising questions, demanding answers. It was none of his business, of course, and it didn't diminish his attraction to her one bit. But he couldn't stop wondering about it.

Even though he'd accepted her proposition of a simple, straight-forward physical affair, he wasn't really that kind of guy. He'd never been like some of the players on his team, ready to jump into bed or the backseat with any puck-bunny that offered. He was sure a shrink would say it had something to do with losing his mother at an early age. Whatever. It was just the way he was.

Behind him, Shawn McMorris rattled papers at his

small desk, muttering under his breath. Justice ignored him.

Maybe Charlotte was second-guessing her decision to be with him. He knew her well enough by now to know that going with the flow, not worrying about what tomorrow would bring, wasn't her usual modus operandi.

Nielson stepped out of his inner office, shrugging into the sport jacket that completed his customary uniform of white shirt and navy slacks. "I've an appointment with the Dean of Graduate Programs," he said. "I'll be back in one hour."

"Yes, sir," Justice replied.

Nielson frowned at McMorris. "Shouldn't you be out on rounds?"

"Leaving right now, sir." He shuffled the stack of papers into order and pulled on his thigh-length winter parka.

Nielson's frowned deepened, but he left without another word.

McMorris laughed without humour. "He's as bad as my wife," he said. "Ex-wife, I should say. Always ordering me around."

Justice grunted a non-committal reply. If the man disliked his job so much, why didn't he just quit? McMorris headed out, steps short and choppy, and disappeared around a corner.

Fifteen minutes later, the radio squawked, startling Justice from his distracted study of one of Nielson's many memos.

Urgency rang in McMorris' voice. "Medical and security services required. Room 10-4520. Immediately."

Justice grabbed a handset. "Message received." He dialled Ambulance Service, confirmed the location of the event, and raced out the door.

****

Charlotte knew Justice was working a day shift. He'd told her so when they'd spoken the night before last. She was tempted to wander down to the security office, see if he had time for coffee. She shook her head at her foolishness. After the way she'd avoided him since the night of her return, she was probably the last person he wanted to see.

She pushed away from her desk and twisted her chair to face the window. A few lights burned in the student residences on the far side of the ring road, including one window almost obscured by neatly stacked beer cans, arranged in such a way that they mimicked the red and white of the flag. Clouds above the residences were dark and sinister, heavy with unreleased snow.

It had been weak and silly of her not to admit to him she had the flu. The morning after they'd been together, she'd woken from a restless sleep just in time to make a weak-kneed dash to the toilet before becoming violently ill. It did no good to curse her distant niece and nephew— they hadn't given her their bug on purpose. But she couldn't remember the last time she'd been so sick. When Justice phoned later that day, she'd used work as an excuse, despite the fact she'd been curled up in bed, shivering with fever and intermittently losing her battle with nausea. Perhaps she was being overly sensitive, but she hadn't wanted him to see her in such a pathetic state.

She was surprised at how much his good opinion mattered to her. It had been part of the reason she'd refused to give him details about her surgery. She pressed her hands against her abdomen, remembered pain ghosting through her gut.

A wailing siren caught her attention. The university sprawled along the ridge of a hill overlooking the city, isolated in academic grandeur. If she could hear an ambulance, that meant it was coming to the campus. She peered out the window as rotating red lights cut through the midday gloom. The vehicle turned onto the ring road circling the main cluster of buildings and disappeared from sight, if not from hearing.

She bit her lip. The university was practically deserted during the winter break, except for administrative staff and a few scattered faculty members such as herself. She hoped whatever the emergency, it wasn't too serious.

She turned back to her computer. The new semester started in a few short days and she needed to finish her lesson plans. Squaring her shoulders, she faced the accusing screen of her computer monitor once more.

****

Adrenaline poured into Justice's bloodstream as he pounded up four flights of stairs, ignoring the elevator.

He skidded around a corner and came upon a small group of people. McMorris crouched next to the prone body of a woman. Standing above them was a young man, shifting restlessly from foot to foot and running his hands through his long, shaggy hair.

"Status," Justice ordered as he dropped to his knees and reached under the woman's jaw, searching for a pulse. It thudded reassuringly against his fingertips, and he felt his own slow in relief.

"No visible wounds, breathing steady but shallow." All the security guards were trained in First Aid, but McMorris had only the bare minimum necessary for the job.

The woman lay face down, sprawled half into the hall,

arms flung over her head. Dark hair, streaked with bright, unnatural blue, glinted in the light tumbling through the open door of Room 10-4520.

The young man crumpled to the floor, legs crossed. "Is she going to be okay?" He reached out a trembling hand then withdrew it, as if afraid to touch her. "I was supposed to meet her here. We were going to a movie."

"What's your name?" Justice continued his assessment. "And hers?"

"I'm Darby Sloan. She's Cassandra. Cassandra Colley. She's got a research project, had come in to work on it."

"Did you find her?"

"No, he did."

Justice shot Darby a quick look, saw him nod at McMorris.

"I came out of the stairwell and he was kneeling next to her," Darby continued. "What's wrong with her?"

"Paramedics are on the way. They'll be able to tell you more." As if on cue, sirens sounded faintly. Justice turned to McMorris. "Go meet them. Get them here fast."

The echo of McMorris' footsteps faded away. Justice ran his hands clinically over the woman's arms, torso and legs. Other than a faint reddening on the skin of her neck, he could detect nothing out of the ordinary.

Darby sat silently, rocking back and forth. With extreme gentleness, the young man lifted long strands of hair off her colourless cheek. Her eyelids fluttered. Consciousness returned in a rush, her fists clenching, her knees drawing up.

"Cassandra!" Darby scrambled to his knees and leaned over her.

"Lie still." Justice placed a hand between her shoulder

blades. "Paramedics are on their way."

"No." She winced and reached for her throat, rolling to her side and curling into a ball. "No, don't..." Her eyes opened. Justice froze at the stark fear in their depths. "Don't touch me, don't..."

He held both hands up, showing them to her. "I'm not. I'm not touching you. I'm only here to help."

Darby patted her shoulder. "Everything's going to be okay, Cassie. He's here to take care of you."

The elevator door slid open. Two paramedics bustled through, hauling a stretcher and carrying red equipment bags. Justice moved out of their way.

McMorris followed, coming to stand at his side. "When did she come round?"

"Just after you left."

Cassandra's panic subsided at the sight of the female ambulance attendants. She clutched Darby's hand, but allowed the two women to carefully lay her on her back.

"Do you remember what happened?" The paramedic with short, iron grey hair flashed a light into Cassandra's eyes, while the other, a younger woman with a slim, athletic build, strapped on a blood pressure cuff.

"I was working," Cassandra replied, voice thready and thin. "I didn't hear anything. I didn't. He grabbed me." Her hand fluttered to her throat. "I couldn't breathe. He dragged me to the door. I think I blacked out."

Justice stiffened. "You were attacked?"

The paramedic shot him a stern look. "Didn't she just say so?"

"I thought she was sick. Maybe had a seizure." He turned to McMorris. "Did you see anyone, before you found her?"

The older man's face was pale. He licked his lips.

"Not to see, no. But I thought I heard a stairwell door bang shut, as I came this way."

The paramedics bundled Cassandra onto the stretcher. Her blue-black hair was vivid against the white sheet, while her face matched its snowy hue.

"She may have a mild concussion. And her heart rate is all over the place." The grey-hair woman gathered scattered gear. "Any questions you have will need to wait until she's seen a doctor."

Justice watched them wheel the stretcher into the elevator, Darby following with a determined expression on his narrow face. The doors closed behind them.

"Call Nielson," Justice said to McMorris. "Tell him we might have another one."

****

The knowledge that Justice was somewhere in the building continued to distract Charlotte. After struggling for several minutes to make headway on her lesson plans, she gave up with a disgruntled sigh. She turned off the screen and grabbed her purse.

Maybe a cup of tea would help. She'd walk off her nervous energy by visiting the kiosk furthest from her office, in the Teaching and Learning Centre. And if that path took her past the security office—well, it wasn't like she was deliberately looking for anyone in particular.

Her heels clicked on the polish cement floors as she wound her way through the corridors. She came in sight of the security office and suppressed a twinge of disappointment. There was no sign of Justice through the glass sentry box. Belatedly, she considered the implications of the siren she'd heard earlier. If there had been an emergency, he would probably be on scene. God, she couldn't even think straight.

The long hallway leading to the Teaching and Learning Centre was deserted. The pewter sky outside made even the corridors walled with windows dim and gloomy. She had taken only a few steps when two figures came into view at the far end.

Justice's size and powerful grace were unmistakable, his long stride eating up the distance between them. The stocky guard hustling at his side was familiar, but she didn't know his name. He held a cell phone to his ear, his eyes on the ground.

As she drew near, her heart clenched at Justice's expression. His eyes were bleak and wary, without the mocking gleam she'd grown to appreciate. She swallowed and twisted her lips into a polite smile. What did she expect, after pushing him away for days?

He stared at her, face blank. She dropped her gaze, intending to pass without comment, but came to an abrupt halt when she caught a few words of the older guard's conversation.

"Hello, sir. McMorris here. There's been an attack."

Justice stopped next to her.

Forgetting her self-consciousness, she repeated in dismay, "Attack?"

The older guard jerked his head up, startled out of his contemplation of the floor.

"Go on," Justice told him as he gestured down the hall. "I'll meet you and Nielson in a minute."

With a disconcerted look at Charlotte, the older guard did as Justice bid.

"An attack, here, on campus?" As she spoke she vaguely remembered an email sent out before Christmas. "Another one?" she asked uncertainly.

Justice took her elbow and drew her into a small

alcove. A tall, narrow window overlooked a chunk of undeveloped land, thickly wooded with spruce and pine. "I don't have time to explain." His face was grim. "Can I trust you not to mention this to anyone?"

She bristled. "Of course you can. But what—"

"Not now." He shot an impatient glance down the corridor. "I've got to get back to the office."

"Can you tell me if anyone has been injured?"

His expression lightened. "Not seriously, as far as I know."

"Thank goodness." She backed up a step. Silence beat once, twice. "You should go."

He nodded, not taking his gaze off of her. "Will you be home tonight?"

"Yes." Her pulse grew thick and slow at the sudden fierceness in his eyes.

"Will you let me see you?" He canted his head to the side. "I'll tell you what I can."

Anticipation bubbled in her belly. "You don't need to bribe me."

"Then I won't. Instead"—he reached out one thick, blunt finger and slid it delicately along her jaw—"instead, you can tell me why you've been avoiding me."

The tips of her ears tingled, the back of her throat burned. "I wasn't. Not really."

"Later." His eyes promised retribution for her cowardice. "I don't know when. It will depend on..." He waved his hand, encompassing events of which she was in ignorance.

"I understand. I'll be working. Call if you can't make it."

"I'll make it." And he was gone.

****

Justice pulled into Charlotte's driveway, headlights illuminating the white garage doors. Other than a modern carriage light glowing next to the front door, the house was bland and blank. Unlike its neighbours, no glittering, multi-coloured lights festooned the eaves, no inflatable Santa glowed on the lawn.

It looked lonely, neglected. He wondered if Charlotte noticed the depressing difference between her home and the cheerful vulgarity of the others.

Muscles clenched tight from the stress of the day ached between his shoulder blades. Tension stretched up the back of his neck to pound at the base of his skull. He rubbed his thumbs into his eye sockets and wondered if visiting Charlotte in his current surly mood was a good idea.

The ominous clouds that had loomed much of the day had finally unleashed their load of snow. Flakes bulleted through the air like tiny chips of glass, hurled by the fury of a raging wind. He took a deep breath, pulled his hood over his head and stepped out of the warm comfort of the cab. The arctic blast seared the inside of his nostrils, and he hurried to the door. Before he had a chance to knock, it opened, and Charlotte dragged him in with a strong grip on his sleeve.

"It's a terrible night to be out. You should have called and said you couldn't make it. I would have understood." She brushed snow from his shoulders, her brows creased over concerned eyes warm as melted chocolate. A bulky sweater in a creamy, not-quite-white colour fell to mid-thigh. She had pushed the cuffs back, revealing slim wrists. Her long, slender legs, clad in the tights he was fast becoming a fan of, stretched deliciously. Fuzzy black socks hid her feet. She looked warm and cozy and delectable.

"I wanted to see you." He unzipped his parka and draped it on the coat rack. "It's not too late?" God, he hoped not. He needed to decompress before heading home. Chaucer was good company, but he needed something more. He needed Charlotte.

"It's barely ten o'clock." She took a step back, gestured to the living room. "Have a seat. You look like you need a drink. Something stronger than hot chocolate."

"Rye?"

"I think I might be able to accommodate." She disappeared down the hall to the kitchen.

The spartan state of her home served as a stark reminder that her life here was only temporary. The living room had two sofas, so tightly stuffed the seat barely dented when he lowered himself onto it. Built-in bookshelves were devoid of knick-knacks and feminine clutter, pale-coloured walls displayed the generic art he'd seen in hundreds of hotel rooms during his hockey days. Charlotte's cluttered, disorganized office at the university was a warmer, kinder reflection of her personality than this bleak room.

She returned, carrying two squat tumblers a quarter full of amber liquid. Ice cubes clinked as she handed one over. "Before my landlord left, he and his wife came for a good-bye drink. He brought a bottle of Canadian Club, because by then he knew my offerings were limited. You're lucky he left it behind." Curling her legs beneath her, she settled beside him.

He sipped the smoky whiskey, letting it linger on his tongue, fumes rising up the back of his nose. It hit his empty stomach in warm welcome, easing the tension in his back and shoulders.

"Can you tell me about it?" Charlotte propped her elbow on the back of the couch, rested her temple in her palm. Her face was shadowed. The only light in the room came from the entrance hall; even though lamps squatted on tables at either end of the sofa, neither he nor Charlotte had turned them on.

"Notice will go out to all faculty and staff tomorrow." He twisted on the rock-hard cushion so he could face her. Her hair was loose about her shoulders, curling riotously. He leaned forward and wrapped one shining ringlet around his knuckle. "Nielson is meeting with upper administration now."

"What's he telling them?"

He unwound the silky strands from his finger, watched them bounce back into place. "He's telling them we have a potential rapist targeting our campus."

CHAPTER THIRTEEN

Charlotte listened with dismay growing into horror as Justice told her about the three attacks. "He's escalating. It was only luck that McMorris, the guard you saw with me"—he raised an eyebrow in enquiry and she nodded. She'd recognized the face but hadn't know his name— "came upon this victim so quickly. He must have scared the attacker away." He moved restlessly, uncurling one long leg from under the other and stretching both before him.

Unease snaked under her skin, raising the hairs on her arms. "This is appalling." She put her now empty glass on the end table and pulled the sleeves of her sweater over her fists. "You've got to warn women—students and staff."

"Nielson's putting the plan together now, he and the President. We don't want to cause a panic, but..." He lifted his shoulders, dropped them wearily. He shifted on the cushion. "Do you sit here often?"

She blinked at the sudden change in topic. "No. Never, actually."

"This is the most god-awful uncomfortable couch I've ever sat on." He rose to his feet, towering over her. "Can we go to the other room?"

"Of course."

He tossed back the rest of his drink, picked up her tumbler, cradled them both in one large palm, and stalked ahead of her, back stiff and taut. After placing the glasses in the sink, he dropped onto the sofa in the small sitting area off the kitchen. In the brighter glare of the overhead lights, she could easily see the lines of worry and fatigue biting deep along the sides of his crooked nose, between his eyes. His cheekbones cut tight through his skin above the dark gold of his beard.

The urge to take care of him, to bring him comfort, had her tapping her fingers on the counter in an uneven tattoo. "Did you eat dinner?"

He grinned faintly. "Do unlimited cups of coffee count?"

Her own stomach roiled in sympathy. "You must be starving."

"I didn't come here so you could feed me. I wanted to let you know what was going on." He rolled his shoulders as if tossing off a heavy weight. His determined blue gaze pinned her. A flutter tickled her throat. "And find out why you've been hiding from me."

She had hoped he'd forgotten that in the confusion of more serious events. "It wasn't on purpose." She turned her back on his stare and opened the fridge, surveying the contents, its air-conditioned breeze cooled her heated cheeks. "Would you like a sandwich? I have ham."

"Sure." Refusing to be deflected, he continued inexorably. "Not on purpose?" His tone was dry with disbelief.

She selected Dijon mustard, roma tomatoes, sprouts and red onion to go with the deli ham and Havarti cheese she'd already placed on the counter. "It wasn't that I didn't want to see you." She untwisted the tie on the plastic bag and liberated four slices of rye bread. They were soft and springy in her fingers, and the scent of yeast and grains made her own stomach rumble. "It was more I didn't want you to see me." She chose two more slices, and set about building the sandwiches.

His gusty sigh blew across the quiet kitchen. "I have no idea what you are talking about."

She risked a quick glance. His elbows were propped on his knees, the heels of his hands pressing into his eyes sockets, broad shoulders slumped with exhaustion.

"I was just being stupid, okay?" she said. "And I hate being stupid." She sliced tomatoes with rather more vigour than necessary, seeds and juice squirting onto the cutting board. "I was sick—vomiting, fever, the whole works— and I didn't want you to see me that way."

She concentrated on layering the fixings onto the bread. After a few moments of silence, a snort from the direction of the sofa drew her eyes to Justice.

He watched her, head shaking slowly back and forth.

"What?" She slapped the top slice of bread onto the three stacks.

"I got nothing." He rose and took the two steps necessary to reach the refrigerator. "Milk?"

"I only have skim."

"Not much better than water, but I'll take it."

She placed two of the sandwiches on one plate and one on the other, and cut them from corner to corner. Justice searched out glasses, moving about the kitchen as if completely at home. They settled at the dinette table and began to eat.

The quiet scratched away at her composure. Swallowing a bite, she laid her hands flat on the table and faced him squarely. "Really?" she demanded. "I put you off, lie to you for days, and when I tell you the silly reason I did so the best you can do is 'I got nothing?'" She imitated his deep, slow voice.

He finished his second triangle and moved onto the

third. "Yup."

She narrowed her eyes at him. "Don't do the dumb yokel with me."

Humour lit his face, easing the lines of stress. "You said you were being stupid. Do you think I'm stupid enough to say I agree with you?"

It took her a moment to sort it out. When she did, she tilted her head, narrowed her eyes. "You think I'm stupid?"

"No." He gulped down the last of his milk. "I think you overreacted."

"Oh." She lifted the top slice of bread, plucked a few threads of sprouts, and nibbled. "I guess I can't disagree with that."

"It's kind of flattering." He flashed a grin, licked his finger and dabbed crumbs off his plate.

"You're welcome," she answered drily. "Do you want another?"

"Thanks, but no. I have to get home. Chaucer still needs a walk."

"Of course." It was silly to be disappointed. She gathered the plates and glasses and carried them to the counter. "Give him a pat for me."

She turned, resigned to seeing him out, only to be confronted by his large, warm presence a few inches away. He leaned against the counter, bracketing her between his arms. His thighs brushed hers and she suppressed a tremble.

Tiny gold flecks lightened the blue of his irises. His lashes were short and thick. The scar slashing his left brow dipped into the socket and she wondered vaguely if he'd been in danger of losing his sight. She breathed out on a trembling sigh as his eyes dropped to her mouth.

****

Justice lowered his head and caressed Charlotte's mouth with his lips. He'd tasted her before—in haste, in lust, in fierce possessiveness—but this was different. He wanted her, could feel his body rise with his need. And yet tenderness was what he offered. What he sought.

Her hand floated to his face, a butterfly's touch. He kept his own anchored on the counter, fingers digging in to the granite surface. He couldn't give in to the crushing urge to take her to bed, yet he hadn't been able to resist one kiss, one connection.

He drew slowly away. Her hand fell to her side, brown eyes luminous as she searched his face.

"I want to stay," he said.

The glow lighting her face deepened.

"I can't." Drawn in once more, he nibbled at the lobe of her ear, inhaled her musky, woman scent. "Chaucer's been cooped up for hours."

"I know." Her breath drifted against his neck, moist and warm. "It's okay. Go, take care of your dog." Her hand fisted in his shirt as he nuzzled the sweep of skin from throat to collarbone.

He found her mouth once more, kissed her firmly and dragged himself back. "I'm going."

"Yes." Her eyes were cloudy, dreamy.

He took her hand, leading her to the front door. Her fingers were long and slim, and fit his palm perfectly. "Good night, Charlotte."

"Will I see you tomorrow?" Her eyes flitted from his face to his chest, and rosiness flushed the hollow of her throat. "I mean, not at work?"

"It's New Year's Eve."

"Oh." She flushed even deeper. "I suppose you have plans."

"Do you?"

She shook her head.

He had asked only to confirm an answer he was sure he knew. Charlotte kept to herself far too much. She needed to get out more, start living life in the now. "Dinner. My house. And then we'll ring in the New Year. Together." He leaned in and kissed her softly, teasing her lips with tiny nips. He wanted her in his bed. Badly.

"Justice..." She whispered his name, her breath sweet along his jaw.

"Tomorrow, Charlotte. Come to dinner." He lifted his head. With frustrated amusement, he noted the bemused, befuddled look was back in her eyes, pulling him in, shredding his control.

"Stay." Her hand in his flexed restlessly. "Tonight. I-I missed you."

The reluctant admission struck a chord of yearning. To be needed, if only for one night. To be the man a woman chose, because of who he was, not who he wasn't.

"Fuck it," he said violently. "The damn dog can wait another hour."

****

Waves of heat swept under Charlotte's skin as Justice's mouth fastened to hers. She gripped his hand tightly, clasping the other around his forearm, desperate for balance, as giddiness zinged bolts of sensation through her belly, weakened her knees.

She welcomed his fierceness, relinquished her will, and allowed him to press her backward, step by step, until she reached the wall. Her body softened, molded itself to his hard edges, jutting angles.

His hands swept down her sides, under the long hem of her sweater, to cup her ass. "God, you feel good." His

143

words murmured against her lips, tugged along her nerves. She wriggled in encouragement, moaning softly into his mouth.

She hadn't meant to say anything about missing him. She had accepted her retching miserableness the last few days with a restless sense of relief. It gave her a valid excuse to avoid him, gave her time to regain her balance after their lovemaking.

Yet all it took was one short evening to rock her off her feet once more.

She ran one stockinged sole along his calf, rucking up the material of his slacks, the strong band of muscle firm under her foot. With welcome shock, she felt the warmth of his fingers at the waistband of her tights. He worked them down over her hips, and groaned when he discovered she wore nothing underneath.

"Bedroom." Two fingers dipped inside her and she shuddered as he rubbed her slickness over her swollen, heated flesh. "We should go—" She felt the dampness on his hands as he worked the stockings down her legs, kneeling to take the heavy socks she wore with them.

"No." She urged him upright, and fumbled at his belt, his fly. "Here. Now."

He stepped away from her. "Condom." She could hear the desperation in his voice. Upstairs was too far away. Neither of them wanted to wait.

"I'm on the pill." A lie, but not a lie. She grabbed for his waistband and yanked him toward her, knowing that if he hadn't wanted to move she couldn't have forced him. She moaned in relief when the heat of his body covered hers once more.

The tinder of tenderness had flared into a conflagration of want. Physical passion she could handle.

Anything more might singe her beyond all recognition.

Never had she had a partner so dominating, in size, in strength, in desire. When he lifted her with bold, firm hands under her thighs, spreading her to take him, she knew no anxiety, felt no qualm, trusted him to support her.

His first fierce thrust snapped her against the wall. Face to face, her legs wrapped around his waist, the intensity in his cobalt eyes stole her breath. "Okay?" he asked huskily.

"God." She held him tighter. "Please."

He circled his hips, holding himself deep within her. Without a latex barrier he was hotter, slicker, iron wrapped in silk. She gasped, arching her back, shoulders hard against the wall. His lips were moist and greedy on the pulse point in the hollow of her neck. Her breasts, crushed against his solid chest, grew heavy, her nipples tight points abraded by the lace of her bra.

She yanked eagerly at his shirt, desperate to feel skin on skin. Her palms skated up his ribs, fingers tangling in the wiry hairs on his pecs. She pinched a nipple, and his hips jerked. Pleased, she pinched again, tightening her core around his cock as he filled her.

Using the strength of her own thighs, she raised and lowered herself, wordlessly begging him to complete her.

He stroked into her, long, smooth motions that almost separated them, and then buried so deep she felt him in her womb. She pressed his head to her breast, feeling the grunts of his exertion hot and moist even through the thick knit of her sweater.

Her orgasm was just out of reach, building in her pelvis, centring on his cock, the friction of the root rubbing her clit.

Her brain whispered warnings she hadn't heard during

their first joining, holding her back from the edge, tying her to reality. As desperate as hormones and lust made her, she couldn't help but remember her despondency when he'd left last time. She couldn't let herself feel that again. Could admit to wanting him. Couldn't admit to needing him.

He jerked against her, his breath heaving out on a long, low growl. "Stay with me, Charlotte." He pounded again, demanding her attention. With a sob she gave in, let her mind focus only on his movements, his strength, tossing consequences and considerations aside.

A scream tore at her throat, held behind her clenched teeth. A rush of pleasure sparked from her womb, sent her careening helplessly in a spiral of flashing fire. Her head dropped to his shoulder, her arms hanging limply at her sides, and still he held her, claimed her, marked her as his, until the shuddering of his body signalled he'd reached his own release.

And still he held her.

He pressed her so tightly to the wall she couldn't distinguish whose heart beat was whose. The skin of his neck was damp, and without thought she licked him, the tip of her tongue tasting salt.

He twitched at her touch, made an indeterminate humming noise. His grip on her thighs loosened. Blood pulsed into the marks his fingertips left behind. She welcomed the stinging pain, used it to gather herself back into her body, so that when he lowered her to the ground she had enough strength to hold herself up.

"I'm sorry." The tips of his ears were red, flushed with blood. "You may be on the pill, but that's no reason to be irresponsible."

"It's okay, really. I trust you." No qualm of remorse

or worry tugged at her. She did trust him. "If it hadn't been safe, you would have stopped, before it was too late."

"Normally I'd agree, but when I'm with you, all bets seem to be off." He tucked himself away, straightening his clothes. "It won't happen again."

"Stop with the guilt trip. I said it was okay, and I meant it. Next time, use a condom, or don't. Or do you want a doctor's note saying I'm clean?"

An apologetic gleam flickered in his quiet blue eyes. "No, of course not." The gleam grew playful. "Next time?"

She huffed and crossed her arms. "Only if you're lucky."

He chucked her under the chin. "Oh, I plan on getting lucky." She rolled her eyes, stifling a flutter of her lips. "And so will you."

CHAPTER FOURTEEN

The air was thin and frozen, cutting into Justice's lungs when he stepped out of Charlotte's house. He waited for the click of the lock, and then strode to his truck with his parka flapping wide, welcoming the chill on his heated skin.

He should regret his loss of control, but couldn't. Her reaction had soothed a part of him that he hadn't known needed soothing. She'd said she trusted him, and the intimacy of that small statement almost superseded the physical intimacy they'd just shared.

Almost.

He would see her again tomorrow night. Too bad tomorrow night seemed such a long way away.

His house was oddly silent when he arrived—no dog bouncing at the door, frantic for attention, barking with hunger. He flipped on the light in the kitchen. "Chaucer?" He found him in the living room, sprawled on his bed, regarding Justice with soulful eyes.

He crouched down and scratched him between the ears. "Feeling okay, buddy? Don't you need to go out?" The dog's tail thumped lazily, but he didn't rise. "What about dinner?" That had the pup scrambling to his feet with a yelp of pleasure.

"I've already fed him."

Justice leaped to his feet, heart slamming in his chest, a breathless curse hissing into the stillness of the room. Tiffani sat on the sofa, a tiny, shadowy figure, out of the cone of light spreading from the kitchen. "Sorry," she said. Amusement quivered in the single word.

He lowered his hands, stretched his clenched fingers. "What the hell are you doing here?" The ripples of shock racing under his skin slowed.

"I need to talk to you." Her voice was soft, faintly defiant. He caught the liquid shine of one eye as she lifted her chin, the rest of her features hidden in the gloom.

"Where's Max?"

"Sleeping over at a friend's house."

Oh, shit. He'd hoped his son was upstairs, an innocent but still useful chaperon.

Justice regarded her warily. "Why didn't you call?"

She shrugged, her abundant fall of blond hair draping over a shoulder, gleaming even in the subdued light, and answered obliquely. "I used my key." He'd given it to her, in case Max needed something from the house. "I got here about an hour ago. Chaucer seemed hungry, so I fed him and let him into the back for a bit."

Justice scowled down at the traitorous dog, who palpitated in anticipation of a second meal. "Nice try. Back to your bed," he said, pointing.

Chaucer slunk onto the cushion, dropping with a disgusted sigh, pinning him with a pained look.

"What do you need?" Unease snaked greasily in Justice's belly. They hadn't been alone since the divorce, and he was uncomfortably conscious of the quiet house, the lack of Max as a buffer.

She floated off the couch, the tan of her thigh-length jacket a light blotch against the black of the window behind her. He could see his own reflection in the glass, a large, looming figure, towering over her. "I want to talk about us." She approached, clutching the edges of her coat, arms wrapped around her torso.

He sucked in a deep breath and let it out slowly. "There is no us." Flashes of the last few months of their marriage—of screams and shouts and tears and tantrums—had him easing away from her. Confrontations with Tiffani could get very ugly, very quickly.

"We were good together, in the beginning." She peered up at him, her lids smudged with glittering makeup, her lashes thick with mascara. "Don't you remember?"

He knew now he'd married her for completely the wrong reasons. He'd thought he could build a family through grit and determination, but it hadn't been enough. His guilt and remorse—that he has survived the crash, and Jake had not—hadn't been the right foundation. "It didn't last," he said.

"It could be that way again." Her mouth tightened, and then relaxed, her lips sticky with gloss. She stepped forward, put one hand on his chest. "I know it could."

"No." He didn't want to be cruel, but he had to make sure she understood, once and for all. "It's over. You don't love me, I don't love you."

"You used to love this." She dropped her arms to her sides, gave a shimmy, and the coat fell to the floor, revealing naked ivory flesh. Delicate black lace cupped her breasts, hugged her hips, emphasizing what it was supposed to conceal.

With the memory of Charlotte's touch, her scent, the feel of his cock inside her, her breathy moans as he'd made her come so fresh in his mind, his overriding emotion was pity. Pity that Tiffani was willing to give up even her pride to lure him back.

She held her shoulders back, chin tilted. Yet her audacious move was undermined by an aura of timidity, even fear, evident in the flick and flutter of her gaze.

"Don't tell me you drove over here like that." He bent forward, keeping his eyes averted, and snatched up her coat. "It's too cold for this sort of a stunt."

She refused to take the offered covering. "I'll do whatever you want." She stepped closer, reaching way, way up to curl her arms about his neck. Her smiling lips trembled for an instant before firming into what he assumed was meant to be a sexy pout. "Remember that time, in the dressing room, after the rest of the team had left—"

"That was Jake."

Her eyes went blank, widening with confusion, and her body, pressed against his, stiffened.

"We never did it in a dressing room. You're thinking of Jake." He reached behind his head, untangled her unresisting arms.

Desperation coloured her voice. "But I want you, now."

"No," he said, shaking his head. "You just don't want to be alone."

"Is that so awful?"

He couldn't talk to her while she was practically naked. "Please, put this on."

"Oh, for Christ's sake." She yanked her coat out of his loose fist, shoved an arm into the sleeve. "What's so bad about wanting to be with someone?"

"There's nothing wrong with that. As long as it's the right someone."

"And I'm not that person?" Fury replaced seductiveness, simmered in her narrowed eyes.

He thought of Charlotte, in her sad and lonely house, yet filled with a strength Tiffani lacked. "Not for me. You broke me, Tiffani, when you asked me to leave. But now I know it was for the best, for both of us."

She buttoned up her coat with sharp, jerky gestures, avoiding his eyes. "I thought we could screw, have a good time. No matter what you say, we were good together. I didn't come for a heart to heart."

She hadn't come simply to scratch an itch, either. Justice knew it, and so did she. But he didn't point out her prevarication

Icy fingers of air clawed their way inside as she stormed through the door and into the night.

****

Charlotte was pleased with her day's work. She'd taken advantage of the relatively deserted library and lost herself in research and writing. Her dissertation was expanding nicely—maybe not as quickly as she'd first hoped, but with a couple months of steady concentration like today, she'd be ready for possible tenure-track opportunities in the fall.

She paid rather more attention than usual to her surroundings as she left the library complex and crossed the road to the parking lot. Justice's announcement yesterday of a potential sexual predator stalking the campus had made her uneasy. She was surprised at how comfortable she'd become around the small university, and how affronted she now felt when that safety might be compromised.

Anticipation curled through her belly when she thought of the evening ahead. She had a couple of hours before she was expected at Justice's—enough time to leisurely get ready for what promised to be a decadent, sensual way to ring in the New Year.

A midnight sky curved overhead, despite the fact it

was only a few minutes past six o'clock. Stars cut through the velvet, pin pricks of diamond-hard light in the amazingly clear air. She buried her nose in her thick, heavy scarf, using its protection to soften the crystalline oxygen pouring into her lungs.

Trudging down the aisle between scattered vehicles, she blinked as headlights suddenly cut across her path, slashing out from a parked truck. She stopped, clutching the straps of her purse and satchel as they crossed her chest. The official memo sent out today by the security director and university president had warned that two of the alleged attacks had involved vehicles, without giving particulars on what type.

She took a hesitant step backward, chiding herself, wondering when caution became cowardice.

The interior light flashed on and she let out a relieved whoosh. Justice sat in the cab.

Ignoring the chill seeping through her thin dress boots, the blades of arctic air scrabbling through her coat, she studied him. It was the first time she'd had a chance to watch him without him knowing.

He rested one elbow on the ledge of the door, the wrinkles in the bend of his jacket sleeve pressed flat against the closed window. His mouth moved, and she caught a glimpse of a cell-phone clasped in one large fist. With his free hand, he rubbed his eyes, pinching the bridge of his nose. The cruel overhead light emphasized every line in his weary face.

His conversation grew more animated. His eyes narrowed and he peered through the windshield, still unaware of her presence, as he spoke with greater and greater ferocity. Now she could hear him, the words muffled, the bitter tone unmistakable. She was about to ease away, belatedly realizing she was intruding on an unpleasant private moment, when he turned his head and speared her with his hot, angry gaze.

No, not anger, she thought, dazed by what she'd glimpsed. Pain, hurt, betrayal. It was gone in an instant, hidden behind a blank, bland blue. But she'd seen it. Felt it.

He looked away from her, checking the screen of his phone. She sucked in a breath, choking as the dry cold seared her throat. With a grimace of disgust, he tossed the phone onto the dash and opened his door.

"What are you doing?" He stood in the space between his truck and the next vehicle, his face shadowed, his bulk silhouetted by the streetlight beyond.

She flinched at the ice in his voice, a grimness she'd never heard before. "I'm heading home."

"Why didn't you ask for an escort?"

"Surely it's not that dangerous, is it?"

He slammed the door, the clang echoing like a gunshot. "Damn it, Charlotte!" He stalked toward her, suppressed fury vibrating in waves from his tense body. "Where are you parked?"

She knew he wasn't angry at her—well, not only at her—but her mouth went dry at his primitive, growling demand. Not in fear. In arousal. "Over there." She pointed, hoping he didn't notice her hand trembling.

He gripped her bicep and marched her in the direction she'd indicated. Despite her own long legs, she had to stretch her stride to keep up. Muttered curses drifted over his shoulder as he dragged her along.

She held mute as they trudged through the ice-rutted lanes. What was it about this man ordering her about that made her legs wobble and her insides turn molten? Made her want to melt against him, trust him to support her, protect her?

When they reached her SUV, he released her with an abrupt motion. "Get in. Lock the door behind you."

Instead of obeying, she stepped around him, stared into his face. His expression was reserved, remote. Slipping off a glove, she raised her hand to his chin. Long whiskers tickled her palm deliciously.

"What's wrong?" Before he could shrug off her concern, she added, "I watched you. I'm sorry, I shouldn't have. But I saw enough to know you were having an argument with someone."

He closed his eyes for an instant, snorting out a long breath through his crooked nose. The exhalation was warm and moist on the chilled skin of her wrist. "My ex. I'm supposed to have Max tomorrow, for New Year's Day, but she's won't let him come."

"Why not?" She watched the muscle clench in his jaw, flex against her hand. Her thumb slid along the hard ridge of his cheekbone, her fingers brushing through his beard, and she felt some of his tension ease.

"She wants something I can't give her. So she's using Max to get at me."

"That's not fair."

The corner of his mouth tightened. She knew him well enough by now to know he smiled more with his eyes than his lips, yet this was no smile. "As my father would say, since when is life fair?" His chest rose and fell on a deep sigh. "I know we're supposed to spend the evening together, but maybe you should take a rain check. I won't be very good company."

The warmth of his skin beneath his beard wasn't enough to keep her fingers from freezing. Reluctantly, she tucked her hand into her pocket. As she did so, the pain and hurt she'd glimpsed in his eyes earlier returned. Only for a fleeting moment, but she saw it.

This was a man who shouldn't be alone right now. He might not know it himself, but he yearned for comfort. And to her amazed surprise, she yearned to give it to him.

"I'll take a rain check on the homemade dinner. But we still need to eat. Why don't we go out?" A sudden flurry lifted the thin skiff of snow from the roof of her SUV and blew it into her face. She shivered, ducking her head deeper into her scarf. "Can we continue this discussion inside my car?"

"Charlotte—"

"Get in, Justice," she said, taking delight in commanding him for once.

She beeped the locks and climbed in behind the steering wheel. Justice folded himself onto the passenger seat, sliding it back as far as it would go, his head brushing the roof. The engine groaned in chilly complaint before it started. She'd turn the heater on in a few minutes, once the motor had a chance to warm the air.

"What are you going to do? About Max?" She snapped on the overhead light, creating a pocket of brilliance in the deep blackness of the winter night outside.

"Wait." He leaned back, tipped his chin to the roof and closed his eyes. "This isn't the first time Tiffani's pulled this kind of a stunt. She'll come round."

"What set her off?"

His eyes remained closed, but the lids flickered. Red flushed up his neck to his under-jaw.

"What did you do?" she asked, astonished.

"I didn't do anything." He slitted a glare at her, and then squeezed his eyes shut again before continuing. "She wants to get back together. And I said no."

****

A breathy gasp reached Justice's ears. Behind his closed lids, ghostly flecks and stripes and stars danced. He knew he was being a coward, but he didn't want to see Charlotte's face when he confessed.

"I see." Her tone made it clear that she didn't. "And she told you this, when?"

"Last night." He couldn't hide any longer. He opened his eyes. "After I left your place."

"I see," she repeated. Her tongue flicked out and licked her lips.

He hitched himself higher in the seat, careful not to bash his head. At least it wasn't a tiny tin can of a car. He had a bit of room to manoeuvre. "Well, if you do, that's more than I can say for myself."

"What do you mean?" She regarded him steadily, her irises black in the dim light.

In as few words as possible, he explained what had occurred the evening before.

Thoughtfully, Charlotte reached out and turned the heater on full. Warm gusts of air blasted from the dashboard vents. "I have a little more sympathy for your ex now than I did at first."

He drew in a heated breath, prepared to defend his actions, but she held up a placating hand. "I don't condone what she's doing with Max. But it must have taken her a great deal of courage to come to you like that. And no matter how gentle you were, she would have been humiliated."

He slumped back. "I know." It had taken him a long time to fall asleep last night, remembering the look on her face.

"You said it yourself. She'll probably settle down in a day or so. She wouldn't—" Charlotte bit her lip. "Never mind."

"Wouldn't what?"

"I just wondered. Not letting you see Max is bad enough. Would she blame you for missing the visit, try and make you look bad in any other way?"

Justice felt a lightening in his chest. "No, she wouldn't." He knew that for a fact. No matter how angry Tiffani was, she wouldn't slam him in front of Max. "We're not strict about visitations. We've changed plans at the last minute before." He knew Max might be disappointed, but she wouldn't have made a scene about it.

"That's good." Charlotte laid her hand on top of his, resting on his thigh, and gave it a friendly squeeze.

Which he felt in a completely different part of his anatomy.

Maybe moping at home wasn't the cure for his frustration. "How hungry are you?" he asked.

"Not very. Not yet, anyway."

"I've changed my mind. Do you own a pair of skates?"

"Ice skates?" Her brow wrinkled. "No."

"No problem. I know where we can get you a pair."

CHAPTER FIFTEEN

Charlotte followed the red glow of Justice's tail lights through the black and white night. When he pulled into the driveway of a snug-looking bungalow, she drew to a stop at the curb.

A carport slanted off the left side of the small home, a minivan parked under the sloping roof. The front window was covered in thin sheers, through which she could see a large television, the distinctive action of a hockey game flickering on its wide screen. Leading from the driveway to the front door was a low ramp.

Justice waited while she picked her way from the icy road to the neatly cleared drive.

"Who lives here?"

"My dad." He motioned for her to step past him.

She hesitated. "You want me to meet your parents?"

"My mom died when I was a kid. It's just my dad." He held out his hand. She instinctively took it, comforted by his grip, and allowed him to guide her past the van to the shallow flight of steps leading to the back door.

Warm air gusted out, redolent with stale cigarettes and yeasty beer. Her nose wrinkled. Justice kicked off his boots but left his jacket on. She followed suit, and he led her down a wide, dim hall.

"Dad? I've brought you a visitor."

The sound of a horn echoed from the TV as she entered the living room behind Justice, his broad back and wide shoulders blocking her view. A rough and gravelly voice greeted them. "Well, at least you've got good timing. The period just ended." The sound cut off abruptly.

Justice drew Charlotte forward with a hand at the small of her back.

"Charlotte Girardet, this is my father, Whitman Cooper."

Rubber squeaked as a white-haired man in a wheelchair twisted away from the screen and rolled a pace forward. She held out her hand. "Pleased to meet you," she said.

His palm was dry and papery, his grip strong but brittle. He grunted, peering up at her from under thick, wild eyebrows. His knees looked uncomfortably high with his feet propped on the footrests. He had probably been a tall man. Not as tall as Justice, but a good size.

"Charlotte's a professor at the university. I want to take her skating. Are any of my old pairs still in the basement?"

"As I haven't been down there for ten years, I wouldn't know for sure." The bitterness was faint but evident. "I haven't given them away, if that's what you're asking."

"What size shoe do you take?" Justice asked Charlotte. His spoke calmly, but a muscle jumped in the corner of his eye.

"Ten."

"Back in a sec."

The tread of his footsteps faded down the hall. Charlotte turned back to Whitman, smiling to hide her nervousness. Before she could decide on which topic—weather or hockey—to fill the awkward silence, he spoke.

"A log pile collapsed."

"Pardon?"

"People always want to know." He waved a hand at his lower body. "I was working in the log yard. Some idiot unloaded a truck wrong. The pile shifted, sent it all sliding down on me. Damn near crushed me to death." His voice held a vicious sort of delight.

She had no idea what to say. Did he want congratulations or condolences? She settled for a mix. "That sounds horrible. You must have been very strong to have survived."

"Damn right." He patted his breast pocket, squeezed out a half-empty pack of cigarettes. He drew one out but didn't light it. "That's what I told Justice. Told him I'd be fine, that he should go back to hockey." He frowned at the cigarette, flipping it over and over between finger and thumb. "Jackass wouldn't do it. Ruined his career."

"I'm sure he feels he did the right thing."

Whitman gave a derogatory jerk of his shoulder. She flailed around in search of a less flammable subject. "Your first name. Does it have anything to do with Walt Whitman?"

"Dad was a reader. Always spouting off poetry or Shakespeare or shit." His need for nicotine finally overcame whatever reasoning had kept him from lighting up before. The lines in his seamed face relaxed as he took the first drag. "All that fancy stuff goes right over my head. Justice seems to like it."

"Like what?" Justice returned, a pair of blocky, black skates dangling by their laces from one hand.

"Your dad and I were discussing poetry."

Justice's brows shot to his hairline. "You're kidding me."

Charlotte met Whitman's gaze blandly. "And Shakespeare."

She thought the old man's mouth twitched. "You betcha." A hacking laugh forced it way out. "The Bard, isn't that right?"

"I see." Justice regarded them both, as if doubting the wisdom of having left them together, and then shrugged it off. "Do you need anything, while I'm here?"

Whitman waggled his hand, the extension of ash at the end of the cigarette miraculously staying attached. "Nah, all good. You go on now."

Expertly spinning one wheel, he manoeuvred into position facing the TV set once more. He picked up a remote from a small table littered with newspapers, a couple of beer cans and an ashtray. Hockey play by play followed Charlotte and Justice out the door.

****

The outdoor rink was surrounded by a tall chain-link fence. Flood lights illuminated the ice with a brilliant blue glare. Next to it, a children's playground crouched, lonely and abandoned, half buried in snow.

"Are you sure this is what you want to do?" Charlotte asked with faint hope. "It is New Year's Eve—shouldn't you be spending it with your father? The three of us could go out to a nice restaurant. A nice, warm, comfortable restaurant."

They had swung by Charlotte's house so she could change out of her work clothes. Leaving her car there, they had made another quick stop for Justice to get out of his uniform, pick up his skates and feed Chaucer. The dog now panted happily in her ear from his perch on the bench seat in the back of the cab of Justice's truck.

Justice laughed. "You won't even notice the cold, once you get going. And my dad doesn't go out much. He can still drive—we fitted up a van with hand controls—but he's happiest at home." He opened his door, letting a polar breeze in and an eager Chaucer out.

A low wooden bench squatted just inside the gate. Justice used his gloves to clear a dusting of snow off the unpainted seat. Charlotte sat down gingerly and began to untangle the laces of her borrowed skates. Chaucer snuffled at the snow piled at the sides of the rink, burying his head almost to the ears, searching for who knew what.

"I'm not very good at this, you know." A slight understatement, as the last time she'd put on blades was a school gym class expedition in Grade Seven. "And I've never used hockey skates before."

"I am good at this, and I'll help you."

He had both his skates laced on before she'd worked her way into one. "Do you need a hand?" She shot him a level stare and he grinned. "I'll just take a lap or two, look for bad patches," he added, and with a quick kick, he was off.

She sat on the frigid, uncomfortable bench, right foot in a skate, left foot in a boot, and watched, mesmerized.

He moved with fluid power, unconsciously graceful, as if the blades were an extension of his body. When he cut a sharp corner, the crackle of steel slicing ice raised the hairs on the back of her neck. He slowed to examine a section, and then picked up speed again, switching directions with a skill that spoke of long, exhausting hours of practise.

He scraped to a stop before her, the edges of his skates kicking up a small shower of snow. "You sure you don't need help?"

His sheer athleticism left her mouth dry. She shook her head and hurried to put on the left skate. With extreme caution, she rose to her feet, ankles wobbling.

Amusement flickered in his eyes, steel blue in the low light. "How long has it been?" His words puffed out in white clouds.

She battened down the faint flickers of panic. "Long enough."

"There are no picks on hockey skates, so you have to use the side of the blade." He demonstrated, pushing off onto one foot. "Here." He held out both hands. She gripped tightly, standing with precarious balance. "Give it a try."

She took a deep breath, let it out slowly. It misted and disappeared. With trepidation, she planted one foot and shoved.

"There you go." Justice coasted backward, moving in tempo to her awkward, choppy pace.

They worked their way around the rink, Justice encouraging, Charlotte determined. Chaucer roamed, checking in once in a while, and then ranging away, but never going far. Houses encircling the small park glowed with light, emphasizing the stillness surrounding them. Every once in a while, a vehicle would pass by, headlights tunnelling into the dark.

After a couple of laps, Charlotte felt confident enough to let go of Justice's hands. He moved to her side, adjusting his smooth, long glides to her shorter, amateurish ones.

"So, what went on with you and my dad when I was in the basement?" His tone was casual, but a thin vibration of tension hummed through the words.

"He told me about his accident." She bit her lip and concentrated as she negotiated a wide arc around the corner.

"And then you talked poetry and Shakespeare?"

She risked a glance up from the ice to his face. "I asked about his name."

"Ah."

"He also told me you gave up your hockey career when he was hurt." She lost her rhythm for a moment and her arms flailed. Justice caught her around her shoulders and held her upright until she steadied. "Thanks."

"You're doing great." He grasped her hand and they set off again.

The tip of her nose was cold, but her blood moved briskly, warming the rest of her just as much as his compliment.

After a short silence, Justice cleared his throat. "Did he also tell you he wasn't happy about that?"

"It was implied."

He snorted. "How diplomatic of you."

"I think it was very loyal of you, to give up a career you'd worked so hard for, to let it all go to care for your dad."

"It was more his career than mine."

She shot him a puzzled look. The glare of a light silhouetted his head, hiding his face. "What do you mean?"

"I loved hockey, don't get me wrong." He released her hand and swung around, skating backward effortlessly. "I had talent, but I was never the best on my team. I had something better, though. I had size. I was always big and strong for my age, and in hockey, being big and strong often takes you further than sheer talent."

He changed direction, skating a fierce, tight circle around her. "I was picked for my first top level team when I was nine. Mom was still around then. She died a couple years later. Cancer."

His voice was matter-of-fact, yet her heart twisted for the boy he had been. "I'm sorry."

He strummed his gloved hand along the links of the

fence as they skated by. "With her gone, the only thing Dad and I had in common was hockey. He worked extra hours so he could send me to special training camps, hired private ice time, signed me up to try out for bigger and better teams." Chaucer ran up, panting, and Justice bent over to scrub his ears. "I wanted to succeed, make him proud. But he had more ambition than I ever did."

"Max told me you had an NHL contract."

He ducked his head in a move that struck her as oddly shy. She didn't think she'd ever seen that in him before. "I was at training camp for what would have been my first season when Dad was hurt." He nudged Chaucer out of her path and led her back to the bench. They removed their skates. "But a contract is no guarantee you'll have a career in the big league. And besides..." He paused, staring out across the ice. She didn't know what he was seeing, but it wasn't an unpretentious little volunteer rink. "I was beginning to doubt myself, whether it was the life I wanted. And a player who doesn't want it, isn't willing to give his all, is worse than useless to his team."

He stood up and rolled his shoulders as if shaking off a heavy weight. He looked down at her, eyes hooded, face bland. "Come on." He held out his hand. "I owe you dinner."

****

"I don't know if it was the skating, the amazing dinner, or that fabulous red wine, but I am so sleepy I don't think I'll make it to midnight." Charlotte stretched long, slender arms over her head, her breasts lifting beneath her blue-green sweater, and then curled like a cat against the far arm of the couch in Justice's living room.

He'd never seen her so relaxed, replete. Watching with appreciation as he sipped his port, he slumped in the club chair set at ninety degrees to the couch. "You only have an hour to wait."

"Chaucer's already down for the count." She grinned at the dog, his head lolling off the edge of his bed, legs paddling as he dreamed doggy dreams.

"He won't move until tomorrow morning."

She propped her chin on her hand and stared at the gas fire flickering behind its protective glass. "Do you remember the first time you were allowed to stay up past midnight?"

"No." Late nights hadn't been on the schedule his father had set for him, and curfews continued during his years with the Western Hockey League. He had seen a few dawns, partying with his teammates when they could get away with it, but had never given the clicking over from one day to the next any special thought.

"I do. I was so disappointed." She laughed quietly. "I don't know what I thought would happen. It was New Year's Eve, and I was ten. My parents and sister and I watched the countdown on TV. There was cheering and clapping and fireworks going off—and nothing had changed." She turned the corners of her mouth down in a self-deprecating smile. "I was so sure something would be different. I didn't know what, but *something*."

A comfortable silence floated over them. For an evening that had started so poorly, it promised to end on a much better note. Charlotte's presence had kept him sane, kept him from angsting over Tiffani and Max. He wished he had the words to tell her how much he appreciated her company. Her friendship, he realized, vaguely surprised at the thought. He'd never had a lover he considered a friend before. It felt... He wasn't sure how it felt.

He placed the shot glass on the table at his elbow.

"Come here."

Her gaze swung toward him, eyes wide. He didn't know what she saw in his face, but her startlement faded to speculation, deepened to sensual interest.

He stayed where he was, reclining with outward nonchalance, and held out his hand.

She rose slowly, paced the few steps needed to reach him. Her fingers were cool in his palm. He tugged her until she stood between his legs, tall, slender, elegant. He laid his head against the back of the chair and let his gaze wander up her body, reaching the pale oval of her face, framed with luxuriant, curling dark hair.

The silence grew. Desire stirred, hard and hot in his groin. His thumb caressed her knuckles. He reached out lazily with his other hand, cupped her hip, and exerted light but firm pressure. As she sank to her knees, he straightened, until they were face to face.

"You won't be disappointed this New Year's." His voice rasped into the quiet room. "I promise."

She shuddered and a soft, gasping breath escaped her opened mouth.

He leaned in. She held still, waiting for his kiss. Instead, he nuzzled her neck, gently scraping the soft fragrant column with his beard. She stiffened, gave a throaty moan, and lifted her chin. He teased his way to the other side, relishing her responsive shivers.

Her hands gripped his thighs, fingertips digging into his muscles. His cock, already uncomfortably trapped behind his fly, reacted to their nearness.

"Undo. My. Zipper." He emphasized his command with tiny bites between each word, working his way up her neck to the seductively scented skin behind her ear.

Her hands didn't move.

"Charlotte," he growled. "Touch my cock."

Her fingers tightened. The pulse point beneath his lips, his tongue, fluttered rapidly. With agonizing slowness, her hands slid to his groin, under the loose hem of his shirt. He sucked in a ragged breath when her cool fingers brushed his abs. She flicked open the button of his jeans, fumbled a moment with the tab of the zipper.

And stopped.

He lifted his head, met her glittering, heated stare. "Charlotte—"

She lowered the zipper a quarter of an inch, cutting off whatever he'd been going to say next. Whether a threat or a plea, he would never know.

Down another quarter of an inch.

She knelt before him, confident as a queen, certain in her power over him. He'd never seen anything more erotic.

"Take off your shirt." Her voice, low and husky, wrapped around him like a heady perfume.

He crossed his arms over his stomach and yanked his shirt over his head. His hips rocked slightly, pressed his cock into her hands.

Another quarter of an inch.

"Now lay back."

He did as she instructed, his hands fisted at his sides, resisting the urge to toss her to the floor and put an end to her torturous teasing.

Tooth by tooth, she drew the zipper down. The pressure on his cock eased, but only until she slipped a hand into his boxers and grasped his shaft. His hips jerked, air hissing between his clenched teeth.

Between narrowed lids he watched her as she caressed him. Her hair hung forward, curtaining her face. She pressed and stroked. He swallowed, clinging to control.

"You haven't given me much chance to explore." She peered up at him, her expression mischievous. "I plan on rectifying that tonight."

Before his hazy brain had time to understand what she meant, she took him into her mouth.

CHAPTER SIXTEEN

Justice wrapped his hands in her hair, a rumbling groan vibrating from his chest. Charlotte smiled, eyes closed, as she licked and sucked. He was smooth and salty, taut and tangy. His pleasure heightened her own, moist heat gathering between her legs, her breasts rising plump and full.

His knees gripped her sides, caging her between his legs. His hips flexed, offering greater access to his cock. She swirled her tongue over the head of his shaft and he held her tighter, urging her on with guttural grunts.

She opened her eyes and came face to face with a hairy, black and white and tan muzzle.

With a muffled shriek, she fell back on her heels. Justice cursed and jackknifed upright. Chaucer joined in with a happy woof, darting from side to side, tail wagging.

Justice grabbed the dog's collar. "What the fuck did he do?"

"Nothing. Nothing." Charlotte's heart pounded with shock. "He just startled me, that's all."

A flush rode high on Justice's cheekbones as he glared at the dog. His t-shirt was rucked up around his waist, his stiff cock quivering, standing tall in the opening of his jeans. A giggle tickled the back of her throat and she coughed to disguise it.

Justice switched his disgusted glare to her. "You could kill a man like that. One minute you're..." he gestured to his hips. She stifled another giggle at his reticence. "The next, you're screaming. Do you know what that does to a guy?"

"I'm sorry." Her voice trembled, and she could feel her cheeks creaking with the effort of holding back her grin.

"Are you laughing?" he said, affronted.

Charlotte collapsed to the floor and howled. In a dim corner of her mind, she was aware of Justice leaving the room, but she couldn't stop. Tears streamed down her face and she clutched her aching stomach.

She couldn't remember the last time she'd laughed with such pure abandon.

Her amusement abated. She hiccupped and rolled to her back, her limbs sprawling, opening her eyes in time to see Justice sink to the floor beside her. He regarded her with wry bemusement.

"I'm sorry." She hiccupped again. "But your face..."

"I can imagine." His eyes smiled, though his mouth remained straight.

She sighed in relief at the evidence of his good humour. "I guess I ruined the mood." A quick glance around showed no sign of Chaucer. "What did you do with him?"

"I locked him in his kennel in the garage." She opened her mouth to protest. He held up a hand. "It's a heated garage, and I gave him a rawhide bone. He's perfectly happy." He lowered his hand to rest on her stomach. His spread fingers reached from hip to hip, and heat radiated into her. Her muscles, just beginning to recover from her laughing fit, went slack again, this time from rekindled desire. "I, on the other hand, was much happier a few minutes ago," he added.

She rolled her hips, watching him through her lashes.

His nostrils flared and his hand slid lower, between her legs. He let it rest there, not moving, simply cupping her. She reached for him.

"Now, where were we?" she murmured.

****

...Wild-beasts and wormkind; away then they hastened
Hot-mooded, hateful, they heard the great clamor,
The war-trumpet winding. One did the Geat-prince
Sunder from earth-joys, with arrow from bowstring...

Charlotte's heart thrilled, the words and rhythm of the ancient poem losing none of their power for being as familiar as her own heartbeat. She wanted to refresh her memory before introducing it to her next crop of first-year students. The grim and bloody saga had first captivated her decades ago, when her father had left a battered copy lying about. The old English text had looked like no language she had ever seen—filled not only with undecipherable words, but odd, outlandish letters. On the opposing page, however, had been the modern English translation, and it had caught and held her childish imagination in thrall.

She turned the page of her own beloved edition, deaf to the occasional tread of staff and students passing down the hall outside her office, until an angry buzzing jarred her out of her absorption in Beowulf's fierce battle with Grendel's mother. She patted the chaotic reams of paper covering the surface of her desk and finally located her cell.

The screen displayed an unknown number. *Probably a telemarketer.* She absently connected the call, her attention already wandering back to the book on her lap.

"Doctor Girardet?" The crisp, professional voice yanked her focus back to the phone.

"Yes."

"Please hold for Doctor Ross-Moore."

Charlotte's pulse quickened. She'd earned her doctorate studying with Arthur Ross-Moore. In the years since then they had only spoken sporadically, yet he had been instrumental in many of her career moves. Not her most recent with UNBC, however. He'd sent one short, gruff email after she'd accepted the position, questioning her sanity.

She jolted when a voice barked into her ear. "What the hell are you still doing in the wilds of Northern BC?"

"I'm fine, Arthur, and how are you?"

"Yes, yes," he replied testily. "I'm alive, aren't I? Let's just take all that balderdash as read." He could speak for hours about the literary culture of the Medieval Period, but had no time to waste on small talk. "Is your book done?"

She winced. "Not quite."

"What the hell have you been doing? You said you took this position because it would give you time to finish it. How am I going to recommend you for tenure-track here if you don't get it done?"

Her chest tingled. "There's a position at York?"

"Meredith Freimuller is heading to Sweden, God knows why. The dean is sending out a call for applicants. Thought you might want to know."

"Of course I do." She couldn't feel her feet, and the tingling had spread from her chest to her hands. She wasn't having a heart attack, was she?

"Update your CV. Include your teaching philosophy. Part of the process will be a guest lecture, so prepare for that. But most of all, you've got to get that damn monograph done."

"I will."

"Damn straight you will. Best graduate student I ever had, wasting her talents at a tiny campus in a backward logging town. I won't stand for it. The website will tell you how to send in your application documents. Do that right away, and then get back to your book. Call me when it's done."

Charlotte wasn't sure if the buzzing was coming from the speaker or her head. She made sure the call was disconnected, and then laid the phone on the desk with the delicate care.

Everything she'd ever wanted, all she'd ever dreamed of, was there, on the other end of that phone call. With Arthur's support, she was guaranteed the tenure-track appointment. Validation, approval, affirmation. A position that proved she was a valued, functioning member of society, no matter the state of her personal life.

That thought led to Justice. He'd kept his promise. She hadn't been disappointed in their New Year's Eve celebrations. She'd allowed him to talk her into spending yesterday with him, and their very own brand of fireworks had left her limp and lazy. She'd dragged herself home that evening, protesting she had to get work done before classes began.

She suppressed a surprisingly fierce stab of regret. Spending time with Justice would have to come second, if she wanted to finish her book. She was close, but there were weeks of work left. It would mean shutting herself away at every available opportunity, but she could do it.

Had to do it, if she wanted her career, her life, to follow the path she'd always planned.

****

The third day of the new year was clear and cold. The sky had been bright and blue during the short hours of daylight, but when the sun disappeared, it hardened to jet, glimmering with quartz stars.

Justice left work that afternoon determined to have it out with Tiffani. He approached the house they had bought shortly after their wedding with a grim sort of calm. He hadn't contested her claim to it in the divorce, wanting to give Max security during those turbulent times. Yet guilt tugged at him, remembering the day he'd left for good, remembering a small boy's confused tears, his own dazed emotions.

A hint of that anxiety returned as he knocked. With any luck, Tiffani had cooled off during the last few days.

Quick, pattering footsteps sounded inside, and the door flung open. "Mom, it's Dad!" His son's boisterousness soothed him with its usual welcome. "You've got to see this!" Max grabbed his hand and yanked. "Come look what Devin and I made."

Justice made suitably admiring noises over the towering stack of Lego he was told was a replica of the Eiffel Tower. Devin, a scrappy centre on the ice, but shy and studious when off, grinned quietly as Max babbled.

"You guys do good work." Justice ruffled his son's hair. "I've got to go talk to your mom. I'll come and say goodbye before I leave."

Leaving the boys discussing their next project, Justice made his way to the family room off the kitchen. A cheesy tomato scent filled the air, along with a hint of garlic. Tiffani sat in a high-backed upholstered chair, flipping through a fashion magazine. He lowered himself to the ottoman in front of her.

"I told you not to come." She licked a fingertip, turned a page, refusing to look up.

"You can't keep me from seeing Max."

She stiffened in mid-page flip. "Maybe. But that doesn't mean I have to talk to you."

"Come on, Tiff." He covered the magazine with his palm, halting her movements. "Do you want me to say I'm sorry?"

Her head jerked at that, her eyes finally meeting his. "For humiliating me? Rejecting me as I stood naked in front of you?" She laughed mirthlessly. "Now why would I want you to say sorry?"

He withdrew his hand, clenched his fists on his knees. "All the reasons we broke up are still between us. Getting back together would be a bad idea." A fucking terrible idea. His stomach curdled at the thought. "And you shouldn't be telling Max we might be."

"I didn't." She tossed the magazine onto the floor. "Well, not in so many words." Bending her knees, she put her feet on the seat of the chair, wrapped her arms around her legs.

She looked tiny and fragile and miserable. He'd done his best to make her happy, but his best hadn't been enough. Would never be enough. He wasn't Jake.

"You know what I mean," he said.

"It's just that…" She pressed her lips together, and then blurted out, "I think I made a mistake, asking for a divorce."

The words were a blow to the chest. "You don't really mean that. You're just lonely, and figure I'm better than nothing."

"No, that's not it, I promise." She curled even tighter into her bent knees.

He couldn't stay seated. Springing to his feet, he paced to the window and back. "When you told me you wanted a divorce, I was stunned. I never saw it coming."

She opened her mouth to reply and he held up a hand to stop her. "That's my fault. I ignored the signs you weren't happy. But it wasn't only you. I wasn't happy, either. After I got over the shock, I had time to think. I finally realized the truth. We should never had gotten married. You still loved Jake."

She didn't deny it. Her eyes filled with tears. "I could have loved you. If only you had loved me enough."

A headache brewed behind his eyes. He hadn't come here to rehash old humiliations. "Tomorrow's Saturday. Max has a game in the morning. After that, I'm taking him home for the rest of the day, and the night. I'll bring him back Sunday evening."

"Fine." She rested her head against the high back of the chair. Her lashes, pale and thin without their usual protective covering of thick mascara, lay against her cheeks.

"Thanks."

Her lids lifted, revealing eyes now dry and sere. "No matter what, you're a good dad to Max."

He knew it wasn't a good time, but he couldn't stop himself. "Don't you think we should—"

"No." Her tone was definite. "We'll tell him when the time is right."

He'd heard that before. When Max was a baby, it hadn't been worth the effort to argue. He'd believed he had plenty of time to convince her to tell Max the truth about his father. But the years went by, and there was always another reason not to explain. He's too young, he's just started school, his parents are getting a divorce.

He was uneasily aware that it might be too late already, but he had to try. "We owe it to Jake."

She flinched. "Do you think I don't know that? But

how is Max going to feel, knowing his dad died before he was born?"

"We should never have kept it a secret. Every day makes it harder and harder to tell him."

She bolted from her chair and stalked to the kitchen, putting the L-shaped counter between them. "Why does he need to know? What good will it do?" She snatched a cloth from the sink and wiped the already clean tile.

"It's the truth. He deserves to know."

A banging door and the thudding of feet gave advance warning of Max and Devin's arrival. "We're thirsty, Mom. Can we have Coke?"

"Not before dinner," Tiffani answered, her eyes on Justice, begging him to keep silent. Did she really think he'd blurt it out, with Devin present? "The lasagna will be ready in fifteen minutes."

"But we're thirsty now," Max pleaded.

"You heard your mother," Justice said. "Juice, milk or water."

Max shuffled to the fridge and chose two juice boxes. Handing one to Devin, he asked, "Are you staying for dinner, Dad?"

The glow of pleasure he always felt when Max called him dad was tainted by his conversation with Tiffani. "Not tonight. I'll see you in the morning. Is Devin staying the night?"

"Yeah."

"Don't go to bed too late—I need everyone on my team ready to play hard."

Max rolled his eyes, but Devin answered solemnly. "We won't, Mr. Cooper."

Tiffani walked with Justice to the door. "I suppose I should say thanks."

"Don't." He shrugged into his coat, his mood only slightly better than it had been when he'd first walked in. "Do you really think I'd tell him with his best friend standing right there?"

"No." She fidgeted with the hem of her t-shirt.

"He'll be ten soon. Promise me you'll think about it."

She squeezed her eyes shut briefly. "Fine, damn it. I promise."

****

Charlotte's lovemaking had an edgy, unruly quality. He was more than happy to go along with her feverish mood, willing to be wooed into forgetfulness after his aggravating talk with Tiffani. His eyes rolled back in his head as Charlotte touched and tasted and tormented him in numerous lust-filled ways, and he'd been pleased to be distracted. But after, when they sprawled across the rumpled sheets of her high bed, panting with exertion and sticky with passion, that odd sense of uncertainty kept his nerves zinging.

"I don't think I'll ever move again." She lay face down, her voice muffled by the mattress. "But, God, I need a drink of water."

He pushed himself upright with arms as slack as untied skate laces. "Be right back." Doing his best not to stagger, he made it to the bathroom, filled and then chugged a glass of water. Refilling the glass, he returned to the bedroom. Charlotte had gathered the pillows—scattered onto the floor during their play—and was leaning limply against them, covered to just above her waist with the comforter, hiding her scar, but leaving her breasts, still flushed from arousal, exposed.

He supposed that said something about her—that she was willing to bare almost everything to him but that small sign of her human frailty. He wondered once more about the operation that had left its mark on her. Had it been necessary to save her life? Again, he shoved his curiosity away. He'd asked more than once, and she only reiterated it was nothing. Revealing how much he needed to know the answer was a step into intimacy he wasn't ready to take.

She took the glass with both hands and swallowed the water in long, breathless gulps. Lowering it only when it was empty, she collapsed back against the pillows. "Thanks." She licked an errant drop of water from her lower lip.

He wanted her again. Right now, while she was spent and sated. He wanted to take her when her muscles were lax and her brain muggy. He was starting to worry that he wanted her in too many ways. The last thing he needed was another complication in his life. Hadn't he learned his lesson with Tiffani?

"I can't stay." *She hasn't asked you to, dickhead.* "Max has a hockey game tomorrow morning."

She tilted her head. "I'm sorry, I didn't think to ask. How did your talk with Tiffani go?"

Charlotte had been on him, hot and hungry, the moment he'd stepped in the door. There hadn't been time to exchange how was your day? before they'd lurched into her bedroom.

"We're back to armed neutrality. After Max's game, he's staying the night and all day Sunday with me."

"That's good."

"I'm sorry we won't be able to spend time together. Unless you'd like to tag along with Max and me?" He snapped his teeth shut. Why had he asked her that? Max had had enough questions the first time he'd met Charlotte.

Questions to which Justice still didn't have the answers.

He was beginning to wonder if he knew anything at all.

"That's okay." She smiled up at him, her fingers pleating the top edge of the sheet in jerky bursts. "I'll have time to work. It's early yet tonight, and then I'll have all weekend to really buckle down."

He hadn't meant he needed to leave right away, yet now he felt obligated to do so. His boxers lay at the foot of the bed. He plucked them up and began to dress.

"Speaking of my book..." She cleared her throat. "I do need to concentrate on getting it done. I had a call today. About a tenure-track position available at my old university."

The unsettled sensation he'd been trying to ignore intensified. He thrust one leg into his jeans.

"The professor who mentored me for my doctorate...he will recommend me. But I have to finish my book. And that means no more..." She circled her hand, encompassing herself, the bed—and Justice.

CHAPTER SEVENTEEN

Maybe other guys would feel relief at her request to keep their relationship on the surface, casual, but Justice's chest buzzed with suppressed anger. "You can't work twenty-four hours a day," he said.

"I came to UNBC deliberately. I didn't want my social life to take away from the time I should be spending on my research and writing." Charlotte pulled the sheet up, hiding her nakedness.

His shirt was crumpled in a pile near the door where she had discarded it in their rush to get undressed. He stomped over to pick it up. "Social life? Is that what you call us?"

"What else is this, Justice?" She brushed the hair out of her face, tucking it behind her ear. It sprung out rebelliously once more. "I want to move on to a tenure-track position, but regardless, I'm leaving at the end of the semester, no matter what. It's not like we have a future."

He stared at her, t-shirt dangling from his hand. "I'm an idiot. You're not telling me you want to see less of me. You're telling me we're done."

"I've spent years working for this moment." Her mouth set in a determined line. "I've sacrificed time with family, relationships, vacations. What would it say about me if, this close to achieving what I've dreamed of for a decade, I gave up, let it slip away?"

"No one's asking you to give up anything." He pulled his t-shirt over his head, exasperation making his movements stilted and awkward.

"Maybe it was easy for you to give up your career. It was only playing a game, after all. And you as good as told me it was your father that had the drive, the aspiration." Her chin lifted, her eyes bright with pride and resolve. "But I'm not like you. I'm ambitious. I want more out of my career than teaching at a tiny university in a small, backwoods city."

He clenched his teeth at the double insults. "That's it, then." He moved to the doorway, repressing the urge to kick the dresser as he passed by. Turning back, he surveyed her, sitting tall, regal despite the sex stained sheets, the tangled hair. "I guess it's been fun. See you around."

A few strides down the hallway, he halted. Had she called his name? He waited a few moments, but the sound wasn't repeated. With an ember of anger burning the back of his throat, he let himself out of the house.

****

Charlotte rested her elbows on her desk and rubbed her temples with her thumbs. The words on her laptop blurred before her eyes and she closed them, concentrating on the dancing suns and stars scattered on the inside of her lids. Just the change in focus distance relieved some of the pressure built up in her skull.

She'd prepared her application documents with fierce obsessiveness. It had taken days to get her curriculum vitae perfect, her philosophy of teaching precise. Choosing a lecture had cost her hours of sleep. And as soon as she'd sent that package off, her world had been subsumed by her book.

Three more weeks of relentless work had put her within reach of the final chapters. Exhaustion had put heavy, dark circles under her eyes, made her snappy with students, and given her a stomach full of acid.

She pushed away the thought that had stalked her for most of that time. That she felt that way because of her last confrontation with Justice.

Swivelling her chair with unnecessary force, she stalked from the bedroom-cum-office into the bathroom. Running the water as cold as she could, she dampened a facecloth and pressed it to her eyes, breathing deeply and regularly, doing her best to calm her cramping stomach, her seizing lungs. Refreshing the cloth with more cold water, she draped it over the back of her neck and wandered wearily back to her office.

The bed was almost invisible beneath reference books and periodicals and printed drafts of what she'd done so far. Her teeth gritted, knowing how much effort was still ahead in the revising stage. But damn it, she would have it done by the middle of February if it killed her.

She was only a little afraid it might.

At the end of the bed a tall, narrow window looked out over the backyard. It was depressingly dark outside, and she longed for light with a wrenching yearning. The weather for the last week had been gloomy and overcast, the heavy atmosphere doing nothing to alleviate her weariness. She could barely remember summer. Grass springy with life under her bare feet, the caress of a warm breeze, the healing glow of heat from a golden sun—her memories were pale and ghostly.

Leaning her forehead against the glass, she took a minute to fortify herself for the sprint to the finish line. Well, one of the finish lines. She'd promised herself once this draft was complete she would take a whole day off—a glorious day in which to do nothing but sleep, read for pleasure, perhaps indulge in a rom-com movie. That would help gird her loins for the editing yet to come.

A desk lamp was the only light in the small room, making it easy to see into the shadowed yard. Her eye was drawn to a faint movement at the far side, near the path leading to the greenway trail. A man stood there, looking up at her window.

Her heart stuttered. *Justice.* But then her head caught up with her hope. Justice had no reason to be skulking about in her backyard, and besides, the figure was shorter and stockier.

The glow from a nearly full moon reflected off the snow, enough to delineate him from the dense background of spruce and pine, but not enough to reveal his features. After that first slight motion, he hadn't moved again.

Her thoughts flew to the attacks at the university, the warning memo issued by the security office. Surely there was no connection. And yet—

She stepped back from the window. The man's still watchfulness had an eerie quality, and her skin flushed with apprehension. From her new position she waited and watched, her breath catching in her throat.

He remained as immobile as the thick trunks of the trees that surrounded him.

Charlotte's muscles spasmed as a loud click and hiss broke the deadened silence. Warm air fanned out of the furnace vent at her feet and her breath whooshed out in relief.

Her legs unnaturally weak, she moved to the desk and switched off the lamp. Pressing close to the walls she sidled next to the window and peered out as cautiously as a rabbit from its warren.

A cloud blotted out the faint moonshine. She waited.

When the light waxed stronger a few minutes later, the faint gleam of metal—a buckle on his coat?—revealed he'd moved deeper into the camouflage of night.

She crept to her desk and palmed her phone. Sneaking with care to the top of the stairs, she glided down, listening with painful intensity, leery of the creak and sigh of each step. No lights broke the gloom of the hallway, and she moved through it like a spectre, her heart beating light and fast, high in her throat.

The moon-washed kitchen held none of its usual warmth and comfort. The stone countertop gleamed tomb-like in the chill, still air. Shadows slashed the tile floor, iciness leaching into the soles of her feet even through her heavy socks.

She found a concealing pocket of darkness near the refrigerator. Through the wide, open expanse of glass that made up most of the rear wall, she could see the entire backyard.

Her hope that the man had given up his frightening vigil during her cautious trek from the second floor shivered into shards when a gust of wind disturbed the snow-covered branches above him. He ducked his head under the flurry, freezing back into stillness almost immediately.

Charlotte waited, hunching into herself, fingering the phone she'd tucked into the pocket of her flannel pajama pants like a talisman.

****

"Come on, guys, that's enough." Justice gripped a gangly young man by the scruff of his jacket and hauled him out of the fray.

"Fucking right that's enough," snarled his combatant, rescuing the glasses knocked off in the scuffle and shoving them back onto his nose. "It's fucking enough that he keeps taking my food, but stealing my cash—" He took a wild roundhouse swing. Justice stepped into it, blocking it with his shoulder. He barely felt the thud. Didn't anyone teach boys how to throw a punch these days?

"Enough."

The boy whose jacket he held wriggled like a worm trying to escape the hook, and Justice gave him a gentle shake. Well, maybe not too gentle. His patience was thin these days, and a sneaky thief and a gullible fool weren't going to gain much sympathy from him.

He was working an evening shift with Elizabeth Paxton. A call from a floor monitor had sent them to one of the dorms, where an obscenity-laden screaming match had degenerated into an unskilled yet ferocious wrestling bout.

"You." He gave Glasses Boy his best hockey enforcer stare. "Stand there." He jerked a chin to the right corner of the small living space. The boy shuffled over, jeans bagging loosely between his legs, muttering under his breath. "You." He released Worm Boy and pointed to the opposite corner. "There."

Elizabeth stood in the door leading to the hall, feet planted, arms crossed. Behind her, curious faces peered into the apartment. When they realized Justice had seen them, they scattered.

He turned to Glasses Boy. "You. Talk."

"This son-of-a-bitch stole fifty bucks from me."

"No fucking way." Worm Boy's face mottled red and white. A scrape on his cheekbone appeared to be the result of a lucky strike by his erstwhile dorm-mate. "I didn't take nothing."

Justice sighed, wishing poor grammar was the only

problem he had to deal with tonight.

"How did you even know where it was? I had it hidden." Glasses Boy thrust his head forward, a shock of straight, dark hair falling over his forehead to his nose. He shoved it back.

"Everyone knows where you hide your cash," scoffed Worm Boy. "So why do you think it was me?"

Round Two seemed imminent. As Justice stepped between the boys, the cell in his pants pocket vibrated against his thigh. He ignored it. "Ms. Paxton, I think we need to separate these two. Why don't you take this one" —he indicated Worm Boy— "to the sitting area at the end of the hall. I'll talk with this one here."

His phone continued to vibrate. He dug it out, intending to shut it off until he'd dealt with the current problem. The call disconnected just as he read the display.

Charlotte.

He hadn't talked to her for twenty-seven days. Not that he was counting. He was positive their last bitter, insulting conversation had been the end of their relationship—social life—whatever the fuck she wanted to call it. If she didn't want to be with him, fine. He'd already had enough drama in his life. He didn't need to search out more.

"Mr. Cooper? Everything okay?" Elizabeth's voice broke into his thoughts. She stood at his elbow, Worm Boy slouched sullenly beside her.

"Yes. Of course." The phone jumped in his hand. Charlotte. Again. "I have to take this. You stay here. See if you can get to the bottom of things. I'll be right back."

Two strides took him to the hall. He swiped the screen, dodging past a young couple leaning against the wall, plastered mouth to mouth, before ducking into the communal area, thankfully deserted.

"Charlotte?"

"I don't know what to do." He pressed the phone to his ear, straining to hear her whisper. "There's a man."

His heart thudded hard and his muscles clenched. "A man?" If anyone had hurt Charlotte—

"He's been standing in my backyard. For twenty minutes, maybe more."

"Where are you?"

"In the kitchen." She hissed in a breath. "He's moving. Damn it, I think he's coming to the house."

"Stay on the line, Charlotte. Whatever happens, stay on the line." Justice pounded down the hall, swinging in to Glasses Boy's apartment. "Elizabeth, I've got to go. Charlotte—Professor Girardet—has an emergency."

She stared blankly for a second, and then snapped into focus. "Of course. Go. I've got this."

The fact that the security office's responsibility did not extend to a professor's private residence meant nothing to Justice at this moment. He felt no guilt at misleading Elizabeth. Hustling through the fire doors, he dashed down the stairwell in long, leaping bounds, one hand on the railing, the other still clutching his phone, his link with Charlotte. "I'm on my way. What's he doing now?"

"Oh, God. He's circling the edge of the trees." Her voice was breathless. "I don't think he wants to cut across the yard."

He switched his phone to speaker, the easier to run and talk. "Do you want to hang up, call 911?" His truck was parked on the far side of the campus. He slapped one-handed at his pockets, relieved to find his keys.

"I don't know. He's stopped again, where the side fence meets the trees."

He sprinted across the ring road, cursing as the treacherous ice on the path leading to the main building forced him to slow. "If he comes any closer, call 911. Don't take any chances." He should probably tell her to do it now, but he couldn't bear to lose his connection with her. Not knowing what was happening would be—well, not good.

"Okay. He's not moving anymore."

"Let me know if he does anything, anything at all." He crashed through the doors, skidded down the stairs of the Winter Garden, and out the doors leading to the Agora. "I'll be there as soon as I can."

"I know."

He didn't reply, saving his breath for the final dash to his truck.

Once in the cab, he tossed his phone on the seat and slammed it into gear. "I'm in my truck. Be there in ten."

"Please hurry."

"What's he doing?"

"Nothing. He's—oh, no. Oh, damn."

He floored the gas, desperately thankful the university road was devoid of traffic at this time of night. "Talk to me. What's happening."

"I don't know where he is." The panic crawling around the edges of her voice leaped into full force. "I looked away, only for a second, and now I don't know where he is."

The thick-treaded tires couldn't hold their grip as he swung onto the main road and gunned it. The truck's rear end fishtailed violently. His phone slipped off the seat and Justice made a wild grab for it as he righted the skid with practised instinct. "I'm on my way. Can you see him yet?"

No reply.

"Charlotte?"
Nothing.

CHAPTER EIGHTEEN

Justice braked to a stop outside Charlotte's house. He dove out the door, slamming it behind him with the force of a gunshot. Maybe he should have been stealthier, maybe he shouldn't have given warning of his arrival. If the intruder was outside, he'd probably be scared off. If the intruder was inside—

If the intruder was inside—

He raced through the gate leading to the backyard, flinging himself around the corner of the house. The snow was blue in the darkness, pocked with deeper pools of navy leading to the back door.

His breath punched like a fist in his throat. He flew up the steps and gripped the doorknob.

"Charlotte! Charlotte, it's me, Justice." He rattled the knob, and the crushing band around his ribs loosened a millimetre as he absorbed the knowledge the door was still locked. "Are you okay, Charlotte? Please, open the door."

No response. He rapped hard on the six-paned window, his pulse quickening once more, thundering through his veins. Had the prowler gained entrance and locked it behind him?

Cupping his hands around his eyes, he strained to see through the glass. There. Crouched in front of the fridge. From this angle he could only see her hip and shoulder, the toe of one foot, a curly mass of dark hair.

He shook the handle and called again, striving to keep the fear from his voice. "Everything will be okay. I'm here.

Let me in, Charlotte."

Surely she could hear him. The night was city-silent, the hum of far off traffic droning through the stillness. "Charlotte," he coaxed.

Her foot twitched. He sucked in a breath of frigid air. "That's my girl. Let me in, Charlotte."

She rolled slowly to her knees, crawled to the counter, and dragged herself up. Her face bloomed pale amid the cloud of her hair, eyes huge and stark. Moving with the stiffness of an eighty-year old, she made her cautious way to the door.

"That's my girl," he repeated, keeping his voice low and soothing, hiding the raging need to find the man who had terrified her. And smash him. With hands and feet and fury. "Unlock the door. Everything's okay now. I'm here."

The deadbolt clunked free, followed by the snick of the latch. He shouldered through and snatched her into his arms, tucking her head against his chest, burying his face in her sweet-smelling mass of curls. "Holy shit, Charlotte. What happened?"

"My phone died." Her voice held the eerie calm of shock. "I must have forgotten to charge it."

He rubbed his hand up and down her back. She stood rigid in his arms. "Can you tell me what happened?"

Her head jerked in a nod, the strands of her hair catching on his beard. "He came to the door. I could see him, through the window." Her voice pitched higher, vocal cords strumming tight as violin strings. "I don't think he saw me. He tried the door. I could hear scratching. And the door creaking. I thought he was going to get in."

She pushed at his chest, struggling half-heartedly to escape his embrace. He held her closer, rocking back and forth. "He didn't. He didn't get in. I'm here now. I won't let you go." And he didn't just mean tonight. He wasn't going to allow her to push him away again.

She gave a muffled sob and sank into him, her arms creeping around his waist. He could feel the catch and heave of her breathing as she struggled to stay in control. "I didn't want to call the police. Isn't that stupid? I didn't want to make a big deal about a man doing nothing but standing and watching."

He agreed with her. She should have called the police. And yet— "I'm glad you called me. That you trusted me enough to ask for help."

Her shoulders jerked as she gave a watery sniff. "And then he was at the door, and my phone was dead, and it was too late—"

"Shhh. Shhh." He murmured the meaningless sound, holding her tight until she calmed again.

"I need a tissue."

With a conscious act of will, he loosened his hold. He wasn't ready to let her go. Not yet. Not again.

A gaudily flowered box perched on top of the fridge. Charlotte made her way there, still a little unsteady on her feet. She blew her nose with dainty snorts and disposed of the tissue. A faint flush coloured the cheeks that had been ghostly only minutes before. Her eyes locked onto her hands, fingers linked together in a vise-like grip.

"Well, thanks." She darted a glance at him, and her blush deepened. "I hope I didn't interrupt you at anything important."

So she thought she could brush him off, did she? He unzipped his parka and draped it on the back of one of the dinette chairs. "I was at work."

She stared at him. "You left work? Because I called?"

"Charlotte." He tilted his head, let exasperation colour

his voice. "You were frightened, and for good reason. Of course I came."

"I-I'm sorry." Her hands twisted together, fingertips red, knuckles white. "About what I said, before. When I broke it off between us. It was cruel and unkind, and I didn't mean it."

He reached out and untangled her hands, rubbing the pressure marks out of her fingers. "I suppose we should talk about that. But not tonight." He walked backward, trailing her with him, until the sofa in the small sitting area brushed against his calves. Lowering himself to the seat, he tugged her into his lap, folded her into his arms. "Not tonight."

****

Charlotte was a big woman, and no one had wanted to cuddle with her on his lap since she was a child.

She wriggled, horribly aware of his solid, thick thighs beneath her. "Justice. This is—this is undignified. Let me go."

"You scared me rigid tonight." He smiled, that small, eyes-only smile that fascinated her. His arms tightened. "Let me hold you. Please."

His big, warm hand stroke up and down her spine, and she shuddered with the desire to arch into his caress like a cat. She didn't deserve his comfort.

"Relax." With light pressure, he urged her to lay against him. Her body succumbed, despite her mind's reservations, and she curled next to the comforting heat of his chest.

He held her, his arms a solid, protective circle. Slowly, the humming silence of the house and the thud of his heart beneath her ear soothed her lingering tension away.

"Better?" His voice rumbled like water boiling in a

kettle, vibrating through bones and sinew. His crisp, starched uniform shirt smelled of fresh laundry.

"I'm sorry. About taking you away from work." She toyed with the button on his breast pocket. "I would hate for you to get in trouble. Should I talk to your boss for you? It's Nielson, isn't it?"

"I'll deal with it." One hand rested on her thigh, its solid heat reassuring, while his other arm cradled her shoulders.

"White knights on shining chargers shouldn't get a scolding when they rescue damsels in distress." She tried to sound lighthearted, but wasn't sure she achieved it.

He sighed. She heard the susurrus of breath leave his lungs, felt it flutter her hair. "It's fine."

Half-hypnotized by the restful rise and fall of his chest, she allowed her eyelids to drift close. "Do you think I should call the police? After all, nothing really happened."

"Yes, you should. But morning will do."

"If you think so." It took an enormous amount of effort to say those four simple words. As the adrenaline faded from her system, it was as if every muscle in her body was weighted down.

"I do. Rest now."

So she did.

****

Charlotte floated out of slumber, her body lax and peaceful even as her mind woke up.

Until she recalled the events of last evening.

Her eyes flew open, her muscles tensed. The sight of her cluttered night table close to her nose calmed her initial panic. In confused relief, she realized she was tucked up in her own bed, with no memory of how she'd gotten there.

197

The display on her digital clock revealed it was just after eight in the morning.

She rolled to her back, and bumped into a warm, heavy weight.

Justice.

He lay on top of the duvet, arms crossed at his waist, fly of his slacks undone, as were the buttons of his uniform shirt. He'd removed his socks, revealing long, slender feet, gnarled and knobbed like a dancer's from all those years of wearing skates.

Any remaining agitation she'd harboured drifted away. Justice was here. He hadn't left her alone. She didn't want to examine how much that meant to her.

Reaching out a tentative hand, she laid it gently on his chest. His breath hitched slightly, and then evened out. His skin radiated heat, and short, curly hairs tickled her palm.

For the first time in a long time, she felt connected to herself. Felt as if all the pieces of her personality had clicked into place. She still had much work to do on her book, but the burning need to finish it no longer churned in her gut. Last night's intruder had scared some sense into her. No matter what she'd told herself the last couple of weeks, her true feelings for Justice had come through. He was the one she'd called to when she needed help. And he'd come, just as she'd known he would, with no regard to his own concerns.

A sense of inevitability filled her. Who knew what the future would bring. But for now, she wouldn't refuse whatever Justice might be willing to offer.

Peace, security.

Passion, intimacy.

Her first class wasn't until after lunch, and if Justice had been at work when she called last night, he was probably due in around the same time. She started to wriggle off the bed, thinking she'd slip to the kitchen and make coffee.

Justice's hand swung up and gripped hers. She squeaked in surprise. Without opening his eyes, he tugged her close again, one muscular arm sweeping over her head to haul her to his side. Her cheek found a natural resting place on his shoulder.

"I didn't mean to wake you," she whispered, breathless with awareness of his hard, hot body pressed along her length.

He hummed deep in his throat, playing sleepily with her fingers, lids still covering those slate-blue eyes.

"I was going to make coffee." If she didn't get away soon, she'd be a puddle of desire, incapable of thought. She couldn't believe she'd denied herself a month of this closeness. Despite the affection in his hold, she wasn't confident enough in his forgiveness to instigate anything more. That would be up to him.

"In a minute." He cleared his throat of its morning hoarseness, twisted his neck on the pillow and finally opened his eyes. His face was so close she had to blink to get him in focus. "Morning."

"Morning." She dropped her gaze, unaccountably shy. His beard glinted in the soft light seeping through the gauzy curtains, the scruff of whiskers under his jaw sparser than that on his cheeks and chin.

"Sleep well?"

"I don't remember coming to bed."

"You're a solid woman."

At that, she lifted her head. "You carried me?"

He dipped his chin in a nod. "You fell asleep on my lap. I figured you'd be more comfortable here."

She dropped her head to his shoulder again, hiding her face. "Oh, God."

"Hey, no worries. I just won't do any bench presses until I recover."

She huffed out an embarrassed laugh and felt the subterranean rumble of his own amusement echo through his bones.

"I'm glad you stayed." She blurted out the words before she had a chance to think better of the admission.

"Did you honestly think I'd leave you alone?"

"I don't deserve your kindness." The arm she was laying on prickled with pins and needles and her scalp tingled where strands of her hair were trapped underneath his shoulder, but she didn't move.

His dry fingers gripped her chin, tilted her face up. Serious blue eyes blazed into hers. "I don't know what bee got into that brain of yours, to make you say those things to me."

"I didn't mean them." She licked her lower lip, swallowed to get moisture into her mouth. "I was afraid."

He frowned. "Of me?"

She shook her head. "Of me. I didn't think I'd be strong enough to stay away from you, so I could do the work I needed to do. I panicked, tried to push you away."

"For a smart woman, you sure are an idiot." His fingers loosened their grip on her chin, slipped to the back of her neck and cupped her nape. "It doesn't have to be one or the other, does it?"

****

The confusion in Charlotte's face tugged at Justice's conscience. He was as much to blame for their estrangement as she was. He should have let her cool off for a day or so, and then insisted she let him back into her life.

"I missed you," he said.

Her eyes widened at his confession.

"I missed this."

He lowered his mouth to hers.

The angle was awkward and uncomfortable. He brushed her lips with his, the muscles in his neck strained. When her mouth warmed, opened to take him in, he shifted her to lay on top of him.

Her worn cotton t-shirt and pajama pants were a thin barrier between them. Her breasts pressed soft and lush against his chest, her knees drawn up on either side of his hips so his groin was cradled between her legs. He'd been hard even before he kissed her, and grew harder still as she pressed against his cock.

She cradled his face in her hands, her palms cool through the bush of his beard, and he let her deepen the kiss.

"Does this mean you forgive me?" She nibbled at his lips between words.

"Stop it." He gave her ass a light slap. She lifted her head on a jerk and stared at him. "We had an argument. Things were said. Now let it go." One palm caressed the rounded globe he'd punished, while his other hand slid under her t-shirt, bumped over her ribs, and knuckled the side of her breast.

Tension seeped out of her and she lowered onto his chest, her face tucked into the curve of his neck and shoulder. "I've been miserable without you. I told myself it was because I was working too hard on my book. But that was only part of it."

"Work is good. But it shouldn't be everything."

"It's all I've had, for a long, long time. It's what makes

me, me."

This revelation, while not a surprise to Justice, still made him sad. And angry, that she should think she was nothing more than a brain doing research on archaic poetry.

"You said something about coffee." His cock was going to be disappointed this morning. It thought it was going to get sex, but she was still too vulnerable after last night. "And then you should go to the police."

Her muscles tightened, and the finger making circles on his pec stilled. "Do I have to?"

He smiled at the dismay in her voice. "Yes. But don't worry. I'll come with you."

CHAPTER NINETEEN

Charlotte's thighs trembled and her heart pounded. With a gasp of relief, she punched off the speed and stepped carefully from the treadmill. The floor heaved under her feet as muscle memory continued to tell her brain she was on a moving platform, despite the evidence of her eyes.

The young man next to her kicked his machine up a few notches, his feet pounding rapidly, smoothly. She avoided eye contact, as one does in a gym, and headed out onto the track. Staggering only slightly, she circled the elevated level, distracting herself from discomfort of both mind and body by watching the rugby game on the artificial field below.

She was avoiding going home, and she knew it. The thought of being alone in the house made her shoulder blades itch.

After a stop at Justice's house this morning to let a very relieved Chaucer out for a run and fill up his kibble dish, they had gone to the RCMP detachment to file a report. It hadn't been as awful as she'd been dreading. Constable Rex Halder was a rec hockey buddy of Justice's and had made the process as simple as possible. He had said he would stop by the house as soon as he could to take some photos of the footprints in the backyard, but other than that only had words of caution.

"I don't want to frighten you, but with your connection to the university, and the incidents that have happened there recently, I think you should take last night's events seriously." Halder had closed the folder and crossed his hands neatly on top. "I'm sure Justice can give you suggestions on simple safety measures."

One of those safety measures had been to alert Justice when she left the office. When she'd finished for the day, she'd done as promised and called him to walk her to her car. Just the sight of him made her feel safer, and she bit her tongue to stop herself from asking if he'd come stay with her again tonight. She was a big girl—surely she wasn't so much of a coward she couldn't live in her own home. He'd seen her safely to her car and returned to the campus building. As she drove past the Northern Sport Centre, however, she gave in to impulse and parked once more, scurrying to the entrance with only a couple glances over her shoulder, her duffel bag clutched tightly in her hand.

Justice also wanted her to do more boxing training with him, but that would have to wait until their schedules coordinated. So for now, she'd decided 5K on a treadmill would help burn off the nerves.

After refilling her water bottle at the fountain, she headed down two flights of concrete steps to the change rooms in the basement. What sadistic bastard had made that decision, she thought, wincing her way to the bottom. Oh, well. She might still be nervous, but at least now she was tired. Perhaps she'd be able to sleep after all.

She spun the combination on her lock and clanged open the metal door. As she dug in her duffel for a towel and a change of clothes, she noticed the blue light indicating a message on her phone. A quick swipe of the screen showed a text from Sonny.

I have news! Give me a call!!!!!!

The exclamation marks had Charlotte's eyebrows climbing. She made the connection one-handed, while pulling out her toiletry case. Sonny answered so quickly she almost didn't hear it ring.

"What took you so long? I texted an hour ago!" The bubbling exuberance in Sonny's tone calmed any nascent worry.

"I was working out. What's going on?" She sank onto the slatted wooden bench and toed out of her sweaty sneakers.

"I already told Mom and Dad. But I wanted you to be next." High-pitched voices interrupted her. "Okay, okay, you can tell Auntie Charlotte. Anthony and Andrea want to tell you. Let me put you on speaker."

Charlotte peeled off her socks and wiggled her toes in pleasure as she listened to fumbling and bumping and giggling. Sonny's voice came again. "Okay, is everybody ready?"

Anthony and Andrea answered, speaking over each other in their excitement. "Yes, Momma. We're ready."

Maybe they're getting a puppy, Charlotte thought.

"Guess what, Auntie?" Anthony's voice was distinguishable from his sister's by the slight lisp of his missing front teeth.

"We're going to have a baby!" Andrea squealed.

The air around Charlotte crystallized. She froze, afraid to move, afraid it would shatter and pierce her, shred her. Tear into her, as her sweet, innocent nephew and niece had just done.

"If it's a boy, we're going to call him Alexander," Anthony confided.

"It's not going to be a boy," interjected his sister. "It's going to be a girl. I want to call her Ariel."

"Ariel's a stupid name. And you don't know it's a girl. You don't know nothing."

"Enough." Sonny's firm voice quelled the incipient argument. "Let Momma talk to Auntie now, all right? You can get the ice cream out." Sonny switched off the speaker. "We're celebrating with sundaes."

Charlotte choked out her first words. "Congratulations. The kids sound thrilled."

"I'm sure it will wear off soon. That's the third time they've had the boy/girl argument already, even though we only told them today. Had to explain why Momma was throwing up every morning." No one sounded happier about vomiting than Sonny did.

Charlotte sat, surrounded by the smell of sweat and shampoo and hot water, and wanted to cry. Proud there was no quaver in her voice to reveal her turmoil, she asked, "How far along are you?"

"Seven weeks. I'm going to be so fat this summer. God, I hope it's not a hot one."

She searched for something else to say, finally fell back on an expected platitude. "I'm happy for you and Thomas."

A hint of anxiety lay just underneath the joy in Sonny's voice. "You're okay with this, right? You're pleased you'll be an auntie again?"

"Of course I am." What was the point of telling the truth? It would only hurt Sonny, and it wouldn't change anything. Besides, she would be happy about the baby—once the bitter bite of jealousy faded.

"Charlotte. I wish—"

She cut Sonny off. "It's great news, Sonny, really." She sprang to her feet and grabbed her coat out of the locker. Whereas, only minutes ago, home had been a place to be avoided, now it looked a sanctuary. "I'm just on my way home, so I've got to go. I'll call you later."

"Tonight?"

God, no. "Tomorrow. I'll have more time to talk tomorrow." And more time to pull herself together.

****

It had been a bitch of a shift. Justice slammed the door of his truck and slumped down behind the steering wheel. On the far side of the empty rows of parking stalls, the university buildings squatted in the frosty dark, exterior lights throwing golden streaks onto the stone pillars, scattered illuminated windows cutting through the gloom.

Fucking Nielson. Justice had barely coded into the office before he'd jumped down his throat about leaving during his shift last night. And he obviously still had connections at the detachment because he knew Justice had taken Charlotte there this morning.

Justice had stood stolidly in front the Nielson' big desk while his boss had chewed him a new one. "You were on duty when you received the phone call. Your obligation is to the university, to the campus. Why did you feel it necessary to leave your partner, especially while in a volatile situation?"

"My assessment, based on Professor Girardet's call, was that her needs were greater than that of two boys brawling."

"You should have consulted with me prior to going to the RCMP."

Justice figured that was what stuck in Nielson's craw the most. He was pissed because Justice hadn't followed what he considered to be the proper chain of command. The confrontation had left a strained atmosphere that tainted the rest of his shift.

He hadn't turned on the ignition and his breath fogged the air in front of him, the interior as cold as the winter night outside. With a sigh that solidified in white wisps, he started the engine and pulled out of the lot.

Nielson's predecessor had been a laid-back, live and let live type, content to let Justice lead as senior guard. It was his own fault he hadn't changed his ways to reflect the different, more unyielding personality now in the director's role. A stronger leader—whether good or bad—changed things. He should have known better—the captain of a hockey team could sway an entire season.

Not that he planned on eating any crow, but maybe he should lie low for a few days. He could take some time off. An extended weekend wouldn't hurt.

He made a quick detour to pick up Chaucer and pack a bag, so it was almost eleven thirty by the time his truck rumbled to a stop in Charlotte's driveway. The house was dark, sleeping, except for a dimly glowing light seen through her bedroom window on the second storey.

She hadn't asked him to stop by tonight. But she didn't need to. He was determined to take care of her, whether she wanted it or not.

He knocked firmly on the door, Chaucer snuffling at the threshold.

No answer.

He rang the doorbell, listened to its chimes echo faintly.

Through the opaque glass in the upper half of the door, he saw movement on the stairs. When the door opened, it revealed Charlotte clutching a heavy fleece robe at her neck, face pale, hair tousled.

"I wasn't expecting you," she said. Chaucer stepped into the entry and nudged her. She patted his head absently.

He didn't plan on giving her an out. Gripping Chaucer's leash, he tugged the dog over the threshold. Charlotte shut the door behind them and leaned against it, as if needing support.

"You okay if I take him off the leash?"

"Sure."

The dog set off to explore. Justice studied Charlotte, frowning at what looked suspiciously like the signs of crying—red-rimmed lids, over-bright eyes.

"What's up?"

She puffed air out her nose. "Nothing."

He wasn't that stupid. "Has something else happened? Did you see the guy again?"

A shake of her head tossed her curls into her face. He brushed them away, letting his fingers linger on her jaw. A faint dampness on her skin told him the truth. "You've been crying."

Her chin lifted out of his hand and her eyes filled. His heart seized—with panic, with the need to fix whatever was wrong. "Tell me."

"It's stupid."

He'd never met a woman so concerned about appearing stupid. "I don't care."

Chaucer clicked back from his examination of the other rooms and sat at Justice's knee, his panting face swinging from one human to the other.

Charlotte pushed off the door and straightened her stance. "My sister is pregnant."

He waited for more. There had to be more, because why would such news make her unhappy?

"She and her husband are ecstatic. Her two other beautiful, adorable children are thrilled. My parents will be over the moon about another grandchild." She met his eyes, her own swamped in misery. "Why can't I be happy, too?"

Chaucer whined and raised a paw to pad at Charlotte's robe. Justice curved his palms over her shoulders, feeling their delicate strength through the thick material. "Why can't you?"

She tore out of his grasp and spun away, striding into the sterile, unwelcoming living room. "Because I'm a bitch, that's why. Because she has what I want." She stopped with a gasp, raising her hand to her mouth. "I'm so jealous I can't breathe. And I didn't even know it until now."

CHAPTER TWENTY

Charlotte couldn't stand still. She paced in front of the couch, hands clenched so tightly her knuckles throbbed. "I thought I was used to the fact I don't have children." She was just coherent enough not to use the word "can't". "I didn't react like this when I found out she was pregnant with Anthony and Andrea. Why is this time so hard?"

Justice remained silent. She couldn't bear to look at him, but was excruciatingly aware of his presence.

"Maybe because it's not just her." She rounded the back of the sofa, bumping it with her hip. "My ex and his new wife are having a baby, too. It shouldn't matter. He doesn't matter. But it's gnawing at me, and I hate it. I hate feeling this way."

"Your ex?"

Justice's cold tone stopped her in her relentless pacing. She rounded to face him. "Yes."

"You were married?"

"No. Engaged." She waved a hand. "It was more than a year ago. He broke it off. I'm over it." That was the truth. She was over him. But maybe she wasn't over why he'd left her.

Charlotte watched Justice, trying to read his expression without success. What was he thinking? She'd just blurted out she was jealous of her sister's perfect life, and then added to the mess by bringing up Richard. Why was she always screwing things up?

The small fire of anger that had propelled her about

the room flickered out. She sank onto the couch, vaguely aware of its overstuffed rigidity.

"I'm a horrible person." Why couldn't she shut up? Her failings were obvious. Did she need to point them out?

Chaucer wove his way past Justice, plopped down at Charlotte's knee and leaned against her. His furry warmth eased a little of the chill aching in her muscles.

"Because you're human?" Justice remained standing in the opening leading to the entrance, his shoulders filling the space, outlined by the light behind him. He watched her with a wary stillness. Probably wondering if she was going to flip out at him again.

She wrapped her arms around her torso, tucking into the pain in her belly. "What sort of human is jealous because her sister has a beautiful family? Because a man who she doesn't love anymore has found someone else?"

"A lonely one?"

Her heart shuddered to a stop. His soft words echoed deep within her, resonating with truth. She gulped down a breath, willing back the tears burning at the back of her throat. Chaucer laid his head on her thigh and she uncurled enough to fondle his ear, letting the velvety fur slip through her fingers.

She cleared her throat and tried to speak lightly. "You think I'm lonely?"

"I think you're one of the loneliest people I've ever met." The rumble of his voice came from above her. She kept her head lowered, concentrating on the dog, who groaned with pleasure as she continued her caresses.

Justice sat beside her, the cushion compressing only slightly under his weight. "When did you find out?"

"About Sonny? This evening." Maybe it was just the shock. Maybe she'd feel different in the morning. She sure hoped so. Right now she hated herself, and she didn't want to feel like that much longer.

"Can I get you something?"

She forced herself to meet his gaze. With relief, she saw only concern and caring in his eyes. No censure, no condescension. "Thanks, but no." A thought struck her. "Why are you here? It's almost midnight."

He shifted on the couch, as if searching for a more comfortable position. "I thought you might want me to stay again."

"Oh." The turmoil of Sonny's news had pushed the fear of the intruder out of her mind. "That was nice of you."

He rolled his shoulders. "If you'd rather I left—"

"No." Her answer was sudden and sure. "No. I want you to stay." Maybe he was right. Maybe she was lonely. But that didn't mean she had to stay that way. She rose to her feet and held out her hand. He clasped hers, his warm, slightly rough palm a comfort. "Let's go to bed."

****

Justice used a finger to mark his place in his book and studied Charlotte. She sat hunched up in the chair in her home office, frowning at the screen of her laptop. Muttering indistinctly, she punched the backspace key repeatedly and hovered her hands over the keyboard before tapping rapidly with all fingers for a few moments. She stopped, frowned even deeper, and repeated the whole process.

He shifted his position on the single bed that shared the space. His back was propped against the wall, his legs dangling uncomfortably over the side. The slight movement dislodged the stacks of books piled on the mattress beside him and he made a quick grab to save it. Chaucer raised his head from his sprawl on the floor and woofed in disapproval, but Charlotte didn't release her focus from her work.

The last couple of days, they'd found an odd sort of rhythm. When he was done his evening shift, he picked up Chaucer and they spent the night at Charlotte's. When she rose to go to the university, he and the dog headed home. When Charlotte left her office, he walked her to her car. The cycle began again after work.

He hadn't asked her if that was what she wanted, but the relief in her eyes when he arrived each night was permission enough. She'd even given him a key. Shyly, diffidently, not pushing it on him, yet pleased when he'd accepted it.

She pulled a pencil out of the curling mass of hair she'd bundled at the back of her neck and made a note on a tall stack of printouts. Her concentration was absolute. Justice had seen the same level of absorption in the best hockey players—a total refusal to let anything get in the way of their goals, and the willingness to sacrifice all to achieve them.

Unlike working out on the ice, sitting at a computer didn't bring the physical exhaustion that contributed to a good night's sleep. Charlotte tossed and turned through the night, and even lovemaking didn't seem to relax her for more than the moment of release. Dark circles bagged below her eyes and he swore she was thinner than when they'd first met.

He had to do something before she simply broke into pieces from over-work, stress and fatigue.

Rising from the bed, he stepped over the snoring Chaucer and laid his hands on Charlotte's shoulders. She continued to scribble on the pages before her. The muscles under his palms were stiff and strained.

"I think that's enough for tonight."

"Almost done." She clicked between two windows on her laptop, grunted, and made yet another note.

"No, not almost. You are done." He leaned over and shut the lid.

"Hey!" She pried at the computer, but he kept pressing. "I just need a couple more minutes."

"It's almost one in the morning."

"It's Friday. I can sleep in tomorrow."

"Since when do you sleep in?"

"I promise." She wrapped her hand around his wrist and tried to slide it off the cover. "I'm almost done this chapter. I won't be able to relax if I don't get it done."

He sank to his knees beside her, the joints popping like muffled firecrackers. "When's the last time you really relaxed?" He gripped her fingers to stop her from lifting the computer's lid. She refused to meet his eyes, staring with a wrinkled brow at the thin silver machine as if determined to finish her work through telekinesis. "I'm worried about you."

That got her attention. "Why on earth? There's nothing wrong with me."

He wasn't going to argue about with her, but he knew better. Whether it was the book, her sister's pregnancy, or the fact the stalker still hadn't been identified, she was brittle, fragile and one stiff wind away from falling apart. "You need to take a break."

She twisted her hands out of his loose grip and rolled her chair back so she could stand. "Fine, fine. We'll go to bed."

He rose to his feet. "I'm talking about days off."

"I had time off at Christmas."

He wondered if she realized she was pouting. "And

215

since then you've been working ungodly hours. I think you need time away from your desk."

"I promised myself I'd have my book done by the middle of February. It won't take much longer. One week." She cocked her head to the side and amended, "Ten days at the most."

He calculated swiftly. "That takes us to Reading Week." The university emptied out then, students and faculty scattering for a needed break in the doldrums of winter. "Don't make plans. You're coming with me."

"Coming with you where?"

"My cabin." It was perfect. No cell service, no Wi-Fi, nothing but tranquil solitude.

"I didn't know you had a cabin."

"I bought it a couple years ago." After he and Tiffani had split, he'd needed a place to heal. The cabin was a place where time fell still, clocks stopped ticking, and life could be lived to the rhythm of nature. He and Max spent every available summer moment there, and rarely visited in the winter. But the more he thought of it, the more he knew the decision was right. Charlotte needed that peacefulness.

****

The cab of his truck smelled of sweaty boy. Not the rank, acrid stench of a teenager, but the lighter, innocent scent of man-child.

"I sucked today, didn't I," Max said, his glum, defeated voice drifting through the darkness. They'd travelled to a nearby town to play a couple of away games, and were now on their way home in the deep winter dusk. It was snowing lightly, scattered flakes as brilliant as the particles of a sparkler in the truck's high beams.

Justice dipped them to low as another vehicle

approached around a winding corner. "You didn't suck." He didn't want to make Max feel worse, yet he had to be honest. "I've seen you play better, though. That can happen to any athlete. No matter what, some days it's just not going to be good."

A windy sigh reached him. "I bet you never had a bad day."

"I had plenty of bad days." And his father had never hesitated to tell Justice so.

"But you were going to play in the NHL."

"That doesn't mean anything. You watch hockey all the time. Does Crosby score every time he's on the ice?"

"No."

"And doesn't Carey Price let in a bad goal every once in a while?"

"I guess." His voice grew thoughtful. "Do you think their coaches get mad at them?"

"I'd bet on it." He shot a glance into the rear view mirror. His son's small face was only a pale circle in the gloom of the back seat. "Do you think I'm mad at you?"

"No." The uncertainly in his tone pricked at Justice's heart. "But I made a lot of mistakes today."

"Mistakes can mean you're trying hard. Did you try hard?"

"I guess."

"That's all anyone can ask. Hockey is supposed to be fun. Maybe it's more fun to win, but even when you lose, like we did today, it should still be something you enjoy. Or it's not worth playing."

They travelled on. The snow grew thicker, and Justice upped the interval on his windshield wipers. He'd travelled this road so many times he knew every twist and turn, and he responded to the demands of driving automatically, his mind caught up elsewhere.

He was still worried about Charlotte. But Reading Week was only a few days away, and she'd reiterated her promise to get away with him then. He'd wanted her to come with him and Max today, but she'd insisted on staying home.

"One more solid day," she'd said, eyes flickering between him and her laptop screen. "I can get it done today. Then one more quick read, and I'll be able to send it away."

She hadn't had a meltdown since the night she'd found out about her sister's pregnancy. But she hadn't talked about it, either. He worried she was using her book to block her emotions when it came to her new niece or nephew.

And then there was the ex-fiancé's child.

He flashed a look over his shoulder. Max had his head down, a blueish glow flickering on his face as he concentrated on the game he was playing on his iPad. His son - not of his blood, but of his heart.

He could never love Max less. But would having a child of his own making be different, in some indefinable way? He and Tiffani had married when Max was not yet a year old. He hadn't seen her pregnant, hadn't felt the baby move inside her, hadn't been there for the birth. And yet that tiny, fatherless boy had become such an integral part of his soul he couldn't imagine life without him.

How would it feel to see Charlotte big and ungainly, beautifully heavy, with his baby? She obviously wanted a family, or why else would she be so upset about her sister and her ex?

He'd have to explore the idea—carefully, oh, so carefully—when he had her alone next week.

CHAPTER TWENTY-ONE

Charlotte's finger hovered over the left mouse button. She read the email once more, double-checked she had attached the correct file. And still couldn't bring herself to tap the small, four letter word that would send her monograph—her now completed monograph—to Doctor Ross-Moore.

She retracted her hand and nibbled at her nail. The words on the screen jiggled before her tired eyes. She squeezed them shut, the sting of dryness easing.

Why was she hesitating? This was the culmination of days and nights of writing, weeks and months of research, years and years of study. A tenure position in a prestigious university had been her goal for so long. She'd already taken the first step with her application. It was in her grasp. Now all she had to do was hit send.

A warm weight plopped onto her thigh. She was smiling before she opened her eyes. "Hey, buddy. How's it going?"

Chaucer grumbled in delight as she rubbed his ears just the way he liked. Justice and Max were at an evening hockey practice, and they had dropped him off to keep her company. As the days wore on without any new developments in either the attacks at the University or her intruder, her fears had eased. She'd stopped jumping at the house's every creak and sigh, and Justice no longer spent every night. She had been the one to insist she was fine, that she would be all right if he returned home.

But, God, she'd wanted him to stay. Which was why she'd had to make him leave.

Still, she welcomed Chaucer's presence. She was much more comfortable with Justice's dog than with his son, she thought wryly. The boy's solemn stare unnerved her. She wondered what Justice had told him about their relationship.

One of the reasons she didn't want to send the email was obvious, and she finally faced it squarely. Once this project was done, she would have hours and hours to think about Sonny's new baby. About Richard and Elyse's baby. About Justice. About the future. She wasn't sure she could handle it all.

Chaucer bopped his head up, demanding her attention, whuffing softly. She rubbed for a few more seconds, and then patted him in dismissal. "Okay, dog, enough loving. Go to your bed." She'd piled an old blanket in one corner of her office to make the hard floor more inviting. "It's time to get this done." He strolled away, tail wagging agreeably, and collapsed with a sigh.

Without pause for further thought, she pointed and clicked the mouse. For a moment she wanted to reach into cyberspace and get the email back. Her hand actually stretched out to the screen. She shrugged off the futile sensation, and with a sense of finality closed the lid of her laptop, smoothing the steel-grey surface with her fingertips.

Tomorrow she and Justice were heading to his cabin. She wasn't sure what she would do without the impetus of her book behind her. Wasn't sure if four days alone with nothing to distract them from each other was a blessing or a curse. Wasn't sure of much, really.

Except for one thing.

Life was about to change.

****

Justice hefted the cooler into the back of the pickup and closed the canopy. It was just past noon, and he was due at Charlotte's any moment. Nielson hadn't been gracious when he'd asked for the day off, but he had a shitton of holidays piled up so his boss had no excuse to deny him. Chaucer had been in a frenzy of joy all morning, hopping in and out of the truck box, not sure what was happening, but determined not to miss out.

His cell buzzed as he opened the passenger door. He dug it out of the pocket of his jacket as Chaucer vaulted in without an invitation and sat panting, tongue lolling happily.

"Cooper," Justice answered.

"It's McMorris." The older guard was covering Justice's shift. "Have you heard?"

"What?" Justice closed Chaucer in and circled around the hood. Maybe Nielson had resigned. That would make what was going to be a good day absolutely great.

"Another attack. Last night. Neilson's talking with the cops right now."

Justice's fist clenched around his keys, the sharp edges cutting into his palm. "On campus?"

A hard edge of excitement sliced through McMorris' words. "No. But a student. I hear she's in bad shape."

"Fuck." He slid behind the wheel and slammed the door. "Any details?"

"She was found in the parking lot of her apartment. The complexes at the bottom of University Hill." McMorris' voice lowered. "She was beaten, maybe strangled. Don't know about rape."

A surge of disgust swept through Justice. The thought

of a man treating a woman that way... He swallowed a mouthful of futile, vile curses.

He tuned back in to McMorris, who was still talking. "—you might want to warn Professor Girardet."

Justice frowned. "What do you mean, warn her?"

Morris coughed, cleared his throat. "Just in case she knows the woman. I heard she was an English Master's student."

Justice was definitely not going to tell Charlotte there'd been another attack, and the victim possibly a student of hers. The next few days were all about unwinding, getting her to relax. He'd tell her once they were back in town. "Thanks for the heads up."

"This guy must be pretty smart, hey? Doing what he's doing, and getting away with it."

McMorris wasn't one of Justice's favourite people, but he never thought he'd hear him say such crap. "He's an asshole and a criminal," Justice snapped. "I hope they put him away for a good long time when they catch him."

"What makes you think they will?"

He'd had enough. "Of course they will. Creeps like this always make mistakes." He cut the connection and put the truck in gear. It was time to pick up Charlotte.

****

Charlotte bit her lip and surveyed the stack of items piled at the front door. She'd done her best to pack light, but winter clothes took up so much space. Justice had insisted she buy "real" cold-weather boots. The pair sat next to her suitcase, taking up almost as much square footage as the luggage. Her parka, with mitts, a toque and scarf tucked up the sleeves for safe-keeping, was draped over top. Then there was the bag of food she'd felt obligated to bring, despite Justice saying he would handle that end of things. And the flat of bottled water. Her pillow. An extra quilt, based on the heavy appearance of the clouds outside, threatening cold and snow.

She glanced up the stairs, toward her office where her laptop was. She knew there was no power at the cabin, but the thought of leaving her computer behind made her twitchy. What was the use of bringing it, though? If there was no power, the chance of Internet access was vanishingly slim. She might—might!—be able to check emails on her cell phone, but the battery on that would be dead before she returned to civilization. She'd packed the adapter that allowed her to charge it from a vehicle, but had the sneaking suspicion Justice wouldn't let her use it. He seemed adamant about going off grid.

A quick look at the clock told her he was on his way. She hesitated a moment more, and then took the stairs two at a time. If she was going to be incommunicado for a few days, she'd better set up an out-of-office reply.

She powered up her laptop, foot jiggling as she urged it to hurry, head cocked as she listened for Justice.

Her email fizzed into life.

And there it was. Big and bold and black. **Subject Line: Tenure Track Appointment—Interview.**

Her breath caught. Her stomach cramped.

Oh, God. It was happening.

Other than a form email a month ago confirming receipt of her application, she'd heard nothing from York University. She clicked and opened the message with a trembling hand.

The selection committee was very pleased with the qualifications she had provided in the documents, and had just learned from Doctor Ross-Moore that she had completed her monograph. Based on that information, an interview had been scheduled for one week from today. She would also be expected to present her lecture to a 400 level class. If the time was inconvenient, another more suitable time could be arranged. A prompt reply was requested.

It said the same when she read it a second time.

Her head whipped round as the sound of a brisk knock echoed up the stairwell. Her legs felt stiff and unwieldy, her head disconnected from her shoulders, as she moved to the door of the office. She called down the stairs, "It's open. Come on in. I'm upstairs."

Cool air swept toward her as Justice entered. He glowered up at her. "Since when don't you check who's at the door before you let them in?"

"Right. Sorry." She barely acknowledged his rebuke as she formulated her reply, combinations of words and sentences bouncing around in her brain. "I'll be down in a moment. Just have to finish one thing."

She accepted the appointment and thanked the committee for the opportunity. Another hurried message was sent to Natasha, her administrative assistant, asking her to book a flight to Toronto. She and Justice planned to return from the cabin on Tuesday. She could leave Wednesday morning, arrive in Toronto that evening, and have all Thursday to prepare.

She even remembered to set up her away message, before slapping the laptop shut and rushing down the stairs.

****

Justice muttered under his breath as he hauled Charlotte's gear to the truck. Her insistence on "finishing one thing" was yet more evidence she needed this time away. She was going to crash and burn if she didn't let it all go, for a few days at least.

He left the food and water for last. She still hadn't come out of her office when he returned. He closed the door and leaned against it, crossing his arms on his chest. One more minute, that's all he was giving her. Then he was going up those stairs and tossing that damn laptop out the window.

With seconds to spare she hurried down the steps, her face flushed, eyes bright.

"I'm so sorry to make you wait. I had a last minute email I couldn't ignore."

He raised an eyebrow.

"I'm done, I promise. No more computer, no more work." She bit her lip. "I don't know what made me agree to this. I'm already freaking out and I haven't left the house yet." She stepped into a pair of short boots, but he saw her shoot a look up the stairs, as if she could feel her office calling her.

And *that's* why they were leaving. Now.

"Coat?"

She flapped a hand. "You brought out my parka already. I hate getting overheated when I travel. This will do." She smoothed her hands down her big, bulky sweater, momentarily emphasizing her curves.

He opened the door and a draft of freezing air lifted the curls from her neck, sending them flying. She stepped past him and he caught a whiff of her scent.

It had been four days since they'd last been together. He wasn't sure he could last one more. But he wasn't jumping her in her hallway again.

He'd wait until they were settled in the cabin.

****

Justice headed east out of town. In fifteen minutes

they were travelling a narrow two-lane highway, covered in compact snow. Ice glared, beautifully dangerous, in scattered patches. Trees lining the road on either side were stark, black-limbed skeletons. In the far distance mountains rose, their peaks sheared off in a grim, flat line by the lowering clouds.

Charlotte sat silent, one foot tucked under the other thigh, hands folded in her lap. Despite her relaxed pose, tension rolled off her, bouncing around the cab. Chaucer, normally pleased to nap in the back seat, seemed to sense her strained emotions, and leaned forward, resting his head on her shoulder. She smiled and reached up to ruffle his ears, dropping a quick kiss on his nose. The dog sighed with pleasure.

They rumbled over a short bridge, the narrow, rocky gorge below bursting with enormous icicles from seeping water. Charlotte continued to rub the dog under his chin, but turned to watch the scenery sliding past her window.

He wanted to hear her voice. Wanted to hear the stress drain away with mundane conversation and trivial chatter. He searched for a safe topic—not work, or intruders, or babies, or love. Definitely not love.

Charlotte beat him to it. "So, exactly where is this cabin of yours?"

"Jack of Diamonds Lake. About three-quarters of an hour on the highway, then half an hour in on a logging road."

"What an odd name."

"When the sun is just right, you'd swear the lake was filled with diamonds, so I understand that part. Who knows when or where the Jack part was added."

"Maybe the first man to live there was called Jack."

"Max likes to pretend I won the cabin in a game of

twenty-one, when the jack of diamonds turned up. Sometimes we re-enact it. Haven't had the right jack turn yet."

"Cute." She wriggled in the seat, twisting to face him, and leaned her cheek against the headrest. Chaucer took the chance to lick her nose. "Uggh!" She pushed the furry muzzle away gently. "Lay down now. I'll give you more loving later."

The steering wheel jerked under his hand as the tires hit a stretch of ice scraped into washboard ruts by a plow. "Max and I go as often as we can in the summer. The road is cleared in the winter—it's still an active logging road to the track leading to the cabin—but we're going to have to haul our gear in a ways."

He cut her a glance and saw her nose wrinkle in suspicion. "How far is *a ways*?" she asked.

"A few hundred metres." Just over half a kilometre, actually, but he didn't want to scare her.

"I suppose I can manage that."

"You'll be fine." The exercise would be good for her. He hadn't seen colour in her cheeks for a long time.

They caught up to a slow-moving sand truck. The blade on the front of the vehicle flung a fifteen-foot fan of snow high into the air, dropping it gracefully into the ditch. A contraption on the back sprayed gravel behind. He stayed a safe distance away, until a wave from the driver indicated it was safe to pull out and around to pass.

The mountains drew closer. Not the towering, grey-stoned slopes of the Rockies, but no less dramatic in their own way, flanks dressed in the dark grey-green of pines and spruce. Hidden in their valleys and behind their rounded peaks were numerous amber-coloured lakes, all of them asleep for the winter under sheets of ice.

"Ever been to Jasper National Park?" he asked.

"Once, years ago, as a kid with my parents."

Most of Justice's travel had centred on hockey in Western Canada, but Charlotte had visited London and Paris, as well as numerous cities in the US. The conversation flowed from places to people to concerts to candy.

"Mars Bar, hands down." Charlotte was definite. "I don't get a chocolate craving very often, but when I do, it's straight to the Mars."

"I'm more of a mint man, myself. Not much into nuts and caramel. But After Eights, or Peppermint Patties? They're my downfall." He checked the rear view mirror and flicked on his right-turn indicator. Easing as far as he could onto the snow-covered shoulder, he let the SUV behind him swing past and then turned onto the side road.

Charlotte, who had grown sleepy and pliant as they'd talked nothingness, straightened in her seat. "We're almost there?"

"By distance, yes. But we won't be able to travel too fast on this road. The lake's still half an hour away."

"Are there other cabins?"

"A few." None of which would be occupied at this time of year, he was certain. He'd only come out in the winter once or twice before, and had been the only one there each time. "It's a bit too far from town to be very popular."

He manoeuvred carefully on the rutted, roughly cleared road. Charlotte fell quiet, peering interestedly out the window. They rounded a wide curve at a sedate speed. Which was lucky, as a large, morose-looking moose stood square in the middle of their way.

She gasped as he hit the brakes, bringing the pickup

to a stop about ten metres away from the animal.

"He's just standing there!" Charlotte's eyes were wide in fearful fascination. "What if we had hit him?"

"He's a she. And at the speed we were going, we all would have probably walked away. But you wouldn't want to do the same on the highway."

The long-limbed creature took a few slow steps, huge ears flicking forward and back, and then broke into an awkward jog, its dewlap swinging comically. It climbed the snowbank on the side of the road and disappeared into the bush.

"I've never seen a moose before," she said. "That was amazing."

Justice was pleased by her reaction. When a city girl met raw nature, you never knew if she'd appreciate it, freak out over it, or simply be bored. He felt a sense of pride, as if he'd arranged the show himself.

CHAPTER TWENTY-TWO

Heart still thumping after the unexpected encounter with the moose, Charlotte leaned forward in her seat, eager for what might appear next. The light was flat and dull, and she wished for sun to set the snow sparkling.

"They have very interesting faces, don't they?"

"Moose?" Justice frowned and slowed the truck even further as he negotiated an especially bumpy patch. Charlotte braced herself with a hand on the door frame. "Ugly is what most people call them."

"So ugly they're almost cute."

He grunted amicably. The cab was warm and cozy and he'd pulled off the snug black knit cap he'd been wearing. His hair stuck up in odd tufts. Without thinking, she reached out to smooth it down. He slanted her a look from the corner of his eye.

She snatched her hand back, her cheeks prickling with heat. "Your hair. It was sticking up."

"Hmmph," was his only answer.

She turned her flushed face to stare out the side window.

The thought of next week's interview punched into her consciousness. She'd tried to forget about it—after all, there was nothing she could do right now. But it hovered on the perimeter of her mind, and jumped out at unsuspecting moments like these. Her stomach muscles contracted and she eased out a long breath, searching for calm.

It was probably a blessing she was spending the next few days away from phones and computers. She would have worn herself out simply waiting for the time to pass. And she knew she needed this break. Justice might have coerced her into it at first, but she recognized fatigue and mental exhaustion had been dragging at her for more than few days.

She snuck a look at him. Her muscles tensed in a much more welcome way when she was with him. Five nights and days together was probably not the worst way to forget about the impending interview.

A small bridge appeared, connecting the banks of an ice-laced creek. On the approach, a wide area to the side of the road had been cleared. Justice pulled into the space, tucking his truck close to the hard-packed mound of snow at the edge. Leading into the trees at her right was a narrow track, cloaked in dull white.

"In the summer we can drive right up to the cabin. Today we'll have to park here." He opened the door and let Chaucer jump out. "If we get a dump of snow, I'll come back to make sure we don't get blocked in by a plow."

Charlotte opened her own door. The fuggy warmth of the cab dissipated instantly, overpowered by the frigid outdoor air, and she shivered. "What happens if we do get blocked?"

"We walk to the highway and hitch a ride home."

Horror froze her in place, until she caught the gleam in his eye. She glared at him through the cab. "Not funny." She grabbed her parka off the back seat and shrugged into it, tucking the scarf around her neck and tugging on her toque and mitts.

His mouth quirked. "It certainly won't be funny if we have to dig it out from behind a packed pile of snow. But

I've got shovels if we need to."

She pulled her new, heavy winter boots from the cab, shut the door and met him at the tailgate.

He stretched an arm inside and lifted out two pairs of snowshoes. "Here." He handed one set to Charlotte.

She eyed the contraptions dubiously. "I've never worn these before." Made of lightweight aluminium and futuristic-looking webbing, they were nothing like her romanticized notion of curved wood and leather lacing.

"The path won't be cleared. You're going to need them."

She pulled off the thin boots she'd been wearing and slipped her feet into the ungainly cold-weather footwear. He showed her how to unbuckle the snowshoe straps and where to position her feet. Then he cranked the harness down tight, snugging her foot to the plastic webbing. "Give them a try."

Feeling self-conscious, she stomped up and down the parking area. Chaucer raced around her, barking encouragement. The gizmos were remarkably easy to walk in, although forcing her into an ungainly waddle, and she felt a bit more confident about actually making it to the cabin.

"We'll have to make a few trips," Justice said, surveying the gear and supplies piled in the box. "Food first, I think."

Charlotte looped the handle of one bag over her shoulder and clutched another in her hand. Justice hoisted a large plastic bin. Thus laden, they trudged to the waist-high ridge of snow blocking their access to the lane. The dog bounded over and headed off to investigate the bushes on the far side.

"Wait." Justice slid the bin onto the bank. Standing

sideways to the berm, he thrust the edge of his snowshoe into it, working it until the snow flattened it into a small ledge. He repeated the process to form a second step, and then moved up to the top of the bank and held out his hand. "Give me the bags." Charlotte passed them up. "Now step up sideways, just like I did."

She manoeuvred with care and puffed out a relieved breath when she stood next to him at the top. They gathered their packages and headed off down the path, Justice breaking trail.

****

Justice grinned at the muffled hissing behind him. Charlotte was keeping up well—he made sure to keep his pace to a slow meander—but he could tell she found the unfamiliar snowshoes awkward by the few muttered comments he could distinguish.

The road they were on followed the creek. He could hear its cheerful chuckling over Charlotte's curses. A breeze rattled dry, bare branches, bringing the crisp, cold scent of snow-burdened clouds. The afternoon was already darkening, and they would have to move quickly to get everything unloaded before evening settled on them.

Chaucer raced past, earning another under-the-breath expletive from Charlotte. He dashed onto a narrow path heading down the slope to their left. The track stayed up on a low ridge, with the cabins between it and the lake. From their higher vantage point, all that could be seen of the nearest dwelling was rust-coloured shingles, half-camouflaged with moss and hidden behind a blue spruce.

Justice sniffed, searching for the scent of wood smoke, but sensing nothing other than the crisp tang of snow and spice of pine and spruce. The air was heavy with damp. More snow was on the way.

He paused and lowered the bin off his shoulder, plopping it into the snow. "How are you doing?"

"Fine." Charlotte halted with him and laid her bags down gingerly. She rubbed her mittened hands as if easing a cramp. "Is it much further?"

He pointed to the red roof. "That's the first cabin. Mine is the third."

Charlotte squinted. "If you didn't know it was there you would never see it."

They hefted their burdens and started off once more. A few minutes later, Justice left the wider trail and made his way down the bank. "Keep your knees bent with your weight over your heels," he instructed. Chaucer reappeared out of the bush, snow scattered on his brown back like sugar on a ginger snap cookie, and bounded toward the cabin.

It nestled with its back to the incline, a deck supported on wooden posts jutting toward the lake. The dark siding was comfortably faded, and its cedar shake roof matched the neighbours' with its coating of moss and pine needles. One small square window looked toward the path, two others peered directly into the bushy bank.

Everything seemed to be exactly as he and Max had left it months ago, and a faint knot of tension at the back of his neck eased. He always felt a niggle of worry when returning to the cabin, wondering if some damage may have occurred, whether caused by nature or man. But all appeared well.

At the foot of a short flight of steps leading to the deck, he lowered the bin yet again and crouched to unbuckle his snowshoes.

"Well, this looks cozy." Charlotte mimicked his actions while studying the building and its surroundings.

"I can't see any other cabins."

"That's what makes it perfect." He came here to get away from people. Neighbours nearby were definitely not on his must-have list.

He pulled off his gloves to dig the keys out of his pocket, feeling the burn of cold on his skin. Propping the bin on one hip, he followed the dog onto the deck. The door was set between two wide windows. The key stuck, as usual, but he worked it until the lock popped open.

Stepping back, he gestured Charlotte inside. "It's not much. But it's quiet."

She moved past him, her expression cautiously eager. He kicked the door shut and dropped the bin onto the table snugged up to the window on the right.

The air in the cabin held the same biting chill as outside. Charlotte's breath puffed out in clouds as she surveyed the room. She twisted the handles of the bags off her fingers and placed them gently at her feet, rubbing her fingers. He watched her expression fade into an almost comical dismay.

Maybe he should have prepared her better. He studied the room, seeing it through her eyes, suddenly wishing it was much, much more.

The walls were fake wood panelling, something you might have seen in a basement during the 1970's. A bed, covered in a faded plaid quilt, was tucked into the corner, partially hidden behind a torn, army green couch set facing the window. The wood stove—used for heat as well as cooking—took up a good chunk of the open space in the middle of the floor. In the far right corner a short counter with curtained shelves below ran along one wall, with the table beside it. A rough-hewn, handmade ladder leaned against the back wall, leading to a loft stretching the width and half the depth of the main floor.

Damned if he was going to apologize. They would be warm and safe. What else did they need? "It's not fancy," he said, unable to keep a note of defensiveness out of his tone.

Her smile wobbled a bit at the edges. "It's fine. I can see why you and Max enjoy it here. It's definitely a guy place."

He moved toward the door. "Are you up for another trip to the truck?" The sooner they had everything at the cabin, the better. Once he had the fire going it would be much more inviting.

****

Charlotte collapsed onto the battered couch, legs trembling, the skin under her arms and between her breasts damp with sweat. Justice had left to collect the last of the gear from the pickup, and she'd only waited for him to disappear off the deck before dropping to the lumpy seat in wordless gratitude.

She'd made two more trips back and forth. The light was fading, and if she'd had enough energy she would have worried about Justice returning in the dark with only Chaucer for company. He'd assured her he had time, and God knew he'd be able to move faster without her.

Before he left he started the fire, briskly crumpling paper and poking thin sticks of kindling into the narrow fire box. He'd also lit two kerosene lanterns, which popped and hissed into life, and now cast enough light to brighten the room.

Heat was beginning to radiate from the heavy metal of the stove, and she struggled to undo her parka. Her arms ached, the muscles in her shoulders strained and throbbing.

The pounding in her ears lessened as her heart settled

into a resting rhythm. Other than the muffled snapping of the fire, there was no sound. The silence was solid, heavy, and her pulse picked up again. The sense of being stranded, entirely alone, plucked at her nerves.

The rustle of her coat and thud of her boots as she laboured off the couch helped fill the quiet. Spotting hooks on the wall by the bed, she hung up her parka. She toed off her boots and placed them neatly by the door. The floor, a ripped, discoloured vinyl, was blotched with thin puddles of melting snow. Dodging carefully around them, she rummaged in the space she considered the kitchen and found a threadbare towel, with which she mopped up the water.

She supposed she could unpack the food and equipment they'd brought, but was unsure where Justice would want it so decided to wait. Instead she climbed, sock footed, up the ladder. Despite its handmade appearance, it was sturdy and firm. Her head popped up through the trap door. To one side a small mattress lay directly on the floor, covered in a Spiderman comforter. On the other side a beat up cardboard box overflowed with toy trucks, a half-deflated beach ball, and other odds and ends. This was obviously Max's space.

The door below clicked open, cold air swooping in and swirling around her ankles. The click of Chaucer's nails on the worn floor preceded the heavier thud of Justice's steps. She hurried down the ladder.

"Here, let me get that." She plucked her suitcase from Justice's hand, and then stood awkwardly, wondering exactly where to put it. He slung the straps of a backpack off his shoulders and tossed it onto the bed.

"Doesn't take long to warm up in here." He pulled off his toque and mitts and shrugged out of his coat. The jacket he hung next to hers, while the rest he clamped to a small clothesline hanging over the stove. Snow dripped off, sizzling on the flat metal surface.

He scrubbed his hands through his hair, causing the sweat-dampened strands to stick up in all directions. The whiskers of his beard glinted with water droplets as the frost that had formed on them melted. Attraction tugged deep in Charlotte's belly. She gripped her suitcase tighter.

"Hungry?" He strode to the table, now piled with supplies. "I brought chili for tonight."

Her stomach growled in ferocious agreement, and he shot her a grin. "I guess I am," she said. Her cheeks flushed, and not only from the heat filling the cabin with coziness.

"Slide your suitcase under the bed." He pulled a metal pot out from behind one of the patchwork curtains hiding the shelves under the counter. Popping the lid off a plastic container he rummaged out of a bin, he dumped the chili, still frozen in a solid block, into the saucepan. Adding a small glug of water from one of the jugs they'd brought, he clanked on the lid and placed it on the stove top. "We'll get settled while this heats up."

In the dark, the two large windows overlooking the deck were obsidian mirrors, reflecting the interior in wavy, shimmery images. The sense of isolation she'd experienced intensified. She wasn't afraid, simply was all too aware of how alone she and Justice were.

The thrill that shivered up her spine was tinged with anticipation at how they might spend this time together.

They moved about the cabin in quiet companionship, organizing gear, putting away food. Charlotte put fresh sheets on the bed, covering them with the old quilt. Justice left a cooler on the deck just outside the door, remarking as he did so that he didn't have to worry about bears at this time of year.

The chili bubbled in its pot and he stirred it. The rich, spicy scent caused Charlotte's stomach to clench in anticipation. She couldn't remember the last time she'd been so hungry.

He poured kibble into a bowl for Chaucer, who attacked it with glee. Then they sat next to each other on the sofa, bowls of the thick, chunky chili sprinkled with shredded cheese cupped in their hands. Charlotte went back for seconds, and cleaned the last teaspoon of juice from the bowl with a slice of bread and butter. Satiated, she leaned back and stretched out her legs.

"God, that was the best meal I've ever had."

Justice grunted softly in amusement. "You're welcome." He plucked her empty dish from her hands and strode to the kitchen, the floor creaking under his feet. "Coffee? Or a glass of wine?"

"Wine sounds lovely."

He uncorked a bottle with economic movements and poured the ruby liquid into a tumbler. "Don't have a proper glass."

"This is fine." She inhaled the bouquet, a full-bodied fruitiness with a hint of cinnamon. The first sip was velvet on her tongue. "Better than fine, in fact."

He rejoined her on the couch, the cushion dipping under his weight and causing her to rock toward him. Connected at shoulder, hip and thigh, she felt another curl of attraction. She'd been so exhausted the last few days that even thinking of the energy needed for sex had flattened her.

She wasn't feeling tired now.

CHAPTER TWENTY-THREE

Justice sipped his wine, hyper-aware of Charlotte's long, lush length stretched out next to him.

And excruciatingly aware of the bed only a few feet behind them.

He had no idea what time it was. One of the joys of roughing it was the freedom to ignore schedules. It was pitch black outside, they were warm and fed. What difference did it matter what a clock said? He could take her to bed now.

He drained his wine. "I should grab more wood for the night." The plywood box by the door was almost empty. "Back in a minute."

"Do you need a hand?"

He couldn't hide a grin at the reluctance in her voice. "Nah. I got it." Shoving his feet into his boots, he decided not to bother with a coat over his heavy flannel shirt. Thoughts of Charlotte would keep him warm. "Come on, dog."

Chaucer ignored him, barely flicking a brow as he lay on his side next to the stove.

"Fine," Justice said, "but you better not ask to go out later."

Firewood was stored under the deck. He loaded an armful, stacking it to his chin, and picked his way carefully up the snow-covered steps. Once this last chore was done he could concentrate on one thing.

Charlotte.

He shouldered his way into the cabin. She had moved from the couch and was searching in the pockets of her parka. He dumped the wood into the bin, bits of bark and sawdust clinging to his sleeves. As he brushed them off he turned toward her, and caught her peering at the screen of her cell phone.

"There's no service," he told her.

"I can see that." She held the phone over her head, as if raising it those few inches would help. "I was hoping..."

He reached her in three quick strides and plucked the device from her hand.

"Hey!"

"I said off-grid, and I mean it."

She stretched on her toes and gripped his forearm, tugging. "Give it back."

He resisted easily, lifting his arm even further, his knuckles scraping the low floor of the loft above. "Why? It's useless."

"It's mine." Determined to rescue her phone, she bounced up and down, her body pressing against his as she clutched at his arm.

"Not until we get back to town." Even covered by her thick sweater, he was enjoyably aware of the softness of her breasts as she strained upward, practically climbing his torso. His cock swelled.

"I'll put it away." Her face was so near her breath fanned his beard. Flecks of bronze flickered in her deep brown eyes, reflected in the steady glow of the kerosene lamps.

He snaked his free arm around her waist and yanked her closer. Her body stilled, lids drooping lazily over her eyes. Her hips rotated in a slow, sensuous twist.

Obviously, he wasn't the only one who'd noticed his

arousal.

He dropped the phone into her parka pocket and wrapped his hand into the curls dangling down her back. "When's the last time you were out of cell service?" He eased her head back, revealing the long line of her neck. He leaned in, revelling in her scent—woman sweat, vanilla, a hint of something flowery.

"Never?" Her voice was breathless. Her hands clutched at his shirt, clutching handfuls of fabric and a few chest hairs.

He didn't pull away, instead nuzzling the silky, fragrant skin behind her ear. "Think you'll survive?"

"I don't know." She sucked in a breath as he scraped his teeth on the tender column of her neck, her breasts lifting.

"Maybe I should distract you." The wide, loose collar of her sweater bared the hollow at the base of her throat and he planted an open-mouthed kiss in that delectable spot, felt the thunder of her pulse under his lips.

Her only answer was a low moan. She clung to him, her body pulsated with heat.

He took that as a yes.

****

Maybe it was the release from stress. Maybe it was the comforting food and the delicious wine. Whatever it was, Charlotte felt herself drifting, lost in Justice's arms, seduced by his mouth on her skin.

The cabin was so silent she could hear every whisper of clothing as their bodies brushed against each other. Every panting breath. Every liquid meeting of lips on lips. Without the noise that permeated every moment of life in the city, in a house powered by electricity and gas, every sound of their joining was enhanced, overwhelming, entrancing.

Goosebumps chased themselves over her ribs and back when Justice skinned off her sweater. The loose yoga pants she wore puddled at her feet. Not to be outdone, she unbuttoned his plaid shirt, worked her hands under the plain T-shirt he wore beneath, savoured the smooth, hard plane of his back as she lifted it off. The button of his jeans was cold against her belly. She wasted no time stripping them away.

"You're cold." Justice's hands cupped her breasts, thumbs teasing their aching points.

"I don't feel it." And she didn't. The heat rising inside her was more than enough to combat the slight chill the wood stove hadn't been able to erase.

"Come." He pulled back the ancient quilt covering the bed. "Get in."

The sheets were so cold they felt damp. She gasped. An instant later Justice's long, large body covered her. Any slight discomfort was forgotten.

He touched her with the confidence of knowledge, but the wonder of newness, exploring the underside of her breasts, the fragile skin where her thigh joined her torso. Her body hummed with pleasure, letting him take and taste and tempt as he would. She felt drugged, dreamy.

The wanting built, until his tender touches were not enough. She moved restlessly beneath him, her hands clutching his shoulders, skimming through his tousled hair.

"I want..." she moaned.

"What?" He breathed the word against her belly. "Tell me."

"Your mouth." Her own was so dry with desire she could barely speak. "On me."

"Here?" He nipped her hipbone.

She tossed her head, speechless.

"Or here?" The other hip.

"Justice..."

"Or here?" And his mouth covered her sex.

She arched her back, her knees dropping to the side, a small shriek escaping. His tongue lapped at her, a long, luxurious savouring that ending with a flick that almost catapulted her from the mattress. He wound his arms under her thighs, spreading her with his shoulders, gripped her hips to keep her in place.

And proceeded to set her sobbing and writhing, the pleasure a delicious pain. She never wanted him to stop. Wanted him to bring her quickly to a crystal climax.

Wanted.

Wanted.

****

Justice was lost in Charlotte's panting breaths, her deep-throated cries. Her thighs wrapped tight around him, tensing and relaxing as he brought her to peak, allowed her to rest. His cock throbbed and jumped, eager for its turn.

He wasn't ready for it to end. Never wanted this wanting to end.

She bucked her hips, hands clamped to his skull, body arched and stiff. A scream burst from her mouth and she collapsed onto the bed, breasts heaving, arms and legs sprawled slack and loose.

He crawled up and dropped beside her, ignoring his body's own demand for release. Her taste was in his mouth, her scent in his nose. Propping his head on his hand, elbow bent, he studied her face. Eyes closed, her lashes fluttered against flushed cheeks. The rosiness extended over her jaw, down her neck, to the tops of her breasts. The pulse in her neck pounded in rapid beats, but even as he watched, it slowed to a more normal rhythm.

He laid a palm on her stomach, swept it up between her breasts to her throat, over her shoulder, down again. She murmured, curling into his chest, giving him access to her long, slender back, the white globes of her ass. His erection pressed between them. He hissed, determined to give her a few moments more to recover. When he took her, he wanted her ready to revel in the sensation as he would, share in their joining.

And then she snored.

At first he thought it was the dog. But when the soft sound vibrated again he drew back, tucking his chin down to get a better view. Her cheek rested on one palm, the other hand a fist tucked under her jaw. Another snore— lady-like but still a snore—ruffled out.

His balls clenched in disappointment, even as he smiled and shook his head. He briefly considered kissing her awake, but remembered the exhaustion dragging in her eyes, even before the efforts of making camp. As it was...

He worked at the quilt with his feet, dragging it close enough to grab without disturbing her. She whimpered softly, a frown creasing the fine skin between her brows, but she settled down once he had the blanket tucked around her shoulders.

He'd brought her to the cabin so she could rest. It was just his bad luck she'd decided to take his advice so soon.

****

The cold woke Charlotte up. It nipped at her nose, prickled across her shoulders. Without opening her eyes, she wriggled deeper into the blankets, huddling them up to her ears. She tucked her knees to her chest and her butt encountered a large, warm object.

Justice.

The sex last night had been—well, awesome came to mind. The flood of hormones and endorphins and whatever else it was that coursed through her had relaxed her better than a month-long vacation. She should probably thank Justice for—

Her eyes popped open. Faint moonlight outlined the windows, the edge of the stove, the couch.

Oh my God, she thought. I fell asleep. Before Justice had a chance to...

She suppressed an embarrassed giggle. Moving carefully to avoid creating drafts, she shifted to her other side.

He lay on his back, chest bare, the quilt bunched around his waist. One arm was crooked under his head, the other stretched out toward the wall. Shadows filled the hollows of his eyes, fell beside his long, broken nose. His torso rose in slow, even movements.

A low whine had her looking over her shoulder. Chaucer sat upright on his bed by the stove, eyes reflecting the moonshine. At the turn of her head, he rose and padded to the door.

"Do you need to go out, boy?" she whispered, realizing at the same moment the dog wasn't the only one who needed a bathroom break. The thought of braving the winter stillness to trudge to the outhouse was daunting. And it wasn't only the cold she worried about. Who knew what creatures might be roaming around the cabin? Seeing a moose from the safety of a truck cab was one thing. Coming face to face with one on her way to the bathroom was a whole different story.

It was quickly apparent she had little choice in the matter. Justice murmured unintelligibly as she slipped out of the warm comfort of the bed. Her nipples tightened in the chill. Buck-naked, she scouted the cabin, finally finding her yoga pants and sweater discarded on the floor. Her coat and boots were easier to locate.

As she searched, Chaucer's whines grew increasingly urgent. Worried he'd wake Justice, she unlatched the door. He shot into the gloom. She wished she had a leash for him. He could have stood watch outside the outhouse door.

The snow was the most marvellous blue, an unearthly colour gleaming under the almost full moon hanging above. She followed the trail Justice had cleared earlier, careful where she placed her feet, searching for the smoothest path.

The night was quiet, but not silent. A breeze hummed through the thick spruce boughs, and the birches chattered to each other. She debated whether to shut the door while she relieved herself. In the end she left it open. She'd rather see what was coming than protect her privacy. After all—who was there to see?

Chaucer was waiting at the door when she returned. The air inside the cabin, while not exactly warm, was definitely cozier than outside. She wondered whether she should put more wood on the fire. With her lack of experience, she'd probably put the damn thing out altogether, so decided to leave well enough alone.

Justice lay in the exact same position as when she'd left. She'd already noticed, in the nights they'd spent together, how little he moved when he slept.

Her skin was chilled, despite the layers she'd worn for the quick trip, and her fingers were icy. Stripping out of her clothes quickly, she wormed her way back under the covers, shivering. Justice radiated heat like a furnace and she longed to cuddle next to him, but that would surely wake him.

Maybe if she made it worth his while...?

She warmed her hands in her armpits to ward off the chill. Carefully walking her fingers over the mattress, she reached his hip. When he didn't stir at her first tentative touch, she wriggled closer and placed a gentle hand on his cock.

Squeezing lightly, she felt it thicken in her palm. She brushed her thumb over the tip. Justice's even breathing hitched and his hips jerked. His brow tightened over still closed eyes. She waited, without releasing him, until he settled, and stroked him, cupping his balls, revelling in her power as his arousal grew hotter, harder, in her grip.

With a sudden start he gasped, back arching off the bed, eyes flying open. For a second confusion filled their depths, until he focused on her face. "Charlotte..."

"I hope you don't mind I woke you." She firmed her grip on his shaft, letting her palm slide over the flared head, down again. "I realized I owe you something."

"No, you don't." His lips pulled back in a fierce grimace. "But, God, don't stop."

"I won't." She slid down, her breasts rasped by the wiry hairs of his thighs, and bent joyfully to work off her debt.

CHAPTER TWENTY-FOUR

Pampering was all very well and good, thought Charlotte. Until it started to drive you crazy.

Which in her world was about thirty-six hours.

It was early afternoon of their third day at the cabin. Justice had instructed her to relax while he took Chaucer to check on his truck. There'd been a light snowfall overnight, and he wanted to make sure all was okay.

She tried to read. In preparation for this time-out, she'd loaded her e-reader with the newest release from one of her favourite authors. It had been too long since she'd had the chance to read simply for fun. But after spending yesterday reading, napping, eating and reading some more, she was no longer in the mood.

Her fingers twitched with the need to get online, check her email, find out what was happening in the world. She'd even snuck a peek at her phone this morning while Justice was out getting firewood, in the unreasonable belief that maybe now there would be service. How pathetic was that?

She propped her feet up on the battered chest that served as a coffee table and frowned in concentration at her e-reader. When Justice got back, she'd suggest they go for a walk. Maybe she was just stir-crazy from not leaving the cabin.

Scant minutes later she tossed the device onto the cushion beside her and growled in frustration. She'd read the same page five times and not taken in a word. It was a waste of time—and ruining what she was sure was a very good book—trying to read in the state of mind she was in.

What if the Selection Committee had changed the date of her interview? What if Natasha hadn't been able to book her flights? She felt increasingly out of control, out of touch. Maybe she should try to talk Justice into going home. If they started packing up as soon as he returned, they could be back in town by early evening.

Her heart thudded uncomfortably in her chest and sweat sprang up on her palms. Was this what a panic attack felt like?

"Oh, for God's sake." She sprang off the couch and snatched her parka from the hook. "I need air." Anything was better than sitting alone with her thoughts.

Her snowshoes were outside, propped next to the door. She carried them down the stairs, plopped them into the top layer of soft, powdery snow, and bent to strap them on.

The tracks left by Justice were clear and obvious. Large depressions off to the side must be Chaucer's bounding imprint. She set off, arms swinging, following their trail.

Her rapidly fluttering pulse settled into a steady rhythm and the sense of incipient hysteria faded away. The sky was a piercing blue, the sun low but brilliant, and she had to squint against the diamond sharp glare bouncing from the snow. Digging in her pocket, she pulled out a pair of sunglasses and plunked them on her nose with relief. Her breath puffed out, streaming behind her in white mist.

She rounded a corner and saw the man and dog heading toward her. Stepping off the narrow path, she waited for them to reach her.

"I thought you were going to relax." Justice had a black toque pulled low over his ears, though the tall collar of his parka was unzipped enough to see the muscled column of his throat.

"If I sit on the couch one second longer I'll go completely insane." She bent down to pat Chaucer's head. "I needed to get out."

"Want to cross the lake? There's a waterfall on the far side."

She cocked a brow. "A waterfall? In winter?"

He shrugged. "I've never been at this time of year. It gives us somewhere to go."

The wide, flat expanse of the lake was just visible through the trees. It could have been a mountain meadow, for all the indication there was water below. Cold, black, deep water. Chills that had nothing to do with the brisk wind snaked down the back of her neck. "Is it safe? Is the ice thick enough?"

Justice started cutting a trail through the trees. "No worries. At this time of year, you could drive a truck on it and not go through."

She picked her way after him, half-reluctant, half-fascinated by the thought of standing on a sheet of ice, only a few frozen feet separating her from the frigid water. When he reached the lake's snow-swept space, he waited for her to catch up. They set off once again, side by side, Chaucer following at Justice's heels.

A muffled boom rumbled under Charlotte's feet. She turned to stone, arms outstretched, listening. "What the hell was that?"

"The ice settling." He held out his hand, encased in a thick nylon glove. She clutched it gratefully. "Nothing to worry about."

Ten minutes later, they were still safe on the surface. Despite the grumbling and groaning rising spookily through the snow and ice beneath her, she was beginning to relax. They stopped and turned to survey the way they had come.

Justice pointed at two mirror-bright reflections where the sun glinted off a pair of windows. "That'll be our cabin."

Our cabin. The simple pleasure that tugged at Charlotte's heart was quickly followed by a wrench of disappointment. He didn't mean her. He meant Max.

"Does he like it here? Max, I mean." They continued on, Justice directing their steps toward a narrow break in the trees.

"He loves it. When I told him we were going, he wanted to come along. He's never been here in the winter."

"Now I feel bad. You should have let him join us."

Justice hummphed deep in his chest. "Are you ready to explain to a nine-year old why his father is spending nights in the same bed as a woman not his mother? And I don't just mean sex. Would you be sleeping with me if he'd come along?"

"Ummmm..." A blush heated her already flushed-by-exercise cheeks and she lowered the zipper of her parka to let out some heat.

"Yeah, I thought so," he remarked drily.

They trudged along, the snowshoes making whispery swooshing sounds in the dry powder snow. The raucous curse of a raven echoed through the wild silence.

"Did you come out as a family? You and Max and your ex?" The question blurted out before she could stop it. She knew a bit about the situation, especially after learning of Tiffani's nocturnal visit to Justice a few weeks ago.

But she wanted to know more.

"I didn't buy the cabin until after the divorce."

"I see." She caught the edge of one snowshoe against the other and staggered, catching herself before she landed on her ass. "Would you tell me—never mind." She waved one mittened hand. "None of my business."

"What?"

"I'm just—curious. About you and Tiffani. How you got together. Why you separated." She couldn't see his eyes behind the dark lenses protecting them, but his shoulders hunched uncomfortably. "And I have no right to ask. So just forget about it."

****

Under the dread that curdled in his stomach at the thought of talking about his marriage, a small warm glow of happiness kindled. Charlotte wouldn't be asking, Justice thought, if it didn't matter to her. If *he* didn't matter to her.

He focused on the pristine snow ahead, felt the soft give of the powder beneath the metal web of his snowshoe. Took a deep breath, and dove in.

"You asked me once where I got the scar by my eye."

Her lips pinched at the corners and he sensed her confusion. "Yes. You said it was a hockey injury."

"Yeah, well, I was a player when I got it, but it didn't happen at a rink." They neared the far side of the lake. A tree had fallen from the shore, its top buried beneath the snow, its wide, thick trunk rising out of the white depths at a shallow angle. He led Charlotte toward it. Brushing off a thin coating of snow, he gestured her to sit and took his place beside her.

"We travelled a lot. All junior clubs do. We had this amazing bus, with tables and bunks and these great reclining seats." The memories of those days were etched so deep they were a part of his very soul. "Most of our travelling was at night. We'd play a game in one town, hit the showers, get on the bus, and wake up in another town, ready for the next game."

Charlotte sat beside him, her gaze off into the distance. Yet he could sense the intensity of her interest. Her shoulder rubbed against his and she leaned into him slightly, as if in encouragement.

"They said afterwards it must have been a patch of ice. I was sleeping in my seat. I remember a horrendous screeching and being flung around the bus. The floor was where the ceiling should be, guys were shouting and screaming." He rolled his shoulders to shake off the weight of remembrance. "I could feel the blood running down my face, getting into my eyes. My shoulder was dislocated—I think I tried to grab hold of something as we were rolling over and over—and I cracked a couple ribs."

Her focus switched to him. He kept his head down, studying the tips of his snowshoes, but he could feel her stare. "You must have been terrified."

"Not at first." He'd read about it, later. Read how survivors of traumatic events described the feeling of being out of their body, of watching as if it was happening to someone else. He knew exactly what they were talking about. "After, once I realized how bad it was, yeah."

"How old were you?"

"Nineteen. I'd been drafted to the NHL the year before, but most players—unless they're superstars—stick with a junior team for another year before moving up." He'd signed his contract a week earlier, and plans had been made for him to attend big-league training camp in August. "It was March, our last road-trip of the regular season. Our team was one win away from making the playoffs."

"I can't imagine what it was like."

An image of the neat and tidy scar slicing the skin of Charlotte's belly rose in his mind. She may not have been in an accident, but she'd suffered in some way. He resolved to find out before they headed back into town.

She was waiting patiently for him to continue. He sucked in a breath of sharp, serrated air, let it out slowly. "It seemed to take forever before the bus stopped moving. Turns out we'd slid down a steep embankment." He pulled off his glove and scooped a handful of snow from between his feet. It was so light and fluffy it refused to form a ball, drifting like sugar from his palm when he opened his fingers. "When everything stopped shaking and shrieking and roaring, the coaches tried to keep things cool, but it was mess. One guy had a broken leg, another a busted ankle. Pretty much everyone was bleeding from cuts and scrapes."

She leaned her head on his shoulder and rested her hand on his thigh. Her silent compassion bolstered his flagging courage.

"My best buddy on the team was Jake Newton. He'd been sleeping in the seat beside me. I looked for him, couldn't see him." Other than the cops who showed up at the accident scene, he didn't think he'd ever told this story to anyone. Not even Tiffani. All these years later, it was still raw. "The windows were all smashed to shit. Jake got tossed out somehow. We found him, about halfway up the slope." He swallowed, hard. "He didn't make it."

"Oh, Justice." She rubbed her cheek against him and hugged his arm to her body. "I'm so sorry."

Too fidgety to tell the rest of the story sitting down, he pushed off the log, lifting Charlotte with him. "Afterwards, the team tried to pull together, but it was too much. We didn't make the playoffs, and to be honest I was relieved when it was over. I needed to get away from the rink, the memories."

He led her along the shore toward what he knew was the creek mouth, even though it, too, was camouflaged under ice and snow. "I went to NHL camp that summer, but my heart just wasn't in it. Then Dad got hurt, and it made the decision easy. So I came home."

"What a horrible few months for you." Charlotte clomped along beside him a few steps, and then added, "But I'm confused. Where do Tiffani and Max come into this?"

Telling her about the accident had been painful. Admitting how naive he'd been would be humiliating. He forced out the rest.

"Tiffani was Jake's girlfriend. About a month after I came home, she had Max." He'd gone to see her and the baby out of a sense of duty to Jake's memory, never guessing how his first sight of that tiny, fragile, fatherless infant would change his life. What did they say about hell? The road was paved with good intentions? "It seemed like the right thing to do—marry the mother of my best friend's son. To take care of them, for him."

****

Justice strode ahead of Charlotte, allowing her a view of his stiffly held back. His declaration had stunned her, stopping her in her tracks.

Max was not his son. Biologically, at least.

Shaking off her astonishment, she hustled after him, searching for the right thing to say. The potential pitfalls were many.

She still hadn't thought of anything by the time they reached the creek mouth. Rotting patches of damp showed through the mounds of white snaking back into the trees.

"We'll have to work our way along the bank," Justice said. "Water's still flowing under the ice. It won't be stable."

Along the bank meant ducking under low hanging branches and stumbling over hidden obstacles. It took all of her attention to simply stay on her feet. A cascade of snow dislodged from the thin limbs of a willow showered over her head, down her neck. She wondered grimly whether Justice was hoping to distract her from the conversation. Well, good luck with that.

She did forget her determination to question him further for a short time when she finally came face to face with the waterfall.

"Oh, my God," she said. "It's a wall of ice." The cliff rose two stories above her head, spread out about three metres wide. A rough, ridged sheet covered the whole of it, trickling water visible behind the opaque glaze. "It's beautiful." Jagged, lacy edges rimmed the narrow pool at the base of the cliff. The dampness in the air brushed her cheeks, making it seem colder in this little pocket of beauty than out in the open.

Justice stood restlessly beside her, frowning at the waterfall, hands thrust deep in his pockets. She bit her lip, certain no matter what she said would be wrong, but equally certain their little chat couldn't end quite yet.

"You love him." That seemed safe enough. She was wrong.

Justice exploded, arms shooting out from his sides, bearded chin raised to the sky. "Of course I love him. He's my son!" He stomped away, heavy footsteps muffled in the snow, turned about and stomped back. "He's mine." He glared at her, jaw jutting. "He doesn't know about his dad, and it kills me. Because he's Jake's, too."

Her mouth dropped open. She closed it with a snap.

"Max doesn't know about his real father?"

"I'm his real father, damn it. But no." He rubbed the heels of his gloved hands into his eye sockets. "It's never been the right time, according to Tiffani. I'm afraid the older he gets, the harder he'll take it."

She agreed with him, but could sympathize with Tiffani as well. How exactly did you start a conversation like that, especially with a child?

The fact that Max was not Justice's child by blood refused to settle, but buzzed around her brain like an enraged bee. "He looks like you." She caught the faint sound of disbelief in her voice and couldn't blame Justice for his slit-eyed look. She added hurriedly, "I believe you, but I never would have guessed."

"Jake and I were similar, at least superficially." He jerked one shoulder in a rough shrug. "I think that's one of the reasons Tiffani married me. She was pretending I was Jake. At first, things between us were okay. By the time they started to go south, Jake's son was my son. He was more than an obligation. He was...mine."

CHAPTER TWENTY-FIVE

Justice brought the heavy splitting axe up over his shoulder two-handed, and swung it down in a ferocious arc that cleaved the chunk of birch in half. He bent forward to retrieve a piece, a drop of sweat plunking from his nose onto the back of his hand as he placed it back on the block, ready to dissect it further.

He'd tripled the size of the firewood pile since they'd come back from the waterfall. Heated by his efforts, he'd shed his parka long ago. His damp t-shirt clung to his chest under his thick flannel shirt, and the muscles in his arms and back and thighs were starting to tremble. He realized dusk had lowered, the gleam of light falling from the windows glowing golden on the snow-dusted deck.

At least the exercise had accomplished its two-fold goal—to replace the wood he and Charlotte had used up, and settle him down after his uncomfortable confession.

Sinking the axe into the chopping block, he stacked the split pieces neatly onto the pile until only an armful remained. These he settled into the crook of one elbow and carried into the cabin.

The scent of baking potatoes and marinating steak caused his stomach to rumble. Charlotte looked up from the cutting board where she was slicing onions. Chaucer sat on his haunches next to her, prepared to send any escaping food to its doom. "Good timing. You're going to have to do the steak. I'm not much of a griller."

The load of wood crashed into the box, the sweet

smell of dead tree adding to the delicious scents filling the cabin. "No worries." He avoided her gaze, the cautious concern creasing her forehead making his skin feel tight.

Stripping off his shirts, he rummaged in his duffel bag for dry clothing. Before he pulled on another plain T, he snagged a towel from the hook near the stove and wiped the sweat from his chest, arms and face. He turned to Charlotte and caught her watching him, head tilted to one side.

"What?"

"Nothing," she said. A faint blush warmed her cheeks and she lowered her eyes to the mushroom now awaiting its dismemberment. "I just like watching you." She tossed him a quick glance from under her lashes. "Especially when you're half-naked."

Perhaps he was overly sensitive—damn it, he *knew* he was overly sensitive—regarding the circumstances surrounding his marriage, his fatherhood of Max. Thank God she seemed willing to go back to the way they'd been before his soul-baring announcement.

She continued to slice vegetables, her movements calm and unhurried. Yet vibes of awareness radiated off her. He paced toward her, and the vibrations amped up. Standing behind her, they were strong enough to raise the hairs on his forearms. In anticipation, in relief, in hope. Her hair was bundled in an attractively untidy knot above her neck. He blew gently, causing small, loose curls to dance.

She shivered, placed the knife carefully on the cutting board and angled her head. "The steak can marinate a little while longer," he murmured against her skin.

****

Justice was warm and solid at Charlotte's back. His arms circled her torso, folded underneath her breasts, lifting them, as he took tiny, tasting bites of her neck. She reached behind and pulled him tight to her, wiggling her butt into his groin.

"How many condoms did we bring?" His heated breath scorched her. Since that time in her entryway, he had insisted on using protection. His mention of contraception now, however, struck her with a new sensation of sorrow. Max was not his biological son. If their relationship ever reached that stage, surely he would want another child. And that was a gift she couldn't give him.

Her thought processes scattered as he cupped her breasts with his big, wide palms. Yet her tumbling thoughts distracted her from his caresses.

"Wait." She gasped as he pinched her nipples, sending a bolt of liquid heat straight to her womb. Her barren womb. "I can't..." She squeezed out of his embrace, stumbling over the dog laying supine, half under the table. Chaucer gave a disapproving woof, unnervingly similar to the grunt of startled surprise from his master.

"Come back here." The passion faded from his eyes when she shuffled further away. "What's wrong?"

"Nothing. I just think..." Her brain scrambled for a reason good enough to explain her change of heart. "You said you were starving. We should probably eat first."

Suspicion sharpened every line of his face. "I'm not that hungry," he said, mildly enough.

"Still. All that needs to be done is sauté the veggies and grill the steaks." She tried a seductive smile, was certain she failed miserably. "We can get back to playtime after."

He studied her a moment longer, and then exhaled strongly through his nose. Without a word, he moved to the stove and lifted the solid plate off the firebox, replacing it with a grill. He transferred the steaks to it, and the scent of barbequing meat sizzled into the air.

Charlotte lowered her tense shoulders. In equal silence, she plopped a pat of butter in a fry pan and set it to heat next to the steaks in preparation for the mushrooms and onions.

The strained atmosphere continued through the meal. Charlotte was miserably aware of ruining what should have been a romantic evening. Justice answered her tentative attempts at conversation politely but distantly, and ate the perfectly grilled steak and fluffy baked potatoes as if they were simply fuel, not something to be savoured.

After stacking the dishes in the plastic pan they used for washing, he returned to the table, sprawling low in his chair, one arm flung over the back. He sipped his wine without lifting his elbow off the scarred wooden surface. "So, you ready to tell me what that was about?"

She drained the last of her own wine in one gulp, the fruity, smoky Malbec heavy on her tongue. "I told you, nothing's wrong." Her smile was better this time. "I thought you might enjoy an appetizer, you could say. Before tonight's main course."

His snort held disbelief, but he didn't demand further explanations. "I need time to digest." A deck of cards and a crib board had been pushed to the edge of the table, up against the wall, to make room for their dinner. He unboxed the cards and began shuffling, fingers dexterous and quick. "How about poker?"

Wary of this unexpected acceptance of her feeble reasoning, Charlotte paused. "I don't know how to play. Not very well, anyway."

"Blackjack's easy. Max plays."

"Closest to twenty-one without going over, right?"

"Basically." He flipped them each one card face down, and then one card face up. "Aces are either one or eleven, whatever works best for your hand. Face cards are ten, all other cards face value." Charlotte had a five up, Justice a ten. "Check your bottom card."

She lifted the corner of the card, so old and worn the pattern on the back was barely visible. A three. "Now what?"

"You can stay, or ask for another card."

"Another, please." The queen of hearts flashed onto the table in front of her.

"If you're busted—over twenty-one—you have to say so."

"I'm not. But I don't want another card. I stay, right?"

Justice raised an eyebrow. "Right." He checked his bottom card again. "I stay, too. Show me what you've got."

She revealed her eighteen. He'd had a seven hidden. "So I win?"

"This round." He scooped up the cards they'd used and handed them to her. "Keep these. The winner keeps the cards used that round. Person with the most cards at the end wins."

"Loser does dishes?"

"Seems fair."

The room fell silent except for the swish of cards, quiet requests for cards or calls to stay, and the dog's breathy snoring from his bed by the stove. A few minutes later, Charlotte counted the thick stack of cards before her, delighted with her success. "No dishes for me, tonight."

Justice snorted. "Playing for chores is like betting with pennies." He took the cards from her hands and shuffled them into the rest of the deck. "Care to make it interesting?"

****

Charlotte worried her lip, cocked her head to the side. "What did you have in mind?"

"Truth or dare. Winner of each hand chooses."

Her mouth pursed and she eyed him through her lashes. "You would have been in trouble if we'd played those rules last time."

Justice knew he'd hooked her. The old adage about gamblers who are first allowed to win lose the most in the end was holding true. He hadn't dealt off the bottom or cheated in any way. He'd simply risked more than he should have—hitting at eighteen, staying at fifteen—and lost a few more hands than he would normally have done in the process. "So you in?"

She paused, nodded, and reached for the cards. "I'm dealing this time."

He handed her the deck, grinning. His good humour faded when he saw how slickly she worked the pack. "You said you didn't play cards."

"No." She arched the deck into a bridge, shuffling swiftly. "I said I didn't play poker very well. I used to play card games with my family all the time."

She dealt out the first four cards with confidence, leaving Justice with a total of eleven. "Hit me," he said. An eight turned up. "Stay."

"I'll take one." She dealt herself a seven. "Stay. What do you have?"

He turned over his nineteen. She smirked and flipped an eight and four to join her seven. "Nineteen. Tie to the dealer, right?"

"Right." He shoved his cards toward her. "Truth or dare?"

"Truth." She tapped her fingertip on her chin. "I'll be nice. Your favourite book."

"*To Kill a Mockingbird*."

She nodded. "Good choice."

They played another hand, and Justice won. He wasn't wasting his turn on something she would willingly tell him. "What was the most embarrassing thing that happened to you in high school?"

Her eyes widened, the flicker of the kerosene lantern blazing in their depths. "Hey! I asked you an easy one."

He shrugged. "Not my fault you missed an opportunity."

She hunched over the cards, shuffling furiously. "The *most* embarrassing?"

He didn't answer, simply folded his arms across his chest and waited.

"Fine." She puffed out a drift of air that lifted her bangs off her forehead. "I was at a pool party. I dove off the diving board, got out of the pool and went back on the board to dive again—without noticing my bathing suit had fallen down and one boob was hanging out."

He was careful not to laugh out loud, but couldn't stop a small snort from escaping.

She glared at him. "I was humiliated. It happened the week before yearbooks were handed out. Everyone wrote about it when they signed mine."

She dealt another hand. His bottom card was the nine of spades. His face-up card, the two of clubs. He tapped the table. "Hit."

And the jack of diamonds flopped in front of him.

"There's your jack." Charlotte smiled at him. "Too bad Max wasn't here. But did it do you any good?"

He flipped over the nine and watched her jaw drop.

"Twenty-one." She glanced at the five of hearts, face up in front of her. "Now what?" she asked.

"Now you have to get twenty-one. Or I win." And then it would be time to increase the stakes.

****

Charlotte snuck a peak at her bottom card. A ten. Her heart beat in a rapid tattoo, jumping and trembling as if more was on the line than a silly game.

"Looking at it won't change it." Humour lightened the blue of Justice's eyes to the shade of sun through ice.

"Fine." She flipped a card smartly off the pile in her hand.

Another five.

"Now what?" Justice's foot nudged her knee under the table. "Play or stay."

With no other choice, she revealed the next card.

A two.

Justice reached over and uncovered her hole card. "Twenty-two. I could see on your face as soon as you went bust."

"Quit gloating." Her pout was only half in jest. "I've already told you my most embarrassing secret. How bad can it get?"

"I could dare you to play the next hand stark naked."

She narrowed her eyes. "You wouldn't."

"You're right." He let his gaze roam over her, that disturbing not-smile teasing his lips. "Too distracting. No, I've got a different sort of dare for you."

Her blood pulsed light and quick, throbbing in her fingertips. She waited in wary impatience.

"I dare you to tell me the truth about your scar."

Her ribs contracted, squeezing her lungs, a tingling sensation suffusing her skin. "My scar?"

"And I don't mean the tiny one on your elbow."

She'd forgotten all about that one—the remnants of learning how to ride a bike. That he'd even noticed it bothered her a little. To have every inch of her body known so intimately...

"A bet's a bet, Charlotte." He crooked a finger. "Spill."

She swallowed, searching for moisture in a mouth gone arid. The memory of Richard's reaction to the very same story brought bile to the back of her throat. She dug her nails into the rough wood of the table as vertigo swayed through her.

"You're starting to worry me." He shoved his chair back and reached a long arm to the counter behind him, snagging a half empty bottle of wine. He filled a glass and nudged it toward her. "Drink. But don't think you're getting out of this. Now I really need to know what's going on."

She gulped the rich liquid, its tart crispness biting back the dryness of her mouth. "It's not something I think about often." Or at least, she hadn't, until the last couple years.

"It obviously still bothers you."

"No poker face, hey?" She twitched a small smile in his direction. "The scar doesn't bother me. But the reason for it does. If I let it."

He leaned forward and cupped her chin in his broad palm. She closed her eyes for a moment, savouring the warmth of his touch. "The scar doesn't bother me, either." Her eyes opened at his quiet declaration. "You are beautiful. Every inch of you."

Tears burned and she blinked rapidly, denying them release. "Thank you."

"I need to know, Charlotte." His thumb traced her cheekbone while his eyes bored into hers. "It's part of you. I need to know *you*."

She couldn't look away. Every molecule in her body yearned for him. Every synapse in her brain screamed she should run. Yet he had had the courage to give her the truth. Recalling his anguish and pain as he told her about losing his best friend and his well-meant but disastrous decision to marry Tiffani, she squared her shoulders. If he could do it, she could. She owed him the same honesty.

"I was sixteen." She drew his hand from her face, lowered it to the table. As she talked, she stroked the hard bones of his knuckles with her fingertips, concentrating on the supple feel of his skin, tracking the veins and tendons leading to his wrist. "I hadn't had my period, yet I started to suffer cramping and discomfort every few weeks. I thought I'd start menstruating soon, but all that happened was the pain grew worse. It got so bad my mother took me to the doctor." Her voice trembled. Justice remained silent, but turned his palms over and grasped her hands. She clutched them, discovering strength in the simple touch. "They discovered a tumour in my uterus. Not cancer, thank God. But they needed to operate." She raised her eyes, met his steady gaze. "I had a hysterectomy." His expression told her he understood, yet she added, "I'm barren, Justice. I'll never have a child."

CHAPTER TWENTY-SIX

Snow swooped off the roof, cascading in ghostly white past the window at Justice's left. Charlotte sat next to him, head bowed, as if awaiting sentencing. Her hands lay limp in his, cold and trembling, her cheeks so pale the curl of hair brushing against it was ebony in comparison.

He'd wanted to know the truth. He hadn't wanted to crush her with the telling.

He pushed her wine toward her. "Drink. You look like you're going to pass out."

She cradled the glass in her palms, staring down at it, avoiding his gaze.

He had no idea what to say. *I'm sorry* seemed ridiculously inadequate. *It doesn't matter* was hideously incorrect. *It doesn't change how I feel about you* was an outright a lie.

It *did* change how he felt. He just wasn't sure exactly how.

"Thank you for telling me." That at least was the simple truth.

She hunched one shoulder, still refusing to look at him. "I couldn't welsh on a bet, could I?" Her nonchalant tone was betrayed by a slight quaver. She cleared her throat. "Shall we play another hand?"

"I think that's enough gambling for tonight." He gathered the deck, slipped it into the box and tossed it next to the crib board. "I'll start clearing up."

"I can help."

"I lost the round, remember? It's up to me."

Charlotte curled up on the couch as he made short work of tidying the kitchen. She appeared to be engrossed in a book on her e-reader, but as he couldn't tell if she was turning pages or not, he wasn't really sure. A hint of colour had returned to her cheeks, yet he could still sense tension in the way she held her head, her jerky movements as she repositioned herself, as if unable to get truly comfortable. Chaucer seemed concerned about her, too. He sat at her feet and dropped his head into her lap with a windy sigh. She gave the dog an abstract smile and toyed with his ears.

The playful sexuality they'd shared when he'd come in from chopping wood now seemed unbearably innocent. She obviously did a good job of forgetting her trauma, must have learned to live with it. Until he'd forced her to retell the story.

He felt like a goddamn jerk. Why had it mattered so much? He wished now he'd never asked. She would have told him in her own time.

Or would she have? After all, she was dead set on leaving. Just look at the way she'd focused on writing her book, to the exclusion of her health, her well-being.

Of him.

He tossed the towel on the counter and started putting away the dishes. He understood now why she hadn't panicked the time they hadn't used a condom. She'd said she was on the pill—

"You're not on contraception, are you?" His voice echoed, overly loud in the quiet of the cabin. She flinched. He moderated his tone. "You told me you were."

She lifted her chin. "A white lie. The outcome is the same."

He had an overwhelming urge to gather her into his

arms, cuddle her on his lap, and simply hold her. Comfort her without words, tell her with his body he still wanted her. But something held him back. She sat on the couch, just a few feet away, and yet it was as if she was separated from him by a glass dome.

There had to be a way to release her from that isolation, without shattering her fragile calm further. He would just have to figure it out.

****

Charlotte's phone came alive about half an hour away from town, vibrating furiously. "Service! Finally." She bent over the display and tapped to read her emails.

The last days at the cabin had been—odd. She wanted to believe she was mistaken, but she couldn't avoid the feeling Justice was treating her differently.

He hadn't been rude, or cold. He certainly hadn't shunned her as Richard had done after he'd learned of her infertility. If anything, Justice had been kinder, gentler, his lovemaking tender and sweet.

As if he'd been saying goodbye.

She choked down the panic that thought engendered, fully conscious of the irony of the situation. Here she was, intending to leave him in a few weeks. And yet she was thrown into turmoil that he might be the one to leave her first.

She scrolled through her messages and saw nothing urgent regarding her interview in Toronto at the end of the week. Her flight itinerary had been forwarded to her from her admin—damn it, she'd have to take the red-eye from Vancouver—and a hotel confirmation email had been sent as well. She should have been relieved. Instead, the faint nausea she'd carried inside for the last few days deepened.

"Did the world keep revolving without you?" Justice's

deep tone held more than a hint of friendly sarcasm.

"Barely." She tried to match his lightness. "One more day, though, and poof." She made an explosive movement with her hands. "Hell in a hand basket." She wondered if she should mention she was heading out of town for a few days. Wondered if he'd care. She opened her mouth to tell him, but he spoke first.

"I hope you enjoyed it. The time away, I mean." He sounded tentative, shy, almost.

"I did." Even with the tensions of the last half of the holiday, unplugging from the world had been the right thing to do. "I feel better than I have in a long time. Thank you."

"You're welcome."

The moment to tell him about Toronto passed. By the time he dropped her off at home, her impression that more than a vacation was ending had grown to such proportions that she had to bite her tongue to keep from asking when she would see him again.

He carried her luggage to the door. She unlocked it and he placed it just inside. "Thanks again. For sharing your cabin with me."

"No worries." He hesitated an instant, and then leaned forward to brush his lips against hers. His kiss was warm and soft and tears welled up behind her closed eyelids. She blinked them away. "See you," he said, and turned to pace down the path back to his truck. Through the windshield she watched Chaucer clamber over the seat to take her place on the passenger side.

"Goodbye," she whispered, loneliness bitter in her mouth.

****

"Hey, Dad." Max sat at Tiffani's kitchen table,

kicking the rungs of his chair with his heels in a monotonous rhythm, staring morosely at a sheet of paper.

"Hey, bud." After leaving Charlotte, Justice had headed home to unload the truck and settle Chaucer, and then come to see Max. Faint guilt tugged at him for the time he'd spent away. "Homework?" He leaned over his son's slumped shoulders, resting one hand on the back of his slender, vulnerable neck. His skin was warm, slightly damp.

"Math. I hate it."

"Long division. Not my strong suit, either. But maybe I can help anyway."

Tiffani had taken advantage of his visit to go grocery shopping. One of Max's favourite programs was paused on the TV, waiting for him to finish his school work.

"I know what to do. I just hate it." He chewed the end of his pencil, before carefully finishing one of the equations. Eyes still on the paper, he asked, "Was the cabin okay?"

"Just fine. Maybe I'll take you on Spring Break."

His head lifted at that. "That would be cool." His smile dimmed and a thoughtful frown drew his brows down. "Did Ms. Girardet like it?"

"I think so." Here was an opening he hadn't thought he'd get so easily. Justice hadn't dated anyone seriously since breaking up with Tiffani, and was still leery about how Max might react. "Maybe the three of us could all go out together."

"I guess." One scrawny shoulder pulled up in a careless shrug. He concentrated on another equation.

Justice sat silently, letting him finish, before asking diffidently, "What do you think of Charlotte? Professor Girardet?"

Another shrug. "I don't know. I've only seen her a couple of times."

He was right. They had spent very little time together. Justice would have to fix that, especially if his campaign to keep Charlotte in Prince George was successful.

She had said nothing about her book while they were at the cabin. He knew she'd pinned all her hopes on it to get a tenure-track position. How did the process work? he wondered. How soon would she find out?

Maybe she hadn't mentioned it because her prospects didn't look good, despite her earlier optimism.

He clamped down on the faint glow warming his chest. What a jerk he was, hoping she didn't get what she'd worked so hard to achieve. Besides, just because one opportunity didn't pan out didn't mean she'd give up her dreams. And as he well knew, she was only on a one-year contract. She couldn't stay at UNBC if there was no position for her.

She was leaving him, one way or another.

Unless he could convince her to stay. For personal reasons.

****

Elizabeth Paxton was typing away at a speed Justice envied when he arrived at work the next afternoon.

"Hey." He hung his parka on the coat rack and tossed his lunch onto the desk he shared with Brent Parvat. The door to Nielson's office was shut.

"Hey." She smiled vaguely in his direction. "Just about done."

"No hurry." He powered up the computer and logged into the shift report. "Nielson in?"

"Late lunch with the President. Said he'd be back around two."

Justice looked at his schedule and saw he'd be working with Parvat and McMorris for the next four days. "Anything doing?"

"One sec." Her fingers flew over the keyboard. "There." The printer in the corner started to churn. "Things have been pretty quiet the last few days, what with it being Reading Week and all. Friday was crazy, though. Cops all over the place, asking questions."

Justice paused, cursing silently. "How is she? The girl?" He couldn't believe he'd forgotten about the last attack. Being off the grid with Charlotte had pushed everything else out.

"She's recovering. Beaten pretty bad, but I heard she wasn't sexually assaulted, which is something. Not much, but still." Elizabeth shook her head, her jagged, cropped bangs swinging over her eyes. "I pray for her. I don't know how anyone ever gets over something like that."

Damn it. He'd meant to mention the attack to Charlotte at the end of their holiday, but the revelation of her infertility had pushed it from his mind. "Any leads?"

"Not that I know of. Nielson doesn't tell us squat, and I haven't heard anything on the news." She pulled on her jacket, wrapped a scarf around her neck, and pulled a flat cap from her pocket. "I gather there's been a lot of random speculation on social media, of course. People wondering if the other incidents on campus are linked to this attack."

"Was there any official communication?"

"Administration sent out another notice, of course, but what is there to say?" She headed for the door. "Being careful only gets you so far. And if the attacker has moved off campus, there's not much we can do."

Charlotte would have returned to her office this morning, so Justice figured she probably knew about the attack by now. He made a mental note to speak with her as soon as he could. Her guard was probably down after so many days without alarms. He needed to remind her to take her own safety seriously.

McMorris bustled in, a half-eaten Boston Crème donut in one hand, a take-out cup of coffee in the other. "Cooper. How's it going?" The scent of sugar and caffeine swirled around him like cologne.

"I'm good." Justice tucked his feet under his chair to allow the older man by. "Elizabeth was just filling me in."

"About the assault? Damn shame." He shoved the last bite of donut into his mouth, chewed happily, and washed it down with a slug of coffee.

Justice suppressed a twinge of disgust. The other guard's indifference irked him, and when taken with his avid report the day of the attack his entire attitude reeked.

Elizabeth waved goodbye as Parvat entered. The three men settled into their routines.

At the usual time, Justice volunteered to take the first walk around campus. He made the Administration Building one of his first stops. As no classes were in session, he had a good chance of finding Charlotte in her office.

The carpeted hallway muffled the sound of his steps. As he approached her office, he noted the closed door. Perhaps she was on the phone, or in a meeting.

"Hello, Justice." Natasha smiled up at him from her desk in the open area in front of the row of offices. "Have a good time off?"

"Yeah." One of the things he liked best about UNBC was the fact it was small enough that you could get to know other staff members, even though you worked in different departments. Of course, that also meant they often knew more about your personal life than you were comfortable with. But if he and Charlotte were going to spend more time together, he'd have to get past that awkwardness. "Is Professor Girardet around?"

Natasha's eyes glinted with wry humour, and he suspected she was laughing at his use of Charlotte's formal title. "She's already gone. Did you forget when she was leaving?"

"She left for home?" He'd expected her to put in long hours today, to make up for being out of touch for so long.

She tilted her head. "No, to the airport. Her flight leaves at four. She wanted an earlier departure, but it didn't work with the connections out of Vancouver."

His breath seized in surprise. "Flight?" He coughed to loosen the tightness in his chest. "Where?"

"Toronto. For her interview at York." Natasha's eyes narrowed. "Didn't she tell you?"

He had to force out the words. "Tell me what?"

"She's up for tenure-track. Her interview is Friday. If all goes well, she'll be a permanent professor at York by September."

CHAPTER TWENTY-SEVEN

The taxi dropped her at home just before nine o'clock Saturday night. She'd left Toronto at four in the morning Pacific Time, but her flight out of Vancouver had been delayed three hours due to blizzard conditions in Prince George. The weather had finally cleared enough to allow planes to land, yet the wind still whipped about her as she walked to her front door, tugging at her jacket and slashing loose strands of hair across her cheeks. Snowflakes dashed helter-skelter through the frigid air.

She dragged her carry-on over the threshold and closed out the bitterness of the black night. With a groan, she unwrapped her scarf and tossed it over the newel post. After a day full of airplanes and airports, all she wanted was a hot shower.

"When the hell were you going to tell me?"

She screamed and spun around, fists clenched at chest-height in reflexive defence. "Justice!" Her terror abated slightly as the looming figure stepped from the front room into the light of the hall. "What? How?" Her heart pounded, using her ribs as an anvil. She had to grip the banister to stay upright, her legs trembling.

"I still have your extra key," he said as he stalked toward her, his blue eyes slate-coloured with anger. "When, Charlotte? After you got the job? Or after you left?"

Right. She'd given him her spare key during the week he spent with her after the stalker. Relief stole the remaining strength from her legs and she collapsed onto the flight of steps leading to the second floor. Justice planted himself in front of her. She was eye-level with his hands, hanging by his hips, the fingers flexing and clenching fiercely.

She crossed her arms at her waist. "It was just an interview. I was going to tell you, if anything came of it."

"Didn't you think I might want to know you were leaving town for four days?"

Despite her guilt at sneaking away without telling him—or maybe because of it—a spark of defiance lit in her thundering chest. She lifted her head, tilting her neck back far enough to see his face. "And did you try and get in touch during those four days?" His face went blank. "No, you didn't. So I'm afraid I can't take your concern too seriously, when you couldn't be bothered to send one single text." She hated to admit, even to herself, how much she had wanted that one text, a single call.

"I was pissed off at you. Still am." He paced to the door and back, his long, powerful strides cramped in the small space. "Why didn't you tell me?"

"Why? Maybe I didn't think you'd care." Ever since she'd told him she was barren, she'd felt him pulling back, stepping away. Tonight's reaction was disconcerting. It was almost as if he still wanted to be with her.

"For fuck's sake." He scrubbed his hands through his beard, over his skull. "Of course I care. Why else would I take you to my cabin? Sleep with you? Find myself thinking of how long it is until I can see you next?" He crouched down, his knees giving off popping sounds like distant gunfire. "What about you, Charlotte? Do you care?"

****

Confusion clouded her dark brown eyes. White teeth worried her bottom lip. Justice waited, gut clenched, for her response.

"It's just that—" She broke off, dropped her gaze to her hands, twisted together in her lap. "You never said anything."

"Said anything about what?" He couldn't keep the exasperation out of his voice. Her shot about his lack of texts or calls while she was gone had hit home, but that didn't mean he was done being angry.

Her mouth thinned and she shifted on the stair. "About what I told you at the cabin. About the fact I can't have kids."

He'd known they'd have to talk about her revelation again someday, but he'd hoped to have more time. The last few days he'd been so pissed off he'd done his best to shove all thoughts of her away. Not that he'd been very successful. "What did you expect me to say?" he said slowly.

She jolted to her feet. "I don't know. But something!" Brushing past him, she headed for the kitchen. He followed more slowly, caution warring with frustration.

Leaning one shoulder against the fridge, he crossed his ankles and watched her fill a glass with water from the cooler. "Your operation. It was a long time ago."

"Yes." She sipped, holding the glass in two hands.

"You've had time to come to terms with it."

The tumbler clunked onto the counter hard enough for liquid to splash over the side. "You'd think so, wouldn't you." Her voice was so soft he almost couldn't hear her. She reached up and pulled her hair out of its loose bun. The thick strands fell forward, draping over her cheek, hiding her profile.

"Did you think it would change how I feel about you?" Not that he'd declared how he felt. *Love* was still a word he shied away from using.

"You wouldn't be the first."

He stopped himself from grunting in bafflement. "What? Who?"

She toyed with the glass, spinning it slowly with her long, slender fingers. "I told you I was engaged."

"Yes," he said, the skin on the back of his neck skittering.

"We'd been together a couple of years. Living together for one." She tucked her hair behind her ear and he saw the corners of her mouth curve up in a deprecating smile. "We'd talked about kids, the way you do. He said he didn't want any, that they didn't fit into his plans. Maybe I was a coward, but I took that as a sign. I didn't tell him about my infertility. I figured it didn't matter."

"He never asked about your scar?" Justice couldn't believe any man would have such a lack of curiosity about the woman he'd asked to marry him.

Her chin lifted. "Once. I simply said I'd had an operation. He didn't ask more, so I left it."

It wasn't hard to deduce where the story was going. He wished he could spare her, but he needed to know for certain.

"Once we were engaged, the subject of babies came up over and over again. Our friends, his parents. In fact, his parents never seemed to stop talking about grandchildren." She sipped her water again. "I noticed he deflected the questions, never saying yes or no. And I began to worry."

"So you told him." He moved to stand beside her. She stood square to the counter, her hands gripping the edge.

"I had to. The wedding was only a month away. And not telling him started to feel more and more like a lie."

"He broke it off." The bastard. But a part of Justice growled in possessive relief. If the jerk hadn't dumped her, they never would have met.

Her knuckles showed white. "Immediately. He stormed about, shouting and stamping, saying I was deceitful and manipulative, accusing me of trying to trap him."

"What an ass."

A choked laugh escaped her. She shot him a quick look. "I might not have tried to trap him, but I did deceive him, did lie to him. I should have told him sooner."

"Is that why you told me?"

She was silent. Her fingertip dipped into the moisture left on the granite by her glass, dragging it into random shapes. "I told you...because of Max."

It hit him like a check from behind, slamming him into the boards. She'd thought Max was his biological child. Now that she knew he wasn't...

"Did you think I would drop you like your jerk of an ex?" he asked slowly.

She seemed to shrink into herself. "Men want sons of their own. I know you love Max"—her voice was so small he had to strain to hear—"but you're young. Younger than me. What if you want more children? Children I—" She broke off.

He blinked back a whirl of vertigo. Charlotte had thought about having children—with him? He had been certain she was one foot out the door. And now this?

She brought her glass to the sink, dashed the dregs down the drain. Tension radiated from her stiff spine, her taut shoulders. He searched desperately for something to say, sensing she was but one wrong word away from total meltdown.

"Have dinner with me and Max on Friday." He saw her shudder and hurried on. "It occurs to me the three of us haven't spent that much time together. I'd like you to get to know him."

"Why?" She twisted to face him, leaning back against the sink and meeting his gaze with eyes that glistened with tightly held emotions.

He couldn't tell her he wanted to prove that a family was made by more than blood. "Just come for dinner, Charlotte."

She searched his face, for what, he didn't know. After long, painful moments, her breath whooshed out in a gusty sigh. "I'd like that."

"Good." He stepped forward, tucked a lock of hair behind her ear, let his fingers linger on the classic curve of her jaw. "I should be furious with you." Her eyes widened. "Comparing me to your deadbeat ex." Her lips parted, and he stopped her retort with the pad of his thumb. He felt the moist heat of her breath, the plumpness of her lip. "Don't do it again." He let his annoyance show in the grim tone of his voice.

She shook her head, mute. He leaned in, replaced his thumb with his mouth. Gentle at first, then harder, marking her, imprinting her with his taste. She might not realize it, but she'd given him reason to hope. Reason to hope for an elusive future, one amorphous and vague. But a future nonetheless.

****

Pandemonium. Charlotte was sure if she looked the word up in a dictionary, she would find a picture of this place.

She stared around her in bemused wonder. The greasy yet tantalizing scent of pizza and steamed hot dogs swirled through air vibrating with the clangs and clatters, bangs and beeps of arcade games. Children shrieked, giggled, shouted and wailed. The plastic chair in which she sat had been designed with small people in mind, and the table in front of her was sticky. With what, she didn't really want to know.

Justice threaded through the brightly coloured tables, looking even bigger than normal surrounded by pint-sized people and scaled-down furniture. He carried a flimsy cardboard box, above the edge of which poked long, golden fries. Max followed, tongue poking out the corner of his mouth in concentration, gripping two plastic cups beaded with moisture.

Charlotte smiled at Max. "The hunters return victorious."

"We didn't go hunting." He deposited the drinks safely on the table. "We just ordered at the counter."

"Max." Justice's tone was mild, but the warning was clear.

"Sorry," she said. "Just a joke. A bad one." She felt her smile slip, but refused to be intimidated by a nine-year old.

Unperturbed, Max slid onto the chair beside her and reached a hot dog out of the box. The bite he took precluded any further conversation. A smear of mustard blobbed onto the table in front of him. Justice handed him a napkin, then offered Charlotte the envelope of fries.

"Here you go," he said. "Are you sure you didn't want anything else?"

She shook her head. "This is a treat. I don't eat fries very often." She nibbled the end, savouring the saltiness.

"Ketchup?"

"Why hide the taste?"

Justice shook his head, eyes smiling. For a few minutes, they munched, their silent table surrounded by cacophony. Max finished first. "Can I go play laser tag?" He wiped his fingers off and pushed his glasses up his nose.

"Sure. Check back here when you're done." Justice watched him rush away, and then turned to Charlotte with a faint frown. "Maybe we should have gone somewhere else. I wanted him to be comfortable, but I should have thought of all the distractions."

"This is fine." It was sweet, the way his forehead furrowed in worry. Determined to make this evening work, for all three of them, she smiled. "After he's finished with laser tag maybe we can hit the arcade. I play a mean pinball machine."

His split eyebrow rose. "You?"

"Hey, don't underestimate me because I'm an academic."

"I wouldn't dream of it."

His grin almost stopped her heart.

****

A children's arcade was not the place to get a hard-on, but Justice was hard-pressed not to as he watched Charlotte beat an ancient pinball machine into submission.

Her hips wiggled as she danced at the foot of the game, nudging the tiny silver ball with practiced slaps, setting it spinning with perfectly-timed flippers. The thin white blouse she wore did nothing to hide the swing of her breasts. She'd rolled up the long sleeves, baring her slender forearms and elegant wrists.

God, he was really in trouble if the sight of her wrists

made his mouth water.

"Keep it going, keep it going!" Max stood by her side, eyes wide behind the smudged lenses of his glasses. His initial reserve had melted away the first time she lit up the bells and buzzers.

Quick flicks kept the ball in play, the score climbing. Justice couldn't take his eyes off her. Her focus, her intensity, pulled at him. As if sensing his regard, her eyelids flickered and for an instant her gaze met his.

The visceral connection between them cut off the arcade's frenetic sounds, as abruptly as an arena door slamming shut.

"No!" Max's cry of dismay echoed faintly. "It's gone down the drain."

With an effort, Justice responded. "Sorry, buddy. That might have been my fault."

Charlotte swallowed, the muscles of her throat moving convulsively. She smiled down at the disappointed boy. "It's probably time for someone else to have a turn, anyway." She lifted the heavy hair off the back of her neck and fanned herself with one hand. "I'd forgotten how much work that was. I need something cold."

Justice ordered three more soft drinks and brought them to the table. Max sipped his and fiddled with the straw. "So, are you and my Dad getting married?" he asked.

Bubbles fizzed up Justice's nose and he choked. By Charlotte's pole-axed expression, it appeared she wasn't in any better shape.

"Max," he managed between coughs, "why would you ask that?"

He shrugged, head down. "Because." The straw made a squeaky zipping sound as he pulled and pushed it through the lid.

"Charlotte and I—" Justice broke off, floundering. He knew he wanted Charlotte to stay in his life, but the details of how to achieve that were pretty vague, especially with the looming spectre of tenure at York University. Could he explain without scaring her off?

Charlotte had found her voice first. "Your dad and I are friends." He waited, wary, wondering. "People who are in love get married. Not friends."

And didn't that just kick him in the nuts.

"It's just I thought maybe Mom and Dad..."

Damn it. He wasn't angry that Max wanted his parents together, but he hated to keep disappointing the boy. "We've talked about that. You know, as much as we love you, we don't love each other enough to be married."

Max shot him a glare. "You used to love each other or you wouldn't have got married at all. And you've never had a girlfriend before. Not until *her*." The glare switched to Charlotte.

"Be polite." No matter what Max's feelings, Justice couldn't allow him to treat Charlotte with anything but respect.

Charlotte's wide eyes pinned Justice with disbelief. "You've never had a girlfriend? Since your divorce?"

"It wasn't that long ago," he muttered.

"I was seven," Max said, "and now I'm almost ten."

"You won't be ten for more than six months."

"That's what I said." Max's mouth set in mulish determination. "I don't want you to have a girlfriend. Devin says now you have a girlfriend, you're going to get married."

A toddler ran by, giggling and shrieking, followed by his harried mother. Serious conversations like these shouldn't take place in a madhouse.

"Let's get out of here." Justice stood. "We'll talk about this at home."

CHAPTER TWENTY-EIGHT

The three of them climbed into the truck, the clicking of seat belts loud in the awkward silence. Justice turned on the radio and spoke under the cover of the Rolling Stones. "Sorry about this. I'll drop you off at home."

Charlotte nodded. "Of course. And I'm the one that's sorry." She hated being the reason for the anger and frustration emanating from the small figure in the seat behind her.

Justice spoke over his shoulder to Max. "We're going to bring Charlotte home before we go to my house."

"I don't want to go with you. I want to go home."

"You're supposed to spend the night with me. You've got hockey in the morning."

"I don't care." The mutinous little voice trembled with a trace of tears. "I want to go home *now*."

Charlotte jumped in before Justice had a chance to reply. "That's okay with me, Max. I don't mind. We'll take you home first."

Justice's fingers flexed on the steering wheel. She wondered if the fact Max considered his mother's house home was as cuttingly painful to him as it seemed to her. "Fine," he said.

A few minutes later, they pulled up in front of an older, split-level house, the drive and sidewalk neatly cleared of snow. Justice parked the truck in front of the wide garage door. "Do you want to come in and wait?"

"No, thanks." Charlotte had no desire to meet Justice's

ex. Especially under the current circumstances.

He sighed. "Don't suppose I blame you." He left the keys in the ignition. "I won't be long. Just enough to get him settled. If you get cold, turn on the engine."

As soon as Justice opened his door, Max pushed out of the cab. Together they disappeared inside the house. A light flared on through the opaque glass at the side of the entrance.

A chill seeped through her warm woollen coat. Cold air had rushed in when the man and boy left, and without the heater blowing it wasn't long before the tip of her nose felt frosty. She was reaching for the key when the front door opened and she leaned back in relief. But instead of revealing Justice on his way to her, a petite blonde stood in the doorway and beckoned.

Tiffani. The ex. Inviting her in. Now what?

She waved with fake cheerfulness. "I'm fine," she called, hoping the other woman could read lips through the gloom. "Don't worry about me. I'll wait here."

Tiffani's beckoning grew more forceful. In the light from the hall, Charlotte could see the gleam of her smile.

God, she didn't want to go in. But if she ignored the other woman, she'd be the one that looked like a bitch.

She slipped the keys from the ignition and opened her door. A brisk breeze swooped under the hem of her coat. She wrapped her arms around herself to keep the cold out and headed reluctantly up the path.

****

Justice's gut churned at the stricken expression on Max's face. The boy sat at the head of his bed, clutching his Transformers pillow. A poster of Spiderman adorned the wall behind him. He looked small and defenseless and vulnerable.

"I'm sorry you're upset," he began cautiously. "I wish I could help you understand. I know it's confusing for you."

Max refused to meet his eyes. His blond hair, a little too long, hung over the frames of his glasses as he stared at the bed sheets. "Is it my fault?"

"Your fault?"

"That you and Mom don't love each other."

The quiet words hit him harder than a sucker punch to the jaw. "No, buddy, it's not. It's not your fault at all."

"You mean it?"

"I would never lie to you. Your mom and I both love you, but we don't live together because we can't get along. It's our fault, not yours."

"Okay." Some of the tenseness left Max's body. "I'm sorry I got mad."

"Everyone gets mad. It's okay. I wish you could like Charlotte, though, just a little bit."

"You like her a lot." Max traced the cartoon characters on the pillow case with one finger.

"I do. I really like her." Justice took a deep breath. "Can I tell you something I've never told anyone else? Not even Charlotte?"

That brought his head up. His eyes grew large behind the lenses of his glasses. "What?"

"I think I love Charlotte."

Max blinked, his bottom lip quivered. "More than you love Mom?"

God, this was killing him. "I love your mom, but in a different way."

"What about me?"

Without thought, Justice scooped the boy up and cuddled him on his lap. His legs and arms were wiry and

291

lanky, yet he still fit under his chin. "I love you more than anything."

"More than Charlotte?"

How to explain the different kinds of love? He searched for the right words. "No matter how much I might love Charlotte, you'll always come first. If you really don't like her, I'll stop seeing her." He held his breath, hoping he'd read Max right.

"You will?"

"I will." He kept the apprehension out of his voice. This had to be Max's decision.

The small body was still within the circle of his arms, the room quiet for endless moments.

"I kind of like her."

Justice released a long-held breath. "That's good."

"She's pretty good at pinball."

"She is."

"She likes Chaucer. And Chaucer likes her. I can tell." He pulled out of Justice's hold and peered up at him, face sober. "Do you think she's mad at me?"

"No, buddy. She understands it's hard for you."

The *Thomas the Tank Engine* alarm clock on Max's beside table told him Charlotte had been waiting for more than fifteen minutes. "Are you feeling better?"

"Yeah."

"Ok. Let's go find your mom. And then I should take Charlotte home."

****

Tiffani gestured Charlotte into the house. "Justice is in Max's bedroom. From the looks of things when they came in, they'll be a while yet. I figured you'd rather wait in the warm. I'm Tiffani, by the way."

"Thanks. Charlotte Girardet." She stood in the

entrance, feeling awkward and out-of-place. Tiffani was barely over five-foot tall with a pale prettiness that made Charlotte conscious of her own extra height and solid build.

"Come into the kitchen." Tiffani led the way down a short hall to the back of the house. "So, you're the reason Max is upset." Her lips smiled, but her blue eyes were hard.

"I suppose so. By association at least." She couldn't deny the guilt she felt. "Did Justice explain what happened?"

"All I know is the three of you went for dinner, and Max came home crying. What did you do?"

Charlotte stiffened. "I didn't *do* anything." Damn it, spending time with Justice wasn't a crime, and she was getting tired of being blamed for it. She could sympathize with Max, but this woman had no say in Justice's life anymore. "The evening was going quite well, until Max asked if Justice and I were getting married."

"Oh." Tiffani tilted her head to one side and scrutinized her with a narrow look. "What did you say?"

"I don't think that's any of your business."

"It is if my son is upset by it," Tiffani hissed, low voiced.

Charlotte kept her tone calm and quiet. "He and Justice are talking about it now. I'm sure they'll tell you all about it. But it's not my place."

Tiffani stalked forward and stared pugnaciously up at her. "Don't get between me and Justice and our son. We might be divorced, but we're still family."

"I know Justice isn't his biological father."

The skin behind Tiffani's carefully applied makeup blanched, leaving the rouge standing out like banners on her cheeks. "He told you that?"

"Yes." Charlotte wasn't sure why she had revealed that knowledge. At least Tiffani was no longer on the attack. "I also know that Justice wants you to tell Max the truth."

Tiffani's fist clenched. "Are you threatening me?"

Charlotte stared. "Of course not."

"Because I'll tell my son when I think the time is right."

A small voice came from Charlotte's left. "Tell me what, Mom?"

****

The sibilant hiss of a conversation snaked down the hallway as Max and Justice made their way to the kitchen. At first he assumed it was the television. But then he recognized Charlotte's voice.

"Of course not," she said, her tone decisive.

"Because I'll tell my son when I think the time is right." Tiffani's reply was clearly audible. Apprehension clutched the back of his neck as he and Max came to a stop at the end of the hall.

"Tell me what, Mom?" Max, worn out from emotions, sensing the strained atmosphere between the two women, sounded on the brink of tears yet again.

Tiffani and Charlotte stared at him with expressions of horror and consternation. In a leap of deduction unfounded on any specific reason, Justice knew immediately they'd been talking about Jake.

Tiffani knelt in front of Max and smoothed the hair out of his face. "Nothing, honey."

"No." Justice had had enough. Maybe tonight wasn't the best time. Maybe Max had had enough turmoil for one evening. But maybe this would also prove to Max how much he was loved. "We tell him. Now."

"Not tonight. Not in front of her," Tiffani pleaded.

Her entreaty should have moved him, but he was so tired of the lie. "It's nothing to be ashamed of," he said. "We should have told him long ago."

Charlotte shifted on her feet, as if wanting to escape, but Justice and Max blocked the exit. "She's right," she said. "I shouldn't be here for this."

"Dad?" Max looked at him, confusion and fear flitting across his face.

Ignoring both women, Justice hunkered down on his heels, face to face with Max, Tiffani on his right. "It's not a bad thing, Max. Maybe we should have told you sooner, but it never seemed to be the right time."

"Tell me what?"

"Remember what I said before, that I would never lie to you?" Max nodded, eyes fixed on Justice. "I want you to know I love you so much. And what we're going to tell you now doesn't change that." He took a deep breath and glanced at Tiffani. She crouched, frozen, staring at the floor. "You know that, to make a baby, you need to have a mom and a dad, right?" Max nodded again. "Well, your mom made you with a different dad. Not me. Before you were born, he died in an accident. I married your mom so I could take care of you. That makes me your dad, too. It's important you know about your other dad, though. He made you, so he's a part of you."

The panicky look on Max's face grew. "You're not my real dad?"

"Of course I am." Justice knew he had to get this just right. "I've loved you since I first saw you. I've taught you and played with you and got mad at you when you were bad. What else does a dad do? It doesn't matter that I didn't make you. I'm still your dad."

Max's eyebrows drew down in thought, the distress fading from his face.

"And he's a great dad." Justice started as Tiffani's voice, quiet but strong, broke the silence. "It's my fault we didn't tell you sooner. I didn't want to confuse you. But he's right. You should know about your first dad."

"Who was he?"

"His name was Jake," Justice replied. God, it felt good to talk about his best friend with his son. *Their* son. "He was a really good hockey player, better than me. We were teammates, and our bus was in an accident. He was killed."

"So he never even saw me?" The idea didn't seem to overly concern Max. His question was a simple request for details.

"Your mom was really sad about that."

"Do I look like him?"

"You do," Tiffani answered. "You know this cowlick?" Her fingers trembled slightly as she brushed the whorl of hair on the crown of Max's head. "He had that. And you have the same nose."

Max ran a finger down the bridge, smiling a bit as he went cross-eyed. "Cool."

"Do you have any questions for us? About anything?" Justice asked.

Max considered for a moment, and then shook his head. "If I think of something later, though, can I ask?"

"Of course you can. Any time. It's not a secret anymore."

"'Kay." He headed for the fridge. As he passed Tiffani, her arms twitched, as if to reach out and hug him to her, but she didn't. "Can I have some juice?"

She rose from her knees. "Sure. I'll get it for you."

Justice stood as well, his head light and disconnected,

like he was just waking up from being knocked out. Charlotte stood next to him, eyes glistening, a smile hovering at the corner of her mouth. He took her hand. Her grip was warm and comforting.

Max downed his drink in a few big gulps. "Can I watch TV?"

"Only an hour," Justice and Tiffani said at the same time. Max giggled and rolled his eyes. The last remnants of tension wisped away.

Justice wondered whether to ask Max if he wanted to stay with him tonight, now that things seemed more settled, but decided against it. "I'll pick you up tomorrow and take you to the game, okay?"

"Yup." Max clambered onto the couch and picked up the remote. "Night, Dad."

Never had the word sounded so sweet.

CHAPTER TWENTY-NINE

The drive to Charlotte's house only took a few minutes. She didn't say anything, still absorbing the scene she'd witnessed. Justice seemed equally preoccupied.

"I'm sorry." She blurted the words the moment he pulled the pickup into her driveway.

"For what?" He left the engine running, but shifted in his seat to face her.

"I told Tiffani you'd told me about Max's father. If I hadn't, Max wouldn't have overheard what he did, wouldn't have asked the question."

"I'm glad it happened." He scraped a nail on the knee of his jeans, cleaning off a speck of dirt Charlotte couldn't see. "I've wanted to tell Max about Jake for a long time."

"It wasn't my place. I don't know why I said it. Tiffani was asking why Max was upset, and I just let it out."

"He seemed okay with it."

Charlotte remembered Max's curious yet calm acceptance, after the first shock of the announcement had passed. "He did, didn't he."

"Kids are amazing. Resilient, adaptable. I'm sure he'll have more questions, after he thinks about it."

"You were great with him."

He ducked his chin. "I just told him the truth."

"You're the only dad he's known. His biological father is just a name to him, not a person. I'm sure that will change, as he gets older, as you have the chance to talk to him about Jake. In the end, though, that's who you are. His dad."

"Do you see now why I wasn't scared off when you told me you can't have children?" Justice's low voice rumbled in the air between them. "Max is not my son by blood. But he is my son all the same."

"Not everyone feels that way." She couldn't keep Richard's angry, damning face from appearing in her mind's eye.

"No. But I do." He cupped her chin with cool fingers. "I do, Charlotte. I believe you can make a family in all sorts of ways. And I'm beginning to think I want to make one with you."

She jerked back, yanking her head from his grasp. "I don't understand." But she did. She just didn't want to.

"I told Max tonight I think I'm falling in love with you."

Panic clenched her lungs, choked off her breathing. "Why did you do that?" she squeaked out.

"Because it's the truth. And you deserve the truth, just as he did."

She scrabbled at the handle and threw the door open. "I can't. I can't talk about this."

Justice gripped her wrist, forestalling her escape. "You don't have to talk. You just have to think. Think about what I said to Max, about loving him no matter what. Think about why you deserve the same chance."

"How can you be talking about love when I'm leaving?" She stood on the driveway. Justice was stretched across the bench seat, holding her wrist and looking at her through the open door with an almost painful understanding.

"Because it's the truth. Because time falls still when we're in love."

She wrenched her arm from his grasp and flew up the path. It took her three tries to get the key in the lock, until she was safe inside.

Safe from the horrible, wonderful, tantalizing temptation of his love.

****

A few nights later, the rumbling, rushing sound of granite on ice led Justice and Chaucer into Whitman's living room. Curling was the sport of the day on his TV screen.

"Hey, Dad."

"Hey." Whitman twisted heavily in his chair so he could peer over his shoulder. "The boy not with you?" Chaucer dropped his head in his lap, and Whitman patted it absently.

"School night. It's science fair time. He and Tiffani are finishing his popsicle stick bridge as we speak." Justice had just spent an amazingly placid and cheerful hour working with them both. He hefted the bag of groceries and case of beer he carried. "I'll put these away."

A grunt was his only answer.

He returned to the living room after stowing the supplies and dropped onto the couch set at a right angle to his father's space. Chaucer had settled at the foot of Whitman's wheelchair, chin resting on his paws. The clack and bang of curling rocks, accompanied by a cheering crowd, declared a well-executed take out.

"I sure like that Brad Jacobs." Whitman had lit a cigarette while Justice was out of the room. It jiggled in his mouth as he talked, smoke curling from the end, drifting toward the ceiling. "Smart skip. Good team."

Justice sat and watched the match, listening patiently to his father's critique of the play. During a commercial break, he took the opportunity to introduce the subject consuming his thoughts.

"Do you remember meeting Charlotte Girardet a while ago? A professor from the university. We stopped by to pick up skates one night."

"'Course I remember. Not senile yet." Whitman plucked the cigarette from his mouth with gnarled fingers, cupping the lit end in his palm as men who are often out of doors do, a habit left over from an earlier life.

"What did you think of her?" Justice rubbed his fist on his sternum, nerves aching in his chest.

Whitman's concentration finally left the TV screen and zeroed in on Justice. "What's it matter?"

"I'm kind of dating her."

"How can you kind of date a woman?" Whitman demanded, smoke-soaked voice gravelly. "Are you sleeping with her?"

"Yeah." He slumped lower on the cushions and cocked one ankle onto a knee, going for casual, hoping Whitman wouldn't sense how important this conversation was to Justice.

"Then you damn well better be dating her."

No one but his father could make him feel like a teenage jerk. "I meant it might be more than dating. I might be thinking about living with her. Maybe marrying her."

"Huh." The commercial break over, Whitman focused back on the TV screen. "Why'd you want to do that? Didn't work out so well with Tiffani."

"Yeah, well, that was then." He leaned over and opened the small cooler next his father's chair. "Beer?"

"Sure."

He handed a can to his father and popped the top on one for himself. The chilled, bitter liquid eased the nervous dryness of his mouth, slid down his throat with welcome familiarity.

"Did you ever think of marrying again?" Justice asked. "After Mom died?" It was a question he'd often wondered, but never had the guts to ask. Yet the answer to it was the real reason he'd come to see Whitman today.

The pause was so long he didn't think he'd get a reply. Whitman's eyes didn't leave the screen, but his gaze was distant, unseeing.

"A week before your Mom found out she had cancer, she told me she wanted to leave me."

Justice stopped dead, can of beer half-raised to his lips. "What?"

"You heard me."

"She was going to leave us?"

"Not us. Me. She wanted to take you with her. But when she realized she was sick, she figured that wasn't fair to you. So she stayed." Whitman's tone was hollow with old memories. "Only until she was better, she said. But she didn't get better."

The last months of his mother's life had swept by like rapids on a river. The weaker she grew the faster the days went, every hour a minute, every minute a second, no matter how hard Justice had clung to those moments. He had always figured his father's bitterness had been against the disease that stole his wife. And maybe it had been. But not all of it.

"I don't remember you two fighting."

"We didn't." Whitman huffed a short breath, precipitating a bout of gurgling coughing. He recovered and went on. "Funny, that was one of the things she complained about. That I didn't care enough to even fight with her."

He knew what she meant. His father's icy sternness had always appeared uncaring, unemotional. As a teenager, it had shrivelled many an argument before it had even begun.

"Still, after she died. Why didn't you remarry?"

Whitman curled the corners of his mouth down. The cigarette smoldered, forgotten in the ashtray. "Didn't meet a woman I cared about enough. And after the accident"— he put down his beer and shifted his paralyzed legs, settling his unfeeling feet more firmly in the rests—"well, let's just say it didn't make it any easier."

Ever since his mother had died, all Justice had wanted was a family. A whole, loving family. While he struggled for his father's approval both on and off the ice, his team had taken the place of that family. After the crash tore them apart, he thought he'd found it with Tiffani and Max. Yet again he'd been wrong.

He might have the use of all his limbs, but he realized he was crippled in other ways. Crippled by doubt, by fear, by lack of faith in himself and in Charlotte. He had to let go of all that and trust in the future. He'd married Tiffani with good intentions, but for the wrong reasons. Maybe his need to help Charlotte heal from her past was exactly what he needed to heal his own.

****

The next week, late on Tuesday afternoon, Madeline Donald appeared in the doorway of Charlotte's office. "Just had a call from York."

For a moment, Charlotte had no idea what the chair of the department was talking about. Then her stomach collapsed in on itself, leaving a gaping hole in her belly. "Oh."

"Seems you made a very good impression at your

interview." Madeline pulled out one of the visitor seats and perched on the edge, movements sharp and defined, giving the impression of a quick, darting bird. "And your guest lecture was reviewed with equal approval."

"Oh," she repeated stupidly.

Madeline's head tilted to one side quizzically. "You seem shocked."

She shook off a faint queasiness. "Of course I'd hoped I'd done well. But you never know." Since she'd returned, she'd thought of that day, of course. In a distant, wondering way, without the burning need to succeed, to be chosen. But her time had been filled with Justice and Max, teaching and planning, and her trip to Toronto had begun to take on the vagueness of an event that had happened to someone else.

"I imagine it will take them a week or so more. But if I were you, I'd be preparing for a move in my future." Her smile was warm and genuine. "I had other good news today. We've received funding to add to our own English faculty. If only they'd made that decision sooner, I might have had a carrot to dangle in front of you. But I know you're set on moving on."

Charlotte found herself wishing she'd been less vehement when telling Madeleine her dream of a position at a major university. "That's excellent news." Her own smile felt stiff and forced. "Congratulations. I'm sure you won't have trouble finding the perfect candidate. I've really enjoyed my time here." The end of that time, which had once seemed a shining goal to strive toward, now seemed a dull, grey wall.

"I'm glad to hear it." Madeline hopped to her feet. "Well, just wanted to pass on my congratulations."

"I won't accept them. Not yet, anyway. Maybe you

misunderstood." After all, Charlotte considered, she hadn't been made a formal offer yet.

"I suppose that's a healthy attitude. But you'll be accepting them soon, take my word for it," Madeline said as she whirled out the door.

Charlotte slouched in her chair and spun it toward the wide window overlooking the traffic circle. The days were finally growing longer, and the late afternoon glow of the sun highlighted the roof line of the residences across the way, staining the snow covered peaks with coral and copper.

She wouldn't think of it, she vowed. If she believed Madeline's certainty, she might jinx the whole thing. Her dreams were about to come true. She didn't want to do anything to derail them.

So why did she feel as if, instead of the beginning of a bright new life, she was coming to the end of something precious?

****

Charlotte locked her office and headed down the deserted hallway. The hum of forced-air heat and florescent lights made a white-noise background for the soft thudding of her boots on the low-pile, industrial-grade carpet.

After Madeline had set off her bombshell, Charlotte had done her best to concentrate on work. It had been a largely useless effort, but she'd kept at it until long after most of the other faculty had gone home. Justice was working the afternoon shift, which meant he wasn't off until 11pm. He'd dropped in for a minute while doing one of his walkabouts, but they wouldn't have much chance to see each other until he was done his tour in a couple more nights.

She hadn't told him of Madeline's prediction. She wasn't being secretive or trying to shut him out. She simply needed time to figure out her own response before she opened herself to his reaction.

Her steps slowed as she reached the double glass doors leading outside. In her abstraction, she'd forgotten to call security for an escort to her car. She'd been taking the precaution for so long it had become habit. Madeline's news had knocked her even further off balance than she had first thought.

As she rooted around in her bag, trying to find her cell, a figure appeared outside. It took her a moment to recognize Shawn McMorris, one of Justice's colleagues. He smiled, pulled the outer door open and called to her through the barrier of the inner door. "Heading home? I can walk you to your car, if you like."

Thankfully, she gave up her search and crossed the vestibule. "What great timing. I forgot to call from my office."

"So no one's coming to meet you?" He fell into step behind her on the walkway, the snow-covered path too narrow to walk side-by-side.

"I was looking for my phone when you showed up." She gripped the iron railing and negotiated the ice-covered steps with care.

McMorris made a noncommittal grunt. A car passed by on the ring road, its headlights cutting day into the darkness. Night had completely fallen, and while street lamps cast circles of light, wide swathes of the parking lot were dim and gloomy. Charlotte shivered, the icy breeze feathering under her collar.

"I'm just over there," she said. Her SUV waited, a dusting of snow powdering the windshield. She quickened her steps, eager to be out of the chill.

A sedan was parked nose-to-tail beside her vehicle. As she approached, she noticed the trunk was ajar. "You should find out whose car that is," she said over her shoulder to McMorris. "They'll want to know their trunk isn't latched properly."

The vicious shove slammed her into the vehicle, her hip banging painfully on the edge of the trunk. Before she could draw breath, her head was twisted back by a stinging, wrenching tug on her hair, and smashed flat into the frozen metal. Pain exploded from her nose, her cheekbones, and she screamed, only to have the sound cut off by a thick, heavy, gloved palm. She struggled for air, her nasal passages filling with blood, her mouth clamped shut by a determined hand. Her boots slipped on the icy pavement as she scrabbled for a foothold, their narrow heels giving no purchase. Her head spun dizzily. The hand released its grip and she gasped, desperate for oxygen. Her attacker grabbed her ankles and tipped her into the trunk. She struggled to roll onto her hands and knees. A punch to her temple dropped her down again. Her satchel was dragged over her head. She made a weak grab for it. It slipped through her fingers.

The lid of the trunk bashed her on the head, and the world ceased.

CHAPTER THIRTY

"You all wrapped up?" Justice saved the last changes to his shift report as Elizabeth Paxton rattled away on the computer next to him.

She tapped the final key with a flourish. "You bet."

"I'll walk out with you." It was almost eleven, and Justice and Elizabeth were getting ready to hand off to the next crew. Brent Parvat checked the run-down chart, while Shawn McMorris perched on the chair in the glass turret. "You and Brent set?" Justice asked.

"We're good." McMorris fidgeted, his knee jiggling. "Nothing ever happens at night, anyway."

"I like the quiet," Brent said as he tossed the chart onto the desk.

"Ever since that English graduate student was attacked off campus, things have settled down." Elizabeth shrugged into her coat. "It can stay that way forever, if you ask me."

"Me, I like a little excitement." McMorris shot Elizabeth a sly glance that had the hairs on the back of Justice's neck prickling.

"Not at the expense of someone else," Justice replied curtly, unable to keep the irritation out of his voice. McMorris' eyes slid toward him. "I suggest you find your excitement elsewhere."

"Don't mean nothing by it." His grin did nothing to reassure Justice. "And don't worry, I make my own excitement, for sure."

Justice and Elizabeth set off for the parking lot. He couldn't shake off a vague feeling of apprehension. Whether it was the conversation with McMorris or something else entirely, he felt unsettled, restless.

And the feeling intensified when he saw Charlotte's SUV still in the lot.

"Hold on," Justice said. Elizabeth looked up at him in enquiry. "Be right back."

He jogged over to the vehicle. Undisturbed snow piled an inch thick on the hood, even though flakes had quit falling more than two hours ago. Surely Charlotte wasn't still at work? When he'd talked to her in the late afternoon, she'd implied she was leaving sooner rather than later.

He returned to Elizabeth. "I'm going to head back in, but I'll take you to your car, first."

"What's going on?" She pulled out a bundle of keys and picked through them as they approached her Chevy van. "Isn't that Professor Girardet's vehicle?"

"Yeah." If Charlotte was still working, he'd be pissed. Was she already overdoing it? "It's late for her to be here. I'll just go check, make sure she's not having car trouble or anything."

Elizabeth beeped the driver's door unlocked. "So, the two of you. The rumours are true, then."

"Rumours?"

"You can't keep anything a secret for long in a small university like this. Everyone knows you're spending time with her. Story is you even went away together during Reading Week, but no one knows where."

Heat flushed the tip of Justice's cold nose. "People should just mind their own business."

She laughed. "You're embarrassed. Never thought I'd see that."

"Go home, Elizabeth." He opened the van door and gestured her in.

"I'm going. And you go find your professor. 'Night."

He headed into the Administration Building. If Charlotte was still there, he was prepared to haul her over his shoulder and take her home, whether she agreed or not.

****

She wasn't in her office. He called her cell and only reached her voicemail. Where could she be? Not even professors had keys to the library after hours, and all the coffee shops and cafeterias were closed.

Spider feet of fear scuttled up and down his spine. He headed back to the security office.

Brent Parvat sat in the office alone, manning the rows of security monitors. "Forget something?" he asked.

"Have you heard anything from Professor Girardet?"

He shook his head. "Were you meeting her?"

"No." Justice felt like a fool. When had he turned into such a freaking mother hen? "Her car's still in the lot."

"Maybe she went out with a friend and didn't want to drive herself."

A possible reason, but one that didn't fit Charlotte. "Maybe." His eyes scanned the monitors, hoping for the sight of her long-legged stride. "Where's McMorris?"

"Doing his walkabout. He doesn't like being cooped up in the office."

"Call him on the radio, would you? Ask him if he's seen anything."

Without hesitation, Brent contacted McMorris. Silently, Justice thanked Nielson for the military-style, obey-all-orders training he'd instilled in the security team.

McMorris' reply rattled from the speaker. "Haven't seen her since I've been on shift." Brent and McMorris had started at 10 p.m., overlapping Elizabeth and Justice by one hour. "Why?"

"Justice is looking for her."

"Sorry. Can't help."

Brent disconnected. "What should we do?"

Short of a full-scale manhunt—which would humiliate both of them when Charlotte was found safe and sound—Justice couldn't think of anything. "Nothing. She's probably with a friend, like you said."

He made his second trip out to the parking lot. Charlotte's SUV stood alone in the row.

"Damn it." Something was wrong. He knew it. Ever since he'd known her, Charlotte was either at work, at home, or with him. She didn't have other friends, and went few places without her vehicle.

He'd check her house, and then call back to the university to make sure she hadn't shown up there, despite all the signs.

And then he was calling the cops.

****

The sickly sweet taste of exhaust blended with the hard iron tang of blood. Charlotte worked saliva into her mouth and tried to swallow away her fear. Her ears rang in the silence of her dark metal coffin.

"Not a coffin." She spoke out loud, seeking comfort in her own voice. "It's just a car." The words echoed oddly in the confined space.

Her nose was swollen, impossible to breathe through, and the coating of dried blood on her upper lip and chin cracked as she spoke. Pain radiated through her head, from between her eyes as well as a throbbing spot on her crown. Her wrists were strapped tightly together behind her back, a narrow, hard plastic tie digging into her skin. He must have done that after the trunk lid had knocked her out.

She didn't think she'd been unconscious long, but that could just be wishful thinking. The car had been moving when awareness had returned, accelerating and decelerating, swaying left then right. The taste of vomit burned at the back of her throat. She'd forced down the nausea, determined not to succumb to her rolling gut, but it had been a close thing.

The black was absolute. She was fairly certain she was in a garage. When the engine had finally stopped, the springs rose as McMorris—it had to be him, unless he had an accomplice, and the thought of two such predators made her stomach turn even more—got out of the driver's seat. She strained to hear, but all that had come through the metal surrounding her was the familiar growling groan of a garage door. After it clanked shut? Nothing.

That had been days ago. At least, it felt that way, until she forced herself to think logically. Her mouth was cotton dry and her bladder tight, but those were manifestations of fear more than symptoms of physical necessity.

"Someone will notice you are missing tomorrow," she told herself. She wished she could depend on it being sooner than that, but she had to be realistic. No one would be looking for her until she missed class in the morning. "And when Justice finds out, he won't let it go until you're found." That she knew for a fact.

The dark pressed in on her, and terror tickled under her ribs. "Help!" Her voice reverberated back at her, with a hollow, deadened sound. She kept calling until her voice broke, hoarse and dry. Tears pooled in her eyes, drops escaping to run down her temples into her hair. With fierce concentration, she drew back from the razor's edge of pain and panic.

She lay on her side, and the arm under her was tingling painfully. She rolled to her back. A band tightened around her throat. Her heart kicked rapidly, her pulse skyrocketing, until she realized it was her scarf. She shifted, lifting her shoulders, raising her head, as she untangled herself. Her face brushed against scratchy, thin material. The light pressure sent agony exploding from her nose.

"Damn it." She drew in deep breaths through her mouth, seeking to control her misery. "Enough of this."

She refused to wait meekly for McMorris to return. Her vague impressions of the car into which she'd been thrust was a fairly recent model sedan. Many of those, she knew, had a gizmo that released the back of the seat so it would lay flat, allowing long cargo to be loaded. Looking for that latch, even if it didn't exist, would at least give her something to do.

First she had to orientate herself. She had no idea which way she was facing. Moving cautiously, she wriggled backward until her bound hands touched the wall of her prison. Stretching out her legs, she found the outer edge. Then, ducking her chin to her chest to avoid banging her already pounding head, she pushed off with her feet, sliding roughly across the floor until her shoulders reached the far side.

She couldn't unbend completely, which wasn't surprising considering her height. But chances were she was lying side to side. "Okay, now let's see if you can figure out which way is front. And why are you talking about yourself in the second person?" Her giggles hovered on the cusp of hysteria and she bit her lip.

She twisted her hands and used her fingertips to explore the wall behind her. Only the gritty scrape of harsh material—no metal, no wires, no straps. She inched around the irregularly shaped space, searching for something, anything, that might help her escape, give her hope. Her muscles trembled from the awkward, constrained movements, her flexibility tested over and over again, and still she searched. She had no way of knowing when she'd completed the entire circuit, no way of marking time or distance. So she kept going, determined to make her way around the entire trunk, unwilling to quit before she was certain she'd covered every square centimetre.

Brain dizzy with effort, emotions dulled by fear, she almost missed the toggle. Her fingers, accustomed to the rasp of the carpet, grasped the swinging loop before her brain caught up with them. Her back cramped from the awkward lift of her arms as she arched to get better leverage.

"Oh, God, please work." She held on tight and shoved her body forward, using her torso to do the work her arms couldn't.

Nothing.

If it worked liked others she had seen, pulling the strap should unlock the seat back, allowing it to fall forward. She twisted her fingers in the band and rocked forward again.

This time, a faint clunking sound rewarded her. Cool air drafted across her hands, seeping through the widening gap. She wriggled backward as quickly as she could and used the pitiful force in her bound hands to thrust it out and away.

Contorting her body, she managed to swing around so she was facing the opening, a lighter grey patch in the charcoal dark. If she could get out of the car she could get out of the garage, she just knew it.

Her shoulders stuck in the narrow space. Squirming, writhing, she worked until her torso finally slid free. Hope ballooned in her chest. Through the windshield, along one wall of the garage, she could see shelves stacked with paint cans and washer fluid and cardboard boxes of all sizes. It was so ordinary, so unassuming, her pulse slowed, her breathing eased.

Without warning, lights flashed on. She cried out, flinching against the blinding dazzle.

****

"I don't fucking care if she's only been missing for a few hours," Justice said, glaring at Nielson. "We need to do something."

"You have to calm down." Nielson met him glare for glare. "We are doing something. We've brought in all available guards, and they're out with Parvat and McMorris, searching the campus."

"It's a waste of time. She's not here. We need to call in the cops."

"We *need* to make sure this is the emergency you believe it is." Nielson jerked a chin at a recalled Elizabeth Paxton, hunched at a desk staring intently at a computer monitor. "We're reviewing the afternoon's security footage, as well. That should give us some indication of where she is."

"Our cameras don't cover everywhere. You know there are huge gaps in our surveillance, especially of the parking lots." The urge to knock the professional calm from Nielson's face almost superseded Justice's gut-clenching fear. Almost. He choked down his frustration and spoke through gritted teeth. "She's not in her office. Her car is still in the lot. I checked her house. She's not home."

"Maybe she didn't hear you knock."

"I have a damn key. I went inside and searched. She's not there."

Nielson's eyebrows rose above the thick frames of his glasses. "What exactly is the nature of your relationship with Professor Girardet?"

"What the fuck does that matter?" Justice paced to the monitors, leaned on his knuckles as he stared blindly at the screens. "Not that long ago she had a stalker, right in her yard. And with the attacks on and off campus in the last few months—" He broke off, gathered his scattering wits. "We can't afford to wait. We have to bring in the RCMP."

"Not until I have a full report of the search on campus."

The head of security's cool, detached tone made Justice want to put his fist through a wall. "Fine. Then I'm heading out there to look. The sooner we finish, the better."

"You'll stay here. We're following a strict search pattern. Teams will be reporting in soon. If we do call the detachment, they'll want to talk to you. I want you where I can see you."

Every second of the next fifteen minutes ached deep in the marrow of his bones. He knew Charlotte was in trouble. *Knew* it. He couldn't sit still, striding from monitors to computer to coffee machine and back. Nielson watched him, silent and stern, leaning against the wall with his arms crossed.

One by one, the pairs of guards trickled in. No one had anything to report. The last one in was Brent Parvat. "Where's McMorris?" Nielson demanded.

"He's taking a pi—uhm, in the washroom." A flush added rosiness to Brent's dark skin. "We didn't see anything. There's no sign of her."

"Are you satisfied?" Justice demanded. "Make the call, Nielson. Or I'll do what I should have done hours ago and called them myself."

CHAPTER THIRTY-ONE

Stuck half in, half out of the trunk, arms trussed behind her back, Charlotte had nowhere to go. Her cheeks tingled as the blood rushed out of her head, leaving her dizzy and faint.

The door in front of her opened. McMorris leaned in. He still wore his uniform, and the normally comforting sight only added to her disorientation. "Aren't you a tricky one?" he said, derision lacing his tone. "You might almost be as smart as you think you are. Lucky I decided to come back when I did."

"Please." She licked her arid lips. "Let me go."

"Well, now, I don't think I'll be doing that." He knelt on the seat and hooked his arms under hers. With a few painful yanks he had her out of the vehicle. He released her without ceremony and she thudded to the cold concrete floor, landing awkwardly on her shoulder. She bit back a gasp of pain and rolled half on her side.

"Here's the thing." He slammed the door, the bottom edge of it brushing over her, so close a breeze ruffled her hair, and stalked around the sedan. Underneath the carriage, she could see his black, ankle high boots, damp with melting snow, pacing back and forth. "I've had it with women thinking they're better than me just because they have a few more years schooling." Metallic clanks and bangs reverberated in the chill air. "It's time they learned some real life lessons."

She twisted to keep him in view as he circled the car.

He loomed over her, a short, stocky man, his face open and friendly at first glance. Until you looked in his eyes.

Or noticed the wicked pair of shears he held.

Charlotte shivered, not only from the freezing damp seeping up from the concrete.

He bent down, his free hand outstretched as if to pull her up. She tucked her elbows tight to her sides and scooted a few inches away. "What do you mean? I don't understand."

"Oh, really? There's something you don't understand?" His tone was mocking. He hunkered on his heels, light from the florescent ceiling fixture gleaming off the wide blades of the tool. "You know how many times you walked by me in the hallway, didn't even nod, say hello? Just like all those others—noses in the air, looking down on me. Weren't so uppity after I got to them, were they?"

She stared at him. "It was you, stalking the women on campus?"

"My wife and I, we got along just fine. Then she decided to go to back to school, improve herself. That's when it all went to shit." He absently squeezed and released the shears, the cutting jaw opening and closing, opening and closing. "Who the fuck cares who wrote some stupid poems so long ago the guy's worm food?" He shrugged. "All of a sudden, I didn't talk good enough, didn't know the right things. I worked in a sawmill most my life—what did she expect? Was my money that put her through all that damn schooling in the first place. I thought maybe if I got a job at the university, she'd think better of me." He snorted. "That just made it worse. She laughed at me. Laughed!"

Charlotte didn't have time to evade when he reached

for her again. He jerked her to a sitting position. "Get up."

She scrambled to her knees, torso bent forward, and staggered to a standing position. Her legs, cramped from hours in the trunk, trembled and shook. "The girl in the lab? That was you?"

He steered her past the car and up a low flight of stairs to a door. "Now, I was pretty smart, there. She never saw me coming. I would have taught her a good lesson, if only that boyfriend of hers hadn't shown up." He reached past Charlotte to open the door and shoved her through. She stumbled on the threshold, but managed not to fall.

"But why? Why her?" She was in a hallway. To her left was the front door. To her right the kitchen. The paint and flooring were eerily familiar. Even the artwork reminded her of her duplex—so much so she thought for a split second he had taken her home.

"Wasn't her in particular. Could have been any of the women up there at the university that don't ever see me. Just walk past me like I'm worth nothing."

He nudged her toward the stairs leading from the front entrance to the upper floor. A living room opened off the hall. The floor plan was a mirror image of her own.

And suddenly she realized what that meant. "Where are we?" she blurted.

His chuckle raised the hairs on the back of her neck. "I wondered if you'd guess."

She started up the stairs, moving as slowly as she dared. "It's my landlord's half of the duplex, isn't it?"

"I'm right handy with tools." The snick of the shears sounded behind her. Her fingers curled into fists and the skin between her shoulder blades prickled. "I picked the locks. No one will think to look for you here."

She threw a glance behind her. He plodded behind

her, face uncannily calm. "They'll be home soon," she said, desperate to distract him, throw him off balance. "They're due back tomorrow. You can't keep me here for long." She couldn't consider the alternative, that he simply needed a place to kill her.

"Nice try. They won't be home until next week." They reached the top floor. With a push, he directed her to a small bedroom. On her side of the duplex, it would be her office, with the rooms sharing a wall. "My ex-wife's friendly with your landlady. Another bitch she met at school. Her and her lawyer husband, spending the winters in Mexico. Giving my ex big ideas, bragging about all their money." He snickered. "Small town, eh?"

The room contained a single bed, neatly covered in a blue satin spread, a narrow chest of drawers, and a silk ficus tree in the corner. A blackout vinyl roller shade hid the window, which she knew from her own side overlooked the greenbelt behind the house.

His familiarity with the house sparked another idea. "Was it you, that night in my backyard?"

"Scared you, didn't I? Stand still." A rough hand grabbed her forearm and pulled her linked hands upward. She arched away, seeking to relieve the pressure. Cold metal brushed her skin and she jolted. "Don't move, I said." He squeezed her wrist tighter.

With a click and a snip, the tension on her arms eased as the strap binding them released. Her muscles, locked for so long in one position, cramped as she tried to bring them forward. She bit her tongue to keep from crying out.

Before she could take advantage of her freedom, she was thrust onto the bed. With brutal efficiency, he knelt on her stomach. Air burst from her lungs. She battled to breathe. By the time he lifted off her and she could draw a full, wheezing breath, she was once again pinioned, this time with her arms over her head, each wrist zap-strapped to the solid wooden bars of the bedstead.

Panic, humiliation, despair, terror threatened to overwhelm her. She had never felt so helpless. He stood over her, surveying his work with a satisfied expression. Her thoughts shied away from what might come next. In desperation, she searched for something, anything to distract him. "And the English grad student? Was that you, too?"

His look of pride was the most frightening thing she'd experienced all night. "That made everyone sit up and take notice, didn't it? I got away with it so easy. No one can call me stupid no more. I take chances, but I'm smart about it." He leaned over her, tested her bonds. "I've been parking close to your car whenever I can. Even watched you a few nights, but that damn Justice was always with you. Then tonight, there you were. Just like you were waiting for me to take you. I saw an opportunity, made it happen."

Her fingers were icy cold, her belly a writhing mass. She swallowed, opened her mouth to say something, anything to keep him talking, but her mind was blank. Blood pounded in her ears. She braced her heels on the bed, ready to defend herself as best she could with only legs and feet.

****

Inside the security office, Justice and Nielson met with Corporal Frank Monkworth from the RCMP's Missing Persons Unit. In the hallway, called-in security guards and a number of constables milled about, waiting for instructions.

Justice flexed and relaxed his fists, aching to be out, to be doing, but willing—for now, at least—to let the experts lead. As the minutes ticked inexorably by with no news of Charlotte, his anxiety threatened to explode into full-blown panic. He reined it in ruthlessly.

"We've sent crime scene analysts to Professor Girardet's office, the last place she was seen." Monkworth spoke with professional calm, his dark blue eyes direct and serious. "A team will be in touch with anyone who works in that building, to see if we can pinpoint when she may have left, as the video surveillance footage was inconclusive. We'll also want to call any friends and family, find out if they've heard from her recently."

"I can handle that," Nielson said. He seemed in his element. Once he'd admitted the need to call in the cops, he'd been brisk and efficient. "I have access to her personal data, next-of-kin and such."

"Her parents are out of country," Justice said, vaguely recalling a conversation that mentioned Europe somewhere. "One sister in Vancouver. She's pregnant."

Monkworth pulled his cuff back, checked the heavy, industrial-looking watch on his wrist. "We can't wait for morning. If Professor Girardet had to leave suddenly because of an emergency, someone in her family should know."

"Charlotte wouldn't have left town without telling me." Justice was certain of that. He pushed aside thoughts of her trip to Toronto. Things between them had changed since then. Hadn't they?

He'd look a right idiot if he was wrong. He knew in his gut he wasn't.

Nielson butted in. "Regardless, we follow procedure. It's the only way to be sure we are doing everything we can to find her."

"We'll need to sweep her home, as well," Monkworth

added.

"I told you, I've already checked there." Damn it, they were wasting too much time, retracing work that had already been done.

Monkworth lasered a look at him. "Inside?"

"Yes. I have a key."

"Been there often?"

Justice jerked a nod.

"Then you can go again, with a Crime Scene Analyst. I take it you'd notice if anything was missing, out of place?"

"I think so."

"Good." Monkworth strode to the door and called the guards and constables to attention.

As the corporal divvied up duties, Justice's eyes restlessly scanned the crowd. Elizabeth was there, looking pale but determined. Brent Parvat stood next to her, brow furrowed in concentration as he listened. Other security guards, faces familiar from years of working together, were scattered about.

It took him a minute to realize a face that should have been there was missing. His eyes swept the group once more. Monkworth dismissed them and people scattered. Justice hurried to catch up with Brent.

"Where's McMorris?" he asked without preamble.

"Isn't he here?" Brent craned his neck, skimming the thinning pack.

"No." Justice dug into his memory. "I can't remember seeing him since you came back from your initial search."

"Now that you mention it, neither can I." A sharp bark from one of the RCMP officers had Brent jolting. "Got to go. I'm sure he's around somewhere," he said as he hustled off.

A uniformed office marched up and regarded Justice. "You Cooper?"

"Yeah."

"You're to come with me. The rest of the team is already on its way."

"Can I take my own vehicle?" They moved quickly through the halls and out into the bitter cold of night. God, he hoped Charlotte, wherever she was, was indoors. At this temperature, frostbite and hypothermia were real dangers. "It's just over there."

"Of course." The officer climbed into his cruiser, parked at the curb. Justice ran to his truck. As he followed the red and blue flashers to the exit, he used voice commands to dial McMorris. His colleague had better have a damn good reason to be missing from the search. They needed every set of eyes available if they were going to find Charlotte.

CHAPTER THIRTY-TWO

Braced for what was to come, Charlotte waited, not daring to take her eyes off McMorris. She twisted her hands, palms slick with sweat, and gripped the wooden bars of the headboard, seeking leverage.

McMorris's gaze swept her from head to foot. Wrinkles creased his brow. "I knew I forgot something. I'll be right back."

The second he was out of the room she began struggling with her bonds. Her wrists, abraded and scraped, burned as she did her best to pull her hands through the straps. Blood, warm and sticky, coated her skin.

Her exertions left her limp and panting, still anchored to the bed. As she lay there, chest heaving, she heard heavy footfalls on the stairs.

And the sound of doors slamming outside.

McMorris rushed into the room, eyes alight. He tossed a coil of rope onto the bed. "This is more like it," he crowed. "Cops are here."

She sucked in a breath and screamed as loud as she could. McMorris dove onto her, one rough palm clamping onto her throat, the other over her mouth, cutting off her cry.

"Now, now, none of that."

She bucked and battled. The hand on her neck squeezed. Wheezing, fighting for air, she weakened. When the palm covering her mouth vanished, her jaw opened and shut. Only mewling cries escaped. Even those sounds were muffled when thick, suffocating material was wedged between her teeth.

She couldn't breathe. Could get barely enough air to stay conscious. McMorris' weight lifted off her, but she experienced no relief. It was impossible to inhale through her nose, and now her mouth was blocked. Wildly she poked at the fabric with her tongue, felt it give at the corner of her lips. A life-giving waft of air snuck through the gap.

She sucked at it greedily, woozy and stupefied. So acute was her need for oxygen that she didn't fight back when McMorris looped the rope about her ankles, fastening her even more firmly to the bed.

"There. That should keep you." He ran his hand over his bristly hair, panting. "Won't this be interesting?" He peered out the door, down the stairs toward the entrance. "I figured they'd check out your house. They have no reason to come to this side, though. No one's lived here for months. The neighbours will tell them that."

Slowly her heart rate subsided, as she managed to breathe evenly, if shallowly, through the gag. McMorris moved to the head of the bed, pressed his ear against the wall. He raised a finger to his lips. "I can't hear anything." He sounded disappointed. "This house must be better insulated than I thought."

Despair dragged at her. Help was just on the other side of the wall. And she had no way to reach it.

The buzz of an angry fly sounded near her ear. McMorris reached into his pocket and drew out an old flip phone. "Bet this is Nielson," he said conversationally. "I'm AWOL from work. Bad stomach bug." He winked as he answered the phone. "Hello?"

His back straightened and he shot a sly glance at her.

"Justice? What's going on?" He turned his shoulder away from her and stepped to the far side of the room.

She had to do something. Had to find a way to let Justice know where she was. The muscles of her throat strained as she worked at the gag with her tongue. Twisting her head, pulling up on her screaming arms, she tried to catch a corner of the material in the crook of her elbow.

"No, buddy, I wish I could help. But when Brent and I were looking for her, I got this awful cramp in my gut. Barely made it to the can. Should have told Nielson, but I was feeling so shitty I just wanted to get home. Dropped onto the couch and haven't left since, except for trips to the head. Watching some old Elvis movie."

Her stomach heaved, bile burning, as the gag dragged against the roof of her mouth. The damp fabric gave, gave a bit more. And then dropped free.

"Justice!" She shouted as loud as she could, her voice cracked and gruff. McMorris spun around, stared. "I'm in the duplex! I'm in the du—!"

The slap knocked her head back. Agony exploded in her skull.

She didn't feel the next punch.

****

Charlotte's voice, barely recognizable in its gruffness, cut through the phone's speaker. Every cell in Justice's body froze. "The duplex! I'm in the du—" The sound of a smack echoed in his bones. Then nothing, as the connection broke off.

He punched the gas pedal through the floor and the pickup leaped forward. Potholes and rough patches rocked the vehicle from side to side. He fought to keep it on the slippery surface with one hand, while he dialled 911 with the other.

The dispatcher answered, her voice collected, professional, completely at odds with the tearing panic ripping through his chest.

"This is Justice Cooper," he shouted. "I need to get a message to Corporal Monkworth."

"What is your emergency?"

The tail-lights of the police cruiser gleamed before him. He swerved to the opposite lane and bulleted past. "Monkworth is investigating the disappearance of Charlotte Girardet. I know where she is being held. I need to tell him. Now."

"Corporal Monkworth is unavailable at this time. If you would like to call the non-emergency line during regular office hours—"

"Fuck it," he roared. "Just call him. Charlotte's being held in the empty side of the duplex where she lives. He needs to know, and he needs to know now!"

"God damn it!" He smashed a fist onto the wheel, welcoming the bruising pain. Had she already been hidden there when he'd searched her side? Bile burned the back of his throat at the thought.

Lamp poles whipped past, flickering blurs of light passing over and through the cab, like film running over the lens of a motion picture machine.

And still he was moving too slow.

****

Hearing returned first. Not that Charlotte could make sense of what she heard. Deep, rumbling tones, a lighter, enquiring voice. No words, just sounds, random, disjointed.

Her head, her face, her gut ached so acutely that nausea threatened to overwhelm her. She concentrated on breathing slowly and deeply. She slowly realized her respiration was encumbered by the band of material stretched across her mouth, dragging her lips back in a rictus. Her head tipped to one side, a lump pressing into the back of her head forcing it over.

As awareness oozed back, so did painful relief. She was still bound, still captive. But she was also still whole, relatively unscathed. Rescue would come. She just had to stay strong, fight fiercely.

She was having trouble seeing out of one eye. The skin was puffy and swollen, and she imagined she was sporting the first black eye of her life. Blinking carefully, she rolled her head toward the door. It was closed. A line of light leaked under the bottom edge, but otherwise the room was in darkness.

The noises outside continued. She strained to hear. One voice must be McMorris. But that meant at least one other person was in the house.

She tried to shout, but could only emit a low, moaning growl. Her tongue was bloated with dryness, her mouth arid. Making any noise at all scraped and tore at her throat.

But she kept at it.

A thunderous thud reverberated from below, rattling the bed on which she lay. Voices bellowed, shouts echoed. Short, sharp syllables resonated—commands, pleas, demands. Steps pounded up the stairs, and now she could hear her name. Hear Justice calling her name.

She shrieked, wriggling and struggling on the bed. It banged against the wall.

The door slammed open, crashing wide, framing Justice between the jambs. Behind his large body she caught glimpses of yellow-striped pant legs, leather belts with holsters, the bulk of protective vests.

Tears she had refused to let fall during her ordeal

overflowed.

"You're safe. You're good." Justice knelt at her side. He slipped his hands under her head, worked at the knot holding her gag in place. "We've got McMorris. He can't hurt you anymore." He eased the gag from her mouth.

"You came. I knew you'd come. You came." The words sobbed out.

Officers cut through the straps restraining her hands and feet. Justice had to help her lower her arms, the pain a welcome sign. Her fingers were bloated, deadened by the loss of circulation.

"He hurt you." His palms cupped her jaw, so gently. His thumbs brushed the tears from her cheeks.

She wanted to grip his coat, pull him closer, but her hands didn't work. "Hold me. Oh, God, Justice, hold me."

He scooped one arm under her shoulders, one behind her knees, and lifted her, then settled on the bed.

A voice above her said, "The EMTs are here."

"Bring them. Now."

Charlotte raised her aching head. "Don't leave me."

"I won't." Justice's eyes burned sapphire blue. She was too tired to decipher the meaning in their depths. "I won't."

****

Justice slouched lower, searching once again for a comfortable position on the dainty chair he'd placed next to Charlotte's bed. It creaked beneath his weight, but the squeak didn't disturb her. She slept on.

God, her face. Violet bruises bloomed across her cheeks, her skin as pale as the butterfly tape holding her broken nose in place. The lid of her right eye puffed out obscenely. An angry red scrape sullied her forehead.

The EMTs and the doctor in Emerg had cleaned her

up, checked her out. They had reassured him the worst of her injuries was a simple fracture of her nose, which would heal cleanly on its own.

His fists clenched on his thighs. The need to punch seethed in his veins. Seeing the crimson and purple stains spreading across her skin, he wanted to beat the man responsible until every inch of his body matched.

And then beat him some more.

She moved restlessly under the covers, whimpering. Deep lines carved into her forehead. He leaned forward, smoothed the furrows away. "Shhh, now. I'm here." The tension eased, and she slid back into deeper sleep.

Morning sun glowed through the window. Dawn had been breaking when he'd brought her home, after hours at the hospital and being questioned by the police. He'd wanted to take her to his place, scared being so close to where she'd been abused would cause her more suffering. She'd insisted all she wanted was a shower and her own bed.

While she was in the bathroom, and despite the early hour, he'd called Tiffani and asked her to check on Chaucer. She'd been shocked to hear about Charlotte's ordeal, and promised to bring the dog home with her and Max until Justice was ready to retrieve him.

His lids drooped and he hauled them up over dry, gritty eyes. He'd planned on sleeping, too, but after tossing and turning next to Charlotte for a few minutes he'd given up, afraid of disturbing her rest. Unwilling to allow her out of his sight, he'd shoved the clothes draped over the chair to the floor and carried it to the head of the bed.

He shifted again, lifting himself upright. His back ached from hours of sitting still, and he leaned forward, resting his folded arms on the high mattress, stretching his spine with a soft groan of relief. The warmth of her body seeped through the covers, and her soft, regular breathing soothed his roiling emotions.

He settled in to wait for her to awake.

****

Consciousness crept back slowly, gently, and Charlotte welcomed it with gratitude. Her body felt relaxed, refreshed, except for residual soreness, centred mainly around her nose. She opened her eyes, discovered that only her right would obey her command.

One eye was enough to see Justice leaning on the mattress, head pillowed on his folded arms, sleeping at her side. His bulk threatened to overwhelm the slipper chair supporting his body. Daylight sneaking past the curtains lit his tousled blond hair with gold, burnished the bristles of his beard, glinted off the stubby, thick lashes that curled above the navy circles under his eyes.

A stiff smile tweaked the corner of her mouth, cracking her dry lips. For a few moments she drifted, luxuriating in a sense of safety, of peace. Then she languidly released her arm from under the covers and brushed her fingertips along Justice's jaw.

His eyelids fluttered. With a startled snort, he jerked up, blue eyes dazed and drowsy. Her smile grew, eased into naturalness, and a soft giggle bubbled in her throat.

"You're awake." He scrubbed the heels of his hands into his eye sockets and shook his head like a bull bothered by blue-flies.

"And so are you, now." She frowned at the sound of her voice, hoarse and rusty.

"Here." He reached for a glass of water from the nightstand.

She propped herself up on her elbow, and sipped

333

thankfully at the tepid liquid. Aware of Justice's scrutiny, she shuffled to a sitting position and used her free hand to shove back the curls tangled about her face. "I must look like a disaster. I didn't dry my hair after my shower."

"You're beautiful." Sleepiness banished, his gaze was fierce and direct.

She drank again, the parched feeling in her mouth and throat easing. "You know, I think I want another." Last night's wash had been necessary to cleanse the taint of her imprisonment and soothe her injuries, but she'd been too tired to enjoy it. "A long, long, hot-as-I-can-stand-it shower."

He rose to his feet and vanished into the ensuite. Moving with caution, she swung her feet to the floor, the soft cotton t-shirt she wore twisting about her hips. Standing up, she tested for the dizziness that had assailed her after her rescue. When it made no reappearance, she followed.

He had one hand under the shower spray, testing the temperature. He watched her, eyes narrowed. "How do you feel?"

Her reflection in the mirror horrified her. "Better than I look, for God's sake." She leaned in, turning her face from side to side. "That's grotesque."

He shut the shower door and stood behind her. "It will get worse before it gets better. But it will go away."

"I know." She crossed her arms under her breasts.

His arms encircled her. In the mirror she watched his eyes close. He lowered his head to hers, and for a few moments simply stood, rocking idly from side to side. "It feels so good to hold you."

Steam clouded at the ceiling and she breathed the warm moistness deep into her lungs. Grasping the hem of her t-shirt, she stretched her arms above her head, wincing slightly as mistreated muscles twinged. She turned to face Justice, who stepped back. She reached for the waistband of his jeans and halted his retreat.

"Care to join me? The water's waiting."

CHAPTER THIRTY-THREE

Justice stared at her, nonplussed. She couldn't possible mean what he thought she meant. "I'll have one after you."

Her cool fingers dipped between his belly and his jeans and his cock jerked. "Don't you want to be with me?"

The ravages marring her face killed him, making it impossible to forget what she'd so recently been through. He searched her expression for revulsion, fear, doubt. In her one good eye—that fucking *bastard*, he couldn't help thinking—was a humorous, teasing glint—and perhaps a touch of trepidation. "You need more rest."

She tugged him forward. It would have been easy to resist, but he found himself standing so close her bare breasts brushed the material of his shirt. His body stiffened further. "I need you. Do you still—" she broke off, dropped her chin, hiding her face.

Was she worried he didn't want her anymore? Didn't love her? Because if there was one thing he had to thank McMorris for, it was showing him exactly how he felt about Charlotte.

Her hips fit perfectly in the palms of his hands, naked skin silky, damp from humidity. She sighed at his touch, tension releasing, and lowered her forehead to his chest. The subtle dip of her waist led to the flare of her ribs, the base of his thumbs sweeping the soft curve of her breasts. Her nipples peaked, pebbling against him, noticeable even through the fabric.

"I still," he said into her hair. "I still." And more, he thought, but didn't say. Not yet. As strong as she was, she wasn't steady enough to have that thrown at her now.

He cupped her ass, pressing her against him so she could feel his want. She made a low humming noise in her throat and nuzzled at his neck, the warmth of her breath hotter even than the steam now enveloping the small room.

"Get in." He opened the shower door and nudged her into the glass and tile stall. Stripping quickly, he joined her, the piping spray making him hiss.

She stood with her back to the flowing water, eyes closed, head raised, rivulets chasing each other down her temples, along her throat, between her breasts to the curls between her legs. His blood pounded, thudding so heavily his vision shook. He dipped his head to suck the droplets clinging seductively to her collarbone. Her hands gripped his neck, the position of her arms pressing her breasts together, an offering he couldn't resist. Bending his knees, he covered one hot, moist nipple with his mouth, toyed with the other, fingers trembling with the need to be gentle, go slow.

****

Charlotte's muscles weakened, even as Justice's obvious desire strengthened her flagging confidence. She clutched his shoulders, thighs quivering. The heat of the water pouring over her was nothing compared to the passion rising inside her as his hands and mouth stroked and tweaked, seduced and tormented.

The last vestiges of panic and pain were swept away by his demanding caresses. Her own hands roamed, claiming every inch of his skin as her own. In the terrorizing dark of the trunk, the humiliating light of the bedroom, thoughts of him had kept her from shattering

337

completely. But she had been broken, had been crushed. And now he put her back together, piece by piece. Built her back into the woman she'd been.

And yet, something more.

His mouth left her breasts. He kissed his way down her belly, from hip to hip. "Justice." Her world focussed on his touch. On the screen of her closed eyelids, she watched as he found his way to her core, her centre.

He catapulted her down a river of sensation and emotion and so much more she could barely breathe. Her hand gripped his skull, drenched hair velvet under her fingers, the coarser brush of his beard deliciously agonizing against the inside of her thigh. When he drove her to the edge she shouted, her voice echoing in the glass enclosure. She collapsed against the tile wall, shockingly cold in contrast to her overheated, over-sensitized skin. Ripples of pleasure shuddered through her as she panted in double-time.

She felt Justice rise to his feet, the fine hair on his chest raising gooseflesh as it scraped lightly on her belly and breasts.

"Open your eyes, Charlotte."

Perhaps the steam had allayed the swelling. When she languorously obeyed his command, she discovered she could see out of both eyes. Justice hovered over her, his face dewed with moisture, stare intent, determined. He nudged her legs apart with his knees, stepped between. Water coursed over them, dowsing his erection as it pressed eagerly into her stomach. Crouching, he clasped her thighs and lifted her. His blue, blue gaze locked on hers, refused to let her look away. As he lowered her onto his cock, she watched in sensual delight as the fierceness in the depths of his eyes went cloudy, opaque. She squeezed her inner muscles and his lids fluttered close.

"Open *your* eyes, Justice."

He dragged them open. She tightened around him again. He groaned, muttered muffled curses. Her hands raced over his chest, his shoulders, raked through his beard, his hair. His hips rocked into her and her ass slapped the tiles.

Unwilling to miss even an instant of the connection, they watched each other as together they fractured, glowing incandescent in satisfied desire.

****

The next morning, Charlotte sipped her herbal tea while sitting at the kitchen table. Beams of sunlight danced through the window, their warmth a comforting illusion. Outside, the temperature spiked low into the negative teens.

She'd spent most of yesterday sleeping, healing. Her eye was still puffy, but she had almost full vision, and while the bruises on her face were at their ugliest—mauve and olive and mustard—she could forget about them. Until she looked in a mirror.

The air rustled about her. Or maybe it was just her own restlessness that made it feel as if the house was waiting, ripe with anticipation. Justice had refused to consider her suggestion that she go back to work. She glared at the innocent golden liquid in her mug. It was okay for *him* to go back, but not her?

To be honest, though, she hadn't fought him too hard on it. Every once in a while, she still needed to simply sit and breathe, long deep breaths that calmed the shudders in her gut.

Her cell phone vibrated on the countertop. She scooped it up, saw Sonny's face on the display, and answered.

"How are you today?" her sister asked, her tone light, but not light enough to hide the sticky tendrils of fear.

"Bored." The RCMP had called Sonny only minutes before Charlotte had been rescued. While she was grateful her pregnant sister hadn't needed to worry long, she couldn't help but wish she'd never known at all. They'd talked briefly that night, and again yesterday.

"Even when we were kids, you hated missing school. Just weird that way, I guess."

"I have work to do," Charlotte said. "Responsibilities. My students need me."

"You need rest."

She didn't feel tired, or sick, or injured. Not right now. "I'm fine."

Sonny sighed. "Tomorrow, you can go back. That was our deal."

Shaking off her self-absorption, Charlotte asked, "How are you? How's that new niece of mine?"

"Your new niece is a nephew."

"Sonny!"

"We had the ultrasound yesterday."

"Andrea was certain she was having a sister. Is she disappointed?"

"Not so you'd notice. She had a friend over yesterday evening and spent the whole time talking about her new baby brother."

A glow of pleasure washed through Charlotte, and with a sense of startlement, she realized the faint taint of jealousy she'd always experienced when thinking of Sonny's children was missing. A life and death struggle really did put things into perspective, she mused. "I am so happy for you all."

"I'm so happy you'll be here to meet him," Sonny said, her voice quavering.

"Are you crying?" Charlotte asked in alarm.

"It's just hormones. I cry all the time." She sniffled and swallowed. "But when I think of that phone call..."

"Don't," Charlotte commanded. "I am perfectly fine. Justice is taking care of me."

Sonny had insisted on speaking with Justice when she'd called yesterday. From the side of the conversation Charlotte had heard, she knew he'd promised to look after her closely. Too closely, she thought with a scowl.

"I like him." Sonny's voice warmed. "He has a good voice—strong, confident."

"Oh, he's confident, all right." As for strong—it wasn't just his voice. Her belly tingled when she remembered how he'd taken her in the shower yesterday, supporting her weight, holding her with ease.

"Have you met his family?" Her innocent tone didn't fool Charlotte.

"His dad. His ex-wife." She took a deep breath. "And his son."

"He has a son?"

"Max. He's nine. And adopted. Sort of."

"What? No, hold on." A rustling and thudding came through the speaker. "Okay, I shut the door. You have ten minutes until the heathens discover I've locked myself away. Go."

Charlotte explained about Jake and Tiffani, the bus crash and baby Max. "You should have seen his face when Max finally found out the truth." The memory of Justice crouched next to his son squeezed at her heart. "He looked calm, but this pulse pounded in his temple. And then"—a soft laugh escaped her—"it was anti-climactic, really. Max didn't seem to care. He was interested, and I'm sure he'll have more questions, but it really didn't bother him."

"I'd say that means Tiffani and Justice have done a great job of making him feel loved, secure."

"I agree." Charlotte hesitated, and then took the plunge. "It made me think."

"About what?"

"That there are ways to make a family other than by giving birth."

Now the silence was on the other end of the line. When Sonny finally spoke, her voice was soft, understanding—and joyful. "There certainly are. I know it's been tough for you..."

"There will always be a tiny part of me that wishes I could have children. To share with the man I love a human being that is equal parts of each of us." The image of Justice rose so strongly before her she had to close her eyes. Her grip on her phone tightened. "But I'm not going to let that hold me back anymore. I'm not going to let it stifle what I could have."

"Does Justice know? About your infertility?"

"Yes." And that knowledge was freeing, liberating. "I had more trouble with it than he did."

"So, what does this all mean? You're together, you're happy—what now?"

"I wish I knew." Restless, she pushed away from the table and dumped her cooling tea in to the sink. "I'm expecting a call any day from York. I had an email from Doctor Ross-Moore." She'd read it in while scanning through her messages in the stingy fifteen minutes Justice had let her use her laptop yesterday. "The position is mine if I want it. I'm just waiting for the formal offer."

"That's great! You really deserve it. I know how hard

you've worked for this chance." Sonny paused, and then added diffidently, "But do you want it? Is it still where you see your life going?"

Charlotte paced from the sink to the back door and looked out over the brilliantly white backyard. She'd come to love the crispness of clear winter days in this northern town, and would regret the chance to discover it in all its seasons. As for the university, what she had once seen as cramped and confining now seemed to have unexplored avenues she didn't want to miss.

That was if she took Justice out of the equation. When she included him in her calculations, the scales tipped even further away from York.

"Charlotte?"

"I'm here." She leaned her forehead against the window. Her breath misted the icy glass. "I'm here, and I'm confused. I had a plan for so long, couldn't see myself deviating from that plan. And now—"

When she didn't go on, Sonny spoke up, her voice consoling. "Now you have decisions to make."

Charlotte's laughter had shaky edges. "I do. But it's not only up to me."

And that was the scariest thought of all.

CHAPTER THIRTY-FOUR

Justice stirred the long strands of spaghetti to keep them from clumping. Max hated sticky pasta.

The boy's small blond head bobbed at his elbow. "I'm hungry."

"That's why I'm cooking," Justice said. "It'll be ready in a few minutes."

Max wandered to the living room and a moment later, Justice heard the tinny tones of the theme to his current favourite TV show.

Charlotte had insisted he spend the evening with Max. "He needs your attention, more than I do," she'd said. "I'll be fine."

Despite her confident words, he'd seen the relief cross her face when he'd promised to be with her by nine. It was a school night, so he would take Max back to Tiffani no later than 8:30.

He hadn't planned on seeing Max, as he'd originally be scheduled to work afternoon shifts this week, like he had the night of Charlotte's abduction. But McMorris' arrest had forced changes in more ways than one, and Justice had finagled his way into a day shift.

He strained the now al dente spaghetti and returned it to the pot. "Come and get it," he called. The TV cut off and Max raced into the room, surfing in his sock feet up to the table before climbing onto a chair. Chaucer followed close behind, whumping onto his butt next to Max, eyes soulful, tail wagging hopefully.

"No feeding the dog," Justice said as he placed the spaghetti pot on the table next to a bottle of olive oil, dish of freshly grated parmesan cheese, and a pepper grinder. He hadn't had time to make a meat sauce, but as he would have been the only one to eat it—Max preferring his spaghetti naked—it didn't matter.

"But he's hungry."

"No, he's not. I just fed him." He poured two glasses of milk and placed one in front of Max.

For a few minutes, they ate in silence. Chaucer gave up and slithered to the ground, eyebrows twitching as he watched alertly for dropped food.

"Is Chaucer coming back to our house tonight?" Max slurped a pale strand of pasta between pursed lips and giggled when the end flipped against his nose.

"Yeah. I'm still staying with Charlotte."

"I thought she liked Chaucer."

"She does. But she needs peace and quiet right now, so he's better off with you and your Mom."

"Mom said a bad man tried to hurt her." Max's blue eyes were wide with curiosity behind his thick lenses.

"He did. But she's going to be fine." Justice twisted a forkful of pasta and thought as he chewed. "You know how I told you once I might love Charlotte?"

"Yup." The idea didn't distract him from trying to capture another mouthful.

"Well, I do. I do love her."

Max's head tilted to one side as he considered the comment. "Is she going to come live with you?"

"See, that's what I don't know." Justice sipped his milk, wishing it was whiskey. This conversation needed something stronger than cow juice. "I think she's getting a job in Toronto."

"Why would she go away?"

"It's a job she really wants. It would be excellent for her career."

"But if she loves you, wouldn't she want to be with you?"

The innocent question arrowed into the heart of the matter. "That's the other thing I don't know. I don't know if she loves me like I love her." He hoped she did, was certain he'd seen signs of it. But he wasn't willing to bet the farm on it.

"So if she leaves, what will you do? Will you go with her?" Worry pinched Max's voice.

"I would never leave you. Not until you're ready to leave me," Justice said firmly, and added, "I'd want to go visit her, see her once in a while. But I would still live here."

"If you wanted to go with her, I'd be okay. I'm almost ten." He sat up straighter, as if good posture made him older. "I'm nearly grown up."

"Not quite, buddy." Justice couldn't help a smile from curling the corner of his mouth. "But thanks for the offer."

"People who love each other should be together." Max's small face was far too serious for a child, and Justice wished he wasn't the cause of yet another anxious moment in the boy's life.

"And that's why I would never move away. I love you."

Some of the tension left his son's thin shoulders. "But won't you be sad, if you can't see her lots?"

"I'll miss her, sure." His gut felt hollow at the thought, and he pushed his unfinished plate away. "But I'll find a way to make it work." He had to, because a life without Charlotte wasn't worth contemplating.

****

A sense of strain permeated the security office. In the days since McMorris went off the rails, Nielson had been even more straight-laced and militant. At the moment, he was ensconced behind his closed door, to Justice's deep relief.

As he monitored the screens an itchy restlessness picked at him, and for the first time he seriously considered moving on. He'd always enjoyed the job, still did, but his patience with Nielson's autocratic ways had stretched to breaking the night of Charlotte's abduction. He wasn't ready to make a solid decision, though. So much depended on her. She hadn't said anything more about the position at York, and he'd been afraid to ask.

He'd managed to keep her at home until this morning, when she'd rebelled and threatened to disembowel him if he didn't get out of her way. As it was Friday, he figured he could let her have the one day. It was also his last shift of the week. Over the weekend, he could make sure she was ready to return full-time.

"Why don't you head out, do the rounds?" Elizabeth Paxton's voice broke through his absorption. "Before you dig a hole in the floor with your foot." She looked up from the computer she'd been working on and sent him a pointed look.

He stopped jiggling the knee he'd been bouncing unconsciously. "It's your turn to get out of the office," he replied.

She shooed him away with a flap of her hand. "You're making me nervous. Go check on her. You'll feel better."

Slightly mortified Elizabeth had read him so well, he decided to take the escape offered, and headed out into the halls.

Just to prove to himself he could, he didn't turn in Charlotte's direction immediately, instead taking his usual route through the medical wing, the teaching and learning centre, through the lab building, and finally winding his way toward the administration block and her office.

She was in one of her favourite poses, facing the window. The bright outdoor light outlined her profile, and the curls of her dark hair caught the sunshine and trapped it like gold amid the coffee-coloured strands. He stood in the doorway for a moment, simply enjoying the sight of her, before knocking on the jamb. "Hey."

"Hello." She spun to face him, smiling, but underneath the welcome he sensed tension vibrating. The bruises were still there, but the butterfly bandage on the bridge of her nose was gone, the swelling in her eye barely visible.

"You okay?"

She nodded. "I'm fine." Her eyelids flickered to the pages strewn across her desk, back to him. "I have news."

He moved further into the room, premonition curling at the base of his spine. "Good?" he asked, keeping his voice light.

She tipped her head back, keeping him in focus. "I don't know." Her shoulders lifted as she drew air in, lowered as she released it on a long huff. "I've been offered the position at York. I just got off the phone with the Dean."

Even though he'd been expecting it, the knowledge still locked his breath in his lungs. "What do you mean, you don't know?" He hoped his smile looked less a grimace than it felt. "That's excellent news."

"Is it?"

Was that wistfulness he heard? "Of course it is." Wasn't it what she'd always wanted?

"You're right. It is. Choices are always good to have." She rose to her feet and circled the desk. She stopped before him, so close he could feel the heat of her body. Her eyes were warm and serious. "Choices mean you have options."

"I'll miss you." He choked out the words, determined to say what was right for her, even if it wasn't right for him. "I'd like to keep in touch." He couldn't let her go completely. He would just have to take what little of her life she was willing to give.

"That's definitely one option." She blinked, and his heart clutched at what looked like tears pooling in the corner of her eyes. She blinked again and the suspicious moisture was gone. "Can you think of any others?" Her hand brushed his jaw, whispering through his beard, sending prickles of awareness through his nerves.

"I can't go with you." Even to his own ears, his voice sounded harsh, unkind. "Max is here."

"I understand." She placed both palms on his chest, worrying the material of his jacket with her fingers. Her teeth bit into the soft, pink flesh of her lower lip, and tiny creases wrinkled the skin between her eyes. "That wasn't what I was thinking."

"What were you thinking, Charlotte?" The pressure under his ribs grew, squeezing, crushing.

"I was thinking I could stay."

****

If she hadn't been so terrified about what she was about to do, about to say, Charlotte would have enjoyed the pole-axed expression on Justice's face. His eyes went blank, his jaw loosened.

"What?" he said. She watched him pull himself together, rolling his neck on his shoulders like a fighter

349

preparing for a bout.

Her pulse pounded in her fingertips and her skin rippled with nervousness. "I said, one option is, I could stay."

"That's what I thought you said." His hands had somehow found their way onto her hips. "Doing what?"

"I spoke with Madeline Donald. There's an opening in the English department."

"Here?"

"She can't guarantee anything, of course. But I put my name forward."

"Here, at UNBC."

She smiled at his dazed tone. "Here."

"You'd be willing to give up York?" His grip on her hips firmed and drew her forward. "What about your plans?"

She wasn't sure her shrug as was nonchalant as she'd tried to make it. "Plans change."

"Not those kind of plans."

"They do, when they aren't right any longer." She drew in a shuddering breath, seeking the courage to tell it all. "I've been doing a lot of thinking, since—since McMorris. That certainly wasn't part of my plan, but it happened. And now I have to deal with it."

"You don't have to do it all on your own."

"I know." And that knowledge was a warm kernel of happiness. "I've also been thinking about families."

"In what way?"

She paused, gathering her thoughts. "I had my surgery so young, I don't think I truly realized how it would affect me," she began carefully. "When you're sixteen, children are something so far into the future that giving them up doesn't seem that much of a sacrifice." She toyed with the zipper on his jacket, aware of his gaze on her face but unwilling to look at him. "But my biological clock didn't stop ticking just because it had pieces missing. With Richard, I thought I'd found someone who would ease that pressure. If the man I loved didn't want children, I had another reason besides infertility not to have them."

"And then he threw you over because of it." His tone was so fierce, her head jerked up. Any befuddlement was gone from his face now. He glared at her. "Asshole."

Her laugh was a choked snort, and the sickening nervousness eased. "Even before him, I'd been focusing on my career. If I couldn't have kids, a family, then at least I'd be the best at what I did. After our engagement broke off, it was all I had."

"You were the loneliest person I'd ever met."

Embarrassment flushed her cheeks. "Was it that obvious?"

Instead of answering, he ran his hands up her back and cuddled her to his chest. She laid her cheek over his heart, comforted by the steady rhythm.

"After you told me Max wasn't your biological son, I had a...well...I guess I had an epiphany." She clasped her hands behind his back, comforted and strengthened by his embrace. "The love you two have is so amazing. And I realized there were other ways to make a family."

"I talked with Max last night," he said. She felt the rumble of his voice through the wall of his chest. "I told him I loved you, and that I was going to try and make things work between us. He said it would be okay if I had to move to a new city to be with you. He said people who love each other should be together."

"Oh, God." She couldn't help it. Tears escaped, moistened the nylon of his jacket. "That's the sweetest, saddest thing I've ever heard."

"I couldn't do it, though. Not as a permanent move."

"I know." She drew away, reaching for a tissue from the box on her desk. Justice refused to let her out of his hold, so they shuffled a couple steps sideways, locked together like teenagers at a high school dance. "And I love you for that."

His arms tightened. "Say what?"

She wiped the moisture from her eyes, met his. "I love you, Justice."

"Holy fuck." The profanity was a prayer. And the last thing either of them said for a very long time.

His mouth was firm and challenging against hers, demanding her body tell him the truth. Her answer was in the way she clung to him, the way her mouth opened to his, giving him what he needed without reservation, selflessly, unhesitating.

When he finally released her mouth she gasped, light-headed, dizzy. "This is a very, very good day," he murmured against her hair.

She felt buoyant. If he let her go, she might float to the ceiling. "I don't think I'll get any more work done."

Reluctantly, he stepped back. His eyes glowed with a deep inner happiness, even though his mouth remained its usual firm, straight line. "I'm supposed to be doing rounds."

"Then you should go." She clasped her hands to stop herself from reaching for him again. "Maybe I should have told you at a better time."

"Don't think that." In a swift move, he cupped her face, pressed his lips to hers in delightful punishment. "There is never a bad time to tell someone you love them." Another bruising kiss. "I have to go. We'll talk to tonight."

And then he was gone.

She dropped, weak-kneed, into her chair. Her lips throbbed and she held her fingers to her mouth.

For the first time in a long time, her career was taking second place in her life. She should have been petrified. Instead, she felt free, confident. There would be so much to discuss, to arrange, to plan. And it would start tonight, when the man she loved, the man who loved her, would come to her. He'd bring his son and his dog, and together they would look to the future. A future full of promise and passion, family and fulfilment.

Also by Brenda Margriet

Mountain Fire

A mountaintop mystery leads two conservationists to dangerous obsessions and violent passions.

Natural resources student June Brandt climbs Longworth Mountain for some alone time. But when Conservation Officer Alex Weaver arrives to look into the death of a grizzly bear, June is caught up in the investigation--and fascinated by Alex.

Alex is attracted by June's competence and coolness under fire--as well as her lithe body and honey-blonde hair. Although their mutual interest in protecting the natural wonders of the area brings them together, they soon realize they view love from very different angles. He offers passion and pleasure, but June wants more.

When one of Alex's colleagues is murdered, June and Alex must work together to find the poacher before other lives are lost. And Alex must look deep inside to discover if he can give June what she deserves.

Chef d'Amour

All Jemma Hedge wants to do is care for her ailing grandmother, and a job behind-the-scenes on the reality show Reservations for Two is the perfect opportunity to earn the needed money. There's one rule—no fraternizing with the cast. Easy enough, until she runs into the show's sexy bachelor, Paul Almeida, the smoldering restaurateur she's already had the displeasure of meeting.

Paul risked more than money when he opened his dream restaurant. To give his fantasy a fighting chance, he accepts the role of Chef d'Amour on Reservations for Two. Flirting with the women vying for his heart should keep him too busy to worry about overstepping boundaries with the crew, until he spots Jemma.

The ingredients for love are at hand. Can Jemma and Paul create the perfect recipe?

The Life She Had Before

A short story – a woman is torn between the bitterness of revenge and the sweetness of a second chance.

About the Author

Brenda Margriet writes contemporary romances with heroes you'd meet at the grocery store. And by that she means real-life men – sexy, smart and looking for the love of their life. Her heroines are bold, savvy and determined to accept nothing less than the man they deserve. A voracious reader since she was old enough to hold a book, Brenda's idea of the perfect holiday involves a comfortable chair near the water (ocean, lake or pool will do), a glass of wine, and a full-loaded e-reader. She lives in Northern British Columbia with her husband, three children (all of whom are taller than her) and various finny and furry pets. Discover more about Brenda and her books on her website – www.brendamargriet.com.

Made in the USA
San Bernardino, CA
07 April 2016